Getaway with Murder

Leo McNeir

Getaway with Murder

Leo McNeir

enigma
publishing

enigma publishing
a division of *specialist* publishing services
Wicken, Milton Keynes, MK19 6BY

First published 2000
Reprinted 2004
© Leo McNeir 2000

A CIP record for this book is available from the British Library.

ISBN 0 9524052 6 1

Printed in Great Britain by Baskerville Press, Salisbury

Dedication

For Cassandra and Dolly

The girl sat hunched on the edge of the chair, fists clenched white in her lap, staring forward, in deep shock. For a few moments she had been left alone in the small, bare room containing only an examination couch, a mobile folding screen and the single chair on which she was sitting.

Outside in the corridor, people were bustling past with the quiet haste of a hospital casualty unit. But in this room there was only the deepest silence centred on the girl, utterly still, scarcely breathing, her eyes wide open and unseeing, accentuating the frailty of the small face and the pale fair hair cut short, almost sculpted to her head. She was sixteen and wore the clothes typical of her generation all over the world, T-shirt, jeans and trainers, the only unusual feature being that hers were smeared with blood, still vivid and fresh. Her hands opened slowly and she looked down to see the palms sticky and red. She breathed in with a shudder.

At that moment the door swung open to admit a nurse, another woman and a man. The girl did not raise her eyes and seemed unaware of their presence.

"This is the girl who found her. She came in with the ambulance," said the nurse in a low voice.

"Is she injured?" asked the woman in the same quiet tone.

"No. That's blood from ... the victim. Doctor said you shouldn't stay for more than a minute. She's very disoriented."

"Will she be able to speak to us?" said the man.

"It's hard to tell. People react to shock in all sorts of ways. She may not even know who she is." The nurse had a homely West Indian accent that seemed strangely reassuring after the horrific events that had taken place. The other woman knelt down beside the girl and put a hand gently on her arm.

"Where's Marnie?" said the girl. Her voice was a harsh, dry whisper and she cleared her throat. "What's happened to Marnie?"

"We need your help. We can't stay long. My name is Cathy Lamb, I'm a detective constable. Can you tell me your name?"

"Marnie?" said the girl.

"No, that isn't your name. What are *you* called?"

"I know that. My name is Anne. Anne with an 'e'." As she spoke, two tear drops rolled down the thin face and dripped onto the blood stains in her lap. She made no sound. The man knelt down on the other side.

"Did you see anybody there?" he said softly. The girl nodded. "Anne, you know me ... I'm Sergeant Marriner. We have to know if you saw anybody when you were in the church. It's very important." The nurse tapped him lightly on the shoulder. He looked up to see that a doctor had slipped into the room. The girl stared blankly forward. "You must help us if you can. You know we're conducting a murder enquiry. Just think." In the background, the doctor gave a slight cough.

"Someone," muttered the girl and began breathing more quickly. Her shoulders slumped and she shook her head.

"Please." The doctor laid his hand on the detective's shoulder and he stood up.

"Anne, we'll come back and see you when you're feeling a little better," said the woman detective. She smiled and gently squeezed the girl's arm. "Is there anyone else we should contact? Do you know anyone in her family?" The girl mumbled something indistinct. "Ben?" said the woman.

"Beth. Her sister." For the first time, the girl raised her head and looked up at the group standing in the room. Her face was vacant, without animation, but her voice had become firm and clear. "I'll have to tell her, not you. What's happened to Marnie? Is she all right?" The detectives turned to face the doctor. His face was grim and he gave only the slightest shrug.

❦ ❦ ❦ ❦

The car turned off the motorway at junction 15 and headed towards Northampton and the casualty department of the General Hospital. As it rushed down the dual carriageway, neither of the occupants spoke. They had hardly said a word during the entire journey from London. Beth stared out of the window, but did not register the fields and the golf course, the hotel and the filling station as they flashed past the window. Paul, her husband, had never driven so fast and once or twice it had crossed his mind that they could easily have been pulled up by the traffic police, but they had raced along undetected and neither of them cared.

Beth tried not to think of her sister lying under a white sheet in some unit where they had laid her. Again and again she went over the events leading up to that moment, wishing she could turn the clock back to the beginning of this episode in their lives. Now, fingering the wallet of photographs that she had grabbed on impulse as they rushed out of the house, she was thinking of all the things she could have said that might have dissuaded her sister from this venture. They could now still be living their usual routine in London, for all its shortcomings, rather than making this desperate journey. It seemed pathetic now, but above all else, she wished she had never uttered those stupid words that day in the spring when Marnie told her that her plans to move were completed, and explained how she was going to carry out her project. She wished she had never said: "Marnie, sometimes I think you'd get away with murder." As they swung off the expressway and followed the signs to the hospital, she heard Marnie's reply as clearly as if she had been with them in the car.

"I like the idea of making a getaway ... but I can do without the murder."

"You've done *what*?" Marnie shifted the phone closer to her ear.

"I've sold her," Beth repeated.

"You've sold *Sally Ann*? Why?"

"Well, for a start, it's winter and we are fair weather sailors. We were talking about the boat to a colleague of Paul's who said he was nuts about narrowboats and canals, and he asked to see her so we took him down to Little Venice. He really liked her."

"What about all the hard work I put into her?"

"Great! That's why we could get a really good price."

"*What?!*"

"No, seriously, you had her practically all last year and you must have got boats out of your system by now, just as we have. Let's face it, Marnie, you've never been the outdoor type."

"I might have changed." Marnie reached over the desk for her Zippo, clutching a pencil in her teeth.

"Not you. Your idea of the great outdoors is a window box filled with geraniums and trailing things or a documentary about wildlife on BBC2."

"Beth, there is such a thing as honour among sisters, you know. I did all that work turning *Sally Ann* into a smart boat ... not to mention the expense. Have you *any* idea how much effort I put in?"

"Marnie, I really appreciated it."

"And now you've gone and *sold* her!"

"Good as ..." There was a pause.

"*Good as?*" Marnie's tone was heavy with suspicion.

"Our friend wants to take another look. He's going down tonight by himself to spend a little time on her and walk around Little Venice. Get to know the place. We can't go with him. We're having Paul's Professor and his wife to dinner. So he's going alone. He can take his time. Maybe it's just as well."

"Well, it's up to you, I suppose."

After they had hung up, Marnie sat fondling her Zippo. It was the nearest she ever came to smoking these days. From her desk she could see out to the canal that went past her office window. winter should have ended by now, but nobody had told it. There had been a frost in the night and most of the surface was opaque and brittle. Down the middle of the channel was a strip of clear water. A boat had passed by in the early hours, heading down to the pool of Little Venice about a mile away, or making for Bull's Bridge and the main line of the Grand Union Canal in the opposite direction. Marnie remembered her own journey the previous summer on *Sally Ann*, a journey that had taken her up through the middle of England and down to Oxford and the Thames. She had taken the whole summer as sabbatical leave to refresh her spirits and had refurbished *Sally* in her own taste, with new curtains and brass lamps, safari-style furniture and a whole set of new crockery, *matching* new crockery.

"Yes, Beth, maybe it's just as well," she muttered to herself and reached across for the diary to see what she had planned for later that afternoon.

❀ ❀ ❀ ❀

It was three-thirty, bright but chilly, when Marnie pulled into a parking bay round the corner from the canal at Little Venice. She paused at the railings and looked down on *Sally Ann*. There were one or two places where the paintwork needed to be touched up, but even so *Sally* had a smart livery. Marnie had painted the roof the previous year, covering the drab maroon with a pale cream and had used the same colour around the bow, along the centre band and round the stern. Above that band the body was in navy blue and below it the hull was black. She was finished off with two broad bands of white and red at the stern.

It had been hard work, as hard in its way as learning to control the boat and work the locks. But Marnie was in no doubt that it had been worth the effort. It had given her a real sense of achievement to learn how to manage forty-five feet of steel narrowboat weighing fourteen tonnes, and a sense of freedom to know that she could take *Sally* on over two thousand miles of canals and waterways. There was a time last year that *Sally* had come to her rescue, when Marnie had been at a low point in her life. The sabbatical summer spent travelling on the boat had been a turning point and, looking down on her from the pavement, Marnie knew how much *Sally Ann* meant to her.

"Surveying your handiwork or making a list of tasks to be done?" With the traffic going by, Marnie had not heard anyone approach, but turned smiling on hearing the voice of Mrs Jolly, the old lady who lived in the house opposite *Sally's* mooring.

"A mixture of both. Actually, I'm thinking of changing her name." Marnie's tone was matter-of-fact, Mrs Jolly's expression unconvinced.

"All right, I'll buy it. What will you change it to?"

"I think *Forth Bridge* would probably be appropriate," said Marnie. The old lady chuckled.

"It was when you started working on her last year that I realised you were serious and not just dabbling."

"Not just a water gypsy?"

"Quite. You've never let me forget that. Anyway, you made a big improvement compared to the way the other people, sorry, I mean your sister and brother-in-law, treated her. By the way, they were here the other evening."

"Yes, I know. I do allow them to come from time to time. It is *their* boat, after all."

"They had someone with them, a friend I suppose, a big burly chap. I just *happened* to be looking out of the window." They both smiled at the unspoken knowledge that nothing happened around *Sally Ann* without Mrs Jolly noticing.

"That was their potential buyer," said Marnie.

"Buyer? For *Sally Ann*?" Mrs Jolly looked shocked. "But surely they can't sell her to someone else?"

"They can. She belongs to them, technically."

"But not *morally*," said Mrs Jolly in a grand tone. "Think of all your hard work, Marnie. In many ways she's more your boat than theirs."

"Fancy a cup of tea?" Marnie asked, leading the way through the gate onto the towpath.

They had hardly sat down in the saloon when a face appeared in the hatchway at the far end of the cabin. It was a man's face, pleasant with a cheeky grin, almost plausible but not quite.

"Come in, Gary. Tea?" He rubbed his hands and hopped into the cabin, looking round as he made his way nimbly to the table and took a seat. He smiled at Mrs Jolly.

"I think you've met Gary, Mrs Jolly?"

"Oh yes. No need for introductions. It was when you let *Sally Ann's* mooring while Marnie was away," she said in an even tone.

"Waste not, want not," said Gary with a nod of the head and a twinkle in the eye. "You know, Marnie, this used to be the scruffiest boat in Little Venice, apart from that houseboat up the other end that's actually sitting on the bottom."

"Thank you. How many lumps?" There was a menacing edge to the question.

"Two please. I said *used to be*. Now she's definitely one of the smartest."

"It's all Marnie's hard work," said Mrs Jolly, turning her head slightly as a shape passed the window on the towpath side.

"We'll have half of Little Venice in here in a minute," said Gary, and, right on cue, a voice came from the aft deck.

"Hallo-o-o. Anyone at home?" This time it was Albert, a retired merchant seaman who lived on a large boat halfway along the towpath with two cats, also retired.

"The door's open, Albert," Marnie called out, reaching for another cup.

"But is there a welcome on the mat?" he said. "There are two of us and you seem to have a full house." Albert stepped down into the cabin accompanied by Jane Rutherford, who kept a narrowboat along the cut, from which she worked as a sign-painter in the traditional canal style. Space was made for them at the table. Gary rubbed his hands together again and grinned.

"This *is* nice. We can have a party … or even an orgy." He winked at Mrs Jolly.

"I'm surprised you have to ask about the welcome," said Marnie, ignoring Gary and handing the newcomer a cup of tea. "I'm not sure if you know Mrs Jolly who lives across the road. Mrs Jolly, this is Albert, who I believe is Little Venice's longest-standing resident." They shook hands. "You know Jane, of course."

"I always think of Little Venice as a village," said Albert, "but really it's two villages, one on the canal and one outside the fence. They don't often meet, which is sad, really."

"To be honest," said Mrs Jolly, "the people on the outside of the fence, as you put it, don't often meet either. They come and go by car and rarely have much contact with each other."

"Same where I live," said Jane. "I don't often see the people who live around me. I suppose that's London for you. Little Venice, *this* side of the fence, is a friendly community like a village."

"Nomads." It was Gary who spoke, in between taking sips from his tea.

"Thank you for that contribution, Gary," said Marnie. "Is there more to come or will you rest on your laurels?"

"Canals are for travelling, so people who use them are like nomads. Little Venice is like an oasis." There was silence while the words were digested.

"So the canal is a community," said Marnie. She felt that Gary had a point.

"It's not static like a village in one place," said Gary.

"It is to some of us who live here all the time and don't move our boats," said Albert. "Or am I like a camel dealer staying at the oasis?" He guffawed.

"Perhaps that accounts for the help and hospitality we give each other," said Marnie, passing round the biscuits. "Anyway, it always feels like a village to me, somewhere secure where everyone knows you and is friendly."

"I think that's a rather idealised view of village life, Marnie," said Mrs Jolly. "I grew up in a village in Hampshire. It was lovely in many ways, just as you say, but there were sometimes tensions under the surface. There were some families who had not spoken to each other for years and nobody could remember why, but it made no difference. Perhaps there are things under the surface in Little Venice, too."

"Fish," said Gary. Mrs Jolly giggled.

"Well, whatever Little Venice is, I may not be in residence for much longer," said Marnie. Three cups of tea paused in their ascent from the saucer. Gary's eyes narrowed.

"You off again?" he said. Marnie and Mrs Jolly both suspected that he was already calculating how much he could make by sub-letting her mooring while she was away.

"Are you leaving us, my dear?" said Albert.

"I'm about to be evicted," said Marnie. Albert looked bewildered.

"*Evicted?* From the mooring? This is the first I've heard of it." Albert always knew what was going on, as if the canal system had long ago become the information super-highway.

"My sister wants to sell *Sally*."

"Is there no chance that you could buy *Sally Ann* from her?" said Jane.

"Most of my resources are tied up in the flat."

"She may not find it so easy to sell," said Albert. "There are half a dozen boats with 'For Sale' signs in the window at the moment, none with 'Sold'. It's probably not a good time."

"But she already has a prospective ..." Marnie paused and looked pensively at Albert. An idea formed in her mind. She got up and crossed to the galley, where she put on the kettle. "Shall we have another cup of tea?"

It was half an hour later that the party dispersed. It was still light when Marnie locked the towpath gate behind her. She glanced at her watch. Paul's colleague would be arriving soon to look at *Sally Ann*. He would be coming alone.

"Yes, Beth, maybe it's just as well," thought Marnie.

❦   ❦   ❦   ❦

The following day, Marnie decided to work late. When everyone had left for the night, she made herself a cup of coffee and went back to her desk. The design for the interiors of the chain of pubs along the Grand Union Canal in the Midlands was virtually completed. Soon the work would be out to tender and she was almost as pleased with the scheme as were the directors of the company.

Through her window she could see the canal, the low evening light reflecting from its surface. spring was in the air and Marnie asked herself if she would really want to set off again on a long journey. Could that really satisfy her needs? What needs? Last year she had felt stale in her work, but now she was involved in interesting projects, her team was young and talented and the company was doing well. At least, they had so far survived the recession. Then why did she feel uneasy with herself?

"Midnight oil, Marnie?" Philip, the senior partner in the practice, was standing in the doorway. "I came in to turn off the lights. Didn't know anyone was here." He walked across the large open-plan office to her desk. "All well?"

"Just tidying up. One or two things I wanted to get finished on the Willards Brewery job."

"Your 'Pub Crawl' project," said Philip.

"Yes. It's about time they came back to us with the really big job, doing their restaurants and head office."

Philip walked round her desk and looked out of the window. It was still quite light, with high pink and grey clouds pulling a thin veil over the evening in the western sky. Already one solitary star was visible above a block of flats in the middle distance and there was a cold brightness in the air. The water of the canal was shining and mirror-smooth.

"I wouldn't be surprised if we were in for another frost tonight," said Philip. "There have been times when we could almost have gone ice-skating on your canal in the last few weeks."

Marnie smiled. She liked the idea of 'her' canal. "It might not be *my* canal for much longer. Beth is planning to sell *Sally Ann*."

"Couldn't you buy her?"

"I don't want to increase my mortgage with the property market falling and

I've invested most of my capital in buying the flat." Philip nodded. He had admired Marnie's acumen a few years ago when she had bought her flat in a good part of London with a view over Hampstead Heath. It had been expensive, but the improvements she had made had helped keep its price at a time when many other homes had lost almost a third of their value.

"Couldn't you persuade Beth to change her mind?"

"You know Beth. Once she gets an idea ..." She shook her head.

"I know you, too, Marnie." He laughed and made for the exit, pausing in the doorway. "If you're still here in the morning I'll bring bacon and eggs."

Marnie switched off the main office lights and used only the lamp on her desk. She made another cup of coffee and worked on for an hour longer. At seven, the phone rang.

"Marnie? It's Anne."

"Anne with an 'e'?" said Marnie. They had met the previous summer when Anne was running away from home to make one less mouth to feed after her father lost his job. Introducing herself that morning, Anne had noted that like the boat she was an Ann, but spelt differently. "How did you know I was here?"

"I guessed when I rang the flat. You'd either be on *Sally* or at work."

"How are things?"

"That's why I'm ringing, really. It's still difficult at home. Dad can only get part-time work and he's ..." she lowered her voice, "... moonlighting to bring in some more cash."

"Perhaps we can get together?" said Marnie. "Have a talk about things?"

"We've got this parents' evening tomorrow night and we've got to decide on next year."

"Well, you know my views on that. I do understand how difficult it is, Anne, but I believe you should stay on at school and do A Levels, so you can go to college."

"Dad says that years ago architects and draughtsmen used to be apprenticed and learn the job that way." Marnie knew he was right, but that system had long since disappeared.

"Why don't we meet soon and talk it over? Could you come down on Saturday? I expect you've got loads of homework to do."

"Not so much that I couldn't visit you," said Anne eagerly.

"Tell you what: why not come Saturday morning and stay till Sunday? You can bring your school work and do it in my study at home."

❦   ❦   ❦   ❦

The worst of the rush hour was over by the time Marnie pointed her Rover in the direction of Little Venice. It took her as long to find a parking space as to cover the rest of the journey. Arriving opposite *Sally Ann's* mooring, she saw Jane Rutherford standing on the towpath beside her boat *Joshua*, silhouetted against one of the windows. Marnie greeted her over the railings.

"The sun's below the yardarm," said Jane in the light of the street lamps. "Fancy a snifter?"

"I see no sun," said Marnie. "I must remember to get a yardarm fitted to *Sally Ann.*"

On board *Joshua,* Marnie accepted a mineral water. "If you hadn't turned up, I was going to give you a ring," said Jane, pouring the drinks. "Last night I met the prospective purchaser of *Sally Ann.*"

Marnie raised an eyebrow. "Cheers." They both took a sip from their glasses.

"Just as we planned, I *happened* to be passing when he came down to look at *Sally*. I asked if he was expecting to meet somebody and said I was sorry, but I thought the owner had already gone home. He seemed surprised and said he didn't think they would be here that evening."

"I hope you kept a straight face," said Marnie.

"Absolutely inscrutable. He asked me if I knew the owners personally and I said that a very nice woman had *Sally Ann* now. He said did she have short brown hair and a husband who lectured at the university? I said she had shoulder-length dark hair and no husband at all."

"Did he go on board?"

"No. He just went off, looking bewildered. That was it."

"I think I *will* have a gin and tonic," said Marnie with a smile. "But just a small one."

Afterwards they both walked along to *Sally Ann*, and Jane waited on the towpath while Marnie went aboard. She emerged carrying two pieces of cardboard.

"I'll look after those on *Joshua*, if you like. They're incriminating evidence if Beth sees them. Anyway, you might need them again." Marnie handed her the cards. Each was the size of A4 paper. One was marked 'FOR SALE' with a line boldly drawn through it; the other said 'SOLD'.

Part 2

The three women were out gathering bluebells and celandine for the decoration of the church on Lady Day when they heard a distant sound that halted them. They were young, with the family likeness of sisters and they stood listening intently, heads cocked on one side. It was a still spring morning with warmth returning. Until that moment when one had raised a hand for silence, they had been chattering gaily, glad to be out in the fresh air, bending to their task. Now they stood upright like wild rabbits sensing danger. The eldest sister, she who had raised her hand, pointed urgently towards the trees and ushered them to shelter.

The sound of hooves pounding on firm dry ground was clear in the morning air. Within seconds the sisters had concealed themselves, crouching in the undergrowth, waiting and watching.

"Can you see anyone?" It was the youngest who whispered. The eldest put a finger to her lips, shaking her head. Moments later they saw them, a large group of perhaps fifty or more. The women ducked their heads into the ferns, though the eldest kept watch for the first sign of danger as the troop rode through the clearing at a canter. The soldiers wore leather coats and most had steel helmets with peaks. The women tasted the dust thrown up by the drumming hooves and heard the clinking of bridles and weapons. It was long after the men had passed before they dared to breathe again.

"Who were they, Sarah? For King Charles or Parliament?" said the youngest as they stood up, brushing the dirt from their dresses. The eldest stepped out and looked in the direction taken by the riders, shielding her eyes from the morning sun.

"I know not," she said. "What matters it?"

❦   ❦   ❦   ❦

Anne (with an 'e') dropped her bag inside the door and walked into the flat, looking around her like a cat entering a building for the first time. At five foot six, she was nearly as tall as Marnie. She wore jeans, a blouson jacket and trainers, had short fair hair, a slight build, sharp features and looked like an urchin.

"Your room's through there and the bathroom is just opposite. I've only got one bathroom, so we'll have to share, I'm afraid."

"We've got one bathroom between the four of us at home," said Anne.

"Okay. That's the kitchen, round there is my room and the living room's in here." Anne went through the door followed by Marnie and stood, turning slowly, in the middle of the spacious room.

"The ceilings are high and the windows are really ..." Anne stopped in mid-sentence.

"Everybody does that," said Marnie. "I usually tell people they've left their mouth open."

Anne closed hers with a snap. "That's the famous one, the one they showed on television," she said simply. She crossed to the fireplace and stared up at the picture. It was the original drawing of the great aqueduct at Pontcysyllte in North Wales on the Llangollen Canal and had been part of an inheritance left to Marnie the previous year by an old man who had spent his life on the canals and who had somehow acquired a collection of 'lost' drawings from two hundred years ago.

"Did you keep any of the others?"

"Just a few small ones. You'll see them around the flat. The collection is in the museum's special gallery. I couldn't resist that one."

"You gave them all to the museum. I'm sure I couldn't have done that."

"Long-term loan. I felt I had to. They were given to me because I would know what to do with them, or so Old Peter thought. I believed the right thing to do was let everyone see them. You would have done the same in my place."

"But you kept this one."

"They have a copy that looks identical. It's the centrepiece of the Peter William Gibson Collection. Shall we have coffee and make some plans or are you tired after your coach journey?"

"Oh yes, I feel a touch of the vapours coming on," said Anne, raising a hand to her brow. "I shall have to lie down for an hour and adjust my crinoline." They headed for the kitchen, Marnie leading the way.

"What would you like to do?" she said, filling the coffee machine.

"I don't mind. It's just nice to be here. Are we near *Sally Ann*?" Anne fetched cups from the shelf and put them on the table.

"Not far. There's a floating art gallery in the pool at Little Venice."

"Do they have any pictures by you?" said Anne.

"No. I think they're all the work of the gallery's owner. They're very good. I only sketch as a hobby or for my job." The coffee machine began making rude noises. "Are you still drawing?"

"When it's not too cold to go out. I'm doing a GCSE project on the canal: locks, bridges and landscape."

"You'd better watch out or you'll end up like me, chugging along on *Sally*."

"That would be great," said Anne. Marnie poured milk into a jug. "Marnie, did you ever want to be an artist, a painter doing fine art?"

"Not really. I think I've always been a practical person. Of course, I like paintings and sculpture, and I go to lots of exhibitions, but I wouldn't find it satisfying to spend my days doing studies in light and colour. If I hadn't become an interior designer I might have gone into architecture. What about you?"

"I think I feel the same, really. I like doing abstract things, but I get more satisfaction from drawing something like a leaf in all its detail. I love that."

Marnie brought the coffee pot over to the table and poured the steaming brew into their cups. "You can keep your options open at your age. You've got time to decide yet."

"That's what they say at school. My mum's giving me a boxed set of art materials for my birthday. This coffee's good."

"When's your birthday?"

❦ ❦ ❦ ❦

An hour later they were in Oxford Street, going from window to window and store to store. Marnie suggested one of the smaller boutiques.

"I can't let you do this," said Anne.

"Just a small birthday present. What do you think of that shirt?"

They spent the afternoon wearing their feet out like shopaholics. Marnie bought Anne a skirt, a flowing creation in bright colours, and a loose-fitting shirt. Anne said it made her feel like a water gypsy.

❦ ❦ ❦ ❦

Anne wanted to help with supper, but Marnie insisted she at least make a gesture towards her homework and installed her in the study. When, ten minutes later, she took Anne a glass of designer water with ice and lemon, Marnie found her immersed in history notes.

"What period are you doing?"

"Modern. I'm just trying to sort out the Irish question."

"Keep trying," said Marnie. "Good luck."

❦ ❦ ❦ ❦

"What do you do with this?" said Anne, laughing. Marnie stirred the vinaigrette and passed her the jar.

"You tilt your plate by putting your fork under the opposite side and pour the vinaigrette into a small pool. Then you pull out a leaf, dip the fleshy part into the dressing and pull off the flesh with your teeth. Like this." She gave a demonstration. "You try it."

Anne copied her, a curious, sceptical expression on her face. As she ate the flesh, she raised her eyebrows and nodded. "It's good. Very delicate taste. I've seen them in the shops, but never eaten artichoke before. A bit exotic for my family, I suppose."

With a slight exclamation, Marnie quickly stood up and went to the fridge. "I nearly forgot." She produced a half bottle of champagne and put it on the table so that Anne could see the label. "I wouldn't normally encourage someone of your age to drink alcohol, but I thought we might have a small amount of this to celebrate your birthday one week in advance. What do you think?"

"Real champagne?"

"Yes. For a special occasion."

"Great! Are you sure you want to open it?" Marnie answered by pulling off the foil cover and popping the cork. As Marnie poured the first glass the foam reached the top of the flute and rolled over the side.

"You see how out of practice I am," said Marnie. "I ought to drink champagne more often." She filled both glasses and passed one to Anne. "Happy nearly birthday, Anne with an 'e', and every success in your exams this summer. I hope it will prove to be a memorable year."

After supper they took coffee into the living room and Marnie asked to see Anne's canal project.

"I've got my sketchbook with me," said Anne. "Can we compare the drawings with the ones you did last summer?" Marnie went to fetch her own collection of pads. They settled on the large sofa with the drawings, Dolly the cat snug between them, and spent an enjoyable half hour going through the books.

Anne accidentally dislodged a book from the pile, and it slid to the floor. She gathered it up and glanced at the contents. "What's this?"

Marnie leaned over and examined the drawing. It showed a group of ruins set among trees, roof timbers visible like a skeleton and walls partly collapsed. "It's just a place I saw on my travels. I did that from memory, actually. At the time, I was hallucinating … a touch of the sun."

"Didn't you go back and find it?"

"No. In fact, I'm not even sure where it is, exactly."

"Was it after you met me?"

"Yes. Some days later on the way to Braunston. Before I got to the Blisworth tunnel, I think."

"It can't be far from where I live," said Anne. "It looks interesting. What is it, or what was it?"

"An old farm, I think. It must have been a big one in its day. It's strange to see it abandoned. After all, it's not in a remote place out in the wilds. Practically the home counties. And it's on the edge of a village."

"Have you got any Ordnance Survey maps?" said Anne. "The ones we use in geography have lots of detail, even the names of farms." Marnie fetched two or three maps of the area and they pored over them, trying to pinpoint the location, but without success.

"Of course!" she exclaimed. "*Sally Ann*. The log. That'll tell us where it was. Just a minute." Marnie went out and returned clutching a cruising guide and a map of British waterways. She spread the map out on the floor and Dolly jumped down to sit on it. Anne traced Marnie's route with her finger while

Marnie consulted her notes in the log-book.

"It must have been somewhere around *here*," she muttered. "The log is blank for a few days. I was feeling groggy at the time and just took it easy."

"Here are some sketches of the tunnel," said Anne. "They're after the ruins in your sketchbook. We must be looking for somewhere between Linslade and Stoke Bruerne." They spotted the village with the canal running round it in a loop like an ox-bow meander. On its southern side there was a farm marked clearly beside the waterway.

"What's the name of the village?" said Marnie.

"Knightly St John."

"That's the place. Is there a name for the farm?"

"Yes. Just a minute, the grid line runs through it. It's … Glebe Farm. Yes, that's it. Glebe Farm, Knightly St John. It has a nice ring to it."

"Mm. I wonder what became of it. Someone in the village told me it was up for sale."

"Perhaps it isn't a ruin any more. Maybe it's been restored," said Anne. "It would be interesting to find out."

"Where is it in relation to where you live?" They checked the map. It was no great distance. Marnie got up and went over to the hi-fi. "Shall I put some music on? What would you like?"

"Oh, Marnie, I nearly forgot!" Anne leapt up and made for the door. "Excuse me a moment. You choose. Anything." She disappeared leaving Marnie bewildered. She selected Palestrina's *Missa Brevis* by the Tallis Scholars and the first notes were wafting across the room as Anne returned, her hands behind her back. She held out a small packet about the size of a ruler, but more bulky.

Marnie pulled the tissue wrapping gently apart to reveal a bundle of packets of joss sticks: sandalwood, amber, jasmine and musk rose. In the packet was a metal holder that looked like silver. "These are wonderful. Thank you *very* much." She kissed Anne on the cheek.

"I didn't know if you liked that sort of thing, but it seemed right for you somehow."

"I haven't had any for years, but when I was a student I often burned them. A brilliant choice. You've given me a new purpose for my Zippo. Since I gave up smoking last year, it hasn't had much of an aim in life."

They spent the rest of the evening listening to music, punctuated by the cat's purring, and looking through magazines they had bought. Marnie persuaded Anne to enter a competition in one of them, *Residence,* to design the interior of a flat in docklands. Anne made some notes and did a few sketches. Later they pored over maps and canal guides, and decided to look in on Knightly St John to find Glebe Farm when Marnie took Anne home the next day.

Anne was in heaven, transported to a world of style and pleasure. Champagne and artichokes, Palestrina and incense, her new clothes. It was all a long way from a small house in a small provincial town. She was beginning to know what she wanted in life and she had no doubt about who could show her the way ahead.

❦ ❦ ❦ ❦

"If I'm not mistaken, there should be a turning to the right somewhere along here," said Marnie. They had made good time up through Hertfordshire and Anne had proved to be a reliable and accurate map-reader.

"About half a mile, I think." Anne looked up for landmarks and glanced down at the map. "There's a church with a tower, but I haven't caught sight of it yet. It can't be far." Marnie kept the speed at a steady fifty and they peered ahead for the first sight of a sign-post.

"It's awkward here," said Anne. "There's a join in the page."

"There's always a join in the page," said Marnie. "They make them like that. I bet if you go to the Sahara Desert, you'll find the maps have pages of sand, and the oases stuck in the corner at the join."

"I think we have to go past and come in from the other side," said Anne.

"It seemed just a small place when I came here last year."

"You were delirious."

"I shall be again, if we don't find it. What's that up ahead?" They approached a cross-roads at a lonely spot where all around they could see only fields. "Let's try this." The road was narrow and Marnie had to keep the Rover in the middle to avoid potholes at the edge. "I have an awful suspicion this is going to lead us into a field," she muttered.

Sitting beside her with the atlas, Anne knew she was supposed to be frustrated or concerned that they could not find the village, but she was ecstatic. Here she was in the leather seat of a Rover GT-i, with classical music coming softly from the CD player and Marnie driving expertly in difficult terrain. Sooner or later they would find the place they were seeking, but for the moment she was happy just to be where she was.

"Look, up there!" said Marnie, changing down for a bend as they caught sight of rooftops above a clump of trees. Anne checked the map, but was puzzled. Several dotted lines suggested a network of small tracks and it was far from clear which of these, if any, was the road they were following. They passed a cluster of stone cottages and found themselves surrounded by trees and small paddocks. The road turned sharply to the left to reveal houses in a terrace at the road's edge and then swung right again, dropping into a gully from which they emerged to find more cottages set back behind long front gardens. Anne glimpsed rows of brussels sprouts.

"I expect we'll come to the centre sooner or later," said Marnie. "Any sign of that church tower yet?" Anne looked all around but by now they were among trees. She shook her head, trying to locate the church on the map, but it was difficult when she had no clear idea where they were.

"It has to be over to our left somewhere," she said. The road bent to the right.

"I think they're trying to hide something from us," said Marnie. Throughout their meanderings they had not seen a single person. Now, some way along the road they could see a solitary figure, an old man walking briskly towards them. Marnie brought the Rover to a halt beside him. She opened the window and they felt the chill air on their faces.

"Excuse me," she said. "Can you point us towards the middle of the village?"

"The *middle*?" said the old man. "Depends what you mean by the middle." His voice was light, with a country accent.

"Where the shop is, or the church," suggested Marnie.

"Church is over there." The old man pointed back the way they had come and over to the left, which gave Anne some comfort. They looked over their shoulders but saw no trace of the church or its tower.

"I can't quite see it," said Marnie. "And I don't think we've passed it."

"You wouldn't. It's just behind those trees." Anne looked down at the map, but it did not give enough detail to show where they were. The old man continued. "'Course, years ago you could have seen it from anywhere round here. In Cromwell's day these were all watercress beds, no trees this side of the church." Marnie wondered if a Mr Cromwell might have been chairman of the Parish Council or something before the war.

The old man noticed their confused expression. "Oh, no, not the Cromwell *you're* thinking of." His face broke into the kind of smile reserved for the backward and stupid. "No. You're probably thinking of *Thomas* Cromwell, the old Chancellor to Henry the Eighth. It's the Protector I mean. *Oliver* Cromwell."

"Right," said Marnie, as if they were talking about a recent occurrence. "Er, is the church near the shop?"

"Just round the corner, over from the pub."

"Very handy," said Marnie brightly. The old man chuckled. "Well, thanks very much." She pushed the stubby gear lever over towards first and smiled up at the old man. He smiled back.

"You can't start from here, mind," he said, still smiling. Marnie thought she vaguely recalled an Irish hitch-hiker story like this and pulled the gear lever back to neutral.

"Is there a problem?"

"There wasn't in them days, but there is now." He pointed across the open land that seemed to be divided into vegetable gardens or allotments. "No road." Marnie heard Anne splutter in the background.

As they made their way back along the winding road, they waited until they were well out of sight of the old man before bursting into laughter.

"Is there a problem?!" Anne mimicked Marnie.

"You can't start from here," said Marnie in a crackly, ancient voice that did less than justice to the man's sprightly tone. "Now, in Cromwell's day, you could wade through the watercress beds. No problem!" Anne shrieked, but kept tight hold of the atlas, determined that this time she was going to guide them onto the right road, whether Cromwell would have recognised it or not. They reached the main road and turned right, continuing for another half mile to a signpost indicating Knightly St John, Village Only. It was a narrow road but they soon found themselves among houses, with a glimpse of the church tower as a backdrop. Rounding a bend, they saw the sign of the pub, the Two Roses, and Marnie pulled up outside the village shop. Anne pushed the atlas towards Marnie so that they could both see it.

"It makes more sense now. We must be about here," said Anne.

"Yes. I see the problem you had, apart from the join in the page. We could really do with a bigger scale." She looked up. "The canal must be in that direction. Shall we walk it?"

They set off on foot past the church, looking up at the honey-coloured stonework. The afternoon was overcast, cold and still, with thin cloud through which the sun was trying to shine. It was a small village of stone, some of the houses thatched, others under slate roofs, with smoke rising vertically from the chimneys. The air smelled of log fires. Soon they came to a gated field where a green sign pointed the route of the public footpath down a gentle slope. Marnie surveyed the land in all directions.

"This could be it."

"Isn't there a proper road?" said Anne.

"Once upon a time maybe. It's only a ruin. Don't expect too much."

🌷 🌷 🌷 🌷

Marnie and Anne followed the track for a few minutes scanning the terrain for a sight of roofs or chimneys. At one point the trail divided and they hesitated before choosing the path to the right, as the other seemed to cut across open land for as far as they could see. Underfoot the earth felt hard. Here and there the dead grass formed tussocks up against the edge of the track. Suddenly a loud bang made them jump backwards. A pheasant, startled by their approach, flew out from under their feet, speeding away towards the spinney that lay ahead of them. Anne pointed. Through the trees they saw the outline of a chimney stack. They had arrived.

"Something has happened here," said Marnie, standing amongst the ruined buildings.

"That's an understatement," said Anne.

"I mean since I was here last summer. I'm sure the place was in better condition than this." Glebe Farm had once been a substantial property, its buildings forming an almost complete square around a broad farmyard. The farm house itself was L-shaped and tall, with stone mullions to the windows, and it extended round two sides of the yard. Across the doorframe someone had nailed strips of old floorboard, with a sign saying 'Dangerous Structure – Keep Out'. Attached to the main house were cottages, though it was difficult to see if there were two or three, for they were in a desperate state, with roofs collapsed, windows and doorways rotted. On the other sides of the yard were barns, only one of which boasted a roof. The others had exposed timbers, blackened by fire, pointing at the sky. The yard was cobbled and uneven, with tufts of dead grass where there were gaps in the paving. Anne picked her way carefully across to the barn with the roof and stuck her head inside the opening, while Marnie remained in the middle, trying to remember what she had seen from the spinney that hot day the previous year when, trying to find shade, she had collapsed under the trees.

"It's similar to your drawings, but more dilapidated," said Anne. "This building's all right, though, for the time being."

Marnie took note of the ominous undertone and strolled over. "*For the time being,*" she repeated.

Anne nodded and walked into the barn, scuffing the ground with the side of her shoe. "Kids have been smoking in here."

"What makes you think it was kids?"

"Who else could it have been?" said Anne. She pointed at the ground. "Adults wouldn't have any reason for coming here and there are too many butts for them to have just been waiting for a shower to pass. Look at the cigarette ends. They're smoked right down to the filter tip. That's just like kids."

"Tramps, perhaps?" suggested Marnie. Anne inclined her head to one side while she considered this and inspected the barn thoughtfully, looking down at the dusty floor. She shook her head slowly as Marnie watched her from the doorway.

"See these footprints?" Anne squatted in the far corner and Marnie walked across. She squinted in the gloom and followed the line that Anne traced with her finger. "Trainers. These are Reeboks like mine. I reckon they stood over here in the corner, out of sight." Marnie nodded.

They walked out of the barn into the daylight and almost collided with a tall man in a tweed jacket holding two large black dogs on leads. The dogs, surprised by the strangers, barked and strained forward on their leashes, while the man struggled to hold them back. Anne, defying all reason, threw herself down on her knees in front of the dogs and opened her arms out wide. Their reaction was to lick her face, jumping around her and rearing up on their hind legs as if they had found an old friend. The dogs' owner stared at the scene. The girl had her arms round both dogs, holding and patting their sides, rubbing their ears, twisting her head from side to side to avoid their tongues.

"Well, as guard dogs go these are a bit deficient," said the man in a light, pleasant voice. "I'd better have them put down and get Rottweilers instead. What do you think?"

Marnie smiled at the man. "I'm sorry if we're trespassing. We just ... happened by and thought we'd take a look."

"Free country," he replied. "As far as I know it's still on the market and you don't look like the yobbos who came and burned down the other parts." His manner was amiable and his smile friendly. He was about six feet tall with dark wavy hair visible from under a tweed cap. The dogs were now calmer and he pulled them back to sit panting on either side of him, their tongues lolling from their mouths, their eyes bright with pleasure.

"Yobbos?" said Marnie.

"Some boys," said the man. "They used to come here to smoke, apparently." Anne exchanged a glance with Marnie. "Then, about three or four weeks ago, the place mysteriously caught fire. The whole lot nearly went up."

"What happened?" said Marnie.

"Oh, the real Dunkirk spirit." He made a sound somewhere between a snort and a laugh. "The whole village turned out with beaters and buckets. A human chain, bringing water from the canal. It's just over there." He pointed over their shoulders. "It was like something out of the Middle Ages."

"Or Cromwell's time," said Anne. The man stared at her.

"This place has a strange atmosphere, rather cut off," said Marnie.

"That's true of the whole village. In fact, part of it *was* cut off in Cromwell's time. There was so much feuding between villages in the Civil War that the old road was closed off to help keep them apart. To this day, you can't get down that way."

"Can't it be opened up again after all this time?" said Marnie.

"I suppose so, but nobody likes change round here. No-one now could tell you where the old road went. It's lost without trace."

"And even the watercress beds have disappeared," said Anne casually. The man narrowed his eyes and looked at her.

"Did you say the place was on the market?" said Marnie.

"That's right."

"It was for sale the last time I came here," she added.

"That can't be right." The man seemed puzzled. "The farm has not been outside the same family for over three centuries."

Marnie laughed. "I'm not quite that old," she said. "It was last summer, actually. By the way, my name is Marnie Walker and this is Anne. We were just looking round out of curiosity and Anne was telling me about the place. She has rare insights."

The man frowned. "Sorry, I'm being rude. My name is Frank Day. This is Cassius and this is Bruno." Hearing their names, the dogs became restless and began to pull forward again. "I think I can recognise a hint when I see one. If you'll forgive me I'd better get on. We have a fair way to go before we're home. The agents are Blackey and Johnson, if you're interested in putting in an offer. I gather the price is rock bottom," he called over his shoulder.

"Hang on a minute," Marnie said to Anne and jogged after the man, catching up with him by the corner of the barn.

"Blackey and Johnson?" she said.

"In town. Market Square. Could be a real bargain."

"Thanks, though I'm not really in the market. I hope our being here hasn't bothered you. We seem to have given you rather a surprise, especially Anne," said Marnie.

"She did surprise me in a way. You'll have to keep an eye on that one. In Cromwell's time, a girl who had rare insights and power over animals, especially black ones, might have been suspected of being a witch. That could be dangerous." He paused. There was a twinkle in his eye and a smile in his voice. "Only joking. It's been nice meeting you. Hope to see you again some time. Sorry if I don't raise my hat. Bye!" Marnie turned back to Anne and, for the first time noticed the sour odour of burnt wood in the air.

Part 3

It was a wet afternoon and the raindrops were dripping into puddles from the eaves of the smithy. The eldest of the sisters, Sarah Anne, hurried in clutching a pot of ale. She set it down on the bench and shook the rain from her bonnet and her shawl. Standing in the glow of the forge, her father was in conversation with three other men, their coats steaming gently in the warmth from the fire. All turned towards her as she came in.

"Now there's a thing, Sarah," one of the men cried out. "We thought you had come with ale for us as well!"

"I did not know anyone else was here," said the young woman with a smile. "But I can go back and seek you some if you would like."

"No, no, but thank you kindly. We shall not stay long. And it would be better if you went out to seek yourself a husband!" All the men laughed together.

"Time enough for that," said Sarah Anne and turned to leave, pulling the shawl tight round her shoulders. The rain was falling more heavily and she hesitated on the threshold. The men returned to their talk.

"I say the vicar could bring trouble to the village," said one of the men.

"He has already," said another. "What with his High Catholic ways. There's no room for his kind in this place." The men grunted their agreement.

"And it is no secret he supports the King." The tone of her father's voice made Sarah Anne look round. A heavily built man, in the firelight he seemed larger, more ominous, forbidding. The others nodded. The blacksmith reached out and turned an iron rod in the fire where it glowed red. "He could bring more than trouble. He could be a danger to everyone. You will have to watch him while I am away."

"So you have decided, then? You are going to the colours?"

"I am," said Sarah Anne's father. "And I am going with two of my boys and both my brothers. Richard will stay to work the smithy."

"It will not be easy to restrain the vicar," said one of the men. "He is strong-willed and accepts nobody's view if it runs counter to his own." Sarah Anne was surprised at how grim her father looked as he pulled the bolt out of the fire with his tongs, set it on the anvil and struck it firmly with the hammer.

❦ ❦ ❦ ❦

"So how was your weekend?" said Beth. The phone had started ringing as Marnie came through the door.

"Very pleasant. How about yours?"

"So-so. We had one of Paul's research students round for supper on Saturday, a very earnest young man, with his girlfriend. He's doing a doctorate in Information Technology and she's doing a Master's in early eighteenth century organ music."

"Their conversation at the breakfast table must be quite exhilarating," said Marnie.

"Which is more than can be said for their conversation at the supper table. Roderick is one of those types who thinks that if you speak in the quietest possible voice you'll be regarded as an intellectual. They were OK, but I was quite relieved when they'd gone."

"Still, it gave you something to talk about afterwards."

Beth gave a snort, ignoring the innuendo. "Paul said they must have a dog's life at home ... all Bachs and bytes! Anyway, that's not really why I phoned."

"Oh," said Marnie. "I thought you wanted to keep me up-to-date on your social life."

"Listen. Mum rang this afternoon and invited us all to go to them for Easter.

Would you like to?" Marnie hesitated. The idea of a fortnight of Spanish sunshine was tempting. She thought about her parents, their sunny garden with its view down to the sea, the meals on the terrace under the bougainvillaea, the mountains shimmering in the distance. She thought about her in-tray, the contracts in progress, the deadlines. "Are you still there?"

"Mm," said Marnie. "Sounds marvellous, but I think I'll have to stay here this Easter. It's not easy to get away just now."

She thought about spring coming at last, the blossom, daffodils and tulips, new foliage, willows trailing fronds in the water. "Perhaps I could borrow *Sally Ann* while you're in Spain? Unless you've sold her, of course." She heard Beth sigh.

"No. We haven't sold her." There was a coolness in the tone.

"Have I said the wrong thing?"

"Let's just say it's a sore point at the moment in this household. One faction thinks we could put the money from selling the boat to better use than just sitting in the water. The other faction has romantic notions without any basis in reality." Beth stopped and waited. "Are you there, Marnie?"

"Yes. I'm just trying to work out which view is yours." There was an indeterminate noise from the other end. It was definitely abusive. "What do you think about me borrowing *Sally*?"

❦   ❦   ❦   ❦

A satellite in orbit eighty miles over the eastern Atlantic Ocean sent information down to the Meteorological Office in London. It transmitted data as radio signals that the computers on the ground translated. This may have been less pastoral than the song of the cuckoo, but it proved to be an accurate messenger announcing the arrival of spring.

The next few days grew perceptibly warmer, and by the weekend the new season had settled in. Almost without thinking about it, Marnie drove up to Knightly.

At Glebe Farm, the small barn where Anne had spotted the cigarette stubs was still almost intact. There was a wooden ladder built into the wall at the far end, leading up to a hayloft. She tried the rungs and decided they were strong enough to take her weight. The loft was taller than she expected and in the light of her torch she saw no traces of intrusion or damage.

Standing among the ruined buildings, Marnie saw them taking shape, walls rising, roofs appearing, roses climbing up to the eaves. Then reality took over, and wandering around she realised how big a task it would be.

She stood in the abandoned farmyard, shaking her head. It was nearly time for lunch.

❦   ❦   ❦   ❦

After a sandwich at the pub, Marnie crossed the road and tried the door of the church. It was locked.

On the wall of the porch were notices about the work of the church in the Third World, a message from the Bishop and the flower rota. The photograph of the Bishop was informal. He was standing in short sleeves surrounded by African children, his arms round the shoulders of a boy and girl. He looked more like a tourist than a senior churchman and could not have been much more than fifty. The heading on the notice referred to a first greeting from Tom Cavendish, installed the previous month after four years as a suffragan in London. His name seemed familiar and Marnie thought she had heard him on the radio. The message was signed "Your sincere friend Thomas ✝" and the small print at the bottom referred to him as The Right Rev Dr Thomas Cavendish MA DD.

"Were you wanting to see inside?" Marnie had not noticed a woman approaching up the path behind her. "I was just going in, if you'd like to visit the church." She was carrying a large shopping bag and wearing a long brown cardigan over a fawn blouse and a tweed skirt, every inch the countrywoman.

"I was just hoping to pop in for a few minutes," said Marnie, standing aside to let the woman pass and open the door with a large iron key.

"It's so sad that we have to keep it locked up like this. Orders from the diocesan office, I'm afraid." She struggled with the lock until it yielded. "You wouldn't believe the vandalism and theft that have happened in some of our churches. If you want to be quiet, I'll not disturb you. I'm just taking away the old flowers. Pretend I'm not there." Marnie realised the woman had assumed she might want to pray. For her this was not medieval architecture, but part of everyday life.

The church was broad with clerestory windows high up under oak beams in the nave and two side aisles. There was a faint spicy smell of incense, and the stained glass windows were mainly Victorian with one or two earlier examples. The list of vicars went back to 1100. An ancient place. There were a few gaps and question marks but a good sprinkling of Norman names: Hugh de Baal, Martin de Chichester, Roland de Chartres. The church had been part of a priory based in Normandy near Le Havre and several of the heads of the order were listed under the title *abbé*. The font was reputedly the oldest in this part of England, depicting Adam and Eve in the garden of Eden, still recognisable after nearly a thousand years.

The apse contained tombs of the local gentry and a plaque commemorating one vicar from the fifteenth century who had gone on to become Archbishop of York. The biggest surprise was the window on the south side, depicting a group of women standing round Mary and the child Jesus. The folds of their dresses were so realistic that Marnie felt she could reach up and touch the cloth. It looked like the work of Edwin Burne-Jones, the Pre-Raphaelite and friend of William Morris, and she walked back to the table by the entrance to check the facts. She looked at every postcard and pamphlet, but there was no booklet telling the history of the church.

"Are you looking for something?" The woman's bag was now stuffed with dead flowers.

"I wanted a history of the church. I've been in a lot of churches not nearly as interesting as this one and they always have a leaflet."

The woman hesitated. "Is there something in particular that you want to look up?"

"The church has such a long history, I'd be interested to read about it."

"There *was* a history leaflet," said the woman. She felt in her cardigan pocket for the church key. "I think it must be out of print." The air outside was warmer than in the building as they walked down the path together.

"There was a window in the south transept near the altar," said Marnie. "It looked like the work of Burne-Jones. I didn't know he had done anything in these parts."

"Oh yes. He designed a number of stained glass windows in the county. I think he had relatives in the area and they got him some commissions."

"It would be good to find out more about his work in this part of the country," said Marnie. "That's one of the reasons why I wanted the history leaflet."

"Ah yes, of course. Well, perhaps you might find one some other time, if ever you're passing this way."

"Yes, perhaps I will. Thanks for letting me in." Marnie set off down the road towards the field track, while the woman closed the lych gate behind her.

Part 4

There were fourteen men in total, six mounted, eight on foot. They assembled at the church gate, but there was no-one to say a blessing. A small crowd of relatives gathered round them, attempting gaiety, as if this was no more than a hunting party. The biggest man on the biggest horse was Jonathan Day, the blacksmith. He was an able craftsman, a kindly husband and father, a patriarch in the village. His aim now was to be a redoubtable warrior in the service of Parliament.

"So many of you leaving," said his wife. "The village will be half empty until you come back."

"But we will come back," he said. "The village will still have enough men to carry on the work, at least until harvest. And there are those who will not join us." He looked around ominously. "There are some who would prefer to hide in their houses, taking sides with the King."

"It is their right to do as they believe they should," said his wife. "We cannot deny them that. They have been good neighbours and will be still, when this is all over and forgotten."

The men embraced their loved ones and set off slowly down the road. As they rode and walked they glared at the houses of those who had chosen not to march with them. With a troubled face, Sarah Anne came forward and handed up to her father a canvas bag.

"This is for you, father. There is pork, ale, cheese and bread, and the last of the apples. Enough for your journey. Go safely." She touched his hand briefly and turned away.

ϙ   ϙ   ϙ   ϙ

Spring

The following Friday, as Marnie arrived home from work, she found Beth and Paul on her doorstep. They had invited themselves round to tell her about their trip to Spain. They had come armed.

Walking into the kitchen, Marnie switched on the kettle for coffee, while Beth placed a bulky carrier bag on the table. "Love from Mum and Dad."

Marnie peered inside the bag and began pulling out a variety of jars, bottles and tins. There were olives of various colours and fillings, anchovies, pâtés, snails in paprika sauce, king prawns, goat's cheese, spicy chorizo sausages and so on and so on. The last items to come out were two bottles of red wine.

"You lugged all these back from Spain for me?"

"All part of the service," said Beth.

Marnie looked dubious. "You must have had an ulterior motive."

Beth and Paul glanced pointedly down at the feast laid out before them. Marnie at once switched off the kettle and rummaged in a drawer, producing a corkscrew. It took less than two minutes to lay out plates, glasses and cutlery. Marnie tipped the food into small serving dishes while Paul opened a bottle and Beth popped two baguettes from the freezer into the oven. It was instant *tapas*.

While they worked their way steadily through the feast of morsels from Almeria, Beth brought Marnie up-to-date on the latest news from their parents. Marnie soon found herself opening the second bottle of wine. The bottle was standing on the workbench beside the accumulated mail and Marnie noticed that the letter on top of the pile was franked with the familiar logo of the National Canal Museum.

"Come on!" said Paul. "We're suffering from grape juice vitamin deficiency over here."

Marnie handed him the bottle and corkscrew so that she could open the letter. "Sorry. I'm intrigued by this." She sat at the table and glanced quickly through the letter from the curator.

"Don't tell me," said Beth. "They've discovered the drawings are forgeries. They've found a little label on the back saying *Printed in Hong Kong*."

"Not quite," said Marnie and put the letter back in the envelope.

"Well?" said Beth. "Is everything all right?"

"They want me to perform the official opening of the new gallery for the drawing collection next month."

Beth and Paul hooted. "Marnie, you've become a canal celebrity," said Paul.

"And you don't even have a boat," said Beth pointedly.

"Quite. All I wanted was a little time to myself to work out what I wanted from life."

"So your journey was not in vain. At least you've sorted that out, haven't you?" Marnie picked up an olive, studied it and put it in her mouth. "Haven't you?" Beth repeated. "Marnie?"

"Well, maybe I have, maybe I haven't. Not completely anyway." She took a sip of wine. "This red is really good. Did you say it was Penedès?"

"Don't change the subject," said Beth.

Marnie said: "Before you remind me about the good job, good salary, smart flat, nice car, etc, etc, it isn't as easy as that."

"But you can't expect to go wandering off in a boat all the time. That isn't a solution to anything."

Marnie examined a prawn on the end of her fork. "It's as if something isn't quite right," she said hesitantly. "As if ... something is missing. It's hard to explain. Take Paul, for example." Paul was sipping his wine, swallowed it the wrong way and coughed, trying not to splutter. Marnie continued. "He has his job and he's done a doctorate. That doesn't mean he's finished with research for the rest of his life. He wants to go on into new areas of discovery and growth. And why ...?"

"Because his professor will nag him if he doesn't," said Beth.

"Or you will," said Marnie.

"*Me?!*" said Beth

Marnie ignored her. "The reason is because he feels he has to," she said. "It's all a matter of personal and professional development."

"How does wandering around on *Sally Ann* contribute to your personal and professional development?" said Beth. "I don't see it."

"It helped me to come to that conclusion." There was a pause in the conversation. Marnie took a piece of bread and mopped the paprika sauce on her plate. Beth pronged an olive. Paul topped up their wine glasses.

"So what do you want to do?" said Beth. "And where does *Sally Ann* figure in your plans?"

"I'm thinking of giving up my job here and starting up on my own outside London."

"Are you *crazy?*" said Beth. "You'd give up everything you've got for some hare-brained scheme to go off to the back woods?"

"Thanks for the support and help!" exclaimed Marnie. Beth grinned at her and Paul laughed. Marnie looked at them. "You *buggers!*" She got up to make coffee and put a plate of *petits fours* on the table. Beth and Paul cleared away the remains of the *tapas*.

"You know," said Marnie, "It was my trip on *Sally Ann* that helped me see things clearly ... gave me something to look after. Opened up new horizons, literally."

"But you can't build a life around a boat," said Beth. "Not when you're a talented interior designer. I can't see you earning a living designing colour schemes for canal boats."

"That isn't what I have in mind."

"What *do* you have in mind exactly?"

Marnie hesitated in the middle of opening the packet of coffee and stood silent and thoughtful as if trying to decide whether she should speak. The phone rang. She handed the coffee to Beth and went to take the call in the living room. It was Anne.

"What's the matter?" said Marnie. "You sound subdued."

"I can't stay on at school."

"Who says?"

"I says."

"Why not?"

Anne sighed at the end of the line. "It's difficult. I should've realised. It was all just a dream, really."

"Has something happened?" said Marnie.

"No, except I overheard Mum and Dad saying how tough things were, trying to make ends meet. Marnie, they can't afford to keep me at school for another two years, then at college for three or four more years. It's not reasonable. I'm going to have to get a job."

"At sixteen? There's not a lot going for sixteen-year-olds."

"There wouldn't be a chance of anything at your company. I realise that. I just like being with you. You seem so secure."

"*I do?* How? Because I have a car, a mortgage and a cat?"

"No, Marnie. Because you're confident. You know what you're doing and where you're going."

"What if I said I wanted to move out of London and start my own business?" She knew at once she had made a mistake. What she had intended was to make Anne aware that nothing was immutable and that the world was in a constant state of flux and uncertainty. Anne knew that well enough already. Marnie cursed herself for her stupidity and knew what she said would do nothing but upset Anne even more.

"That's great!" said Anne.

"What?"

"It's great! I *said* you knew what you wanted to do. That's marvellous. I could come and work for you. I wouldn't want much and I could learn from you like an apprentice, like in the old days."

"Well, er ... Anne, I mean ... it's not quite as easy as that."

"I don't expect things to be easy. I've learnt that much already."

"No, of course. It's just that I have very little capital at the moment. I couldn't afford staff, at least not at first, except maybe a few hours of secretarial help each week." She bit her tongue, realising that what she was saying had no basis in reality.

"Well that's fine," said Anne. "I could do that. I'm really good at typing. I always get the best marks for word-processing and office skills."

"Anne, don't get carried away. Listen. I haven't firmed up my plans yet. There's a lot more to be considered and it may never happen."

"Right. I get the picture. But when you have a better idea, I hope you'll tell me about it."

"Sure."

"Promise?"

"Of course."

Beth and Paul were chatting in the kitchen but stopped as soon as Marnie returned.

"Everything all right, Marnie?"

Lying in bed that night, Marnie went over the conversations with Anne and Beth and Paul, wondering where she was going. She had said far more than she intended and had talked about ideas that she had not fully considered. Time passed. Ideas ran through her head. A restless night.

Thirty miles away, Anne closed her book, switched off the bedside lamp and snuggled down under the bedclothes. The day had had an unexpectedly happy ending after a bad start. She slept soundly.

Marnie got up after a while and went to the kitchen for a glass of sparkling water. Standing by the window in the darkened room, with only the light from the half-open door of the refrigerator, she tried to see into the future. The image of Anne's smiling face floated by. She was sitting in an office surrounded by computers, a monitor, a printer, a photocopier. Marnie sighed. She did not even possess a typewriter.

Part 5

Sarah Anne could not sleep for the anguish she had felt since her father and the other men had left the village to go to war. Silently, so as not to disturb her sisters, she rose from her bed and dressed. She wanted air and light to clear her head.

The path beside the watercress beds was narrow, and she had to watch where she trod to avoid the mud that seeped through the tussocks and spread in patches across its surface. It was good to be out on this fair morning, with only the singing of the birds for company. Her walk would take her to the edge of the woods where clusters of daffodils grew in profusion.

At first, she did not see him coming, nor did he notice her, his head bowed in thought. Before her, on the track leading out of the woods, partly camouflaged by his brown coat against the trees, was the vicar, walking back towards the village. Towards the village? They could not help but meet on the narrow path. Even so, when he caught sight of Sarah Anne, the man seemed to pause in his stride, just for a second, as if he might wish to avoid her, but he walked on. Sarah Anne stopped to let him by.

"Good morning, Vicar."

"Good morning to you, my child."

"A lovely day, sir."

"Indeed, and you abroad so early. The sun is barely risen."

"I wanted to gather flowers for the church. My mother is decorating it for the Easter service tomorrow. She said she wanted to fill it with daffodils to ..."

"To help us forget the ugliness of the world?"

"To make it joyous."

"Quite so, quite so." They stood in silence, neither seeming ready yet to move.

"You are also walking early, Vicar." He looked down. "Are you contemplating your sermon?"

"I am always on God's business, my child." At that, he raised his hand and placed it lightly on the side of her arm. Without thinking, Sarah touched it with her own. The vicar smiled and passed by.

After he had walked on, Sarah still seemed to feel the faint pressure of his hand. She turned and watched him striding along the path. So early to be out walking, even on God's business.

❦ ❦ ❦ ❦

Marnie looked in on Philip on Monday morning.

"Come in, Marnie. Have a seat. Now why do I think you've got something on your mind?"

"You're as bad as Beth, my sister. I sometimes swear she's psychic."

"So I'm right?"

"You're right. I'm not quite sure how to put this, mainly because I'm not sure about all the details myself."

"I recognise the symptoms, Marnie. Remember, I used to work for another company years ago before I started up this one with Alex. Have I hit the target?"

"I like it here, Philip. In fact, I can't think of another company I'd rather work for. It's just that perhaps I need a new challenge."

"Has someone made you an offer?"

"Oh, no. Nothing like that. I just have this feeling that ... maybe I'm ready to do my own thing."

"Well, you're only in your early thirties, so it's too soon for a mid-life crisis. I'm ten years older than you and I'm still saving up for mine."

"As soon as we see the sports car magazines on your desk, we'll know it's happening," said Marnie.

"Or in your case, it'll be canal boat magazines," said Philip. "I think perhaps your sabbatical did help you to sort yourself out, after all. So what do you have in mind?"

"I'm not sure. The idea's only just developing."

"In your *conscious* mind, maybe. But it's been fairly obvious to me ever since you came back last autumn." His voice was gentle, but the words took Marnie by surprise. "I think it was inevitable that this would happen, or certainly there must have been a fifty-fifty chance it would. Although it's not in our best interests, for you it's probably the right thing to do. But it may be a difficult time to set up on your own."

"We've built up a good interior design team. More than one of them would be capable of taking over the group. I'm not indispensable."

"Okay. But I'd be sorry to have you as competition, Marnie."

"I wouldn't be near enough to be competition." The more they spoke, the more Marnie realised how little thought she had given to the ideas that were forming. Why was she going down this path?

"This arrived this morning." He passed her a letter on the familiar headed note-paper of Willards Brewery, the large company for whom they had carried out some major projects. She read quickly. It was the job they had been waiting for, refurbishment of their chain of restaurants, complete renovation of their head office in Leicester. This was the kind of contract that, working alone, she could not hope to win. She looked up at Philip, whose expression was enigmatic.

"Turn over and read the second page," he said quietly. "Read it out loud."

She read: "We have had very good customer reaction to the refurbishment of our canalside inns and we are confident that the good relationship that has developed with your company over the past year will produce the desired results." The rest concerned the timetable for drawing up a contract and preparing the brief. "He's right," said Marnie. "We've all worked well together. And he knows that a lot of the ground work has been done."

"That isn't what he's saying, though, is it?" said Philip. "It's a vote of confidence in you, Marnie."

"Backed up by a first class team," said Marnie.

"Yes. But essentially they want you and, let's not forget it, they want access to the drawings that you were left by the old guy in his will. They're a key part of your design."

"Philip, if I did go and start up on my own, I would let you have access to the drawings that I inherited. If that's what Willards want, it's fine by me. I wouldn't let you down."

Philip smiled. "You said you wouldn't be near enough to be in competition, or something like that. That made me think you had your ideas fairly well worked out. But maybe I misunderstood."

Marnie outlined her ideas and Philip listened without comment or reaction until the end.

"You're not sure if this farm is still for sale and you don't know the asking price."

"That's right."

"But it's a ruin. That's definite, is it?"

"Yes."

"And it's uninhabitable. That's another certainty."

"Yes."

"Possibly unsafe and likely to collapse."

"You'd make a poor estate agent, Philip."

"It's what I would call a *courageous* decision, I think."

"Isn't that the management way of saying the idea is completely mad?"

"Bold, perhaps."

"On the face of it, it all sounds pretty stupid, doesn't it?" said Marnie.

"Well, you didn't see this place when we first took it over. Alex and I put everything we had into it. But it was in a good position at a good price."

"Are you telling me the farm idea isn't completely mad, or that it's in a bad position, may not be a good price and is not worth thinking about?"

"I'm telling you that a start now isn't going to be easy, but with the Willards project to get you launched, you might just make it, depending on the price they want for the farm complex. We might even be able to offer you the odd spot of consultancy. You've got some more thinking to do."

❦   ❦   ❦   ❦

On the following day after work, Marnie drove to Little Venice with *Sally Ann's* curtains, freshly washed and ironed, on the back seat of the car. She had planned to spend the evening on the boat, tidying up and getting her ready for the summer. She had wanted to think things over by herself, but Beth had phoned to say that she would be going to the boat that same evening.

"I thought you'd have been here sooner," said Beth. "It's gone half-past-six."

"It's the best time. The parking meters have stopped." She dumped the curtains on the bed.

"When I got here and saw the curtains had gone I thought we'd had burglars. I know how much you must have paid for that material. At least no-one would ever have thought of stealing the ones we had before."

"Not unless there was a national shortage of dish cloths," said Marnie, "and the underworld was desperate to clean up. Sorry, no joke intended."

"None noticed."

"So, what brings you here?" said Marnie.

"It's my boat."

"Ah, yes ... I remember. You said you had things to do. Such as?"

"Oh, this and that. You know what it's like on a boat. There are always loads of jobs to be done."

"What do you have in mind?"

"I'll ... put the kettle on for coffee."

"It's a start," said Marnie. "Do you want to help me put up the curtains? Or did you want to get on with fitting new pistons in the engine?"

"I thought diesels didn't have pistons."

"That's carburettors."

"Oh ... I knew something didn't have pistons."

"Make the coffee, Beth." Marnie unscrewed the ends of the brass rods and began hanging the curtains. They looked as good as new. Beth poured coffee and sat down.

"Marnie ... I was wondering ..."

"Ye-e-s ...?" The tone in Marnie's voice betrayed suspicion. Beth looked hurt.

"I only wanted to ... to ask you ... you know, about your plans ... if you'd got any further ... or if you'd ..."

"Come to my senses?"

"Yes ... no!"

"Come on. Let's have it. What's the matter? If you go on biting your lip like that, you might bleed on my curtains. Then I'll turn nasty." Beth smiled a brief smile and drew breath.

"Well ... after your separation I worried about you taking on the flat. It seemed such a big responsibility, and so expensive."

"It was a bargain."

"Only because you worked solidly at renovating it."

"It helped take my mind off things. I enjoyed it. As an investment it's been good."

"But at the time I thought, *we thought*, you were killing yourself with overwork."

"I didn't work on it the whole time. I took a break between rooms and relaxed while I planned the next one."

"That was the next worry."

"You thought, *you both thought*, I was getting too idle?"

"No. We both thought you were drinking too much." Marnie's jaw dropped. "We did, really."

"Anything else?"

"When you were … *restless*, I think you called it, at work … we thought you were unable to cope with executive stress. I thought you might be going to have a nervous breakdown." If Marnie's jaw had been capable of dropping further, it would have been in free-fall until it hit the ground.

"So what with the stress and the drink, allied to the manic overwork on the flat, you became more relaxed about things when I borrowed the boat for my sabbatical and went on a pleasant trip. Right?"

"Not quite. Remember we were in Boston and all we ever heard from you was about the boat. I worried that you were becoming obsessive about *Sally Ann*."

"You think being obsessive might be a family trait?"

"I was glad, *we both were*, when you came back and got on with your job. You looked so much better, you were more confident. We came back to find you were in the newspapers, on the radio, on the television news, because of the drawings you inherited. You're practically an institution."

"Good."

"But now you seem unsettled again."

"I am," said Marnie. Beth groaned. "But, against my better judgement, I think I'll have to tell you what's on my mind."

Beth looked suspicious. "You started to tell us something the other day, but then you clammed up."

"Well I'll tell you now," said Marnie. "The only thing is, you have to promise not to interrupt or gesticulate or huff and puff. Otherwise you'll have to go home."

"By that you mean I'll have to get off *my own boat* and go back to my house."

"Exactly."

"Go on, then."

"I take that as your promise," said Marnie. As concisely as she could, she explained to Beth about finding Glebe Farm and her plan to renovate it to create offices, a home for herself and some cottages to sell or let. By now the idea was starting to seem less improbable and she felt more confident about explaining it. During the narrative Beth sat impassively at the table. "Well, that's about it. Of course, it is just an idea and a lot will depend on whether the place is still for sale, how much it costs and whether I can sell my flat."

"Well, you seem to know what you're doing," said Beth thoughtfully.

"I wouldn't go that far," said Marnie.

❦ ❦ ❦ ❦

"Marnie, hallo! Welcome aboard!" It was after work on Thursday that Marnie found herself back in Little Venice, stepping onto Roger Broadbent's sixty-foot narrowboat *Rumpole*. Roger was the solicitor who had dealt with the will of Old Peter and had informed Marnie of the bequest of the collection of drawings by

William Jessop. A keen boat-owner himself, Roger spent many evenings on *Rumpole*, moored on the other side of the pool from *Sally Ann*. Marnie had phoned him that morning, while working through her list. They settled themselves in comfortable armchairs in the saloon.

"So, what can I get you, tea, coffee, or something warm?" Roger blossomed in the evenings once he had changed out of his conventional office suit and traditional canal hospitality took over.

"I think something warm might be a good idea," said Marnie. They decided on gin and tonic with lots of ice. "Marjorie not joining us?"

"She's gone late night shopping in the West End. By the time I see her again I expect I'll be bankrupt. Unless she's left the credit cards behind. What can I do for you, Marnie? You said there was something you wanted to talk over." She outlined the plan and Roger listened carefully, his face resuming some of its professional seriousness.

"So you'll be leaving us and giving up *Sally Ann's* mooring?"

"She's not my boat, remember. She belongs to my sister."

"Of course, I was forgetting that."

"Beth thinks I have a tendency to do the same."

"And you have no problems with contracts from your present firm, no restrictive clauses, that sort of thing?" Marnie shook her head. Roger sipped his drink. "Don't think I'm prying, but do you have a sound financial base, loans lined up with the bank, perhaps some invested capital?" Marnie shook her head again.

Roger sipped his drink again before he spoke. "So the intention is to sell the flat and use the proceeds to finance the purchase and the move. Mmm ... That's what I would call ..." They both chorused in unison: "a courageous decision."

"Ah," said Roger. "You've been through this conversation before."

"What I was wondering," said Marnie, "is what you think of my plan."

"Presumably you would wish me to keep within the laws of libel?"

"Preferably." They both took another sip of gin and tonic.

"Well," he sighed, "I've heard better propositions in my time. It's a big risk. You'd be putting all you've got into a derelict collection of ruins. Nowhere to live. Starting a business in a new part of the country where you have no contacts. Would that seem a fair summary of the proposition?"

"As far as it goes. You've missed out the *bad* news. I haven't yet got a buyer, or even an estate agent, for my flat." Roger stood up and fetched the bottles of gin and tonic. Frowning, he topped up their glasses. Marnie did not object.

"Actually," he began hesitantly, "I wonder if I might be able to help you there." He looked vacant as if searching his memory. "Yes ... Robin."

"Robin?"

"Our new partner. He's been with us about six months. Commutes in from Alton every day. He's getting cheesed off with it. From your part of town he could do it in twenty minutes or so. I'll mention it to him, if you're sure about it."

"Thanks. You never know. Mind you, I'm not sure what the value is at current prices."

"Trust me," said Roger, tapping the side of his nose. "I'm a solicitor." Marnie raised her glass with a dubious expression. "And look on the bright side. You're not going to have any problems with the bank."

"You think they'll see it as a sound investment?"

He beamed. "No! It's so ... *courageous*, no bank's going to touch it. One less thing to worry about."

Marnie contacted the estate agents about Glebe Farm and the details soon arrived in the post. It was described as the rare opportunity to acquire a farm complex in need of refurbishment. Roger phoned to confirm his colleague was interested in seeing the flat. Marnie looked in local estate agents and gained a fair impression of asking prices.

After work on the following Friday, Roger rang Marnie to say that Robin and his wife were keen to see the flat over the weekend. Marnie set about tidying up with a fervour normally only reserved for *Sally Ann*. She even groomed Dolly, to their joint surprise. When the doorbell rang on Sunday morning, Marnie had a quick glance round, concluded that the flat had never looked so desirable and, muttering under her breath that she must be mad ... no, *courageous* ... she pressed the button to open the front door.

🌹 🌹 🌹 🌹

It was nearly ten o'clock that evening when Roger rang up. Robin and Gwen were desperate to buy the flat and would confirm their offer to her the next day. The price was generous and subject to the flat being taken off the market immediately. Almost as soon as the conversation ended the phone rang again.

"Marnie, what did you say was the name of that village where the ruins are? Is it Knightly St Somebody?" Beth sounded quite animated.

"Knightly St John. Why?"

"It's just been on television. You'd better not go there. The place is *heaving* with suppressed passion."

"So are Penge and Bromley, for all I know."

"Quite. It was a snippet at the end of the regional news. It seems the vicar is in dispute with his parishioners, some ancient row over prayerbooks, or something. They interviewed him ... he's very good looking ... and some old buffer who said the vicar didn't properly believe in God."

"Those are the ones who get promoted to Bishop," said Marnie.

"Yes, well, I thought you'd like to know, anyway. They showed the church surrounded by daffodils. It looked lovely. It has a very tall tower, doesn't it?"

Part 6

The singing in church that morning was less vigorous than when all the men of the village were attending the service. Now, with so many of the congregation away at the war, those remaining struggled to raise their voices to fill the church with song. And many now present could not find in themselves the power or the will to sing out. Sarah Anne had enjoyed coming to church since as long as she could remember, had enjoyed the feeling of being together with all the people she had always known, had enjoyed sharing and giving thanks for what they had been given. On this first Sunday after the band of men had left, she was glad the hymn was finished and she could sit down on the cool hard pew and drift away in her private thoughts.

She saw Mr Goldsworthy mount the steps of the pulpit and she heard his voice, but she paid no attention to what he was saying. Perhaps her inattentiveness was a form of blasphemy. After all, you were summoned to church to hear the word. But what good would it do if you did not listen? Her father and brothers and uncles could be dead at this moment and it would be some time before news ever reached the village. Perhaps the King's soldiers had been told of them travelling and had lain in ambush to kill them before they could even make contact with the regiment. It was said in the village that someone was giving intelligence to the Royalist army, someone who placed the interests of the King above the safety of their own people.

The vicar was holding forth. Sarah heard him speak of faith and loyalty: faith in God and loyalty to those appointed by Him to rule His people. There were murmurings in the congregation. Some around her were muttering that he was right; other voices said he was speaking against the people.

Sarah watched the vicar raise his hand in emphasis, his long white hand, long white fingers that had never done a day's toil. He was pointing up to Heaven, warning of the judgement that would fall on those who turned their backs on the true faith. Sarah could smell the incense in the air. Such beautiful hands he had, and such a fine head. His voice was clear and strong and could always be heard above all others during the singing of hymns. It was as if the vicar was the embodiment of all fine things dedicated to the service of God and the King. She was unable to take her eyes away from his beautiful hands.

When the first man stood up in front of her, she jumped with shock, thinking that she had missed the announcement of the next hymn. She began gathering her skirts to rise, but saw that her mother and sisters were still. Other men rose from their pews and walked out of the church that Sunday morning. There was muttering, cries of 'shame!', and more walked out. The vicar continued to speak as if he had not seen them, his hand still raised in the air. His beautiful hand.

🌷 🌷 🌷 🌷

Marnie arrived early at Knightly St John that Saturday morning and left the car near the gate to walk down the field path. The air was clean and she breathed in the scent of young leaves, new grass and the smell of the earth beneath her feet. The farm buildings were deserted and she walked on through the spinney. The canal was still, reflecting the first shoots now appearing on the overhanging branches. Some way up the cut a water vole was making a pathway of the vegetation beside the water. The sun was breaking through the light clouds in brief bursts that dappled the surface of the canal. Marnie shut her eyes, enjoying the smell of the water, the cool air and the peace of the morning.

Behind her she heard a car arrive and she turned back to Glebe Farm. Two men were waiting for her. Mr Dyson was about her own age, early thirties, pink-faced and fair, dressed in dark blazer and flannels, smiling broadly and extending a hand. He introduced the older man as Mr Fletcher, the owner of the property. Marnie found her hand enveloped in the huge firm grip of the farmer, who looked her straight in the eye. Though not tall, he gave the impression of strength from his broad shoulders and his way of standing four-square on the ground. He looked like a man who had lived all his life on his own land and knew his place in the scheme of things. Dyson, still smiling, took out the details of the property from his folder.

"Shall we begin with the farm house itself? As you see, it's a fine structure, seventeenth century, with stone mullions, constructed of local limestone under a roof of Welsh blue slate."

"Where it has a roof," added Marnie. Dyson inclined his head, conceding the point. He went up to a window and peered in.

"Now, if you look through this window, you'll see that the reception rooms have good proportions." He led the way to the next window and put his nose close to the glass, cupping his free hand round his face. "This is the dining room, with easy access to the farmhouse kitchen."

"*Was* the dining room," said Marnie in a quiet voice. Dyson picked his way carefully over fallen pieces of masonry to see through to the kitchen from the next window.

"The kitchen itself is a good size, plenty of room for an Aga, if you like that sort of thing," he smiled broadly, "with charming views out to the, er ..." he looked down at the particulars.

"Sky?" suggested Marnie, peering up at the gaping holes in the ceiling.

"Herb garden," said Dyson with a flourish.

"I'm impressed," said Marnie. Dyson looked gratified. "That's a real feat of the imagination," she added. During the inspection so far, old Mr Fletcher had not spoken a word. He held himself at a distance, looking down at the ground or gazing across the yard and the fields.

"Now, if you'll come this way, we can see the farm cottages," said Dyson. Again, he peered in from the yard, the only difference this time being that there were no windows impeding the view, just empty window frames, though he was quick to point out the stone mullions. "This is the larger of the three farm workers' dwellings, as you can see, based on the traditional two-up two-down pattern much favoured in the period ..." He droned on as they went from building to building, cottage to barn.

"This cart barn is one of the earliest buildings on the site at present ..."

"*Former* cart barn," interrupted Marnie. Dyson stopped and turned to face her.

"I beg your pardon?"

"Well, it isn't a cart barn at present, is it?"

"Subject to renovation," said Dyson, evidently put out and seeming to find Marnie's objection unreasonable.

"Mr Dyson," she said evenly, "it has three walls all full of holes. The roof has collapsed and the only remaining rafters are badly damaged by fire. At best it's a shell, at worst it's going to have to be demolished and rebuilt from the ground up." From behind her Marnie heard the old farmer give a snort or a cough. Dyson looked as if he was about to launch into a defence of the qualities of the property. "Can we go inside some of the buildings now, please?" said Marnie.

Dyson looked uneasy and cleared his throat. "Actually, that isn't possible, Mrs Walker. There's a technical problem, I'm afraid. The local authority has declared the buildings to be structurally unsound in their present state."

"Condemned as unsafe and unfit for habitation?"

"As things stand at the moment, yes."

"If something isn't done very soon, there won't be much standing here at all, will there?" She wandered over to the one barn that still boasted a roof. Dyson muttered something inaudible to Mr Fletcher and they slowly followed her. "Evidently someone comes here," said Marnie, pointing at the cigarette butts still lying where she had seen them.

"Probably ramblers taking shelter, caught by a sudden shower, I expect," said Dyson.

"When did the vandalism happen?"

"*Vandalism?*" It was the first time that Marnie had heard the voice of Mr Fletcher.

"Several of the buildings show signs of fire damage," said Marnie, addressing her words to the farmer.

"Oh, there's been fire here. All along."

"Well, only in one or two places," added Dyson cheerfully.

"It must be difficult to protect a place like this from vandalism," said Marnie.

"Vandalism?" said Dyson. "Mrs Walker, where you come from is very different from here. This isn't London, this is the country." This meeting was becoming tedious and Marnie was beginning to think she had made a mistake. These people were not going to be reasonable in negotiating. They probably took her for an ignorant townie with more money than judgement, who had some romantic notion of the country gleaned from glossy magazines that never mentioned the inconvenience of not having a supermarket up the street or a doctor's surgery nearby.

"Mr Dyson, even in the country I don't think buildings are susceptible to spontaneous combustion. My worry is that already they've reached a serious state of dilapidation. Anyone making an offer on Glebe Farm could well find conditions have deteriorated badly by the time they complete. There has *obviously* been vandalism here." Dyson opened his mouth to speak, but the words came from Mr Fletcher.

"You're quite right. There has been fire and vandalism. This house has known fire in its time. It was burned when it was new, it was burned after the war and now it has burned again." He lapsed into a sullen silence.

"I only wondered if something couldn't be done to prevent it happening again," said Marnie. "No-one's going to buy a property that may have been turned into a pile of ashes before they can take it over. It would be such a pity if the whole lot were destroyed."

"Short of mounting guard on it, there isn't a lot we can do, Mrs Walker." Dyson now seemed genuinely worried and Marnie was sure he could see his commission in the imagined pile of ashes.

"Well, I think I've probably seen all I can see today. Thank you for showing me round."

"But you haven't seen the other barns or the extent of the gardens and grounds," said Dyson. "It goes right over to that line of trees and back round by the canal to those bushes by the docking area and then up to the back of these barns. It's nearly two acres in all."

"Fine. You've given me a great deal to think about." They turned to leave, making their way across the uneven tarmac of the yard. Marnie felt deflated at the thought of all the work needed to restore the place. Here and there the tarmac had crumbled to reveal ancient cobbles below the surface. There seemed to be much lying beneath the surface in Knightly St John.

In broad daylight the idea looked increasingly impractical. Suddenly she stopped. "Do you hear that?" she said. The old farmer shook his head. The younger man strained to listen. "Bells," said Marnie. "Church bells. I wonder what it can be on a Saturday. A wedding perhaps?"

"Not here," said Mr Fletcher. "Hardly any young people in the village. Can't afford to live here these days. Everything's too expensive. Probably just practice."

"I'd like to look in at the church before I get back to London. It looks a lovely old building. Wasn't it in the news last week? My sister said she'd seen your vicar on television." Dyson looked away.

Mr Fletcher frowned. "This village is cursed!" he cried. "Has been ever since *they* tried to take it over. Came here with their fancy ideas. Ruined everybody's lives. Now it's all starting again." The three of them had come to a halt while the farmer delivered his tirade. An uncomfortable silence fell over the group when he had finished.

"I'm sorry," said Marnie. "I seem to have spoken out of turn." She heard the farmer draw in a deep breath.

"Not at all, Mrs Walker," said Dyson, trying to retrieve the situation. "I'm sure it's just a little local difficulty. These things happen from time to time."

"Huh!" said the farmer. "This village has been cursed for centuries. You'll find no peace here. Vicar's stirring it all up again. Ought to get rid of him!" Without another word Mr Fletcher set off across the field leaving them where they stood.

"I really had no idea ..." Marnie began. Dyson interrupted her.

"He's a queer one and no mistake. I've never seen him like that before. Usually he says hardly anything. He's put people off just by being here, but he always insists on coming. I'd better go and talk to him. Sorry about this."

"My fault," said Marnie. Dyson set off, but stopped abruptly after a few paces and turned to look back at her.

"You did say you were a cash buyer, no chain involved?"

"Yes. But I'll have to think about it ..." Dyson nodded and walked away briskly.

Think about it! What was there to think about? The entire scheme was crazy. Marnie wandered slowly around the yard, kicking up some of the loose tarmac with the side of her boot. If the whole yard was cobbled underneath it would make an attractive courtyard garden. But that would probably mean digging up all the cobbles and relaying them. She shuddered at the thought of the expense.

Why had she been so taken with the place? She could not say she had no idea of the realities of doing up derelict buildings. Where would she start? Where would she live? The trouble was, a place to live would take so much of her resources, she would have little left over for the other conversion works. Everything she earned from the Willards Brewery contract would have to be spent on the renovation of Glebe Farm.

Her wandering had taken her back to the canal, to where she had first pulled over in *Sally Ann* on a hot day the previous summer. Then, it had been a touch of the sun that had addled her brain; now, it was the bewildering permutation of possibilities that was having much the same effect. She strolled along the bank. According to Dyson, all this was part of the property ... *as far as the docking area* ... what docking area? He must have meant the place where the trees thinned out and a boat could be pulled over, as she had done last year. A row of bushes now formed a barrier across her path, seeming to form a hedge in the undergrowth, a straight line that was oddly out of place in a spinney. She stumbled and was surprised to discover an iron ring protruding from the soil. She knelt down and pulled at it, but it was firmly fixed to a metal plate in the earth. A mooring ring.

The bushes ran in a straight line back to the canal, as if they had been planted ... *as far as the docking area* ... Could it be that she was looking at it now? She leaned forward and parted the undergrowth. The roots were in water.

Just then, she heard dogs approaching. Two black Labradors came bounding towards her, followed by the man she had met there once before, striding along behind them. The man called the dogs back and they walked obediently at his side as he approached.

"Good morning. We meet again."

"Hallo. Yes. I can't seem to keep away."

"Do I take it the property's on the market again?" said Frank Day. "It's difficult to keep up with the situation."

"It is, but it's full of problems, not the least of them being the owner. His idea of the hard sell is to tell prospective buyers that the place is cursed and anyone who comes here is doomed. I expect you know Mr Fletcher."

"Well ... slightly. But you're seriously interested?"

Marnie looked round at the buildings and the land sloping up to the horizon. "As I said, it's full of problems. Even if the price could be agreed, it could be destroyed by vandals. Then there's the question of where to live in the meantime. And I'd have nowhere safe to put my furniture."

"At least you're not put off by the thought of it being cursed."

"No. No, I'm not."

"In that case, maybe there's a way I could help with one of the problems. Of course, I don't like to push myself on you, but storing furniture is in my line."

"Your line?"

"Yes. I have a removals firm. You may have seen our vans. Days of Yore."

"Days of Yore." Marnie shook her head. "I can't say I've seen them."

"We're well-known hereabouts. The Days have lived in these parts for generations. Yore is the next village going north."

"Right. I'll bear that in mind."

"Good. You'd find us quite reasonable. We're not as expensive as London up here. I'm afraid I haven't got a card with me."

"Don't worry. I'll find you in the phone book. It's an easy name to remember."

"That's the idea."

❦ ❦ ❦ ❦

Back at the car, before driving off, Marnie took out the particulars on Glebe Farm and read through them. She passed quickly over the asking price, winced inwardly, and turned to the narrative.

"... Glebe Farm was built by the Earls of Knightly circa 1640 to service agricultural expansion ... at that time it was surrounded by thick forest and water-meadows ... it was sold out of the estate shortly before the Second World War to the tenant farmers who had worked it almost since new and are the present owners ... stone barns reputedly built by ex-Napoleonic War prisoners of the Earl, who worked on the estate in the early 19th century ..." She skipped quickly on, scanning the text for mention of the docking area. There it was. "... some nine years ago the docking area (80 x 6 x 12ft with gate) was completely rebuilt to become a working canal dry dock capable of serving narrow boats up to 72 feet ... concrete slip ... low block area ..." It was unrecognisable as the muddy, overgrown patch of shrubbery and rushes that she had seen.

Part 7

The three sisters walked out of the village in their good clothes. That day they would not collect berries or flowers. It was the Sabbath and no work was done. The Fourth Commandment: Remember the Sabbath day, to keep it holy.

Sarah Anne had little to say, though her sisters spoke of the men and women who had stood up in the middle of the vicar's sermon and walked out of the church. On the Sabbath day! These were hard times. Nothing seemed to be sacred. Nothing seemed to be certain.

From the rising land they looked back and saw nothing of the village but the church tower standing tall among the trees. Sarah caught sight of movement in the distance. She raised a hand to shield her eyes and see better. Smoke smudged the horizon. Someone was busy on the Sabbath. Sarah knew beyond any doubt that it was no ordinary work. In time of war there were no commandments. The smoke was the sign of fighting. It was the Devil's work.

❦ ❦ ❦ ❦

It was mid-morning on Monday, and Marnie rushed into the office like a typhoon, glancing at her watch while juggling three files of papers and muttering under her breath. Her meetings were already behind schedule. Lois, the design group's new secretary, was hovering over Marnie's desk, reading the diary.

"Oh there you are, Marnie! I thought you must have left for the meeting in Bloomsbury."

"Problems with Foster Sinclair. They're dangerously close to reaching a decision. It's almost a precedent. Why couldn't they have gone to Heal's?"

"There's a Mr Dyson for you on the phone."

Marnie sighed. "Tell him I'll ring him back."

❦ ❦ ❦ ❦

"Ladies and gentlemen, I want to end where I began." It was Wednesday and the official opening of the new gallery at the canal museum. At the hint that the Chairman's speech was coming to an end, the audience stirred. To be fair, the speech had not been long, nor had it lacked its witty moments, but half the guests at the official opening of the gallery were keen to view the exhibits. The other half were keen to sample the food on the buffet table and help it on its way with a glass or two of chardonnay or claret. "There would be no Peter William Gibson Collection in this fine new gallery if it had not been for the generosity of our benefactor, Mrs Marnie Walker. It gives me great pleasure to invite her now to perform the official opening." Applause broke out as the distinguished elderly gentleman stepped down and everyone present hoped that performing an official opening, in whatever form it took, would not be a long-winded affair.

There was a buzz as Marnie came to the rostrum. She was wearing a navy blue velvet jacket and skirt, with a cream silk shirt open at the neck to reveal a simple gold chain. With her dark wavy hair and little make-up, the impression she gave was of youth and energy. Most of those present had expected an older woman. Silence fell as she leaned towards the microphone.

"Good morning everyone. I don't intend to make a speech." There was a flurry of applause and Marnie smiled. "This collection was left to me by an old man who lived in a caravan beside his boat at Little Venice. Old Peter, as we knew him, lived very modestly and kept to himself. He died last September. For longer than anyone can say, he also kept safe this collection of original drawings, about two centuries old. No-one knows how he came to possess them.

They have become known as the Lost Drawings of William Jessop. They have been described as priceless and exquisite. They are. But for many of us, they are also the epitaph to our friend, Old Peter, and it is in his name that I am here to open his gallery. Thank you for being here today. I know he would want you to enjoy the exhibition." She stepped down and the Chairman shook her hand.

There was a gap before the applause, the guests unsure if the proceedings were completed. The simplicity of Marnie's words and the brevity of her address had come as a surprise. People who had had thoughts only of the refreshments suddenly found themselves anxious to see this unique collection and pressed forward as Marnie walked to the elegant double doors and opened them under the lights of the television cameras and the flashing bulbs of the photographers. There was further applause.

As the guests surged forward, Marnie found herself isolated in the middle of the crowd. A young woman approached, carrying a clip-board. She was dressed in a black trouser suit and exuded confidence.

"Marnie, hallo. I'm Alison McGee, BBC Television News for the south-west. Can we interview you briefly?"

❦ ❦ ❦ ❦

That evening, after supper at Beth and Paul's, the three of them gathered in front of the television to watch the evening news. A ministerial scandal, the Balkans and the Bay of Biscay were the leading stories.

Beth finished pouring coffee and nodded at the television. "Shall I turn this off now?" The presenter was coming to the end of a summary of financial markets. Beth put down the pot and moved towards the set just as the presenter was coming to the last item.

"And finally ... a lost national treasure goes on show for the first time in two hundred years. Alison McGee reports from the west of England." The screen was filled with the drawing of the great viaduct of Pontcysyllte and the scene changed to the opening of the gallery at the National Canal Museum. Instead of the routine interview, the report focused on the drawings themselves with a commentary on their importance and how they had come to light. Suddenly, there was Marnie stepping up to the rostrum as the reporter explained: "It is thanks to one woman that the collection can now be seen by the public: the owner of the drawings, Marnie Walker."

"I do believe you're blushing," said Beth.

"Sh-sh-sh!" said Paul, pointing at the screen. Marnie was at the microphone. Paul grabbed the video controller and pressed the record button.

"... was left to me by an old man who lived in a caravan beside his boat in Little Venice ..."

"It'll have finished before the machine gets started," said Beth. On the screen Marnie was still talking.

"... and kept to himself. He died last September ..."

"We'll get as much as we can," said Paul. They sat in silence as Marnie continued her speech, expecting it to be faded out at any moment, but it ran on to the end.

"... Thank you for being here today. I know he would want you to enjoy the exhibition." As the audience applauded in the background, Alison McGee ended the report. Back in the studio, the presenter rounded off the programme.

"That was the first time we have ever shown an entire speech from beginning to end on the evening news. On a day when so much has been said by world leaders to so little avail, it's good to end on that generous note. From all of us here, good night."

"Well!" said Beth. "You'll be doing the Barclaycard adverts next." Paul got up, switched off the television and rewound the tape. Marnie blinked a few times and cleared her throat.

"I liked your speech," said Paul. "I wish our Dean would come to you for lessons in public oratory. We'd have much more time for research. I think I've got most of it recorded for posterity." He pressed the eject button and pulled it out of the slot. "I'm sure you'll want to keep this as a memento." He held the tape out to Marnie, but before she could take it, he looked down at the cassette and groaned. "Oh, bugger!" Marnie stared at him curiously.

"What's up?" said Beth.

Paul looked at her and rolled his eyes. "I've taped over the beginning of *Casablanca.*"

🌷   🌷   🌷   🌷

Back in the office next morning, Lois had arranged a collection of messages and notes in priority order in the message-tray. There were three from Dyson at the estate agents. As she was reading the notes, the phone rang on her direct line. It was not yet eight-thirty.

"Ah, Mrs Walker. It's Dyson from Blackey and Johnson. I was starting to think we'd never speak. I'm glad I've caught you. I wonder if you've had any more thoughts about Glebe Farm." Marnie knew it was probably the most unwise decision she would ever make.

"I've been having a busy time these last few days, Mr Dyson. I'm sorry you've had difficulty reaching me."

"If you wanted to make an offer ..." he began. Marnie said nothing. "... there could be scope for some flexibility on price."

"I think there would have to be, Mr Dyson." Marnie's heart was beating faster. "Have you received any offers so far?" The directness of the question took Dyson by surprise.

"No. Well, that is to say, not exactly, at the moment. Though we have had a great deal of interest."

"There would have to be a great deal of flexibility on price for me to be interested."

"How much flexibility, Mrs Walker?" This was the tricky part. Too low a figure and they would not treat her seriously; too high and it could make the whole project unviable. Just then, the other phone rang, startling Marnie in her concentration. She moved her hand to pick it up.

"Excuse me just a second, please," she said to Mr Dyson and spoke into the other phone.

"There's someone for you, Marnie. It's a poor line. Shall I ask him to ring again later?"

"No. Probably a mobile. I'd better take it. Just a moment." She turned back to Dyson, but before she could speak, he broke in.

"Mrs Walker, would you be thinking of an offer, say five per cent less than the asking price?" Marnie did a calculation. No chance. It was hopeless. She saw the whole thing slipping away. Now she had nothing to lose.

"More like twenty!" she muttered. "Look, I'll try to get back to you later this morning. I really must go now." Dyson said he would be in his office till lunchtime and they hung up.

Marnie turned back to her other phone. "Is it Willard's, Jackie?"

"Something like that. It's really not a good line."

"Okay, put him through, thanks." The line clicked. "Marnie here, good morning."

"You sound as if you were expecting me to call." The voice was low, cultured and vaguely familiar, though the background noise of traffic made it indistinct. Marnie struggled to attach a name to that voice and frowned into the receiver.

"I'm sorry, there's a lot of interference on the line."

"Yes. I'm in a phone box and obviously you *weren't* expecting me to call. It's Ralph Lombard. You've probably forgotten our meeting last year." *Forgotten!* thought Marnie. How could you forget pulling someone out of the canal at dead of night, someone who had attempted to commit suicide? Ralph Lombard was not the sort of person it was easy to forget.

"No, of course not. I just thought you were a client I was expecting to ring me. Where are you?" The traffic noise increased in volume as if he had turned his head towards the road.

"I can't see a street name, but I'm somewhere in Little Venice."

"Any other clues?"

"Well, I'm near the tube station and the phone box is full of visiting cards advertising all sorts of exotic personal services. It gives a whole new meaning to the expression *strapped for cash.*" Marnie could picture the cards, probably garish yellow, illustrated with highly fanciful drawings of voluptuous young women in fishnet tights. She laughed at Ralph's joke, though she had always found the cards rather sad.

"It's nice to hear from you. What brings you to town?"

"A meeting of external examiners, and then I'm looking at a boat. I got an early train to Paddington and walked over to see it before the proper inspection."

"You're thinking of buying a boat?"

"Yes. You might remember we talked about the idea once." Marnie recalled him mentioning a sabbatical. "Oh, my phonecard's running out. Are you around at lunchtime by any chance? Could we meet?"

"Twelve-thirty?" suggested Marnie.

"At the phone box by the tube station?" said Ralph.

"Fine. If you're not there, I'll know where to find you." Ralph was cut off. Marnie in her office reached for the filofax. Ralph in his phone box pondered what she had said, caught sight of the bright yellow cards and chuckled.

❦ ❦ ❦ ❦

"Marnie, hallo, you're very punctual. Good to see you." He wore a charcoal grey double-breasted suit, a striped shirt in maroon and white and a tie of deep burgundy. His black shoes were hand-built by Northampton craftsmen. Dr Ralph Lombard, Reader in economics and political science and Fellow of All Saints College, Oxford, did not look like the usual academic. One reviewer had said of him grudgingly that his writing was as elegant as his clothes.

They settled for a small Italian restaurant in a side street not far from *Sally Ann's* mooring and took a table by the window. Ralph noted, but did not comment on, Marnie's appearance. She was wearing a dark green and blue striped jacket over a white blouse buttoned to the neck and a short navy blue skirt.

"Tell me about the boat and your plans," she said, as the waiter poured San Gimignano into their glasses.

"It's quite simple. The university has granted me a year's sabbatical from the end of the Lent Term. I intend to write a book. You gave me the idea of taking time to travel. Since we last met I've thought about living for part of the year on a narrowboat. That's it, really." They chinked glasses.

"So you're free from Easter?" He nodded. "And you've looked me up to advise you on choice of boats," said Marnie. "Well, I know what to look for, but you'll need a survey by an engineer to be certain."

"Yes. Something like *Sally Ann* would suit me fine. The boat for sale in Little Venice is rather similar." Marnie knew of several boats that were for sale, and they spent some time discussing their various merits over fettucine and crespelle.

"Little Venice is like a separate town tucked away all by itself," observed Ralph. "I'd never been here before today."

"This is positively a metropolis compared with Little Venice the other side of the towpath railings," said Marnie, turning her head in the general direction of the canal. "There's almost no contact between the people on either side of the fence."

"You make it sound like the divided communities in Belfast," said Ralph in a quiet voice. Marnie looked up sharply.

"I think it's rather different," she said quickly. "There's no animosity between the people here."

"I often wonder if there is really so much animosity between all the people in Northern Ireland at the human level," said Ralph. "All organised communities tend to be prone to some kind of conflict within themselves ... divisions in society. Erecting physical barriers does little to bring people together. Sorry, I'm being boring. Conflict is one of my things."

"Not at all," said Marnie. "It's something that worries me a lot, too. At the moment I'm thinking of moving out of London and buying a place in a village beside the Grand Union about fifty miles north. It's a pleasant place, but there are strange undertones and I'm not quite sure what to make of them. The owner of the property says the village is cursed, and sometimes you'd think the Civil War was still going on."

"Barriers," said Ralph. "I shouldn't imagine they'd affect you as a newcomer. Of course, you'd always be regarded as an outsider, however long you lived there."

"But I always thought villages were friendly places. It's like that in Little Venice. Couldn't be friendlier ... on the canal side."

"Yes, but they're different," said Ralph. "The boat people's world is nomadic. I experienced that kind of hospitality from you last year. Nomads don't pry into each others' lives. They don't *own,* they just *are.* In a permanent village there's a tendency to know about your neighbours and sometimes you can know more than is good. Introduce an element of conflict into such a world and you have a dangerous mixture. Northern Ireland, the Civil War, religious rivalries, clan feuds; they're all the same thing." Marnie sat back in her chair as the waiter hovered with the menu. They ordered coffee.

The owner arrived and beamed at Marnie. "We saw you on TV last night, Marnie. It was very nice, the drawings, your speech." He put down two glasses of liqueur beside the coffees. "A little glass of Amaretto, on the house." He gave a slight bow.

"That's very nice of you, Luca."

"Is good to have some nice news for a change." He smiled broadly at Marnie, bowed at Lombard with a muttered "Signore" and withdrew. After the direction their conversation had been taking, Marnie now felt a surge of warmth at this kind gesture. She picked up the glass and took a sip. Rich almonds.

"He's quite right," said Ralph. "I saw you as well. It was a charming speech. I hope that doesn't sound patronising."

"Is that what made you think of coming to see me to help you with the boat?"

"I didn't come to see you because of the boat," he said. "The boat was a coincidence. My reasons were purely personal." He sipped the Amaretto. "I've often thought about you since we met. I only wish the circumstances had been different. Tell me, did you find things had changed for you as a result of your sabbatical?"

"The job was much the same, I suppose, but I saw things differently, I think."

"Your plan to move out of London ... is that because you still feel restless? Did *Sally Ann* contribute to that?"

"*Sally Ann* made me feel more ... independent, more capable, perhaps less willing just to fit in as part of someone else's team. Be careful, or your sabbatical might unsettle *you*, if you spend it on a narrowboat." She smiled and sipped her coffee.

"Do you have time to look at the boat I've come to see?"

"I can stay for half an hour. Would that help?"

❦ ❦ ❦ ❦

As Marnie crossed the entrance hall, Jackie at the reception desk called over. "Oh, Marnie, your Mr Dyson rang again. He rings every half hour."

"When's he next due?"

"Any minute."

Marnie sighed. "Wonderful."

Jackie was right. The phone rang. It was her direct line. "Mrs Walker? It's Tony Dyson again. I'm glad I've managed to contact you. I've spoken to my client and explained that you were interested and wished to make an offer." Dyson paused and Marnie waited. "Well ... you suggested a figure ... somewhat below the asking price, Mrs Walker." Dyson did not like being in the position of making an offer when he was acting for the vendor.

"Yes."

"My client would be prepared to accept a compromise somewhere between the five per cent reduction that *I* suggested and *your* offer of a twenty per cent reduction." *Twenty per cent reduction!* thought Marnie, boggling. He had taken her seriously. She hesitated and Dyson went on. "Mr Fletcher would consider an offer ... ten per cent below the asking price." Ten per cent. Marnie made a quick mental calculation. It was right on her limit. She was on the point of accepting when she thought of *Sally Ann*. Marnie closed her eyes, took a deep breath and heard herself say, "It would have to be fifteen per cent."

"Mrs Walker, that would not be acceptable to my client."

"Are you sure of that?"

Dyson scribbled the figure on his pad. It was almost derisory. In his mind he saw the decaying buildings and overgrown site of Glebe Farm and knew that it could only deteriorate further if it was not taken over very soon. "I'll ask him," he said. "I'll 'phone you back as soon as I can."

Marnie assembled the papers to prepare for her meeting, making a real effort to concentrate. She found herself repeatedly reading the same sentence and almost jumped when the 'phone rang. It was Dyson again. She listened, gave the briefest of replies, ended the conversation and put the 'phone down. She stared at the receiver for a few seconds, picked it up and pressed three buttons.

"Philip, can I see you for a moment?"

In his office, Dyson put down his receiver. He looked at the figure he had scribbled on his pad. It *was* almost derisory, but it was better than nothing.

That evening Marnie went round to Beth and Paul for supper. She handed Paul a package that he opened to discover a boxed set of the video of *Casablanca* with a book on how the film had been made. It was a special presentation to mark the film's fiftieth anniversary.

"No wonder you're my favourite sister-in-law," he said, kissing her. "Brilliant."

Over supper Marnie tried more than once to bring up the subject of her move to Knightly St John and Glebe Farm, but each time, the conversation moved in a different direction. When the chance eventually came, it was not the way she wanted. Paul was again worried about his position at the university. Marnie had asked how his research had been going and spotted the warning sign of a brief exchange of glances between Beth and Paul.

"The actual research isn't going too badly," said Paul. "The question is, will it be completed in time to preserve my job? It's the usual rumours of cuts … in research funding … the departmental budget … staffing. You'll soon be the only one of us left with a steady job, Marnie. I hope you're feeling fit." It was the moment of truth.

"Actually," she began, realising that Beth had noted the tone of voice in an instant, "actually, I'm contemplating a change myself."

"Seriously contemplating?" said Beth. Marnie nodded emphatically. "The place in the village where the vicar has all the trouble and the buildings are falling down?" Marnie nodded again. "You've made an offer on it?" A nod. "You've got someone to buy your flat?" Same again. "You've made an appointment with a psychiatrist?"

Marnie raised her chin for the start of a nod. "What?"

"Have you actually resigned your job, your *steady, well-paid* job?"

"I've discussed it with Philip, yes. In fact, he's going to put a contract my way, the biggest contract I have on my list at the moment. It'll be a good start."

"But I thought you said the whole place was a ruin … *uninhabitable.*"

"Ye-e-s."

"Have you thought about the small problem of having a roof over your head, somewhere to live while the ruins are turned into a hovel?"

"Oh yes. That's the easy part. No problem." Marnie took a sip from her wine.

"Marnie," said Beth. "Where are you going to live?"

Marnie took another sip. "Guess," she said.

Beth and Paul frowned. Suddenly, Beth looked Marnie straight in the eye. "You mean …?"

Marnie nodded and smiled charmingly.

Beth gave an exaggerated exasperated sigh. "You know, Marnie, sometimes I think you'd get away with murder."

Marnie smiled at her sister. "I like the idea of making a getaway … but I can do without the murder."

❦   ❦   ❦   ❦

It was ten minutes later that Philip, with a serious expression on his face, walked into her office. "I've just had Willards on the line, Marnie. There's been some trouble. Do you know *The Irish Navigator?*"

"I don't think so."

"It's one of their restaurants on the canal. There's been a fire during the night. Quite bad. Part of it is almost gutted. They want to get on with repairing it as a matter of urgency. I said we'd get someone up to have a look at it today, only we haven't got an architect free just now. Any chance of you going? The interior design would be, *will* be, one of your jobs."

Marnie checked her diary. "Do we have the address?"

Philip passed her a note. "Here," he said. "It's not far from your new place, I think. All we need do today is find out how bad the damage is and assess what steps we can take to sort it out PDQ. The manager's called Henderson and he'll be on site."

"I'll go straight away." Marnie took a notepad, mobile phone and Polaroid camera from a drawer and checked the address. She stood up to leave as the phone rang.

"I have a call for you, Marnie."

"If it's Dyson, tell him I've gone for a site meeting in Timbuktu."

"It's a girl. Says her name is Anne." The call was put through.

"Anne, hallo! How are things? Are you revising hard?"

"Not exactly. Would you believe I've been told to rest for a few days? The doctor says I've been overdoing it. I kept getting headaches through working late at night. I just rang to say I've sent off my design for the magazine competition, the flat in Docklands. Sorry to bother you at work."

"I'm very pressed at the moment, so I can't really talk just now." She glanced down at the address of *The Irish Navigator*. "Do you know Fawley?"

"Yes. Near Leighton Buzzard."

"Do you have a headache at the moment?"

"No. I've only just got up. I'm supposed to go for a walk and get some fresh air. Why?"

"Suppose I pick you up after my meeting and take you for a spot of lunch. I've got some news I want to tell you." There was a pause at the end of the line. "Anne? Are you all right?"

"Yippee! Yes, yes! I'm fine. When are you coming?"

"I just left."

꧁ ꧁ ꧁ ꧁

"How was your meeting?" said Anne. She was looking tense and pale and her sharp features seemed even more pinched than usual. They had found a pub on the canal just outside Leighton Buzzard.

"Not very pleasant, to tell you the truth. The police were there. Suspected arson, possibly terrorists."

Anne's eyes seemed to grow larger. "That's terrible."

"Yes, but I've got some better news. I'm going to buy Glebe Farm. My offer's been accepted."

"*Wow!* But that's great, Marnie! You must be very excited."

"Not quite the word I would've chosen, but I'm pleased ... at least I *think* I am."

"When will you be moving?"

"That depends on a number of factors, not the least being whether the buildings, such as they are, manage to remain standing. It looks like a mid-June completion, probably the fifteenth."

"My exams finish on Tuesday the thirteenth." Anne pulled a face.

Marnie nodded. "Right. The company is letting me keep the contract with Willards Brewery, which will give me regular work probably for the first year of operations. I shall have to get part of the farm ready to serve as an office straight away, so there's a lot to be done."

"Where will you live while this is going on?" said Anne, sipping her drink.

"Ah, well, that's one of the problems. Let me tell you what I have in mind ..." Marnie outlined her plan to use *Sally Ann* as a base while the initial works were carried out. The first task would be to make a barn ready for occupation as an office. She explained that the docking area would have to be dug out as a mooring for the boat and listed the other operations needed.

"Does this mean you're going to buy *Sally Ann* from your sister, then?"

"Ah ... *slightly* sore point ... I think the best answer I can give you there is ... *sort of* ..."

"You mean you're borrowing her?"

"Let's just say it will be a kind of long-term loan, until my finances are sorted out. I have to put all I've got into Glebe Farm."

"It's very generous of your sister," said Anne.

"Well, like I said, it's a slightly sore point at the moment. Even that isn't easy. I've got to get the dock cleared and that will be quite a task."

"Do you know about Canal Action Network?" said Anne. "They volunteer to do work on canals, you know, restoring the towpath, clearing trees, that sort of thing." Marnie raised an eyebrow, inviting Anne to continue. "I've come across them a few times on my exam project. They might be able to help with the docking area and get it ready for you so you can move there as soon as the place is yours."

"That sounds like a very good idea," said Marnie, all thoughts of putting the lid on Anne's enthusiasm now departed. "I wonder how they might be ..."

"Leave it to me," said Anne.

Part 9

It was after darkness had fallen that Robert Tarry came rushing to pound on their door. It was his wife's first pregnancy and he dared leave her only for a few minutes to run to the nearest neighbours for help. She was sick with pain and feared she was bleeding. Sarah Anne helped her mother assemble a bag of herbal remedies, sage, lady's mantle, wormwood and poppy. She struck a flint to light a torch, standing well clear of the thatch eaves as she waited briefly outside for her mother to come. Robert ran on ahead, afraid to leave his wife in her bed of pain for another moment.

The two women made their way as quickly as they could along the lane, the massive bulk of the church looming over them as they passed the lych gate, both of them praying for Margaret Tarry under their breath. This was a dangerous time for any woman. Sarah's mother stumbled over a tussock half hidden in the shadows and she stopped to steady herself. Reaching forward to take her mother's arm, Sarah's attention was caught by a flash of light high above them. She hesitated for a second.

"Come, Sarah. We must hurry. What is it?" Her mother was breathless. Sarah looked up at the tower, but there was no light.

"Nothing, mother. I thought I saw something. But it must have been a spark from the torch flame." She took her mother's arm and they set off again. These were dangerous times for everyone.

❦   ❦   ❦   ❦

"It is written, then," said Philip in a prophetic voice when Marnie gave him an update on progress with the move. He said it more than once. In fact, he only just stopped himself saying it the fourth time she put her head round his door and gave him the latest piece of news. The first time he said it, she had smiled weakly. The second time, she had put on a slightly pained expression. The third time, something in her look warned him he was in danger of becoming a cliché. Marnie knew that Philip was on her side and accepted that this was the best time for her to go, if go she must. But she preferred to think of it just as a change of job, rather than a push in the back from the hand of Destiny.

It seemed to Marnie that from the moment her offer was accepted, everything moved quickly and irrevocably towards the move from London to Knightly St John. Where things could have gone wrong with the sale and purchase of the two properties, nothing went wrong. Contracts were even exchanged one day earlier than planned and all the technicalities leading to the completion date in mid-June were carried out without the slightest hitch.

Marnie rang the sixth-former who worked with CAN – the Canal Action Network – and obtained the name and phone number of the local group's organiser, Dave Perryman. Far from dismissing the idea, he was delighted to accept the opportunity of a small restoration scheme and agreed to meet Marnie on site one evening after work to weigh up the task. Marnie's offer to pay for the work was politely rejected, but her offer to provide refreshments whenever she could be with them was accepted. The vendor agreed to the works being carried out in advance of completion and co-operated with connections of electricity and water. Nothing, it seemed, would stand in the way of the move.

About a week before the Big Day, Beth rang and invited Marnie to look in after work. They settled in the kitchen for coffee.

"Paul set off this morning for Edinburgh and Dundee … examining," she said. "He's not back till the end of next week. So, how are things going? All packed and ready for off?"

"Amazingly, yes, more or less."

"What about your man in Oxford? Is he still in touch?"

"Ralph? Yes, from time to time. He's actually quite interested in a boat someone's offered him, but he hasn't got time to think about it at the moment. He's been lecturing in America and now he's up to his neck in examining."

"A familiar everyday story of university folk," said Beth.

"Look, you didn't ask me to call round to find out if my cups had all been wrapped up in newspaper. Something's on your mind. Is it Paul's job ... a problem at work?"

"No." She paused. "I suppose ... I'm concerned ... about you."

"Me?"

Beth nodded. "You're taking this big step in your life and I'm doing nothing to help you. All *I've* done is tell you it's not a good idea and you're giving up a good job and security to chase after something that might be a ..."

"Yes, fine," said Marnie quickly. "I don't need the reminders."

"That's what I mean," said Beth. "I ought to be doing something useful, supportive, standing by you, you know, the sisterly bit. Instead, all I do is go on about our own problems."

"Beth, is this leading somewhere? I mean, it's nice to know you care about what I do, but I don't want you to worry. I don't want you to feel you aren't being a real sister if you're not worrying, if you see what I mean. Things will work out or they won't. If they don't, I'll find another job. But this is my best chance to try to do my own thing."

"Fair enough," said Beth. "You always were braver than me. First one up the tree, first to learn how to swim, first to try skiing ..."

"First to fall down the ski-slope," added Marnie.

Beth nodded. "That's why I'd like to help you now." She leaned across the table. "How would you like a crew?"

❦   ❦   ❦   ❦

So it came about that on the morning of Saturday, 10th June, bright and early, Marnie and Beth set off in convoy in separate cars, heading north out of London in light traffic. Within an hour they were turning off the motorway, taking the A508 west until they reached the signpost for the minor road to Knightly St John. They parked beside the church opposite the pub.

"This is a very convenient arrangement," said Beth. "All the essentials on hand." She shielded her eyes with her hand to look up at the church tower. "It's certainly very beautiful. Look at the strength of that tower. It's massive, built to last for ever. Can we look inside?"

"I think you'll find it's locked," said Marnie. "But we can try." They walked through the lych gate and up the path to the side porch in the quiet of the morning, to the accompaniment of birdsong. They tried the black iron handle on the great studded door. It turned easily and swung open. In a quiet voice Marnie said: "I expect someone's inside changing flowers, or something."

Sunlight was pouring through the windows, splashing colour from the stained glass onto the stone flagged floor and the polished pews. Beth walked over to study the list of vicars while Marnie made her way down the centre aisle. Marnie pointed out the carving on the font and the Burne-Jones window. For several minutes they strolled around the ancient building, reading inscriptions on tombs, admiring displays of flowers. On their way out, Beth pulled the purse from her shoulder bag and put money in the offertory box. She picked up the top copy from a neat pile of booklets standing on a table by the door and gave it to Marnie.

"Souvenir of our visit," she said. "All the gen on the local history scene." Marnie took the booklet.

"Thanks." The paper was crisp and white with a line drawing of the church on the cover.

They passed through the porch, went out onto the path and looked back at the tower. "It's strange, isn't it, Marnie. Inside, it's domestic and cosy. But that tower is almost out of proportion, it's so ... so *substantial*."

Marnie squinted up in the sunlight. "Maybe."

"Did you notice the gap in the line of vicars?" said Beth. "In the 1640s there was one who only lasted a year ... Joseph Goldsworthy ... and then two years without a vicar at all ... interesting. That booklet will probably explain it all." Marnie put the booklet in the glove compartment of the car for safe keeping and they set off down the road to inspect Glebe Farm.

"They certainly don't waste any time," said Marnie, standing by the canal at the point where it joined the docking area. She had led Beth round the back of the barns to see how much progress the volunteers from CAN had made. The transformation was complete. No undergrowth obscured the borders of the side channel and the dock was full of water. The soil on both sides had been cut back to reveal a concrete edge, cracked and pitted, but still solid enough to provide a firm bank.

"So this is where *Sally* will stay when you're living on board," said Beth.

"I think it'll be okay for the summer. I want to get as much work as possible done on the cottages to make one of them habitable before winter." They wandered back towards the buildings. One of the barns, the only sound building on the site, now boasted sturdy doors freshly painted black and fastened with a heavy brass padlock. Marnie undid the padlock and led the way inside, quickly pulling the door closed behind them.

"Hey, it's dark in ..." Beth's voice faltered in surprise as the barn filled with light. She turned towards Marnie who, with a flourish, gave a slight bow.

"What do you think of it?" Beth was unprepared for the sight that greeted her. Where she had expected a dirt floor, there was coir matting from wall to wall. Instead of dusty cobwebs on the walls, she saw fresh white emulsion, a year planner, not yet very full, and bright posters depicting parts of the canal network. The empty space she had thought to find was occupied by office furniture, two desks, a phone, filing cabinets, a drawing board, a low table, some chairs, all new. A computer was standing in its box in a corner. The dark interior had been transformed by lighting from two tracks of spotlights.

"Marnie, it's great! You must have been working like a slave to get all this done."

"Actually, it didn't take long. While the CAN people were working on the docking area, I came in here and got the office commissioned. I filled the holes in the concrete to make the floor level and the rest was just cleaning and painting. No trouble at all. The electricians only took two days to put the light and power in. When I'm working here, the new barn doors will fold right back like shutters, and the floor-to-ceiling glazing units will give loads of light. When I stop work, I can close the barn doors to make the place secure."

"It's brilliant. What's that over there?" Beth pointed to a wooden ladder attached to the end wall, leading up to an opening in the roof.

"I've just repaired and varnished it. It goes to the hayloft above. I've cleaned it all out and it has a power socket. I'm not sure what I'll use it for, but I thought I might as well get it decent while I was working on the rest."

"You know, Marnie. I think you're going to make a go of this. I know I've sounded a little doubtful on occasion ..." – Marnie pulled a face – "... but I really do believe that if *anyone* can make this work, you can."

"Thanks, Beth. And I'll do everything I can to make it work ... if it kills me." At that she laughed and pulled a thermos flask from her bag. "Let's drink to it.

Only coffee, I'm afraid."

They garaged the Rover in one of the derelict barns and Beth drove them back to Marnie's empty flat to collect Dolly before setting off on *Sally Ann*. The telephone rang eerily on the living room floor. Marnie's footsteps echoed as she walked across the room to pick it up.

"Shouldn't you be studying, young lady?" Marnie's tone was mock reproof.

"I'm having what my mum calls a 'Marnie break' ... yes, honestly. It's to stop my head getting overloaded. Anyway, I'm over the worst of it now. There's only RE and the last French paper, then ... freedom!"

"How have they been so far?"

"Not bad. Bit of an anti-climax really. I was *very* nervous on the first day. Didn't know what to expect, but the papers weren't so different from the mocks and I was lucky with the geometry. Anyway, how about you? All ready for your big move next week?"

"Actually, it's today."

"*Today?!* I ... I thought you were setting off on Thursday the fifteenth." Marnie explained about Beth's offer to share the journey on *Sally Ann*. Anne made no reply.

"Anne? Are you there?"

"Oh ... yes. I just thought you'd be coming through this way by about Saturday. I thought I might ... see you as you passed ... have a chat ... that kind of thing. I wondered if I could help with the move ... get your office ready."

"That's nice of you. What if I give you a ring after your exams are finished and we fix something up?" After Marnie hung up she sat for a few seconds looking at the phone. It rang again.

"Did you forget something?"

"Hallo, Marnie. You were expecting someone else again?"

"Ralph, hallo. Sorry, I was talking to a friend and had just put the phone down. How are you? Presumably back from your travels?"

"Yes. I got back last night. I just thought I'd ring to catch up on your news, your move being imminent."

"Immediate, in fact." Marnie gave Ralph her new numbers. So many new things. A fresh start. It seemed that they had always been having this conversation.

"It must be very exciting for you, Marnie. I shall be thinking of you. Good luck."

"More than just thinking, I hope. Keep in touch." It was only after she had put the phone down on the last conversation in her flat, the last conversation of her old life, that Marnie realised she had spoken only of *her* news and wished she could give a quick ring back to ask for *his*. For once, the filofax containing Ralph's phone number was not with her.

"Do you usually go into meditation like that after every phone call?" Marnie had almost forgotten that Beth was there. "Are you willing it to ring again? Is that your system?"

"I didn't give Ralph a chance to tell me *his* news. All I did was go on about myself. Oh, well. Too late now. Time to go." She stood up, slung the kitbag over her shoulder, picked up the holdall and Dolly and headed for the door.

"Do you want to take one last look round the flat?" asked Beth. "Say good-bye and all that?"

"Don't look back," said Marnie.

❦   ❦   ❦   ❦

Beth drove Marnie to Little Venice with Dolly and the kitbag. They swung the boat on its nose to face west and while Marnie unpacked, Beth set off home.

They would converge within the hour on the supermarket beside the canal at Kensal Green, Marnie on *Sally Ann*, Beth on a double-decker bus. They met in the supermarket as Marnie reached the checkout. Outside, they dumped the bags on *Sally Ann's* deck and Marnie opened up. Beth was smiling.

"You know, Marnie, this is like an adventure. Do you remember Guide camp when we were kids? You were always the first to be ready. Even in those days you had everything organised ... and everybody."

As Beth spoke, Marnie picked up some of the bags and pulled open the cabin doors with her foot. "Nonsense. I'm not really like that." She indicated the remaining bags with a nod of the head. "You should be able to manage those. Follow me."

The weather remained fine for the whole journey. *Sally Ann* behaved impeccably and they shared the workload by alternating at locks. Marnie was surprised that Beth was not more adept at handling the boat, initially finding it difficult to steer her in a straight line and tending to wander off towards the bank. At locks she was no more expert, and checked the order of the operation with Marnie each time they made their approach and she stood, windlass in hand, ready to jump onto the bank.

But Beth was impressed with Marnie's skill and judgement, her handling of the boat so that it ran on rails hidden beneath the surface, her efficiency at the locks, always seeming to be one move ahead. Gradually, under Marnie's guidance and example, Beth found herself steering down the middle of the channel without deviation.

❦ ❦ ❦ ❦

After supper one evening, they took a stroll along the towpath in the pale evening light. As they walked they spontaneously linked arms, something they had not done since their teens. The air was mild and still, scented with the greenery of early summer and the cool smell of the water. In front of them lay only a pastoral landscape, little changed since the canal was built two centuries ago, rolling countryside with the Chiltern Hills as a backdrop.

"I know it's silly, but I can't help feeling what an adventure this is," said Beth. "You make things happen, Marnie, and you just seem to take it all in your stride. Being with you on this trip makes me see how it all somehow makes sense." They turned back to the boat, neither of them ready for the evening to come to an end.

"Beth? I don't suppose you feel like going on a bit further? It's going to stay light for a while yet."

They made *Sally Ann* ready and set off across the mirror-smooth surface into mid-channel. Ahead, they faced a sequence of locks rising up to the Tring summit and they decided to go as far as they could while the light lasted. They had negotiated three locks before the dusk came down.

"Two more locks and we'll be at the top," said Beth, studying the cruising guide. "Then we have a clear run over the Chilterns."

" It seems a pity to stop in sight of the Tring summit," said Marnie. "Feel like going on?"

"Have you done locks in this sort of light before?"

"No, but I was travelling alone. We could try one and see how it goes."

It went well, and Marnie hopped back on board for the short trip to the next lock. The sky was clear and the first stars were appearing. Marnie gazed up, leaning against the hatch, feeling free and untroubled. Whatever the future held, for this moment she had no worries. Her job, her home, her life, her whole career, were set aside for another day and another place. The Starship *Sally Ann* cruised the galaxy and left the world behind. It was a tap on the shoulder from Beth, pointing ahead, that brought Marnie back to earth.

The final lock was full when they reached it and Marnie had to bring the water level down. The paddles were stiff and the gates were heavy, needing all her strength, and it was some minutes before she could signal Beth to come forward. Breathing deeply with the effort, she sat down on the balance beam with her back to *Sally Ann's* headlamp, listening to the rushing of the water flooding the chamber. Gradually, with the light of the headlamp creeping slowly higher as *Sally Ann* rose in the lock, she lit up the whole of the lock area like a new dawn.

❦ ❦ ❦ ❦

The next day they travelled through the almost deserted wooded scenery, seeing a solitary angler on the bank and a heron patiently waiting for breakfast to swim by. Across the summit and past the Victorian workshop buildings at Bulbourne, they began their descent towards the Vale of Aylesbury. *Sally Ann* was running smoothly, or as smoothly as a geriatric two-cylinder diesel can run, and they passed the bridge where Marnie first met Anne with an 'e'.

"I have to be careful not to give her the wrong idea about my new set-up. She really ought to stay on at school and go to college. The trouble is, she thinks she can work for me, but there's no chance of that happening, not for quite a while, at least."

"Do you think she's got the message?" said Beth. "Youngsters can be very determined."

"Yes. I think she understands ... though I half expected to see her lying in wait for us. It would be just like her."

❦ ❦ ❦ ❦

That afternoon, as they chugged round Milton Keynes, Beth turned towards Marnie. "Today's the day, isn't it? The contract will be completed and you'll be the new owner of Glebe Farm."

"Yes. Tomorrow morning starts a new phase." They watched a heron flap away from the bank, tucking its neck into its body. "Now that the time has come, I'm really looking forward to it."

"So am I," said Beth. "But why tomorrow? If we wanted to get there this evening, could we make it?"

"It's not all that far, and there is only one lock after Milton Keynes, at Cosgrove."

"Then why not follow your motto?" In unison, they said: "Just do it!".

They travelled on at a steady pace, and Beth used the mobile to check her answerphone messages at home. "Eight-twenty tomorrow morning. Paul's shuttle lands at Heathrow. That's two days earlier than expected. Must be fewer people to examine."

"You'll be wanting to get back," said Marnie.

Beth looked thoughtful. "I shall be sorry to go. Of course, I'll be glad to see Paul, but I'm really enjoying this trip and I wasn't sure *Sally* was really my scene. I just came for the ride, maybe to ... show solidarity." She grinned at her sister. "Now I feel sorry I've got to think about returning home."

"When do you want to do that?" said Marnie. "Crack of dawn? I could get you on a milk train, if there is such a thing ..."

"I suppose it would be more sensible to get a train this evening and avoid the morning rush, if you didn't mind, Marnie."

"No problem."

Beth guided *Sally Ann* on the final leg of their journey. It was a mild evening as they passed under the last bridge before Glebe Farm. Through the tops of the trees, Beth caught sight of the honey-coloured stone gable of the main building and she offered the tiller to Marnie to bring *Sally Ann* into her docking area for the first time. Marnie shook her head and set off along the gunwale. By the time Marnie had secured the bow rope, Beth was in the engine compartment turning the stern gland.

"Welcome to Glebe Farm," said Marnie.

"Welcome home!" said Beth, and the two sisters hugged each other as the shadows lengthened among the ruins and Dolly emerged from the cabin to sniff the air on her first evening as a country cat.

❦   ❦   ❦   ❦

It was about ten miles to the nearest station and the roads were almost empty.

"Thanks for coming, Beth. It was nice to have you aboard. You know you're always welcome."

"Thanks, Mar ... What do you mean, *I'm always welcome?* It's my bloody boat!"

"Sorry, I was forgetting."

"As usual." Beth grimaced in mock ferocity. "Seriously, though, I've really enjoyed these few days. It seems ages since we set off."

"But you'll be home in no time. Give me a ring to let me know you're back."

Night was falling as Marnie waved her sister off and returned to the car. The signpost to Knightly St John appeared in the headlights and she pointed the car down the narrow road. Turning by the pub, she headed for the field gate and the track down to the farm. She rounded the bend and saw the dark bulk of the buildings among the trees and bushes. For a moment she thought she saw a reflection of her headlights in a window. But there were no windows on that side, only barns and walls. How odd.

Marnie parked the Rover behind the barns. It was a clear, still night and she paused for a moment before switching on her torch. Suddenly in the corner of her eye she saw what could have been a shooting star very low in the sky away to her right, if the buildings hadn't blocked out the sky on that side.

Marnie stood still and thought through the situation. Could there be someone lurking among the ruins? She dismissed the idea. Psychopaths, rapists and potential axe murderers would hardly lurk in a place where no-one was likely to pass. What would be the point? Who then? She compiled a shortlist. Poachers, kids out for a clandestine smoke, a courting couple. All of these were possible. Who else? She dredged her imagination and brought up drug dealers, devil worshippers, a coven of witches, general perverts and miscellaneous deviants.

No purpose would be served by standing in the darkness, and the thought of unwanted visitors skulking around *Sally Ann* all night made it improbable that she could simply go to bed and forget about them. Marnie stepped silently forward, expecting at any moment the crack of a twig under her feet. She gripped the torch firmly, thankful that she was wearing flat shoes in case she had to make a run for it. She paused at the corner of the nearest derelict barn and waited.

This was the moment of truth. In the dark silence she waited for a sound, anything to reveal the presence of an intruder. The seconds slipped by without a murmur and Marnie wondered if she had been mistaken. *This is absurd*, she thought. I'm probably standing beside an empty barn. I can't stay here all night. She took a deep, silent breath, flexed her shoulders and turned the corner, at the same time raising the torch and pressing the switch. The instant the light came on, the torch was knocked from her hand. She gasped and instinctively dropped down on one knee. Grabbing for the torch, she heard another gasp nearby inside the barn. She looked up to find herself confronted by the intruder, squatting at the back of the barn, dimly lit in the beam of the torch. Marnie stood up as the intruder spoke, steadying herself on the jutting hinge that had made her drop the torch.

"Sorry to give you a fright."

"*Anne!*" said Marnie.

"With an 'e'," said the girl smiling faintly as she rose from the floor.

❦ ❦ ❦ ❦

Marnie poured steaming hot tea into mugs in the saloon of *Sally Ann* and passed one across the table to her visitor.

"Would you like anything to eat?"

The girl sat with Dolly purring in her lap. "Oh, no thanks, Marnie. I'm okay."

"How long have you been here?"

"Since about … two o'clock."

"So you've not had supper?"

"Well, no. But I'm fine, really."

Marnie got up and opened the food cupboard. "The choice is enormous. In fact, I haven't eaten since a sandwich at lunchtime, so let's celebrate taking over Glebe Farm." She rummaged among the stores. "Any preference?"

"You choose, Marnie. I'm easy. Honest."

Marnie began to pull out the ingredients for an impromptu supper. She started by partly slicing a baguette, and while it developed into garlic bread in the oven, she mixed a tuna salad. Anne laid the table, slightly subdued at the thought of the questions and explanations to come.

"Why not tell me about it?" said Marnie, mixing vinaigrette in a bowl.

"I haven't run away from home or anything like that."

"Good. What about the last two exams?"

"Not bad. The French was better than I expected. RE was okay."

Marnie checked the oven and the aroma of garlic bread wafted past her. "Okay, so no crisis."

"No. I just wanted to … wish you success and happiness in your new home."

"And your parents know you've come?"

"Oh, yes. I told them I was coming to see you."

Marnie took the garlic bread from the oven. "Right. Before we eat, use the mobile to ring home and ask if it's okay for you to stay here for tonight. I'll drive you back tomorrow."

They ate at first in silence and Marnie remembered the remains of the designer water in the fridge. They chinked glasses and sipped.

"Is there something else you want to tell me?" said Marnie.

"I'm very happy for you, now you've got Glebe Farm." Anne smiled and looked down. "I know it's silly, but I was wondering … if I could … well, work for you … like an apprentice, you know." She cut a piece of garlic bread and ate it without looking up. For all its flavour, Marnie knew her young friend did not notice the taste.

"Anne, it's difficult at the moment. There are so many imponderables. I'm not sure how things will turn out." It was Marnie's turn to frown. She hated sounding so negative. Anne ate and nodded. "Look. I promise you I'll talk to you about it again, once I have a better idea of how the work's going. That's a *firm* promise."

"Thanks, Marnie."

They had just finished the main course when the phone rang.

"Hi Marnie! I'm home. Thanks for a wonderful cruise. How are you … not too lonely?"

"Guess what?" said Marnie cheerfully. "I've got my first visitor." Beth immediately became suspicious. She lowered her voice.

"Is everything all right?"

"It's Anne. My ... my designer friend."

Beth became more suspicious. "The one you told she really ought to go to college but that wants to work for you?"

"Yes." Marnie's voice sounded a little strained.

Beth continued. "The one who fully understands there's no chance of that happening? The one who wouldn't run away from home?"

"That's right." Marnie hoped her voice sounded convincing to both the people listening to her.

"Marnie?"

"Yes?"

"It's a good job you were careful not to give her the wrong idea ..."

❦　❦　❦　❦

During her first conscious moments the next morning, Marnie had to make an effort to remember where she was. She reached up onto the shelf above the bed and pulled down the travel alarm. Six-forty-five. The first day. In her mind she went through a list of tasks, meetings to be arranged, people to ring. From now on every part of her work depended entirely on her, every phone call, every message. She would do it. Just do it. But first, there were matters to be resolved. She turned onto her side and called Anne softly round the corner of the dividing partition.

There was no reply and Marnie lay back on her pillow, wondering if she could let the girl sleep on for a while, but there was no way of preparing breakfast or moving about the boat without disturbing her. She called her again, a little more loudly. There was a sound of movement, an intake of breath, very faint. "I think there are some croissants and cereals, but I suspect we're out of orange juice."

As she spoke, the face of Dolly appeared beside her, the cat's front paws resting on the bed as she stood on her hind legs and blinked at Marnie. "Good morning, Dolly. Time for your breakfast, too." She stroked the soft ears and the purring began. Marnie swung her legs from under the cover and sat up to look round at Anne. The bed was empty. Marnie frowned, got up and quickly put on jeans and sweatshirt. The doors to the cratch were unbolted and pulled together. Anne had left via the bows.

It was a fine, mild morning with a light haze on the water, and the buildings of the farm, glimpsed through the bushes and trees, looked abandoned and desolate. Marnie walked towards them. The door to the barn was shut, but it yielded as soon as Marnie pushed it. Anne was sitting at the desk, sorting through piles of papers.

"How did you get in here? This is my top security wing."

"You left the key on the workbench in the galley. The label said 'office'. Your filing's a bit behind."

"It can't be. I haven't started yet."

"Well, the paperwork you brought with you is all over the place."

"It's nothing important. I'll deal with it as I settle in."

"You won't *be* settling in if you don't sort those out." Anne pointed to a small collection of papers on the corner of the desk. Marnie picked them up. The telephone connection bill (she'd wondered where that had gone), the mail redirection form for her flat, the invoice for her professional indemnity insurance ... She replaced them on the desk. "I think you ought to do them straight away," said Anne, "and I'll go to the post box so they catch the first collection."

"*After* you've had some breakfast," said Marnie. "We'll drop them off on our way."

"Okay."

Marnie looked round the barn. "You've been tidying up."

"It needed it. There's a black bag over in the corner next to a pile of paper that I *think* is rubbish. You'd better have a look before we throw it out. When do the bins get collected round here?"

"Er … I'm not sure. I've got to check up on that sort of thing." Anne reached out for a pad and made a note. "What's that?" said Marnie.

"Queries list."

"It's rather long, isn't it?" Anne looked pointedly at the 'urgent' pile and the papers still waiting in front of her to be checked and gave a theatrical sigh.

As they walked back to *Sally Ann*, Marnie breathed in the fresh morning air while Anne carried the bundle of urgent papers, glancing through them while taking care not to trip over uneven cobbles. Marnie gave Anne a rundown on the options for breakfast and waited while her friend pondered.

"Marnie … in business studies at school they taught us the most important problems facing small firms. You're a small firm aren't you?"

"About five foot seven," said Marnie. "That's quite tall, really."

"I'm being serious. Mrs Alderman said the number one problem is cash-flow. Would you agree with that?"

"Do I get a GCSE if I give the right answer?"

"Do you *agree*?" Anne persisted, realising that Marnie was floating on a cloud of excitement on this first day of a new life. She felt the same herself, tinged with the knowledge that for her the first day was about to end in half an hour with a drive home.

"Yes, I suppose it is," said Marnie. "Don't people call it the 'life-blood of the enterprise'? That's rather good. I think I deserve a GCSE for that." Anne handed her a paper from the bundle. "What's this?" said Marnie taking it.

"A blocked artery," said Anne. "It's an invoice to Willards Brewery. It's got Friday's date on. Does it need a covering letter? I could set up a template on the computer."

The conversation continued through breakfast. Marnie hastily dealt with the most urgent bills and forms ready for posting. They set off at eight. Anne got out of the car at the post box and read the notice giving details of collections. Buckling her seat belt, she gave Marnie an outline of the service.

"There's a collection at eight-fifty. The afternoon post goes at five-fifteen and the sub post office closes at one o'clock on Wednesdays." Marnie's brow furrowed as she tried to take in the information while guiding the car onto the road leading out of the village. Anne scribbled the times on her list, which by now had a number of items crossed out. "I'll leave you the list so you can check it over later." She put it in the glove box and almost immediately took it out again to add another entry.

"What's that?" said Marnie.

"It's the computer helpline."

"But the computer's still in its box. I don't even know if I'll need the helpline until I get it out."

"That's why you'll need it."

They drove down the dual carriageway and turned off towards the Chilterns and Anne's home town. Soon, they were pulling into her street, an ordinary street of ordinary houses, a million miles from the strange ruins and isolation of Glebe Farm.

Jackie opened the front door, smiling warmly, with the smell of coffee lurking in the hall. As if on cue, two slices of toast jumped in the toaster as they entered the kitchen and Marnie was offered a chair. The house seemed so solid and permanent.

Anne excused herself, saying she wanted to change into clean clothes, and went upstairs. Bundling a fresh shirt, underwear and jeans under her arm, she went to the bathroom and washed. She brushed her hair, not noticing her reflection in the mirror. She would go down, say good-bye to Marnie and watch the car drive up the road and round the corner. Behind her, she could hear footsteps on the stairs. Her mother was coming up to see if she was ready.

She turned to see Marnie standing in the doorway. Instinctively, Anne held out her hand and attempted a smile. Marnie came forward and held Anne's hand in both hers.

"I think," Marnie began, glancing towards the wardrobe. "I think you'd better pack some warm things. It can get quite chilly in the evenings on the canal ... especially by the end of summer." Anne struggled to make sense of the words. "Oh, and it's a good idea not to go around with your mouth open like that. You might swallow a fly and ..." Marnie had no chance to continue as Anne leapt forward and hugged her so tightly she could hardly breathe.

❦   ❦   ❦   ❦

"And it's not just for the weekend," said Anne.

Marnie threaded her way through the morning traffic and pulled onto the dual carriageway. "No. You can certainly stay for the summer and longer if you want. We can decide how long when we see how things settle down."

"That's great."

"I think we ought to agree on a basis for your stay."

"I don't want anything," said Anne quickly. Marnie ignored the interruption.

"It would be great if you could sort out the filing, as you were doing this morning, and help me to organise the office."

Anne reached into the glove box and pulled out her list. "I can get the computer set up and running," she said.

"Right. Now, I will pay you a weekly amount, say ..." Before she could finish, Anne put her hand on Marnie's arm.

"Marnie, you don't know how much you'll be earning at first. Board and lodging will be fine, if that's all right." Marnie shook her head. She suggested an amount.

"No, no," said Anne. "Board and lodging, like an apprentice, like Telford or Jessop."

"Blimey," said Marnie. "I'm having an industrial dispute on my first morning. I think I've just taken on a shop steward. Look, I'm the employer, I set the conditions. Now, do you want the good news or the bad news?" Anne was puzzled by the question. "Well?" said Marnie.

"The bad news, I suppose," said Anne.

"Okay. You're going to get the worst pay and conditions of anyone in the whole of the British interior design industry."

"Right. And the good news?"

"I'm back-dating it to the start of the week."

Part 10

Sarah was already awake, or perhaps it was the noises that woke her. She rose silently from her bed, trying not to disturb her sisters and looked down into the lane in the pale light. It was scarcely dawn.

From the furthest bed one sister called out to her in a whisper. "What is it, Sarah?"

"Horses. I can hear horses. The men returning!" No longer concerned with silence, she put on her shoes and pulled a shawl over her nightshift. By the time she reached the front door, the house was awake and she was followed into the lane by her sisters and her mother, half smiling, half anxious at what they might discover.

At once they knew this was no homecoming. There were raised voices, women screaming, men shouting, the stamp of horses and the rattle of harness. Above it all rose a pall of smoke and flame that they saw before they came to the road. The smell of burning filled the air. Sarah held the arm of one of her sisters to prevent her rushing ahead. They stopped at the end of the lane, eyes staring, hands raised to their mouths. Soldiers on horses were throwing lighted torches onto the roofs of houses. One man begging them to stop was struck down with a pistol barrel. Men and women and children were running among the horses, others standing by the roadside wailing in despair.

"Who are they?" said Sarah's mother.

"They must be the King's men," said Sarah and in that moment, two of the men detached themselves from the main party and galloped towards them, one holding a torch, the other with sabre raised. Sarah heard her sisters gasp and reached for their hands. "Get behind us, mother!" she called over her shoulder and began shouting at the soldiers. Her two sisters joined in, a weak, thin line of girls in shifts blocking the entrance to the lane, daring the men to charge them. The girls lifted their hands in the air, screaming like demons, frightened and frightening. The soldier lobbed the torch over their heads and it fell short by yards, spluttering on the dusty path. His horse shied. The other soldier reined in and they turned back. The sisters and their mother clutched each other, trembling where they stood.

"What do we do?" said a sister.

"We must stay," said Sarah.

"How long?"

"As long as it takes ... until they go. We must be steadfast."

❦   ❦   ❦   ❦

Thursday 15 June

The first day of the New Life almost began with a head-on crash with the post van by the field gate at the top of the track. The postman gestured to Marnie to come on while he reversed into the field to let her pass. She drew level and opened her window.

"Sorry. Didn't expect to run into anyone."

"Same here. It's been years since any post went to Glebe Farm, but there were so many letters I thought it had to be right. I've left a bundle against the wall by the barn door." He was an older man with a country accent and a brass badge bearing the name Alan.

"My name's Marnie Walker. Nice to meet you. This is Anne. We only got here last night. I'll go round to the post office this morning and let them know we're here."

"Right. Well, I hope you'll be happy down there." He paused as if trying to find the right words. "Where are you actually ... er, living?" Marnie suspected that this would only be the first of many occasions when she would have to explain about living on *Sally Ann* while refurbishing the buildings. His reaction, just short of incredulity, would probably become familiar in the days to come.

"I think we ought to record an explanation on tape and just play it to people when they ask that," said Anne as they opened the barn doors. She dumped her holdall on the floor by the desk.

"Okay," said Marnie. "Let's work out a programme for the morning."

Anne said, "I can finish sorting through the papers, if you like. Then I can get the computer unpacked and try to get it working." Soon, Marnie was startled by a loud crack as Anne cut open the packing to remove the computer from its box. She smiled as Anne shook her head at the sight of the spaghetti of wires, and returned to her list of phone calls. The next surprise was to find a cup of steaming hot coffee on the desk beside her, as she was speaking to the Head of Marketing at Willards Brewery.

She tore from her pad the list of completed phone calls, screwed the note into a ball and threw it onto the floor at the place where the bin had been standing before Anne had commandeered it. "How's the computer coming on? Found the plug yet?" Anne pointed towards the table behind Marnie, who turned to find the computer set up on the table ready for action, its screen glowing.

After coffee they walked up to the sub post office in the shop. Marnie half expected people to stare at her and Anne, as strangers to the village. Instead, there was a glance and a polite half-smile from the two women chatting in the corner, a muttered 'good morning' from the man passing them on his way out and a welcoming nod from the woman at the counter. Marnie introduced herself and Anne.

"I've just moved in ... *we've* just moved in, that is. We came yesterday evening. You should be getting mail here redirected from London."

"It's Richard who's the sub-postmaster." The woman indicated her husband sitting in a small glazed booth at the end of the counter. He came out to meet the newcomers.

"I'm having another phone line put in any day now and various building jobs done. No doubt people will be coming to ask directions."

"Don't worry. We'll point everyone in the right direction, won't we, Molly?"

"Oh yes. We hope you'll be very happy here. If there's anything you need, just let me know," said Molly. "We can deliver groceries if you're out at work and don't have time to shop."

"Thank you. I'll remember that. As a matter of fact, I'll be working from home, at Glebe Farm."

Molly glanced at her husband. "But I thought it was ... derelict and you were just going to be renovating it. Surely there isn't anywhere to live?"

Marnie gave the usual explanation. Anxious not to let the conversation develop into an interview, she enquired about facilities in the area and Molly was glad to advise. In the course of her speech she pointed towards the shop window. Outside, the man who had left the shop as they arrived could be seen in conversation with another man dressed entirely in black.

"If you want good meat, you won't do better than Mr Stubbs. That's him there talking to the vicar." She picked up a poster lying on the counter. Reading it upside down, Marnie saw it was an announcement of a special meeting of the Parochial Church Council to be held that evening.

"He's also a pillar of the church?" she suggested.

Molly looked at her husband before replying. "Doesn't quite see eye-to-eye with the vicar on some matters. Likes things to stay as they are. You know, tradition, family values, roast beef and Yorkshire pudding for Sunday dinner, one o'clock sharp." She laughed.

"Oh dear," said Marnie. "I tend to eat very little meat these days and red meat hardly ever."

"I don't eat meat at all," said Anne.

"Well, you won't be popular with Mr Stubbs then," said Molly cheerfully. "He sells free range eggs from his own hens and he has contacts who do really good fish. But he still says a meal isn't a meal without meat. Never mind. He's nice when you get to know him, but he does like to have *opinions*, if you know what I mean."

Marnie had a fair idea. "So the meeting is to discuss a village event, perhaps?" she asked.

This time it was Richard who replied. "It's to discuss the *changes*." He nodded to emphasise the word. Anne turned sideways to watch the two men through the window. Mr Stubbs looked in his late fifties, as far as she could judge, like her grandfather. He was of medium height, thickset and balding, with a bull neck that was wrinkled at the back. This was in marked contrast with the vicar who was about a head taller, with short dark wavy hair over a sharp profile. As he spoke, he leaned forward to give weight to the points he was making and Anne had the impression that there was no great display of Christian brotherly love in their words.

Marnie said "I'll just take a few bits and pieces for the moment. Anne, is there anything you need while we're here?" Anne shook her head and Molly smiled at her.

Marnie gathered up the bag with her bits and pieces. Outside, Mr Stubbs was looking thoughtfully at the back of the vicar as he walked away. He was wearing a full length black cassock, as worn by priests long ago, and the tall, thin figure seemed an odd sight in the modern world, like a glimpse back to another age. As they made to go past, Mr Stubbs turned and looked at them.

"Good morning again. Fine morning." His voice was deep and pleasant, hinting at roast dinners and thick gravy. "May I ask are you new to the area, or just passing through?" Marnie explained briefly. As she spoke, Mr Stubbs had one eye on the retreating back of the vicar, as if keeping him under observation. They shook hands and Anne felt vulnerable as his broad, fleshy fingers enveloped her slim hand. She thought of thick-cut pork sausages and smiled at the idea. His face lit up.

"Did Molly tell you about my own business?" He beamed at them. "For generations we used to slaughter in the outbuilding at the back of the house, but we stopped that in '69. Now I get all my meat from the local abattoir. They're very good, but it's still important to know your source and the farmers."

"I'm sure we'll be in touch with you," said Marnie, hoping it did not sound too much like a commitment. She glanced round in the direction taken by the vicar, who was now crossing the road opposite the church. "It's a lovely village," she added, trying to steer the conversation away from meat.

"I wouldn't want to live anywhere else," said Mr Stubbs. "In fact I never have, except when I did my National Service. Even then, I only went as far as Weedon depot."

"And a beautiful church," added Marnie. At that, Mr Stubbs drew breath audibly.

"For the moment," he said. "While it's all in one piece." His smile had gone. "You've not met our vicar I suppose?"

"That was him, presumably." The black shape had now disappeared into the churchyard.

"One for *changes*, all sorts of *changes*, our Reverend Hughes." Marnie felt unable to back out of this.

"And not everyone likes changes," she said in a neutral tone.

"It would not be the first time this village has taken action against its vicar." Mr Stubbs pursed his lips and his thoughts were far away. Marnie was curious, but she had no wish to begin her residence of Knightly St John with a gossip in the street. It was time to move on.

"I believe you sell free range eggs, and fish?"

"Fish to order, oh yes. I'll let you have a list. Then you can drop it in any time you like and I'll have it delivered within a day or two. My chap's very reliable and good value."

"Actually, we will be needing some eggs." Marnie glanced at her watch.

"I could fetch them," suggested Anne. "Tomorrow perhaps?"

"If there aren't any at the shop we have them at the Old Farm House, straight up the road," said Mr Stubbs pointing. "Side door. Come any time." He raised his hat, turned and set off.

"Better get back and do some work," said Marnie. "That was a good idea about the eggs. You can have a nice chat with Mr Stubbs. He's probably never seen a vegetarian before, in the flesh. You'll have lots to talk about."

Anne winced. "Of course, but he'd prefer *you* to go. He liked you all right, Marnie. Couldn't take his eyes off you."

"Oh no. Not at all. I'm sure you're wrong. Not enough meat on me for his liking!" Laughing, they almost collided with the tall black shape of the vicar as he stepped out from the churchyard gate.

"I'm sorry … I wasn't looking … I didn't see you coming along." He smiled apologetically. At close quarters he looked less youthful than he did from a distance. Marnie reckoned him to be in his late thirties or thereabouts, with dark hair and sharp features, a strong beak of a nose giving him a thrusting, inquisitive expression like a jackdaw. He had dark eyes and pronounced cheekbones. A fine, intelligent face was made firm and uncompromising by the austere black cassock. For all the diffident manner and the courteous tone, Marnie judged that this was not a man to be flexible on matters of principle.

"No, no. It was my fault, really," said Marnie, offering her hand. "I'm Marnie Walker. This is my friend Anne Price."

"My name is Randall Hughes." They shook hands in turn and this time Anne found the firm grip of the long, cool fingers more agreeable.

"We've just arrived," said Marnie. "We're at Glebe Farm, or rather what remains of it."

"Of course. Mr Fletcher mentioned he had finally sold it. Oh, sorry … I mean after it had been in his family for generations."

"And it had been on the market for a long time too," said Marnie.

"Quite." The vicar hesitated for a second. "Mrs Walker, I was wondering …"

"Yes?"

"Am I correct in understanding that you're an architect or a designer?"

"I'm an interior designer," said Marnie. "We've been admiring the church. It's a fine structure."

"Well, you see, that's just the point. It *is* a beautiful building, of course, but it has lots of problems and needs attention … serious attention."

"Appeal for the church roof, that sort of thing?" Marnie could see the collection plate floating into the conversation.

"Actually the roof's okay. It was redone about ten years ago. No, the real problem is the porch and also the tower, plus various internal things that can't be ignored for much longer. I have a file two inches thick."

"It sounds like maintenance work," said Marnie.

"Look, I'm sorry to accost you in the street like this. You must think me rude and I'm sure you're very busy."

"That's all right. I'll be glad to help if I can. Perhaps we ought to have a talk and see what can be done."

"Thank you. Shall I call by some time, perhaps after the weekend? Give you time to get your bearings?"

They went their separate ways and Marnie quickened her pace, anxious to return to work. Lunch was casual. Marnie ate a sandwich at her desk, organising her workload for the first month. The jobs list grew steadily. Between bites, Anne installed the remaining software onto the computer, tidied the collection of leads and wires out of sight and formatted a box of disks. Her list of jobs to do went into a second page on the pad.

"Marnie, I think we're in business. We ought to talk about your system when you've got a moment."

"System?"

"How you want your computer files organised, what directories you want set up, how the diary's to be kept, you know." In her previous life Marnie had never given a thought to how the office ran. How *were* her computer files organised? What directories *had* been set up?

"I'm not sure. I'll have to think about that."

"Shall I put something together for you to look at?"

"Do you know how to go about it?"

"Sure. We did all that in business studies. I got an 'A' in my coursework."

"An 'A'," Marnie repeated. She felt uneasy about the future management structure of the Walker Design Conglomerate being set up by a sixteen year-old who had left school two days earlier. "Er … well, that's very good. Perhaps you could do that and we can talk about it later on." What made her more uneasy was the knowledge that Anne had a better idea of what to do than she did. At least Marnie was confident that she had revealed nothing of her feelings and doubts.

"Did you bring any disks with you from the office in London?" said Anne. "I can use the same system. Then you won't be so worried about me messing things up." It was said without rancour or sarcasm and Marnie swallowed.

"I had no such thought," she protested cheerfully.

Anne met her gaze and held it unflinchingly. "Fine. So where are the disks?"

"In the car, I think. Try the boot. Or they might be in the large brown envelope on the back seat." Anne took the keys and was gone for some minutes, eventually returning laden with a box and the envelope perched on the top of it.

"Any luck?" said Marnie.

"They were in the glove compartment. I thought I ought to deal with these, too." She spent the next hour sorting through the pile. By the time she reached the end of that job, Marnie was still on the phone and Anne had reached the point where she could make no further progress without a consultation. Marnie finished her call and turned to find Anne engrossed in reading a small booklet.

"Marnie, did you know the vicar was murdered?" Anne said without looking up. "This little book was in the glove box with the disks."

"The vicar?"

"Yes. The vicar here in the Civil War … Joseph Goldsworthy. He was murdered in the church one night in 1645 … killed in the tower."

"Who by?" said Marnie. Anne quickly scanned the page.

"Nobody knows," she said. "It says here: '*The identity of the murderer is unknown to this day. It remains one of the great unsolved mysteries of those turbulent times.*' Do you remember what that Mr Stubbs said about it not being the first time the village had taken action against the vicar?" She had a sudden vision of Mr Stubbs raising a butcher's knife high above his head and bringing it down savagely to stab the vicar through the heart. She shuddered and gasped for breath.

"Are you all right?" said Marnie. "You've gone quite pale." She pulled a bottle of mineral water from a cupboard and poured some into a glass.

Anne sipped it and smiled self-consciously. "Sorry, I don't know what came over me." She took several deep breaths and began to feel better. She told Marnie what she had imagined and felt foolish.

"Is that how it happened?" said Marnie. "Dreadful." She took the booklet and put it on her desk. "Why don't we go and get some fresh air? It's a fine day. We can post our letters and do some more sorting out when we get back. Come on! It'll do us good."

On this second outing they found the village alive with activity. On their way back from the postbox the children were pouring out of school. Cars were parked at odd angles up and down the high street. Mothers were chatting in small groups. Several of them greeted Marnie and Anne as they passed and were slowed by the congestion on the pavement. A cluster of the smallest children brought their progress to a halt like a flock of sheep stopping a car on a country road. A woman stepped forward in the playground, stood in the gateway and urged the children to make space, smiling an apology at Marnie.

"They just aren't aware at this age, I'm afraid." She had a pleasant but firm manner, a woman of around forty, about Marnie's height in a summer dress with a light cardigan draped over her shoulders. The image of a village school mistress.

"That's okay," said Marnie. "I didn't expect such a small village to have so many children."

"Not all from this village," said the woman. "They come from two other villages, Yore and Hanford, as well."

"How odd," said Marnie. "I had the idea that Yore and Hanford were larger than Knightly St John. I'd have expected them to have their own schools."

"Quite right," said the woman. "But that's another story. I don't believe we've met, have we?"

"No. We're new to the village. This is our first day here." They introduced themselves and Marnie explained about living temporarily on *Sally Ann*. The woman was the Headteacher, Margaret Giles.

"What kind of boat is *Sally Ann*?" she said. "Would you call it a barge?"

"No. She's a narrowboat. Forty-five feet long, seven feet wide. A barge would be longer and about twice the width." Mrs Giles seemed genuinely interested and was about to speak when another woman appeared from behind her and told her she was wanted on the phone. The Head turned to leave.

"Mrs Walker, perhaps we could have a chat some time when you have a moment? I'd like to know more about *Sally Ann*."

"Yes, of course."

"I'll be in touch," said Mrs Giles and strode off.

"You're looking a bit more human now," said Marnie glancing at Anne as they walked on.

"Perhaps I'd been staring at the computer screen for too long." Anne dropped the letters into the post box and they turned back. "It's funny. I had such a clear picture in my mind of Mr Stubbs and that knife. It was horrible."

"Well, I shouldn't go on about it, if I were you. It's a long way for me to have to carry you back to Glebe Farm if you pass out."

"I wonder what the headmistress wants to ask you about *Sally Ann*."

"I expect I can guess. She probably wants the children to do something on the canal, local history project, wildlife on the waterways ..."

"With a boat trip to make it more fun?" said Anne. "A cruise to Stoke Bruerne with me serving refreshments on deck!"

"That sort of thing, I suppose. We'll see, but I can't think what else she'd have in mind, unless she's planning her summer holiday." They were walking along the field track and the roof timbers of Glebe Farm were just coming into view.

"We need a routine," said Anne suddenly.

"Exactly what I was thinking."

"I can free you to do design work and deal with the clients. That would help, wouldn't it?"

"Yes it would. You know, I must say, Anne, I've been very impressed with how you've got on and done things. It would've taken me days to get the computer sorted out, probably the whole weekend." They crossed the yard and Marnie unlocked the office door. "I wonder if this is really necessary ... locking everything up like this when we go into the village. It's not as if we're in the middle of London."

They settled down to getting the computer system fully operational. Anne asked for a few minutes to complete what she was doing. Unable to settle down to any other work until Anne had finished, Marnie browsed through the church history booklet. She opened it and read to herself the part referring to the canal.

"... until in 1793 the squire of that period became a sponsor of the Grand Junction Canal Act and contributed to the building of the canal that now passes round the parish on three sides. Throughout the nineteenth century the canal enhanced the wealth of the area, helping farmers to carry produce to local markets. To this day, Glebe Farm retains the docking area that was built for this purpose. Nowadays the canal is used almost entirely for leisure and the only indication of it is the gentle chugging of the long boats as they carry holiday-makers on their journey towards the great tunnel at Blisworth ..."

"Long boats!" thought Marnie. She turned back to earlier times and found the reference to the Civil War and the incident that led to the murder of the vicar. She read the episode twice to make sure she had not missed any of the details. There was no mention of any knife and no description of how the vicar was killed.

"... rushing into the church they found the vicar lying at the foot of the steps leading up into the tower, mortally wounded, in a pool of blood. He died without speaking another word and never named his assailant. The identity of the murderer is unknown to this day ..."

Marnie leaned back in her chair. Where had Anne got the idea that the vicar was killed with a knife? How *had* the vicar been killed? *Who* had killed him? Why should anyone want to kill a vicar, *any* vicar?

"I think we need a disk for each major project. I know it seems a lot of capacity for just one job, but it will probably save time in the long run ..."

More than anything, it struck Marnie as really strange that one small village deep in the country should have had so much conflict between the church and the community. An agnostic herself, she still expected those who *did* believe to conduct themselves in a manner approaching the ideas of brotherly love, or at the very least, not go round killing each other.

"... I have the impression I'm not getting through here ... Marnie?"

"Oh, sorry. I was thinking about something." She was not anxious to open up the conversation about the murder again. "Did you see the passage about the canal? Ridiculous ... 'the gentle chugging of the long boats as they carry holiday-makers ...' I mean ... Long boats! I ask you ... it's bad enough being regarded as water gypsies. At least we don't have to dress up as Vikings and wear helmets with horns on!" Anne laughed at the idea, and Marnie was relieved.

"Do you want me to tell you my ideas on the computer and how to use it?" said Anne, like a parent indulging her child. Marnie settled back to give Anne her full attention. For the next half hour they went through Anne's list point by point until they had a clear policy on running the office. They had almost finished when the phone rang. Marnie took the call. For much of the call Marnie listened, muttering agreement, until she finally thanked the caller and hung up.

"The best news we could have had! The plumbers are coming on Monday morning first thing to install the loo!" Great was the rejoicing. Marnie looked up at the clock. It was just after five-thirty. "You know, I think I've had enough for one day. Why don't we have a drink and go for a trip on *Sally Ann*? Then I can make supper and we can have a pleasant, quiet evening to the accompaniment of a little Mozart or Bach. How does that sound?"

"Wonderful," said Anne, and really meant it.

❦ ❦ ❦ ❦

At the moment when Marnie and Anne sat down to supper on board *Sally Ann*, the members of the Parochial Church Council were filing into the village hall for the special meeting. It was a subdued group that evening. There were eight members present, but everyone knew that the main protagonists would be Albert Fletcher and George Stubbs, who had organised the meeting.

As the members of the PCC arrived, the vicar greeted them with formal courtesy, well aware that while some were plainly embarrassed at the circumstances, a few were openly hostile to his views on nearly every subject. Only Valerie Paxton, churchwarden and secretary of the village school, fully supported his ideas and she lacked the strength of character to stand up to any serious attack from the older members of the group.

The vicar took his usual place at the head of the table and opened the meeting. At once, George Stubbs leapt in, speaking in a rush.

"Thank you, Vicar. I've called this meeting because ..."

"Mr Stubbs." The voice of the vicar stopped him in mid-flow. "Although this is an extraordinary meeting, that does not mean we should conduct ourselves any differently from our normal practice." George Stubbs opened his mouth to protest, but found himself confronted by the bowed heads of the other members. "Let us pray," said the vicar. "Our heavenly Father, we ask you to bring wisdom to our deliberations, balance to our judgement and the spirit of love and companionship to our assembly." Mr Stubbs drew breath to utter 'amen'. "Help us to find the path of reason, remembering that our only duty is the service of Your will. In the name of the Father and of the Son and of the Holy Spirit. Amen."

"Amen."

"My friends, this meeting is being held at the request of Mr Stubbs, who wishes to discuss the use of Church funds. Before I invite Mr Stubbs to address the meeting, I would remind you that the duty laid on us is to devote all our resources to the upkeep of the church in the community. That includes the building itself and its related activities. George, please go ahead."

Mr Stubbs cleared his throat. "As I see it, we are losing sight of what 'the community' really means. In the last three years we've spent large sums of money messing about with building works and paying travel costs for speakers to come here and talk about being 'born again', whatever that's supposed to mean." Mr Stubbs looked from one to another and was disappointed to find that all except Albert Fletcher were staring down at the table before them. "The real community is *people*. What we *ought* to be doing is spending our resources on them, especially the children."

"I have to remind the meeting," said the vicar, "that *our* responsibility is to preserve the church and *its* needs, not to provide a social service. We have a thriving Sunday school, a Mothers' Union, a Brownie pack and a Cub pack. We have a playgroup in the church hall two mornings a week ..."

"But that doesn't compare with what people get in the *town*," said Mr Stubbs. "People expect more these days and if we can't provide it, they'll drift away. Look at the conditions in the school. They've got outside toilets, small classrooms, a tiny hall ..."

"But Mr Stubbs, George, those are the responsibility of the governors and the local education authority, not the PCC."

"But it's a *church* school, Vicar."

"It's a *voluntary controlled* school. There is a difference."

❦   ❦   ❦   ❦

On board *Sally Ann*, Marnie looked up from her magazine and moved closer to the lamp. "Can you see all right, Anne?"

"Just about. Can you?"

"More or less. We should have the mains extended down here some time next week. Then we'll be able to see what we're doing. There's such a lot to be done."

"Yes, but it's a nice place to be doing it," said Anne.

"Good. I think so too." She set the magazine down in her lap. "I can't help thinking about the children this afternoon. I was really surprised to see so many from such a small school."

"Didn't the Head say they came from other villages as well?"

"They don't have schools in Yore and Hanford, even though they're bigger villages. *But that's another story.* I wonder what she meant by that?"

"You can ask her when you go to see her," said Anne. "I still think it must be nice to go to a little village school. It's small and friendly in a village."

❦   ❦   ❦   ❦

At the PCC meeting Albert Fletcher raised a finger and the vicar nodded at him to speak.

"George is right. If the school was closed, no-one with small children would want to come here. It's bad enough as it is. Young folk can't afford to buy property in the village and there's nowhere to rent."

"I think that's rather an exaggeration, Mr Fletcher," said the vicar. "In any case, as I've already explained, the County Council is responsible ..."

"No!" George Stubbs banged his hand down on the table. Valerie Paxton jumped in her seat, but the vicar remained unmoved. Mr Stubbs continued. "My family have lived in this place for generations. We cannot let it be run by newcomers who haven't been here five minutes. We don't *want* change for its own sake when it's not needed, or wanted."

"Mr Stubbs," said the vicar in a calm voice. "The church is God's house. That has nothing to do with where it's located or who is the vicar at any given time. It is in our temporary stewardship and I must care for it as I think best, naturally taking account of this council's advice."

"Other vicars have been opposed," said Mr Stubbs.

"Of course. But they were weak. I'm not such an easy target."

❦   ❦   ❦   ❦

On *Sally Ann*, Marnie stood up and put the kettle on. "My eyes are going funny in this light. I think I'd better stop reading before I go blind."

"That would be a disadvantage for an interior designer," said Anne.

Marnie smiled back at her with exaggerated sweetness. "What would you like to drink? The choice is coffee, tea or some indeterminate stuff in a packet left on board by Beth and Paul, probably about five years past its sell by date. It purports to be a malted milk drink based on skimmed milk and guaranteed to be almost entirely fat-free. The same goes for taste, I expect."

"Sounds tempting," said Anne.

"This is probably the best place to drink it," said Marnie. "In this light we wouldn't be able to see it properly."

"That's certainly something to bear in mind," said Anne.

"So that decides it, then?"

"Definitely. Tea, please."

❦   ❦   ❦   ❦

The vicar raised both hands, but not in surrender. Valerie Paxton was passing round cups of coffee that the members of the council took without a word. She finally set down a plate of biscuits in the middle of the table where they remained untouched.

"I think we've got as far as we can this evening," said the vicar. Albert Fletcher was watching him steadily. George Stubbs looked from side to side at the others. "I've noted your views, Mr Stubbs, and will bear them in mind, but I have to say that in my judgement the church funds must be used to carry out essential works to the fabric of the building in the interests of safety. That is my responsibility."

"You could get a diocesan grant for that, if it's so unsafe," said Mr Stubbs in a low growl.

The vicar, shook his head. "The money was donated specifically for the fabric. It would be quite wrong to spend it on school maintenance when the local education authority is responsible for such matters. I believe there's nothing more to be said on the subject." George Stubbs grimaced, angry that no-one else had taken up the fight, though he knew they nearly all supported his views.

Albert Fletcher was staring down at the table in front of him and the vicar began to gather up his papers as a signal that the meeting had come to an end. "Not quite," said the old farmer. "I move that we put it to the vote."

"This is not a matter to be decided by ballot," said the vicar firmly. "It's an issue delegated to my judgement."

"We can still vote on it," said Mr Fletcher. "That way, you'll know the strength of feeling on the PCC. It'll be in the minutes, recorded for future reference." Molly Appleton shifted uncomfortably in her seat. George Stubbs narrowed his eyes as he looked across the table at the old man. The vicar acquiesced. The resolution took some minutes to agree. Finally the vicar put it to the group.

"The proposition is as follows: 'The advice of the council is that church funds be allocated by the vicar as required for the upkeep of the fabric of the church building in accordance with his judgement and discretion.' Will all in favour please raise their hands ... unless, of course, you would like it to be a secret ballot, Mr Fletcher?" The old man shook his head. "Very well. Those for the proposition? ... Thank you. Against? ... Thank you. That is all. I declare the meeting closed." He picked up his papers and left the room.

❦   ❦   ❦   ❦

As Molly Appleton turned out the lights in the village hall and locked the door, Marnie and Anne were making up an inflatable bed on the floor of *Sally Ann's* saloon.

"Of course, we'll have to work out a better arrangement than this," said Marnie. "I hadn't expected to have anyone staying here with me when I planned the move."

"I've got an idea," said Anne." The truth was that Anne was thrilled to be spending another night on *Sally Ann*. She had not wanted to mention it because it might seem childish to Marnie. It was something she had not done since her family hired a boat for a holiday when she was about nine years old.

"So what's your idea?"

"I thought I could maybe use the upstairs room in the barn ... turn it into a little bed-sitter. Unless you have other plans for it."

Marnie considered the idea while brushing her teeth. She emerged from the shower-room, drying her face on a towel. "It doesn't have a proper window. Only a vent. But there's a power-point, so you could have a lamp."

"Perhaps I could get some plastic and cover the vent to keep out any rain. I don't think that's a big problem at this time of year. The main snag is furniture, but I could use this mattress, if that's all right."

"Well, I've got rugs, lamps, a small coffee table. It all sounds feasible." She turned out the lights and got into bed. "Good night, Anne. Sleep well."

"Night, Marnie. And you."

"We'd have to be sure it was comfortable enough as a bed-sitter for you ... check there are no bats living up there."

She heard Anne giggle under the duvet. "Marnie, there's nothing that could possibly spoil things here for me."

❦   ❦   ❦   ❦

The landlord at *The Two Roses* was calling last orders. One or two customers ambled over to the bar. In the furthest corner, George Stubbs and Albert Fletcher paid no attention. Each sat with a half pint of beer in front of him, the little they had consumed, untasted.

"I don't see how he *can* go ahead, not now, not after the vote," said George Stubbs. "That puts a different complexion on things. It was a good idea, forcing that vote on him."

"Don't you believe it. I wouldn't put anything past that one. I just wanted proof that he was acting on his own."

"He only got one vote. That's proof enough, all right. That Val Paxton would stick her head in the gas oven if the vicar said to." He took a sip of beer. "The question is, what do we do now?" Albert picked up his glass and stared into it.

"We could go to the Rural Dean ... tell him the school ought to have the church funds, rather than the *fabric of the building*. Huh! *Him* sitting there telling *us* it's God's house and his decision. We've been attending that church since before he was born. We were christened there. And he comes along and thinks he owns the place." He drank most of the beer in his glass in one swallow.

"I'm not sure the Rural Dean would be the best one to approach," said George. "I thought he gave him the job in the first place. He's another of your *born again* variety. We'd be wasting our time."

"What then?"

"The bishop, I suppose."

"Would he listen?"

"Perhaps he would if we sent a petition signed by all the members of the PCC."

"All except Val Paxton," said Albert.

Part 11

"Sarah! Sarah!" The cries of her mother running down the lane brought Sarah Anne to the door, dropping the sewing and overturning the chair in her haste. "Horsemen, Sarah! They're back!" Sarah Anne hurried out, her head spinning. She took hold of her mother by the shoulders.

"Did you see them? Where are they?" She felt her mother slump in her arms, shaking her head. "How many are there?" Her mother gasped for breath.

"I only saw one, I think ... but I saw his uniform ... a soldier ..." Sarah Anne guided her mother into the house and sat her down before making her way quickly and quietly up the lane to the high street. She at once found herself confronted by the soldier, a lone horseman, holding no weapons, his leather coat reaching to the top of his thigh boots, his horse snorting and damp with sweat. She looked up into the man's tired face, half hidden, enclosed in a cage of iron. He pulled off the peaked helmet and shook out his long hair.

"Madam," he said. "I am looking for Mistress Day. I have news. They said I would find her in the smithy at the end of the lane."

"That is my mother, sir. And that is the house. Will you come?"

"I have little time and far to ride."

"Then give me your news, if you can. I hope you bring good news, but I fear you would not have come here just to tell us that all is well."

"Indeed not," he said. "I am to tell you that William is dead." Sarah Anne went pale at mention of her uncle's name, her father's youngest brother. She bowed her head.

"Is there more to tell?"

"And Jonathan is wounded."

Sarah raised her face. "How wounded?"

"They say he will live, but his right arm is shattered. He lies in Huntingdon with the other wounded, left behind by the regiment. I was there two days ago. I am sorry to bring this news."

"Will my father ... Jonathan ... fight again?"

"No, miss. He will not. That is perhaps a blessing."

"A cruel blessing," said Sarah Anne. "A blacksmith without two strong arms is not a blacksmith." More than anything she wanted the man to leave now. "Will you take some refreshment before you ride on?"

"I cannot stay, but thank you." He turned his horse and set off at a trot. Sarah Anne turned back to the house, heavy with the weight of the news.

❦ ❦ ❦ ❦

Friday 16 June

"Mrs Paxton?" The Headteacher, appearing in the doorway of her office, found herself addressing the back of the school secretary, who was standing at the window. There was no response. "Mrs Paxton? Is everything all right?" Thoughts of a scuffle in the playground crossed her mind and she began to advance towards the window. The secretary turned suddenly, a startled look on her face.

"Sorry to alarm you, Mrs Paxton, but I'd like you to do a note to Mrs Walker."

"Mrs Walker? I don't think we have a parent of that name." The Headteacher frowned. In a school of less than seventy pupils, everyone knew everyone else.

"Mrs Walker is the young woman who's moved into Glebe Farm."

"Glebe Farm?" Mrs Paxton repeated.

The Headteacher sighed. "She has bought Glebe Farm from Mr Fletcher senior, whom you know, and I spoke with her briefly in the street yesterday afternoon at home time. You came out and fetched me to the phone while we were talking. Don't you remember?"

Mrs Paxton looked confused. "I'm not sure. I was busy with other things." She shook her head in a gesture that could have been taken for annoyance. "Anyway, how could this Mrs Walker move into Glebe Farm? It's derelict. There's nowhere to live down there."

"Apparently she has a canal boat, and she's living on that while she does things to the house." This was quite beyond the imagination of Valerie Paxton. To her, a house had to be comfortable, with a fitted kitchen, central heating, a roof. How anyone could move into a *ruin* was unthinkable.

"Does she have children coming to the school?"

"No, but she has a *boat*. And before you ask what that has to do with it, I'm thinking of asking her to let a group of the children visit her to find out about boats, canals and so on."

"Didn't you do that last year?"

"We just looked at the wildlife. This would be different. It would be about canals as transport. Mrs Walker seems an intelligent person. Perhaps she could explain that sort of thing to the children."

"You want me to make an appointment?"

"Yes, please. Only I don't suppose she has a phone installed yet and in any case I'd like to give her some idea of what I have in mind, so she's prepared in advance for our meeting. That's why I want to write. Perhaps after assembly you might like to practise your shorthand?" The Head returned to her office and Mrs Paxton sat down to resume sorting the small pile of mail on her desk. She slit open the envelopes with her paper knife.

The Head stepped briskly from her office with a folder under her arm, on her way to assembly. She looked down at Mrs Paxton as she passed. They had known each other for five years, since Mrs Giles was promoted from deputy head at a school in Brackley, and they had developed a good working relationship, without ever becoming friends outside the hours of work.

"Mrs Paxton, you will be sure to keep that knife shut away in your desk when you're not using it, won't you?" The secretary looked at the knife. It was a dagger with a black handle, its end shaped like the head of an eagle, its blade bright and shiny. They had had this exchange on other occasions and the Head wished she had asked Mrs Paxton years ago not to keep it at school, but she had missed her moment and now it seemed too late to raise the matter without causing bad feeling. Even so, Mrs Paxton resented the implied criticism that she could not be trusted to take care of her possessions, or that she might do anything to put the children, or anyone else, at risk. Assuring the Head that she would be careful as she always was, she bent to her task, slit open the last envelope and put the dagger, the *paper knife*, as she regarded it, into the top drawer out of harm's way.

❦   ❦   ❦   ❦

At the far end of the village, at Rooks Farm, Mr Fletcher's daughter-in-law Maureen was pouring tea for their visitor. She had known George Stubbs for ten years, since first she had come to live in Knightly St John as a young bride newly married to Albert Fletcher's older son Leonard, but she still thought of him as Mr Stubbs and probably always would. Leaving the pot on a tray on the side table, she withdrew to her kitchen and left the men to their talk. The ins and outs of the local church were no business of hers and of no interest, either.

"Well, George, what's next?" The old farmer seemed subdued, almost resigned to being beaten.

"I rang Emily's boy, the one who works for the newspaper in Northampton, and told him what happened last night. He thinks there could be quite a bit of interest. Apparently, stories about vicars usually go down well, especially in the summer when there's not much real news about."

"So what do we have to do?"

"I gave him an account of our meeting and told him we were thinking of writing to the Bishop. He thought that was a good idea and said we should go ahead. When we get a reply, he'll do a story, depending on what the Bishop says. Trouble is, he thinks the Bishop will first try to put a damper on everything, calm it all down till after the holidays and hope everyone will have forgotten about it after they've had two weeks on a beach bored out of their minds."

"Who's going to write, then?" said Albert. George produced an envelope from which he extracted a piece of paper. He read the letter out loud while the old farmer listened. It was short, summarising the main points of contention. At the end it described the vote taken at the meeting and asked the Bishop to intervene to stop the vicar going ahead with any more changes.

"When it's written down like that, it all seems trivial," said Albert.

"*Trivial?* Bricks and mortar against the interests of the whole village? And the *attitude* of the man. Anyone would think we were heathens, the way he goes on. Talk about *holier than thou!*"

"I'm not saying we're not in the right. It's just that, well ... a letter ... I prefer action to words."

"I was wondering whether we might get up a petition, too," said George. "We could get most of the village to sign it, I reckon."

"I'd rather go up and have it out face to face. Better than *letters* or *petitions*. Bits of paper!"

"It's worth thinking about," said George. "And we couldn't get to see the Bishop as easily as that. My nephew reckons the Bishop might want to do something. Might act quickly. He's already brought in one or two ideas while he's new to the diocese. His *honeymoon,* they call it."

"Changes of his own, you mean? Looks like they're all at it. Can't leave well enough alone." Albert took another sip of tea.

"What does it matter if it helps us?" said George. They both drank and looked at each other thoughtfully.

"Well, we'll see what happens. But don't expect any miracles."

❦   ❦   ❦   ❦

"You know," said Marnie, "I think you had a point about recording an explanation of what we're doing here to answer everyone's questions. I could've used it today on the phone. My calls took twice as long as they should have."

"It's a pity we didn't think to send out a press release with the change of address announcement."

"That's a thought ... but I didn't have you with me then, did I? Would you know how to do a press release?"

"Sure. I did that sort of thing at school ... Media Studies. I got an 'A' for the coursework."

"I might have known. So, how's your list going?"

"Nine points to deal with at the moment. But nothing urgent."

"Right. It's four o'clock. Time for an executive decision. Do we have a cup of tea now, or go to the village and have it when we get back?"

"Mm ... tricky one," said Anne. "I'm easy."

Marnie read her own list. "Suppose we go now? That'll give us time to look in on Mr Fletcher, just a courtesy visit, post the letters and go to the shop. Okay?"

"Fine."

Their route took them to the other side of the village, about twenty minutes on foot. Rooks Farm was large and businesslike, with a long driveway lined with oak and ash and fields of sheep and cows. There were outbuildings of varying sizes, glimpses of tractors and a combine harvester in barns old and modern, cow-sheds, stores and Dutch barns half filled with hay. The centre of the complex was a fine stone farmhouse, standing in gardens stocked with delphiniums and roses, sunflowers and hollyhocks, each flower bed neatly bordered with bedding plants, the cream stone a perfect backdrop for the blue and pink, the white and red and gold. As they approached the house, they saw a woman gathering in washing from the line. It was the picture of an English farm on a summer's afternoon. There was even a black and white collie lying in the corner of the yard outside its kennel. It watched the newcomers without stirring.

"Good afternoon," said Marnie. The woman turned, noticing them for the first time. She smiled, an open, friendly, countrywoman's smile.

"Hallo." She folded a towel loosely and dropped it into the basket at her feet.

Marnie made the introductions. "I was hoping to see Mr Fletcher, if that's possible. He doesn't know I'm coming. It's just a casual visit."

"I have two of them about the place. Which one did you want: my husband or my father-in-law?"

"Mr *Albert* Fletcher, who sold me Glebe Farm. I've just called to say hallo."

The woman bent down and picked up the basket. "I'll call him for you," she said.

"I hope I'm not disturbing anything," said Marnie.

"That's all right. He's probably in the tool barn. He often goes there when he's got something on his mind."

"I could come back another day if he's busy."

"He'd be sorry to miss you. It may not always seem like it, but he likes a bit of company." She put her basket down by the porch and indicated an old outbuilding. "Let's see if he's there." As they approached the barn, she called out "Dad! Dad!" and Mr Fletcher appeared in the entrance, an unlit pipe in the corner of his mouth. He looked dour and preoccupied but on seeing his visitors he smiled. While Maureen returned to her chores, he shook hands with Marnie and with Anne and asked if they were all right at Glebe Farm. Marnie assured him they were.

"I wouldn't know what to do with the place myself," said Mr Fletcher, "but I daresay you've got your own ideas about that. This is my home."

"It's a very fine place," said Marnie. "Whatever we do, Glebe Farm will never be like this. Still, we'll do our best."

The old farmer looked thoughtful. "You see, I like young people to come in and bring new ways with them. I've had my turn ... now it's yours. I don't mean to criticise everything, just because it's different."

"I wasn't aware that you had, Mr Fletcher."

"Of course not. I want you to ... *succeed,* do the things you want to do. I wouldn't want to interfere."

"Is there something I'm doing that you don't like?"

"Oh no. It's not you." He had a faraway look. "It's all the other changes coming in the village ... changes that nobody needs ... all unnecessary ..."

"Would this be to do with the church, perhaps?" He sighed. Anne, who was standing beside the entrance to the barn, turned her head and looked inside. Marnie, feeling similarly out of touch, followed her friend's gaze and was surprised to see an ancient tractor standing in the middle of the barn. It looked like new and she made a small sound of admiration.

"Is that an old Fordson?" she said.

A raised eyebrow from Mr Fletcher. "Yes, it is. 1948."

"Someone's worked hard to restore it to *that* condition."

"It's beautiful" said Anne. "Look at the seat. It's got holes in like a colander!" The farmer smiled at her. They walked in and stood round the machine in the cool, shady barn. A piece of sacking was spread out on the ground under it, partly covered with tools, rags and boxes of parts. The air smelt of oil and diesel, not unlike the engine on *Sally Ann*, but the tractor was clean down to the grooves on the tyres and had been freshly painted a dark red.

"I'm getting it ready for the County Show in September. This is how I spend my time now, bringing back the past. Only ... you can never bring things back, really."

"That's what I shall do when I've finished Glebe Farm," said Marnie. "If I survive the experience!" She laughed gently.

"Restoring tractors?" said Mr Fletcher.

"Not tractors, no. I've got an old sports car partly dismantled, in my sister's garage. MG TA, 1936 model. I'll have a lot to learn, but I'll get there in the end, I hope." Anne was looking at the other things in the barn. Over by one wall was a wooden plough, also restored, and bits and pieces of equipment and machinery that she could not recognise. Another wall was covered in hooks on which implements had been hung. They shone dimly in the half light.

"People don't usually come in here. No-one ever sees these things."

"That's a great pity," said Marnie. "But I hope we're not intruding into a private place."

"You're very welcome here," said the old man looking directly at Marnie. They crossed over to the wall of hand tools, sickles, scythes, shears and others that were beyond the recognition of the visitors. Each had been restored, sharpened and oiled as if they might be needed at any moment.

"Some of those are nigh on a hundred year old. That hand scythe was my grandfather's." Marnie pointed at one of them. "No, the one below it. You can hold it, if you like." She took it carefully down from its hooks. The blade was long and curved, well worn but very sharp, and tapering to a fine point. The handle was smooth and comfortable to grip. She weighed it in her hand.

"Is it all original? All of it the same age?"

"Of course." He seemed puzzled by the question.

"I was just remembering a story," said Marnie. "I heard of a farmer's wife sweeping the yard with a broom, telling someone what a good broom it was. She had had it for thirty years and in all that time it had only had three new heads and two new handles." The old farmer laughed throatily and shook his head. Marnie passed the scythe to Anne who touched the side of the blade and pulled a face. She held it away from her and was glad to give it back to Marnie, hoping she had not given offence to Mr Fletcher.

"That's right, my girl. You do right to treat it with respect. There've been plenty of accidents with those, some bad luck, some caused by stupidity." He took the scythe gently from Marnie and hung it back in its place. Anne liked the old man and felt pleased to have been admitted to his inner sanctum. She smiled at him and he put his arm on her shoulder as they walked to the entrance and out into the daylight, where the air was warmer and the smells of the farm took over from the tang of the machinery.

On the way down the drive, Marnie looked at her watch. "We stayed longer than I expected. We'd better get a move on." They strode out, breathing in the good air, enjoying the rolling countryside, the sheep and cows, the trees on the horizon and the broad ridges extending across the meadows.

"I thought Mr Fletcher was nice," said Anne. "I wasn't sure at first, but he liked showing us his tractor and all the tools."

"He must be a very good engineer. I'd like to have seen photos of that tractor before he started work on it. I bet it was a pile of junk. There's hope yet for my old MG!"

"That scythe was really scary," said Anne. "I thought if I dropped it I might cut my leg off!"

"Yes. Certainly not something to be handled too casually. Still, it's not dangerous in the right hands." Anne pulled a face, still imagining the injuries the scythe could cause. Marnie laughed at her. "I wasn't sure what he was talking about when we arrived. Hidden depths in Mr Fletcher, I think. Something on his mind."

"To do with the church," said Anne.

"I wouldn't be surprised."

❦ ❦ ❦ ❦

"Hallo again. Settling in all right?"

"Not bad. I'm greatly helped by having Anne around. She keeps me organised." Marnie turned to look at her friend and found her already working her way down the shelves, list in one hand, basket in the other.

"I see what you mean," said Molly Appleton and called out to Anne: "If there's anything you can't find, just ask."

Anne's face peeped round the corner. "I'm looking for the eggs, actually."

"If there aren't any on the end there beside you, we must have run out again." Molly lifted up the counter and went down to join her. "Oh dear. I didn't notice they'd all gone. Did you need them for today?"

"Don't worry. I can make something else," said Marnie.

"Sorry to let you down. I'll ask Richard to pop over to Mr Stubbs and drop them in on you later."

"I can go for them, if you like," said Anne. "I know where to go. Just up the road."

"Well, if you're sure, my dear. I know he's there now, making up an order. Will you tell him we'll collect some more later on?"

"All right. Shall I go now, Marnie?"

"Sure. I'll see you back at the office."

Anne had not been along this part of the high street before and enjoyed the walk, looking at the old cottages. Most were of light cream stone under slate or thatched roofs, some set back from the road behind small gardens crowded with flowers. Others fronted onto the pavement and she glanced sidelong in at the windows, catching sight of comfortable sofas and polished tables. It was a far cry from the dilapidation of Glebe Farm, but Anne saw all this as a taste of things to come.

The Old Farm House stood at the far end of the road, set at right angles. Anne walked up the drive past a herbaceous border that hummed with bees in the afternoon sun. She made her way along a path of slabs like stepping stones leading to a group of outbuildings beyond the house. Passing a window, she caught a glimpse of a large room with french windows, the light pouring in across armchairs and carpet towards an inglenook fireplace. The path turned the corner and brought her to a small stone barn, covered with a climbing rose of delicate pink. It all looked so inviting that Anne wanted to throw herself into the restoration of Glebe Farm with every ounce of her strength to restore it to this condition. For a moment her patience deserted her and she could not bear it that they had only arrived two days ago. It had to be done *now*. It *had* to be just like the Old Farm House.

She came to a door, wide, heavy and studded. Over the lintel hung a tin plaque, weather-beaten and peeling, a skull and cross-bones, like an old pirate flag. She struck the door twice with her clenched hand but it was so hard that the sound she made was almost imperceptible. She waited in the still, warm air that seemed to become heavier, making her drowsy and lethargic, and was on the point of trying again when the door opened soundlessly on well-oiled hinges. Mr Stubbs recognised her and smiled.

"Good afternoon, young lady."

"Good afternoon, sir." It was an automatic reaction, like speaking to a teacher at school. She bit her lip. "I've come from the shop. Mrs Appleton has run out of eggs and we need a dozen, please." Mr Stubbs stood back and held the door open. Slip of the tongue or not, she had evidently pleased him.

"Of course, come in. I won't be a minute. I'm just making up an order for Molly now." He returned to his table and picked up a knife. His apron was immaculately white but streaked with red across the front. The barn was spacious and clean with large refrigerators along the back wall and kitchen units with worktops of stainless steel and white marble. The floor was of quarry tiles, scrubbed and shining. A fastidious man. On the workbench in front of him he had laid out on greaseproof paper a row of joints and steaks and was carving and weighing the last of these. Anne swallowed and tried to look away without revealing her distaste. The smell of the meat was making her feel nauseous.

"Mrs Appleton said they'd come for some more eggs later on."

"Jolly good. I'll be with you straight away. This is the last of the steak. Just look at this. You won't find better produced beef anywhere in the county." Anne forced herself to look as he cut it from the full piece, taking a knife from the block, slicing through the red flesh with ease. "What do you think of that, now?"

"Wonderful," said Anne, swallowing again. "I was noticing the skull and crossbones over the door when I knocked."

"Oh, that. I put that there when I was a boy, still at school." Anne smiled, relieved to have turned the conversation away from the bloody steaks on the bench.

"We used to slaughter in here in those days. That's why I put the sign up. The animals came in through that door. You see those hooks up there on the beam? We hung them there to bleed into the gully and collected the blood in a vat over there."

Anne could feel her face change colour as if her own blood was running out and the room began to sway. In some dim recess of her mind, she knew she had to hold her ground and not show weakness. She wished she could breathe in deeply, but knew that would be the end of her resistance. She wandered as casually as she could over to the wall units, as if she was following his story. When she was sure she was out of his direct line of vision, she closed her eyes and breathed in slowly through her mouth, trying not to smell the meat and the blood, trying to shut out the vision of what had gone on in that place for generations. The movement was enough to steady her.

"Are you enjoying it here?" The question could scarcely have been more unfortunate.

"Yes, thank you. It's very nice. We like it very much." Her voice was steady.

"You her little girl, are you?" Anne could not decide whether the tone was friendly or mocking.

"No, I'm her assistant, her colleague." Anne hoped her tone would be taken as matter-of-fact. She strolled nonchalantly back to the table.

"Right now. That's that." Mr Stubbs put the last steak into its bag and smiled at her as he licked his fingers, the blood making a red ring on his lips. "Shall we see about those eggs? A dozen?" Anne could not speak. He wiped his hands on a damp cloth, walked across to a cupboard, from which he deftly selected the eggs from a tray and put them into a box. Returning, he handed them across the table to Anne.

"Thank you. What do I owe you?" She put them in her bag, glad to be able to look away.

"Nothing. The large free range are one pound twenty a dozen. That's so you know for the future. These are with my compliments. To welcome you both to the village. I hope I'll often see you in here."

"Thank you very much. That's very kind of you. Are you sure it's all right?"

"Of course." He opened the door and wished her good afternoon, watching her until she turned the corner. Anne heard the door close behind her and took a deep, deep breath. Roses had never smelled so sweet.

❦ ❦ ❦ ❦

After leaving the shop, Marnie had set off home at a brisk pace. Walking down the field track, she stretched her vision to the horizon where trees and meadows gave way to a hazy sky. In the nearer fields crops were ripening and it seemed incongruous to her, a Londoner, that she could be here earning her living, risking everything she had in an enterprise that had been conceived the previous summer while suffering a mild sunstroke. Oh my God! Do serious people really do things like that?

She walked across the yard, past the office-barn and through the spinney towards *Sally Ann*. From the edge of the buildings to the canal was about thirty metres and the docking area came into view when Marnie was halfway through the wood. But something had changed. Moored against the bank behind *Sally Ann*, and completely blocking her in, was another boat. Confident that she would discover a neighbour from Little Venice who had recognised *Sally* in passing, Marnie advanced towards the bank. She dropped the bags of shopping on the deck and stepped off to take a good look at the newcomer.

It was a handsome boat, with a low hull and long fore-deck. The paintwork was new, an attractive dark sage green with deep gold linings and the hull a semi-gloss black. The brass mushrooms on the roof were brightly polished and matched the port-holes. The chimney had bands of shining brass against the glossy black funnel and the tiller handle was brass with a grip of dark polished wood. Marnie had a feeling that she had seen this boat before.

Her thoughts went back to Little Venice and the boats she had seen there. And quite suddenly she knew beyond doubt. She moved nearer to inspect it. Yes. This was Old Peter's boat. She had seen it many times passing by, and had once sat on it talking to the old man who had bequeathed to her the original papers and drawings of William Jessop that now hung in the museum.

Old Peter had died during Marnie's summer-long trip, and she had never seen him again, though she had blundered into his funeral cortège in thick mist on her return journey by the cemetery at Kensal Green. Invited to his mooring to receive her bequest, Marnie had found his boat gone and had suspected it had been 'taken over'. She had her suspicions about who that person might have been.

"Hallo! Anyone at home?" She knocked firmly on the door. "Gary! Are you there? Come on! I know you're on board." She noticed the name on the stern. Whatever she had expected to find there, she did not expect the boat to be called *Thyrsis*.

"Sorry to disappoint you, Marnie." The voice came from close behind and she started in surprise. Marnie looked up into the face of Ralph Lombard, who kissed her gently on both cheeks. "Aren't you going to tell me this is an unexpected pleasure?"

"I will when I get my breath back! This is certainly unexpected. I thought you might be someone I knew from Little Venice."

"Gary, yes, so I gather. Why did you think that?"

"Well ... this boat ... it belonged to someone I knew ... and I thought Gary ..."

"Restored it?" suggested Ralph. "A marvellous job, don't you think?"

"Wonderful. You'd scarcely recognise it." Marnie suspected that was part of the plan and she wondered how much Ralph had paid Gary. She did not like to think that Gary had stolen the boat then sold it, taking advantage of Ralph.

"Would you like to see what I've done to her? Have you time to come on board?" Ralph led the way down the steep steps into the cabin and offered Marnie a hand as she followed him. He pointed to a door behind them. "That's where I sleep, typical boatman's cabin. I've left it much as it was, apart from redecorating. It's even got a cast iron range."

"You had it decorated?"

"I did it myself. This is the dining area, linking up with the galley." Marnie liked the style, light coloured wood finishes, a sage green carpet and tiles like terracotta in the galley. The shower room made her envious, sparkling new with white tiles, shining chrome fittings and folding glass screens. No wet, flapping curtains here. The built-in units were of beech and mahogany with glass shelves. By now, Dolly had joined them and was rubbing her flank against Ralph's trouser legs.

The sitting area had a built-in sofa in old rose and fitted cupboards. It was bright, with a porthole on each side and a roof light with brass fittings. "I mainly use this for keeping my clothes." He pointed at the cupboards as Dolly jumped up onto the sofa.

"A narrowboat with a dressing room," said Marnie. "Whatever next?"

"Mock not," said Ralph, grinning and pushing open the door into the next area. "I had to plan the boat to meet my needs. This is the business end." He stood aside to let her into the front cabin.

"Blimey!" she said. The front cabin was as long as two of the other spaces, perhaps a little more than sixteen feet. Half of one wall was equipped with built-in bookcases from floor to ceiling. Apart from the door leading out to the cratch, the furthest wall was taken up by an L-shaped desk with a computer and a library lamp with green glass shade, faced by a leather chair. Further back towards the bookcases was a printer and a hi-fi system, with racking above it for tapes and discs. In one corner on a tiled surround stood a wood-burning stove with framed prints of Oxford either side of the flue. Light poured in from roof lights and portholes. It was an inviting workspace. In the evenings, with the stove lit and the brass wall-lamps switched on, it would be magical.

"It's extraordinary, Ralph. Marvellous. You've created a floating Oxford college!"

"Exactly," he replied, looking out on the canal side. "In fact, wherever you moor, you can see Magdalen Bridge from the porthole ... on a clear day."

They strolled over to *Sally Ann* for coffee. "Well, I must say, for all his faults, Gary's done a fine job."

"Not Gary, actually," said Ralph.

"Who did the restoration, then? One of the boatyards in Oxford?"

"Actually, I did it," he said.

"You? I thought you implied that Gary had been involved. At least, that's what I understood."

"No. In fact, Gary's involvement with *Thyrsis* has been rather less than he would have wished ... in all sorts of ways."

"So you bought the boat from him and did the work yourself?"

"Nearly everything. I had the engine serviced in Oxford and some work done on the wiring. Also the new roof lights. I did the decoration." There was something about the colour scheme that Marnie found familiar. "I'd never have thought of doing this at all, if it hadn't been for you, Marnie. My contact with the canal in Oxford when you fished me out was meant to be my last."

"I know where you got that colour scheme ... it's just like a Harrods carrier bag!" Ralph raised his hands in mock horror, aghast. "You poser!" she said.

"*Moi?*" he replied. "*Poseur?* Actually, it's meant to be the colour of a Barbour jacket but I mixed the wrong colours at the paint shop." Marnie restrained herself from striking him firmly in the ribs.

"Tell me about it over coffee."

While the kettle heated up, Ralph installed himself in a chair and explained how he had had to learn decorating as a young academic doing research and newly married. He became interested in DIY, as his wife, a postgraduate student herself, had no inclination towards practical things, much preferring medieval lyric poetry.

"So you just got on with it," said Marnie. "What about Gary, then? What happened to him?"

"Ah, yes, Gary. Well, he told me about this boat he knew that was going to be restored. It wouldn't be cheap, but it would be good. I agreed to have a look and my suspicions were aroused when I had to go to a place in Birmingham that was *very much* off the beaten track ... or whatever that may be in canal terms. I asked who owned the boat and Gary said it belonged to a mate who did not want to be on the water any more and needed the money. I said I'd think about it."

"What colour was it then? Was it faded green and grey?"

"Yes, it was. The outside was sound. The interior was clean. The engine was fine."

"So you bought it and took it down to Oxford."

"Not immediately. Something strange happened. I asked about the registration certificate and Gary said it had got lost and they'd have to register the boat as new. It would be 'less hassle' that way. I realised that something odd was going on and said I'd think it over. Gary did not know that I'd seen a registration plate lying in the corner of the main cabin. The next day I rang British Waterways and asked them if they could tell me who owned the boat with this number. They said the registration had not been renewed last year and they'd written without success to the owner. They couldn't give his name over the phone."

"I could guess what the name was," said Marnie.

"No doubt," said Ralph. "Anyway, I rang Gary, told him about my conversation with BW and said I didn't really think I could go ahead in the circumstances."

"That would've pleased him."

"He was *horrified*. Wanted to know if I told them where I saw the boat, who had it or any other details."

At that moment *Sally Ann* rocked gently at her mooring and a shadow appeared in the stern doorway. "Hey, Marnie, whose is that boat blocking us in?" Anne came down into the cabin and caught sight of Ralph. He stood up and held out his hand.

"Good afternoon. I'm Ralph Lombard."

"Hallo. I'm Anne. Anne Price. I'm Marnie's assistant."

"Have a seat. I'll pour you some coffee," said Marnie.

"I don't want to interrupt your conversation."

"That's okay. Ralph was telling me how he acquired his boat, the one blocking us in."

"*Lovely* boat," said Anne, sitting down, putting a letter on the table. "It's funny, I've often thought that Harrods colours would look nice in a canal setting."

Ralph laughed. "I see it's no use claiming originality for my design. I can't fool you two." He turned to face Anne directly. "I take it that you are also a designer?"

"Anne is much more than that," said Marnie, bending down to open the fridge. "She's helping to set up the office and work with me before starting her formal training. Oh dear. You know what I forgot at the shop? There's no milk. What a nuisance. It'll have to be the emergency powdered stuff, I'm afraid."

"No," said Ralph. "I've got plenty on *Thyrsis*. Your cat is certain to want some. I'll go and fetch it." After some protests it was agreed that Anne would go.

"Now," said Marnie, "where were we with the story? You told Gary you weren't prepared to buy stolen property, and he was worried that BW might be able to trace the boat to him."

"Correct. I also hinted that as you were Old Peter's heir, in a sense, perhaps the boat rightfully belonged to you. Just as I was about to put the phone down, Gary said that sometimes boats are abandoned and taken over by other people. 'Like a salvaged wreck at sea?' I suggested. Gary agreed. I wished him luck with trying to dispose of it that way, and he said would I not like to buy it on that basis."

"What difference would that make?" said Marnie.

"At salvage value? I asked. Gary wasn't keen, but knew it was all he'd get, at least from me. He also probably thought I might tell you about it and then he might risk losing the whole thing. In the end I gave him five hundred in recognition of his salvaging the boat."

Anne's footfall could be heard on the aft deck and she re-appeared with the milk. "What did you think of the boat?"

"Beautiful," said Anne. "I love the way she's been fitted out." A sudden wary look came over her face.

"I'm glad," said Ralph. "I meant to suggest that you might look her over." Anne looked sheepishly at Marnie, who poured her coffee and put some milk in a saucer for Dolly.

"I was going to ask you about the name," Marnie said to Ralph.

"Matthew Arnold," said Anne. They both stared at her. "The poet. Oxford. *The Scholar Gipsy* and all that. We did him in English Literature. I got an 'A' for the coursework." At that, Marnie laughed, went over to Anne and hugged her.

"Can anyone join in?" said Ralph. Taking her place again at the table, Marnie quickly gave Anne a résumé of Ralph's story of how he acquired *Thyrsis*. Anne sat glancing at Ralph like a fellow conspirator. Eventually, until Ralph stood up, saying he had interrupted their day and was sure they had many things to do. Anne looked disappointed.

"Are you doing anything this evening?" said Ralph.

"The choice of nightlife is a little restricted in Knightly St John on Fridays," said Marnie. "There are only two casinos, and the night-clubs are usually fully booked."

"How about supper at the pub?"

"Sounds good to me."

"Would it be convenient for both of you?" he asked.

Anne looked uncertain. "Oh, you don't have to include me. I've got lots to do."

"I'm sure you have. But I wouldn't have asked if I didn't mean it and if you can come, I'd really like that." They agreed to meet at seven-thirty on *Sally Ann*.

"What a nice man," said Anne. "I've never met anyone like that before. What does he do?"

"He's Reader in Economics at one of the Oxford colleges ... very well known in his field. Quite a celebrity, really."

"And that's why his boat's called *Thyrsis*," said Anne. "What should I call him? 'Mr Lombard'?"

"He's *Dr* Lombard, actually." Marnie thought about it. "I'd avoid calling him anything at first. See how it goes."

"His boat looks like a library at the front. It doesn't look like a holiday boat at all."

"It's not a holiday. He's on sabbatical leave, writing a book."

"Travelling alone?" said Anne.

"Yes. Like me last year."

"What about his wife?"

"He's been a widower for some years. Why do you ask?"

Anne hesitated. "I just wondered." She turned to clear the coffee things from the table, putting them carefully on a tray. In her mind was the photograph she had seen on the small black range in the sleeping cabin. She had certainly been a beautiful woman.

❦ ❦ ❦ ❦

At the end of the school day, most of the children were off the premises by about four o'clock. It was then that Valerie Paxton liked to have the place to herself to finish her work in peace and quiet. The Head had left promptly for once, the cleaners had not yet arrived and even the caretaker was not in evidence.

Now it was as quiet as the church on the days when she did the cleaning and changed the flowers. The church was filled with the deepest peace, centuries old. Why could the village not just let the vicar do what he wanted? What did it matter if he wanted to use a different prayer book, or take out the old pews or use different words in the service? It was not as if the congregation was really listening to what he said. They were just thinking about the Sunday lunch or going out in the afternoon. Why could they not just leave him to get on with his job? Suddenly she was filled with an anger that made her want to shout out loud that everyone should just get on with their own lives and not cause trouble for others.

In her mind she saw the vicar, kneeling at the altar in prayer at evensong. She heard his voice clearly intoning "... and grant us a quiet night, O Lord ..." It was one of her favourite lines.

"You still here, Mrs P? I thought the place was deserted. Quiet as the grave." The caretaker stood looking at her from the doorway. She busied herself to conceal her surprise, gathering papers from her desk and putting them in the drawer, pushing her paper knife to one side. She picked up a small bundle of letters and a shopping list.

"That's everything for now," she said. "I'm off. Bye."

"Have a nice weekend, then."

"Thanks. And you." She swung a bag over her shoulder and left. Walking across the small playground, she caught sight of the vicar passing the school and quickened her pace to intercept him by the gate.

"Good afternoon, Randall."

"Hallo, Val. Finished for the day?"

"I'm sorry about the meeting last night."

"Oh, these things happen. Just one more cross to bear." He sounded casual enough about the situation, but Val sensed his disappointment.

"What do you think will happen now?"

"Well ... that depends on other people, doesn't it? It depends what they do about the vote that was taken. I appreciated your voting for me, Val, but I have to face the fact that things aren't looking good at the moment."

"But what can anybody do?"

"They *could* do all sorts of things ... complain to the Archdeacon or the Rural Dean, approach the Bishop, even."

"Will it make any difference? Any *real* difference, I mean."

"You never can tell. Things may not go my way. Perhaps my days here are numbered. We shall have to wait and see."

"... *my days here are numbered* ..." The vicar's words echoed in her mind as Valerie continued her way down the road to the shop. In her preoccupied state she almost posted the letters before remembering that she had first to buy stamps. There was only one other person at the counter.

"Richard's just out the back, Val. He'll only be a minute."

"Fine." She put her letters and bag down on the counter. "I only need some stamps. No great hurry."

"Have you met Anne? She's living down at Glebe Farm. Just moved in. This is Mrs Paxton from the school."

Valerie said 'hallo' with as much enthusiasm as she could muster and gave Anne something approaching a smile. "Glebe Farm? Down by the canal?"

"That's right. I'm working with Marnie Walker. We're an interior design company." Anne expected to have to give the usual explanation but Mrs Paxton picked up her bundle of letters, sorted through them and handed her one.

"Could you give this to Mrs Walker, please? It seems a pity to use a stamp when you're going that way."

"I'll make sure she gets it right away." As Anne left, Molly called out her thanks for passing on the message to Mr Stubbs about the eggs and for coming in to report back.

"Did you say eggs?" said Valerie after Anne had left.

"We've run out and Anne went up to tell Mr Stubbs. She's a very nice girl. Were you wanting some eggs, then?"

"Among other things."

"Probably won't have any in the shop until tomorrow, unless you can wait for Richard to fetch them."

"No, it's all right. I can wait till tomorrow. I'll have to. It's just one more cross to bear ..."

❦ ❦ ❦ ❦

After Ralph returned to *Thyrsis*, Marnie and Anne went back to the office to finish work. Marnie read the Headteacher's letter.

"Just as I thought," she said and passed the letter to Anne.

"'... *and so I was wondering whether it would be possible for a group of older children to see your boat and learn about life on the canals* ...' Yes. You were right. I bet they'd like that. Will you do it?"

"I don't see why not. We could give them a tour of *Sally Ann* and maybe go for a trip. What else would they like?"

"Why don't I type a programme?" said Anne, pressing buttons on the computer.

"Good idea. We can start with a visit to look over the boat."

"Hang on a minute," said Anne, setting up the document. "Right. That's Item One."

"Then a short talk about the canals and how they were built."

"And why they were built," added Anne. "Item Two. We can do that in the barn."

"Yes. More room than on *Sally*. I wonder how many there'll be."

"Twenty?" Anne suggested.

"I could give them tea in the barn, or beside the boat ... a picnic if it's dry."

"Item Three."

"Then a trip up the canal and through a lock."

"Item Four. They'll *love* that. What about life jackets?"

"Oh, yes. Pity to spoil the day with a mass drowning. We'll have to see about that. Then they could do some drawing at the lock or back here."

"Great!"

"*I know*," said Marnie. "I can show them a few of my slides of Jessop's drawings. The great aqueduct – I've got a video of that somewhere. A tunnel. Bridges. Just a few. Nothing too technical. Old shots of horses pulling barges." The phone rang and Marnie turned to take the call while Anne printed the programme. It was Beth.

"Congratulations. The end of your first week. Well, almost. How's it going?"

"We're up and running, largely thanks to Anne. She's turned out to be a computer wizard." Hearing this, Anne looked up from the machine and pulled a face. Marnie told Beth about the work they had done and the people they had met.

"Not too lonely, then?"

"No. Far from it. We've even had a visitor."

"Let me guess," said Beth. "The vicar. Has your name been added to the flower rota?"

"No. Not the vicar. Ralph Lombard. He's come here by boat."

"Are you *serious*?"

"He's on sabbatical. You should *see* his boat. And you'll never guess whose boat it is ... or rather *was*." The line went silent for a count of three.

"Old Peter's?" There were occasions when Marnie was convinced that Beth could read her mind.

"How did you know?"

"How many boats do I know that have gone missing suddenly, with Gary somehow involved?"

"You're doing it again."

"What am I doing?"

"Answering all my questions with a question."

"Am I? How long have I been doing that?" Marnie uttered a low growl. Beth continued: "Anyway, tell me about Ralph."

"He just called by to see us and show us the boat. He's renovated her himself. Or perhaps I should say 'him'; it's called *Thyrsis* ... for obvious reasons."

"Of course. He'll be inviting you out to dinner next."

"We're going to the pub this evening."

"He must be keen."

"We're all three going."

"Well, have a nice time, all three of you. I'd better get on. Just wanted to see how things were going."

"Thanks for phoning, Beth. I'll ring you in the week. Bye!"

"Oh, Marnie ... you'll have to tell me all about the vicar and the flower rota some other time."

"The vicar? Well, that's another story."

"And you'll have to explain what *Thyrsis* means too. Bye!"

❦ ❦ ❦ ❦

At about the time when Marnie and Anne were getting changed to go out, Valerie Paxton was standing at the sink in the kitchen, gazing vacantly out into the garden. Her husband was pottering about in the vegetable patch. He was regarded as a good man by the whole community. But ... but ... he was predictable in everything he said and did. Everything. He had no bad habits, but no capacity to surprise her. He never quarrelled with anyone, but he never expressed an original opinion, either. In fact, she could scarcely recall him expressing an opinion at all. He was thoughtful, to a degree. He would bring her a magazine when he went for the Sunday papers and he only smoked his pipe outside in the garden, because he knew how much she hated the smell. There was no time she could remember when he had ever trodden mud in from the garden and he always left his slippers by the back porch.

She wiped the draining board with a J-cloth. It was the third time she had done it in the last five minutes. Try as she might, she could no longer avoid the truth that the arrival of Randall Hughes in their world had changed her attitude to her life, to her husband and to herself. It was almost laughable. Almost but not quite. She was no longer young, but not yet middle-aged. She had kept herself trim and prided herself that she still wore the same size clothes as when she was eighteen.

She was twenty-three when she got married fifteen years ago and had fasted for weeks to look good in her wedding dress. It had hung in the wardrobe ever since. Last week she had taken it out of its cover and slipped it on. It still fitted and she compared herself with the wedding photograph on her dressing table. The only disappointment came when she looked at the tall, slim young man standing beside her in the frame. He looked too boyish to be taking on the responsibilities of husband and perhaps one day, father.

There was no question of Jack fitting into *his* wedding suit now. The slim figure had given way to the comfortable stockiness of a man contented with his life, his wife, his home. Already looking older than his years, he would remain like this until the day he retired. Val knew that when he reached forty next year, he would start counting the years he had to go to retirement. He would be counting his life away, and hers with it.

The porch door opened and Val heard Jack come in from the garden and struggle out of his wellingtons. He came into the kitchen and set a bunch of carrots down on the draining board. Irritably, Val put them in the sink and wiped the surface with her cloth.

"You're a bit quiet tonight, love. Anything the matter?"

"Why should anything be the matter?"

"No reason. Only you usually chat about what's been happening at school."

"I don't feel like it, that's all. I've got a headache."

"Oh, I'm sorry, love. Let me get you an aspirin."

"No. It's all right. Don't fuss." *For God's sake don't be so understanding*, she thought. *That only makes it worse.*

❦   ❦   ❦   ❦

"What do you fancy?" Marnie looked at Anne over the top of the menu. "They've got vegetarian dishes."

"Ah," said Ralph. "How strict are you?"

"Not very. I just don't eat meat."

"Fish?"

"Yes. Actually, the Mediterranean fish bake sounds interesting," said Anne. "Vegetable lasagne might be a bit heavy."

"I've often noticed when dining in hall," said Ralph, "that chefs seem to think vegetarians have *enormous* appetites. Or perhaps they aren't used to cooking for them and get the quantities wrong."

"Perhaps we do have vast appetites," said Anne. "After all, the biggest animals on earth are veggies."

"True enough," said Ralph, making no comment on her sylph-like figure. All three opted for fish bakes and Ralph asked Marnie to choose the wine. She suggested a white Bordeaux, Entre-deux-mers, and Ralph went to order at the bar.

"Marnie, Ralph – I mean Mr Lombard, *Dr* Lombard – didn't have to invite me as well. I don't want to get in the way."

"You're not. He wanted us both to come. If he didn't, he would've invited me some other way."

"But I add to the expense."

"I don't think an extra fish bake is going to worry him unduly. There are times when you just accept hospitality and enjoy it. We can invite him another time."

"Okay. I'm not used to eating out very much … it's part of my education."

"Good. I'm sure you'll get an 'A' for the coursework." Anne was stifling a guffaw as Ralph returned.

"You two look radiant this evening. Knightly St John obviously agrees with you."

"I think it does," said Marnie. "Time will tell, but so far we're enjoying it, after two whole days."

"It's a picture-book English village," said Ralph. "Stone, thatch, cottage gardens. The church is very fine. Is it Norman?"

"It was part of a priory based in Normandy near Le Havre."

"My wife used to take me round looking at churches, or anything medieval. I was quite knowledgeable about them at one time."

"The font here is nearly a thousand years old," said Marnie. "And there's some good stained glass by Burne-Jones. You'll have to visit it."

"Yes. I like the mixture of Early English with Decorated Gothic. I'm surprised it didn't suffer more in the Civil War."

Anne leaned forward in her seat and spoke in a quiet voice. "The vicar was murdered here at that time."

"*Murdered?* You mean a casualty of the war?"

"He was killed in the church … 1645."

"By which side?" said Ralph.

"I'm not really sure." She looked at Marnie for help.

"We haven't found an account of what actually happened," said Marnie. "No-one knows for certain who did it."

"An unsolved murder," said Ralph. The waitress appeared and showed him the label on the wine bottle. He nodded and she began removing the cork. Ralph continued, "Well, I don't suppose we'll ever find out who did it now, unless you decide to play the detective, Marnie."

"Would you like to taste the wine, sir?" Ralph indicated Marnie's glass. She sipped and smiled at the waitress, who poured the wine for each of them, including Anne. Ralph leaned towards her. "I hope that's all right for you, Anne. I didn't think to ask if you'd prefer something different."

"It's fine. Perhaps if I had some mineral water I could gradually turn it into a spritzer."

"Good idea." Ralph ordered a large bottle.

"Talking of detectives," said Marnie, "Anne's the one with those talents." The conversation moved on to the ruins of Glebe Farm and Anne's deductions about cigarette stubs and trainers. From there it progressed to Marnie's plans.

"How long will it take to do all this?" said Ralph.

"I'm aiming to complete the work in phases, so that each stage provides the finance for the next. I have to move carefully because I'm undercapitalised. The income from the Willards contract should keep me going for about a year, enough time to get the first units rebuilt and let."

"Am I right in thinking you've put everything you've got into this venture?" said Ralph.

"I think you're about to tell me how *courageous* this action is. Am I right?"

"No. I don't think you're completely mad. If you are, we could use a lot more mad people in the country."

"Anne thinks it can be done, don't you?" said Marnie, squeezing her hand across the table.

"Yes. But I've got no real experience of work. I just believe in Marnie. She makes things happen. She's a very special person." It all came out in a rush.

"You know, Anne, I think you're *absolutely* right," said Ralph picking up his glass. "I would like to drink to your success, your *joint* success."

As Marnie raised her glass, she noticed that Anne's face was slightly pinker than usual. "What about *your* plans, Ralph?"

"Quite simple. I shall be writing a book and travelling around on *Thyrsis*."

"Don't you need libraries for your kind of books? Or is *Thyrsis* linked into the information superhighway by satellite dish?"

"Yes and no. I've brought enough material to keep me going for some while and I can pop back to Oxford from time to time, when I need to."

"There's a lot to be said for dropping out and going on the canals," said Anne.

"I agree. At least, I do at the moment. Like you, I'm new to this way of life."

"How long will you be staying?" Anne's question had also occurred to Marnie.

"Well ... this is just a short visit. I have to get *Thyrsis* to a boatyard for a new battery, possibly two. In fact, I ought to set off tomorrow." Anne looked disappointed.

"I can lend you a generator for a few days, if that would help," said Marnie. "There's nothing worse than running out of power."

"That would be very helpful. I had thought of going down to a marina to sort out the battery problem and going on from there down to London, along the Thames and up to Oxford."

"Sounds good," said Marnie.

"On the other hand, if I did borrow your generator, I could drop it back to you shortly and set off after that. One thing I've learnt is that time is different on the canals."

The meal arrived and was surprisingly good. At the end Ralph invited them back to *Thyrsis* for coffee. Outside, the air was pleasantly warm, and they stood briefly opposite the church, looking up at its dark outline against the sky.

"Strange to think this is the scene of an unsolved murder," said Ralph. The subdued glow reflecting across the road from the pub made the church look homely like a picture on a Beautiful Britain calendar. The lower part of the tower stood in darkness, partly obscured by the yew trees in the churchyard. Although there was no breeze, one of the trees seemed to sway. Marnie narrowed her eyes to focus in the dark and saw movement in the shadows. One part of the blackness had detached itself from the rest. It was gone in an instant, leaving Marnie unsure whether her vision had been deceiving her. "Still, it looks peaceful enough now," Ralph added.

Marnie glanced in his direction, aware of Anne standing beside her, and said nothing. On an impulse, she linked arms with them both and led them off towards the field track that would take them back to *Thyrsis* and *Sally Ann*.

Part 12

Word had passed round the village that the people should assemble outside the church. Most came, standing in family groups while a captain of the New Model Army addressed them on horseback. He was flanked by two other officers, and the rest of his unit, fifty or more men, sat under the trees further down the road with their horses tethered in the shade. The vicar was not present.

"And so I tell you to be vigilant," said the captain. "There are Royalist squadrons in this area, as you know all too well. They have spies everywhere and they will stop at nothing to harass all who stand in their way." The people stood in silence, wishing that the Roundheads would be away and leave them in peace. The sharp odour of burnt timbers still soured the air, an ever-present reminder of the dangers of a civil war where one neighbour could be your enemy, while another was your friend.

"One of my officers will buy provisions from you." The soldier on his left raised a hand. The captain continued. "We will pay for everything we need. The army of the Eastern Association does not rob the people ..." As he spoke, Sarah Anne let her gaze wander down the road to where the soldiers and their horses were resting. Even though members of her own family wore the uniform of Parliament, she and all the villagers regarded any soldiers as a danger. She shuddered at the thought of what would happen if the Royalist army attacked the Roundheads here in this place now. Perhaps there were spies among the people standing beside her. She thought of burning thatch, smoke and flames rising into the sky, the sparks floating across the village ... a torch lit at the top of the church tower, one flame burning and then concealed at dead of night. What could it mean? That night she dreamt of fires, smoke, witches burning at the stake, the stench of war, the flames of Hell.

❦   ❦   ❦   ❦

Saturday 17 June
"Did you hear that, Marnie?" Anne's hoarse whisper rose from her makeshift bed in the saloon of *Sally Ann*.

"Footsteps. Someone passing," said Marnie from the sleeping cabin, wide awake. She rolled out of bed and opened the curtain just a slit with her finger. Anne scrambled up from the floor and peeped through the curtain in the saloon. "Ralph," said Marnie and glanced at the clock. "Quarter to seven."

"I hope I didn't wake you," said Anne.

"No. I was lying there thinking." Marnie filled the kettle and lit the gas, while Anne cleared up her bedding. "You know what day it is?"

"Saturday," said Anne.

"Saturday. Yes. I realise that, being self-employed, I have complete freedom to work seven days a week."

"Fine by me," said Anne. "I've got loads to do. You should see my list."

"No doubt, but I don't think it's right. I can't expect you to keep going without time off."

"I don't mind. It's all fun as far as I'm concerned."

Marnie put croissants into the oven and made a pot of coffee. She pulled open the curtains in the saloon. Outside, the canal was still and smooth. Sunlight was poking among the trees in the spinney. "Breakfast on deck?"

Anne beamed at her. They quickly changed into sweatshirts and jeans. Marnie laid a tray with three sets of crockery. Anne noticed this and put three chairs round the table on the aft deck.

Coffee was steaming in two of the cups when Marnie went below to fetch the croissants. At that moment, Ralph came back from his walk, striding towards the boats.

"Morning, Anne!"

"Hallo, Ralph. Sorry, I mean Mr ... er no, Dr ..."

"Ralph will do fine." He stopped by the stern rail, breathing deeply.

"I think Marnie's going to invite you for breakfast. She's just gone in to get the croissants."

"Wonderful! I'll be back in two minutes. There's something I want to show you."

When he returned, a basket covered with a blue and cream napkin stood in the middle of the table. "Couldn't you sleep?" said Marnie, pouring his coffee. "Or do you always go out so early in the morning?"

"I usually have a walk at this time. Clears the head. And Oxford is delightful before everyone's up. What about you?"

"We have no trouble sleeping." She passed Ralph the croissants. "Our problem is finding enough hours in the day. There's such a lot to do. We'll be working today, I expect."

"It'll do you no harm, at least for a short time. I remember when I began my research. For the first few months I worked almost non-stop."

"Then what happened?" said Anne.

"Someone reminded me it was Christmas. This is delicious. I usually just have a coffee. And for years I had a cigarette to go with it." Anne raised an eyebrow.

"Me too," said Marnie. "Now I've given up for good." Anne gave her a mock frown.

"Changing the subject," said Ralph, "I did a little research last night after we got back." He tapped a book that he had put on the table. "Have you read this? It's a history of the county." Marnie shook her head and Anne squinted to read the title upside down. "This place was a hotbed of violence, intrigue and betrayal during the Civil War. You wouldn't think so now, would you?"

"Oh, I don't know," said Marnie. "Passions seem to run high round here, especially where the church and the vicar are concerned."

"Interesting ... you see, that was the cause of all the problems in those days, too."

"Apart from the fact that there was a war going on, presumably," said Marnie. "Quite."

"I don't really understand about the Civil War," said Anne. "What if you're on one side and your neighbours want the other side to win?"

"*That* is the problem," said Ralph. "And it happened all the time. In some parts of the country the great majority were for the King or for Parliament. Those who took a different view either left or kept quiet and tried to go about their business."

"What happened here?" said Marnie.

"There were some pockets in favour of King Charles, particularly in rural areas. Northampton was mainly for Parliament and some places wanted nothing to do with either side, if they could help it."

"*A plague on both your houses!*" said Anne. "We did it in history."

"That's right. But the problem here was that some villages were High Church, where the vicar supported the Royalists and others were mainly non-conformist, the puritans who sided with Cromwell."

"They wouldn't all automatically be on the same side just because they lived in the same village," said Marnie.

"Not at all," said Ralph. "The book doesn't go into detail about this village, but it mentions the conflict between the puritans, who went to chapel, and the churchgoers. They rarely fought each other, but there were always accusations about people spying on troop movements, or sheltering messengers, hiding priests. It must have bred suspicion and distrust."

"Horrible to live like that," said Anne. "You'd never know what would happen next. I'd hate it."

"Well, if you want to know more about those times, I can lend you the book. Or you may prefer not to think about it, of course."

"We can educate ourselves when we rest our weary bones at the end of the day," said Marnie and passed Ralph the last croissant. "What are your plans for today?"

"Is the offer of the generator still open?"

"Certainly."

"Then I'll set off for the marina and be back in a few days. If you need it, you can ring me on the mobile and I'll bring it back by taxi."

After breakfast they installed the generator on *Thyrsis* and Marnie showed Ralph how to use it. Within half an hour he set off. Marnie stood for a few moments beside the canal as the sound of the diesel faded. Through the spinney it was almost impossible to see the buildings of Glebe Farm at this time of year with the trees in full leaf. Marnie loved the place despite the local squabbles. What did it matter if the people did not like changes? No-one could be harmed by moving some old pews and she did not believe that hatred and evil could hang in the air all these centuries.

Yet there was something about the church that niggled at the back of her mind. Yesterday she had come close to identifying what it was, but it had eluded her like a half-remembered song and she had decided not to pursue it in case it worried Anne. Marnie set off to join her in the office barn, putting out of her mind all thoughts of St John's church and its square stone tower.

"Marnie, I'm happy to sort out the office and I'll get it all running the way you want it, but could I ask you something?"

"You want to be more involved on design matters."

"Just so I learn about that side of the work, too."

"Sure. Let me get this scheme worked out and then we can go through it together. That way, you'll see how I do it and talking it over with you will help clarify my thinking." Anne's face lit up. "But," Marnie continued, "We aren't going to work the whole day. If it stays fine like this, I think we should have a trip on *Sally Ann* this afternoon. Agreed?"

"Great!"

They made good progress. From time to time, Anne glanced over at Marnie and watched her sketching, noting, selecting materials and colours from her collection of samples and catalogues. Anne longed to work like that, totally absorbed. It seemed a marvellous way of life, and she felt lucky to be there, lucky to have met Marnie by the merest of chances that day last summer. At ten-thirty they began going through the scheme while Anne took notes. She could hardly believe it when Marnie looked at her watch.

"Twelve-fifteen. Not bad. I think that should do it for today. How about you?"

"*Twelve-fifteen?* Oh blow! I forgot to make coffee again. I meant to show you what I've done on the computer. I ought to show you how it all works when you've got time."

"Perhaps we can do that tomorrow. Oh sorry, I was forgetting. Tomorrow's Sunday. Perhaps you'd like me to take you home for the day?" Anne looked surprised. "You do remember home, don't you? The place where you live? Your family ... remember them?"

"Yes, of course, but we've only just arrived. I thought we had a lot to do. We were going to work this weekend, weren't we?" Just then the conversation was interrupted by the arrival, bounding across the yard, of two black labradors, who sniffed their way to the entrance and stood in the open doorway, panting and wagging their tails. Marnie stood up and walked over to them, while they barked on the threshold. She squatted down and stroked their heads.

"I'm sorry if they're being a nuisance." Frank Day appeared, walking hurriedly. "I was going to skirt round the farm now that you're here, but Bruno shot off along the familiar route and Cassius followed him."

"That's all right." Marnie stood up and shook hands. "In fact, I was going to phone you. I need to get some of my things from the store."

"No problem. If you'd like to give me a list I can sort them out. Anything large?"

"I need the spare bed, a low table, a lamp, bedding, a few rugs ... I'd better come over and choose."

"You've completed the rebuilding works already?" he said with a smile.

"Partly. Anne is going to have her own room, so we need to furnish it." Marnie half turned her head into the office and Anne waved from her desk.

"And how do you propose fetching the things over?" said Frank. Marnie hesitated, trying to remember where she had put the roof rack.

"Can it wait till tomorrow? If so, I can collect what you want in our van."

"Tomorrow's Sunday," said Marnie.

"That's okay. I often have to deal with business matters over the weekend. And we're practically neighbours. It's really no trouble." Marnie thanked him and offered coffee, but he declined. The dogs sprawled out in the sun while Frank admired the office, impressed with their fast work.

"Do you think you're going to like living here? Not too sleepy for you after the bright lights of London?"

"It's certainly not dull. In fact in many ways it's rather interesting, so many strange things in the air."

"What do you mean?" There was a slight edge to his voice.

"Oh, nothing much. I was just thinking of the first time we came here and asked an old man for directions into the village. He spoke about Cromwell as if he'd been around in living memory."

"There are quite a few stories of the Civil War time in these parts. My wife and I were once out walking in the Chase. It's an old hunting forest not far from Northampton. It came on to rain and we were miles from anywhere, so we took shelter under the eaves of a cottage, thinking it was deserted. To our surprise the door opened and we were invited in. An old couple lived there, a retired gamekeeper and his wife. They explained they were about to leave, couldn't bear to live there any longer."

"Obviously not noisy neighbours," said Marnie.

"They'd become increasingly depressed by things they saw and heard, by what they called 'the visitor'." Marnie shivered and felt her cheeks tingle. She was especially concerned about Anne, with her vivid imagination and wished somehow the conversation could stop. It did. Frank turned without warning to the dogs. "Come on," he said and looked back at Marnie. "I mustn't keep you with my boring old stories. If you want to ring the office and give them your list, I'll bring the things over tomorrow. Bye now!" And he was gone, the three of them disappearing as quickly as they had come.

"That was rather sudden," said Marnie, quite bewildered.

"Perhaps he remembered something he had to do," said Anne, joining her in the doorway.

Marnie shook her head. "Nowt so queer as folk," she said. "It's strange round here."

"It's *lovely*," said Anne, turning her face to the sun and closing her eyes.

Marnie went back into the office to clear her desk and Anne called out, her eyes still closed, "Marnie, what do you fancy for lunch?"

"How about some home-cured bacon to go with those eggs?" Anne shrieked and almost jumped into the air at the sound of a man's voice close beside her. She gasped and found herself confronted by George Stubbs. He was dressed in tweed jacket and flannels despite the warmth of the day and in his hand held a packet wrapped in white paper. "Oh dear, did I make you jump, young lady? I *am* sorry." He looked unrepentant. Anne felt foolish.

"Mr Stubbs," she said. "I nearly passed out! I didn't see you coming."

"You did have your eyes closed, my dear." His way of scoring points and patronising her at the same time was becoming irritating. She smiled wearily and was relieved when Marnie joined her.

"Hallo, Mr Stubbs. Are you terrorising my colleague?"

"Peace offering," he said, holding out the packet.

"I didn't think hostilities had broken out," she said.

"Indeed not. It's really a house warming present."

"That's very nice of you." She sniffed the packet. An unmistakable aroma. "Your own home-cured bacon? I'm sure it will be wonderful. You're very kind."

"Not at all." He was beaming at her, and Marnie smiled back unperturbed. Anne watched how Marnie handled him, keeping a balance between friendliness and formality.

"We were going to have a drink before lunch. Would you like to join us?"

Mr Stubbs looked at his watch. "I am on my way to a meeting," he began. "But I would very much like to accept … for the pleasure of being in your company a little longer." Anne tried not to wince or throw up. There were times when the adult world was quite a strain. She offered to tidy the office, lock up and follow them over to *Sally Ann*. By the time she reached the boat, Mr Stubbs was unfolding the table, with three chairs already set out on the deck. Glancing up at Anne he gave her a brief smile and called down into the cabin.

"Our young lady has arrived!" It was only her friendship for Marnie that made Anne resist the temptation to put her foot on his rump and push him over the side. Marnie handed him a tray of glasses and small dishes of olives, cheese straws and cashews. They sat out in the dappled sunshine under the trees in the warm air and sipped their drinks.

"This is most civilised. Ladies, your very good health and every happiness in Knightly St John." They raised their glasses and wished him good health. "This is a first class gin and tonic. I'm sure you do everything to this high standard, Marnie."

"It's not a rehearsal," she said simply. The reply caught Mr Stubbs unawares and he had to think about it.

"No, it's the *real thing*," he said. "But not like that drink in the adverts on television, eh?" Anne laughed at the spectacle of the older man trying to be trendy and he was clearly delighted at what he took to be her enjoyment of his joke. "So what are your plans for Glebe Farm, Marnie … if you don't think I'm prying, of course?"

"I'm going to try to make it habitable, so that I can live here and work here."

"It's a big place for one person, or even two," he said with a conspiratorial wink at Anne.

"I'll have to take it step by step. These are early days."

"Very wise. Quite right. It is a lovely spot. I used to play here as a child, you know."

"You lived at Glebe Farm? I thought it belonged to the Fletchers for generations."

"That's correct. Old Albert Fletcher and I are second cousins. The Stubbs and

93

Fletcher families have farmed and worked in this area since time began." He laughed.

"You must regard me as an interloper."

"Not at all. There's a limit to how many houses a family needs. It's the land that counts. Despite what you may hear, we don't think all change is a bad thing. It's just a matter of respecting what ought to be preserved. New blood can be good for a place. I'm sure you've got your own plans." He took a mouthful of the gin and tonic and Anne tried not to think about blood.

"So you remember Glebe Farm in its heyday, Mr Stubbs," said Marnie.

"George, please. Oh yes. In fact, I used to help load and unload boats at Glebe Farm, on this very spot, when I was a boy. I often used to have a ride on the working boats and then walk back with my brother. Now that's going back a few years, I can tell you. More than I care to remember. The village was prettier then, quieter. Hardly any cars, but lots of horses." He shook his head and Anne wondered what she would remember when she was old. He must be getting on for about sixty, she thought, and could not begin to imagine so many years ahead. "Strewth!" he added. "I'm starting to sound like an old man. I'm supposed to be in my prime."

Marnie refrained from comment. "Was there much commercial traffic on the canal in those days?"

"Boats were going by the whole time, some still using horses. What do you think about that? Most were diesels, though. It was in the war and I'll tell you another thing; there were a few boats crewed by women, helping the war effort. It's no surprise to me to find ladies running canal boats. I'm all for it. Why not?"

"Did they ever come to the farm?"

"Not to my knowledge. I think they mainly carried heavy loads like coal and steel. Jolly hard work and it could be dangerous, too. Do you know what they called them?" He paused for effect.

"Idle women," said Anne. Mr Stubbs stared at her. "Marnie met one last year," she added.

"*Idle women.* That's right. But I was forgetting. I'm in the presence of two boaters. Of *course* you'd know about them."

"Do you know why they were called that, Mr Stubbs?"

"No, Anne, I don't think I do. I thought perhaps because they were from what we used to call 'good families'. They certainly spoke well but they weren't idle, I can tell you."

"It was from the badges they wore. They had the letters 'IW' on them. Inland Waterways."

"All these years and I never knew that!" He finished the gin and tonic and looked at his watch. "Time to love you and leave you, I'm afraid." He rose and Anne wondered if he was going to kiss Marnie's hand. To her disappointment, he merely shook hands with both of them and stepped carefully onto the shore.

When he had gone, Anne cleared the table while Marnie organised lunch.

"You certainly have an admirer there, Marnie."

"You think so?"

"Don't you?"

"I would say Mr Stubbs thinks he almost got what he wanted, but not quite."

"I'm not sure I follow," said Anne.

"It's a long way to come to bring half a pound of bacon," said Marnie. "What would you like for lunch?"

While Marnie was cracking four free range eggs into a mixing bowl, the shiny Range Rover was pulling into the drive of Rooks Farm. George Stubbs went straight to the back door and knocked twice. Almost at once he was let in, making complimentary noises about the smell of baking as he passed through the kitchen to join Albert Fletcher in the living room.

"Well, George, how's it going? Did you get your petition?"

"No. Not yet. I didn't want to hold things up. I think we should keep that in reserve, wait and see what comes from the Bishop. That could be the next step, if we need to press our case."

"You posted your letter?"

"This morning," said George. "I decided to sleep on it. I read it again after breakfast and sent it off."

"I slept on it, too, and I think you're right. We'll wait for the Bishop. But if he doesn't do anything, I'm going to take action myself. I'm not just going to stand by and let people come into the village and trample on the rest of us."

"Let's see what the letter produces. The Bishop can't ignore us." The old man made no reply. "I must say, Albert, not all newcomers bring problems. I've just been down to Glebe Farm to see your Mrs Walker. No *Mr* Walker around, just the girl who works for her."

"I never had dealings with a husband. Probably divorced, I expect. Still, I must say, she was very straight to deal with. A good head for business."

"A *fine* head, I would say. Very attractive young woman. She's already got the office set up as if she'd been there for ages. They've made a good job of it, too. Very smart."

"I wonder what she's going to do with the place," the old farmer muttered.

"Well, I can't see someone with her style turning it into a caravan site or a holiday camp."

"Did you think she might?" said Albert.

"I suppose you're going to tell me you had restrictive covenants put in the contract to prevent her from doing that."

"No way I could. There was a farm, cottages and a boatyard. Residential with light industrial or commercial use. Anyway, I wanted to sell it and people've got a right to make use of their own property. She'll do no harm, that one. She's all right. Unless she's bitten off more than she can chew."

"If she has, she'll not be the first one round here to do that," said George.

"We'll see what the Bishop says. And he'd better not take his time. I'm giving him one week."

❀　❀　❀　❀

In the middle of the afternoon clouds began to appear, huge billowing white cumulus, drifting across the sky in flocks. A light breeze sprang up, barely enough to ripple the surface of the canal. For some time they saw no other boats and, apart from the occasional angler, no-one at all. Anne volunteered to operate the locks while Marnie steered and Dolly lay curled up on the hatch.

Waiting for the first lock to fill, Anne lay on the balance beam, a huge tree-trunk cut square and painted black with a white band at the end. She lay flat on her back, her ears filled with the sound of the water roaring into the lock, watching the clouds through eyes half-closed. She could almost imagine herself drifting along with them. Gradually she was aware only of the sound of her own breathing, until a loud clatter made her jump. The windlass had slipped from her hand onto the paving. She sat up with a start.

"I think it's full now," Marnie called to her. Anne bent down to retrieve the windlass. "Are you all right?"

"Yes. Yes, I'm fine. I nearly dozed off, I think."

"But you're feeling okay?"

"Oh yes. *Wonderful.* Everything is wonderful, Marnie. It couldn't be better. Everything is perfect." As Anne pushed open the gate, Marnie pulled *Sally Ann* into forward gear, pressing the accelerator to set her on her way.

Part 13

Sunday 18 June
"One hour," said Marnie in a firm voice. "It's not healthy to work all the time without a break."

"All right," said Anne, switching on the computer. "But Ralph said it wouldn't do us any harm. And we did have a trip on *Sally Ann* yesterday." Marnie was standing at the window of the office barn, looking out at the grey sky and the wet cobbles in the farmyard. There had been a downpour in the night and the rain beating on the roof had woken her. She had been almost quick enough to close the windows. That was around two in the morning and it had taken her a long time to get back to sleep, lying in the dark cabin in pyjamas that were damp in patches, trying to doze off, her mind full of strange shapes scurrying round the church in wind and rain like lost souls. Eventually she had dropped off, not waking again until nearly eight. Anne was still soundly sleeping and she had waited another half hour before stirring from the bed.

"Would you like me to take you down to see your parents?"

"They're not expecting me to go back this weekend. Of course, if you'd like some time to yourself ..."

"Oh no," said Marnie. "I just thought you might want to have a break from our routine, that's all. Everything would still be here when you got back. You don't have to renounce the rest of the world completely."

"Well, I'd just as soon stay here, Marnie. Really. As long as I'm not in the way."

"That's fine." Marnie sat at her desk preparing for her meeting with Willards the following day. She was checking the costs for the third scheme when Anne put a cup of coffee on the desk.

"Oh, thanks. I'd lost track of time."

"It's gone eleven," said Anne. "Time we were packing up."

"I just need another ten minutes or so."

"We've already gone on for longer than you said."

"But Ralph did say it wouldn't do us any harm at first."

"Well, just ten more minutes, then," said Anne in a firm voice and ducked so that the rolled-up ball of paper missed her head by inches.

❦   ❦   ❦   ❦

"In the name of the Father and of the Son and of the Holy Spirit. Amen." Randall Hughes brought his sermon to a close, crossed himself and descended from the pulpit as the choir incanted a short anthem. On this, as on every other Sunday, the church was full and Valerie Paxton, sitting in the middle of the congregation, found herself wondering whether half of those present each week came only to keep an eye on the vicar and make sure he did not get up to anything peculiar during the services. The other half, including herself, were stirred, no, *inspired*, by the whole atmosphere that he brought to the church.

Valerie realised she was trembling inside at the power of the sermon. The vicar had taken as his theme the notion of sacrifice and woven a skilful message bringing together sacrificial rites in ancient times, the biblical scapegoat of the Old Testament and the renouncing of personal interests for the greater good of the community. He had brought his argument together in the sacrifice of the crucifixion, blending history, philosophy and theology in a way that made them relevant to the everyday lives of the people living in the village.

She suddenly realised that the congregation was singing a hymn and was surprised to notice her book open at the right page. Her husband was singing steadily in a light tenor voice, only needing to glance down at the words from time to time. As he sang, he was thinking about the cauliflowers in his vegetable garden and the terrible problem he was having with slugs. After church, he would have half an hour down there sorting them out, while Val got lunch ready.

In the second row from the front, Albert Fletcher was singing softly. These days, if he tried to sing out, his voice would give way and he would become breathless and start coughing. You had to hand it to Randall Hughes, he thought. Whatever you may say, for all his unwanted changes and his strange ideas, he really knew his job. Albert could remember vicars in that church going back seventy years. Some of them were kind to the children and organised special services where the little ones received gifts of oranges or candles. Others were for ever organising fêtes and garden parties for this or that good cause. Almost without exception, their sermons were unmemorable or patronising or just plain boring. He could not honestly recall a single word from any of them.

Now Randall Hughes, he was quite different. Even if you could not remember all the subjects he chose, you always came away from his services with an understanding of the scheme of things. He had a clear vision of how faith held the world together, gave life a meaning, and he knew how to put his message across. Watching the vicar singing the hymn with his head raised, leading his congregation like a watchful parent, Albert knew that this man would one day be a Bishop. And Albert suspected that Randall Hughes probably knew it too.

In front of Albert, George Stubbs was booming out in his Sunday best baritone. He was conscious that he had put on weight in recent months and his Sunday suit was becoming uncomfortable, especially constricting him around the shoulders. His shirt collar seemed to grip him like a hand at his throat. For all his animosity towards the vicar, he granted that he always gave a good sermon and had a strong presence. That was one of the main problems, as far as George was concerned. The services had become focused on the vicar. He liked vicars who went over the bible stories, explaining what they meant. This one was too clever by half, always acting as if he knew more than anyone else. Always acting. He did not want a vicar who made himself centre stage all the time.

❦ ❦ ❦ ❦

"Do you fancy exploring?" said Marnie. The rain had given way to light clouds and a cool breeze.

"Anything is fine by me," said Anne. They had taken delivery of some of the furniture, leaving it dumped in the office for the time being, and now they were walking through the spinney.

"I was just wondering about putting a picnic lunch together. We could go for a drive, have a look at the county, find a National Trust place to visit, perhaps. You always get a good cream tea there."

"Sounds great … if you're sure you don't want to stay and do things here."

"We can organise your furniture later. It's too pleasant to be indoors on a day like this. I think it would be nice to look further afield."

❦ ❦ ❦ ❦

"Depart in peace to love and serve the Lord."

"Amen," murmured the congregation.

The organ began a restrained anthem. There was a pause lasting several seconds as the congregation remained in their seats, heads bowed in private meditation, while the vicar stood beside the font at the rear of the congregation with eyes closed and hands held together at his chest. As he straightened his back and dropped his hands to his sides, the congregation began to stand and move towards the door. The members of his flock moved into the aisle, crowding together and shuffling slowly out, some of them speaking in muted tones, some exchanging nods with neighbours, all of them seeming still under the spell cast by their vicar, who waited now outside the porch to send them on their way.

Part 14

The vicar had been away from the village for nearly two weeks. Mrs Lockyer who kept house for him told everyone that he was in Stafford, visiting his father who was very ill and may not live. Few believed her, for she was the vicar's devoted servant. For her, he could do no wrong. Some said that the vicar had been seen in Yore, others said Northampton. A drover thought he had seen him in Sibbertoft, at the other end of the county beyond Guilsborough and Naseby. All these were far from the road to Stafford.

It was on a warm Tuesday afternoon that Sarah Anne saw him return. She had been to visit Margaret Tarry, still weak in her sickbed, and was walking home filled with concern for her neighbour. The vicar rode slowly down the high street. He was dusty and, to judge by the state of his horse, he had travelled far. Both looked worn and weary, the vicar unshaven, his face gaunt under the shade of his hat. He touched its brim as he passed her and she stopped to bend her knee. He rode on without speaking. For all he was fatigued from his journey, he sat upright in the saddle, his shoulders square and his back straight.

Sarah watched him progress away from her, thoughts of Margaret Tarry now gone from her mind. She saw only the black cassock and the grim, determined expression on his face. She saw the eyes glance briefly towards her as he touched the edge of his hat with one long, pale, elegant hand.

🌷 🌷 🌷 🌷

Monday 19 June
"I reckon if I set off by nine-thirty I should be able to do it without having to break the land speed record." Marnie was assembling everything needed for the meeting at *The Irish Navigator*. "So you slept okay in your new room?"

"Fine. You weren't too lonely on *Sally Ann*?"

"No, but I'm sure Dolly was snoring in the night. Let me know if there's anything you need for the room. I can get it on my way back." Together, they had made a comfortable bedroom for Anne in the hayloft, with reading lamp, cupboard and bedside table. The narrow ventilation slit made it gloomy in the daytime, but at night it was cosy with the lamp lit and oriental rugs spread over the floor.

Anne was perched on a stool ticking off points on her list. There were still forty-five minutes to go before Marnie's departure. "Let me know when you're ready for me to tell you about the things on my list," said Anne.

"Just give me a minute or two and I'll be with you. Ah, what's this?" Marnie pulled a small book out from among her papers. It was the history of the church. She put it on the desk and returned to her task. Finally, she put her filofax and the office file on top of the other documents. "That's it. Right. The list. Fire away."

"Would you like a coffee before you go?"

"I'll get one there, I expect. "

"You were going to look in at the school on your way out and tell the Head you'll have the children here to visit *Sally*." Anne gave Marnie a sheet of paper. "That's the programme we drew up for her."

"Great. I hope she likes it."

"We just have to agree a date," said Anne.

"I'll ask her to let us know as soon as she can."

"The vicar's calling round some time this afternoon. Do you know when you'll be back?"

"Probably soon after lunch," said Marnie. "I should be here in good time."

"Okay. You're due to send Willards an invoice this week for the two restaurants near Leicester. And they ought to start talking to you about the redecoration of head office." Marnie made a note. Anne continued. "They may want to start the project for the new restaurant at the Grand Union Marina. It's on their planning list. I think your associate designer may already have some ideas about that. It's in a very historic position."

"Historic?"

"It's the centre of the whole canal system."

"Yes, of course," said Marnie. "It's just along from … *associate designer?*" She looked up from her notes. Anne was smiling, her impish face making her look more childlike than ever. "Some ideas, did you say?"

"A few," said Anne.

"We'd better have a look at them when I get back, then." Anne's smile broadened and she returned to her list.

"I'll do the invoice and a covering letter while you're out."

"Okay. Good," said Marnie. She glanced up at the clock. "I'd better get ready."

Anne enjoyed learning from Marnie, watching her meticulous approach to every part of her work. This morning, after showering, Marnie had begun the day in jeans and sweat-shirt, putting her clothes out ready for the meeting.

Anne walked around the office thinking how she could improve their standard of organisation. She realised it was all a matter of detail and placed a note pad with a pencil beside each phone. She filled the paper tray in the photocopier and checked the roll in the fax machine. While she was doing this, the phone rang.

"Hallo."

"Marnie?"

"No. This is Anne Price. I'm her colleague."

"Is Marnie available?"

"She's out of the office at the moment. Can I take a message?"

"Has she left for the meeting?"

"No. Are you from Willards?"

"Roger Brooks. Marketing manager. Can you get her to ring me before she goes? She has the number."

"I'll ask her to ring as soon as possible."

"Right." Gone. On the pad Anne wrote his name and looked up the number on the file. Were all business people so abrupt? He sounded fraught. She set off for the boat.

"Hallo, Roger?" Marnie listened, muttering and taking notes on the pad by the phone. "Already? I thought you wanted it later in the programme." She continued muttering and scribbling. "Yes, of course it can be included. That's fine." She glanced over at Anne and raised an eyebrow. The conversation came to an end and she hung up. "You were right. Head office *and* the marina restaurant. Apparently their accountants advise them to go ahead now for tax reasons."

"Do you want to take the files with you?"

"Please. It might help reassure Roger." Marnie laughed. "He sounds stressed."

"Are clients always like that, clicking their fingers and expecting us to jump?"

"It happens. Roger's all right usually. He's just under pressure. This will mean much more work for him to manage. People react differently when they're put under stress."

"Are you under stress because of this, Marnie?" Anne was pulling files from the cabinet.

"No. I'll have the nervous breakdown later. It's time I was off. Golden rule:

never be late for a meeting, especially if you're a woman." She took the files from Anne and made for the door.

"You won't forget to look in at the school, will you?" Anne called after her.

"Oh, God. Now I *am* under stress!"

"Shall I phone for you?"

"No. It's okay. I'll ring her on the mobile. Thanks. See you!"

As Marnie backed the Rover out of the barn, Anne appeared alongside and held up a piece of paper. Marnie took it through the window.

"School phone number," said Anne.

"Great! By the way, I liked the pad by the phone ..." Her voice was whisked away by the burble of the engine, and her hand waved out of the window as she set off. Anne could see her fastening the seat belt and keying in the number on the mobile as she bounced up the field track.

❦ ❦ ❦ ❦

"I hope it doesn't mean an epidemic," said Valerie Paxton, replacing the receiver.

"Oh, I don't think it's as bad as that," said Mrs Giles. "Probably just coincidence."

"Well, that's three calls already this morning. What a way to start the week!"

"It's not unusual," said the head, turning to go back to her office. "A spell of fine weather ... running around outside ... not keeping warm enough. It's easy for them to get a chill." As she pushed open the door, the phone rang on the secretary's desk and she waited while Valerie took the call.

"Yes, I know. You're coming in this morning." She listened and the Head waited for the outcome. "You've been held up. I see ... Sorry, could you repeat that please ... a programme did you say? ... Oh, in the car ... yes, I understand." She looked out of the window and the Head followed her gaze. At that moment, across the short expanse of playground, they saw a dark blue car accelerate past in the direction of the main road. "There's usually someone here until four-thirty, sometimes later ... that would be helpful. Thank you. Good-bye."

"Mrs Walker," said the head.

"Phoning from the car." Valerie looked slightly affronted. "I had to wait while she changed gear."

The Head laughed. "I take it she's not coming this morning."

"No. Held up by work. But she's prepared a programme for the visit and she'll try to call in later. She sends her apologies."

"And she'll let us know when she's coming?"

"Yes. From the car on the way back."

"Oh well. That's something different. We don't get calls from people passing the window every day." She smiled at the thought, but saw that Valerie was frowning. In fact, she had been less than cheerful ever since they arrived at school that morning. "Is anything bothering you?"

The secretary shook her head. "No. It's just that everybody's in such a rush these days. People have to phone each other from one part of the village to another and drive through it *far* too fast."

"I'm sure it was just so as not to let us down," said the head. "After all, we are asking her to do us a favour. This must be a very busy time for her. And I don't think she was *really* going too quickly."

Valerie looked up at the Head and for a moment there was anger in her eyes. She sighed. "It's just ... those who want to make real contact with other people aren't understood ... nobody wants to know ... it just isn't right, that's all." In total bewilderment, the Head crossed the room and put a hand on Valerie's shoulder. She could not begin to imagine what was the meaning of all this, but she suspected it had nothing to do with the numbers of children absent with summer colds or Marnie Walker's use of her mobile phone.

❦ ❦ ❦ ❦

Anne looked up from her work as she heard the car approach. Marnie had been gone about twenty minutes and Anne had converted her normal working space into a design area by the simple expedient of laying a large, flattened cardboard box on top of her desk to use as a drawing board. She put down a pattern book and went to the door.

"Mornin', Anne, my love. I need a signature for this one." The postman held out a slip of paper for her to sign.

"Marnie's out this morning. Is it all right if I sign for her?"

"'Ms Anne Price' it says on the envelope." He held up a large Recorded Delivery envelope the size of a magazine. Anne signed and took the post.

"Settling in all right?"

"Fine, thanks. It's very nice here." She wanted more than anything to open her special packet, but did not want to show her impatience.

"Got the telephone in?" Anne smiled and nodded. "Good. That's the main thing. Just in case you ever need anything. You never know. Oh well, see you tomorrow, me dook."

Anne slit open the envelope with care. It *was* a magazine, *Residence*. The cover showed the interior of a huge flat in London's Docklands, a living room the size of a parade ground, with arched windows onto a balcony like the deck of an ocean liner. Diaphanous white drapes were wafting in the breeze, giving views of the Thames curving away towards Tower Bridge. There were cream sofas and a polished mahogany floor, vast canvases on the painted brick walls and vases bursting with sunflowers. *It was her design, reproduced by computer!* The envelope dropped out of the magazine at the moment her eyes caught the names of the contributors. New Wave – Young Designers: Competition winner Anne Price.

Her mouth dropped open and she stooped down to pick up the envelope. It contained a letter from the editor hoping she liked the article ('see page 54') and listing the other enclosures: an invitation to a private view at one of the major fabric companies, their newest collection of curtain fabrics, at their headquarters behind Oxford Circus; free membership for one year of the Friends of the Victoria and Albert Museum; first-day tickets for a whole series of exhibitions in London and the National Exhibition Centre over the coming twelve months; an invitation to a seminar on post-modern design at the Royal College of Art. The final enclosure was a voucher for fifty pounds to spend at any branch of House of Fraser. *Wow!*

This was too much for a Monday morning. Anne sat down, overwhelmed, and turned to the article. It *was* her room. There was no doubt about that, but it looked quite ... well ... *stylish*. And there was the photograph of Anne herself that she had had to send in the top right hand corner. They had somehow even made her look like a designer, instead of a schoolgirl. The only sadness was having no-one to share it with her until Marnie got back.

She wrote a 'thank you' letter to the editor and turned to her drawing board. The sight of the outsize piece of cardboard immediately brought her back to earth and she laughed out loud. "Let that be a lesson to you, my girl," she said, mimicking the accent of Alan the postman. Still laughing, she returned to her work, but this time she felt different. She knew she would be a designer, not at once, but one day. And she knew that it had all come about as a result of a chance meeting last summer with Marnie and *Sally Ann*.

❦ ❦ ❦ ❦

That same Monday morning, Rosemary Upton sat at her desk in the palace, opening the envelopes and putting the post into priority order for the Bishop. She kept apart the items marked 'private', leaving them unopened, and noticed that one envelope, light blue and of good quality, had an address on the reverse. She was vaguely aware of Knightly St John at the far end of the diocese. The Bishop's meeting with the Dean and the Archdeacon of Towcester had gone on longer than anticipated and any minute she expected a journalist to arrive from local radio for an interview on the Bishop's first impressions of his new role.

The sound of voices and the rattle of the door handle heralded the exit of the two clerics and the Bishop stood in the doorway to see them out, a warm smile on his face. Rosemary was impressed by his ability to handle even these two tough old reactionaries. What had they called the Bishop in the national press when his appointment had been announced? A *fixer*. Yes, that was it. A *fixer*. She remembered asking herself what that really meant. She had heard of him as a suffragan Bishop from the London diocese and recalled a speech he had made at a diocesan synod, reported widely in the church press for its vision in an age when very few people had it in them to make sense of the times. Now here he stood, quietly having a final, friendly word with two men who, not six months before, would have been expected to oppose his views.

"Bishop, may I give you your mail before Mr Stoddart arrives?"

"Yes, of course." He quickly scanned the top half dozen there and then and handed them back to her. "These are routine. Usual replies, please. What's this?" He picked up the blue envelope. "Knightly St John? Now there's a coincidence! Who could be writing to me from there? I'll take these through. Could we have coffee when the BBC man arrives, please?" He went back into the vast office with its floor to ceiling bay window and perched on the corner of the huge mahogany desk.

"*My Lord Bishop* ... (probably correct, but very outmoded, he thought) ... *I am writing to you on a matter of great importance to our whole community ... we regard it as scandalous* ... (oh no, not choirboys, not so soon after my arrival) ... *repeated and unnecessary changes to almost everything we hold dear in our church* ... (a schism?) ... *pews removed, prayerbooks replaced, refusal to baptise infants of people whose families have lived in the village for generations on the grounds that they are not churchgoers* ... (always a tricky one, especially when half the graveyard is filled with their ancestors) ... *I could go on for pages* ... (spare me that, please) ... *but now, the latest in a long line of disputes ... the vicar is refusing to spend church funds on the village school – a Church of England School in fact – saying he wants to spend the money on works to the porch. Vicar regards the needs of the schoolchildren as less important than the maintenance of the church building. We regard this as a blatant waste of money ... difficult enough to get young people with families to come here and those that do, send them to private schools in the town ...*"

The Bishop finished the letter and frowned. He knew that it was a matter for the education authority and the school governors to finance school building works. Why were the good citizens of Knightly St John up in arms like this? Every instinct told him that there was more to this than just bricks and mortar ... *the latest in a long line of disputes*. He walked to the door.

"Rosemary, can you arrange for Randall Hughes to come in and see me in the next few days, please. He's the incumbent at Knightly St John. No sign of our reporter yet?"

"He's due any minute." The Bishop withdrew and shut the great door silently behind him.

Standing by the window, he looked down at the garden. The herbaceous border was just beginning to come into its own and the arbour leading into the space beyond was covered with bright yellow roses. Through the beech hedge he could glimpse the familiar outline of his wife's gardening smock as she knelt beside a flower bed. Behind him there was a soft tap on the door and Rosemary put her head round.

"A car has just driven in, Bishop. I think it's him. Would you like me to remind you when it's time for your next appointment?"

"Five minutes beforehand, please, Rosemary. It's always an effort to get these fellows to wind up." He smiled pleasantly.

"Certainly. I've spoken to Mr Hughes. He's giving a paper at a seminar at the university tomorrow, but he can come on Wednesday. I've put him in the diary for ten-thirty. That should give you a good half-hour before you have to leave to catch your train to London."

❦ ❦ ❦ ❦

"Hallo, Marnie? Sorry to interrupt your meeting, but Mr Hughes has arrived to see you." In a hushed tone, turning slightly away, she added: "The vicar." As Anne spoke, the vicar stood tall and immobile in the middle of the office, like a long black statue. "Okay, I'll tell him ... yes, yes ... right ... About what time? ... Where? ... all right ... yes, okay. Oh, Marnie? You won't forget you've got to call in at the school? Or shall I ring them and explain? ... Fine. See you later." She turned back and found the visitor glancing down at the magazine on her desk. She wondered if he might recognise her name. He looked up.

"Have I come at a bad time?"

"Marnie apologises. They've kept her much longer than she expected."

"That's quite all right. I realise I'm intruding on her working day. It's only vicars who are supposed to work one day a week." He spoke amicably with an ironic half-smile, and Anne very much wanted him to notice her name on the cover of the magazine.

"Marnie says if it's convenient she'll call round and see you on her way back. She'll ring me when she's on her way and I can let you know what time she should get to you. Would that be all right?"

"That's fine. Let me write down my phone number."

Anne gave him a notepad. "You can use that magazine to rest on," she said. He leaned forward and quickly wrote the number in elegant black figures on the white paper. Visible below the pad was the heading that clearly showed the name: Anne Price.

"It's Anne, isn't it?"

"Yes. Yes it is. *Anne Price.*" She smiled eagerly, waiting for him to go on.

"Well, thank you, Anne. You've been very helpful." He looked down at the magazine and reached towards it. Anne was agog with anticipation. The vicar picked up the pad and handed it back to her with the pen. "I'd better leave you to get on. I'm sure you have a great deal to do."

As he walked across the farmyard towards the field track, Anne could hear half snatches of conversation in her mind. *Anne Price? Not the Anne Price, the interior designer? Well yes, actually, as a matter of fact I am ...* A faint sound brought her back to reality and she looked down to see Dolly rubbing her flank against the door jamb. She bent down and picked up the cat, walking back into the office.

"Right. I've got to tell someone, so it might as well be you, Dolly." She carried the cat in with her and went over to her desk. "You see this magazine, well, that's my name on the front. Yes, I'm famous." Dolly wriggled free and sat on the desk, licking a front paw. "I knew you'd be impressed." Anne put the notepad back in its place and pinned the page with the vicar's number onto the office notice board. She turned back to find Dolly curled up on the magazine.

❦ ❦ ❦ ❦

"Anne, hi, it's me. How are things?"

"All under control."

"Good. I've just turned off the main road and I'm heading for the school."

"What about the vicar?"

"Could you let him know I'm back and ring me on the mobile if there's any problem."

"Will do. I'm sure it'll be okay. He's expecting you."

Marnie pulled the Rover into the school lay-by and got out just as the Head and secretary were appearing in the doorway across the small playground. They paused as they saw her coming.

"I'm sorry to be late."

"Don't apologise," said Mrs Giles. "I feel guilty at imposing on you."

"Everything's a rush today." Marnie reached into her bag and pulled out a folder. "We've prepared an outline programme of what we think we could do." Mrs Giles scanned the paper.

"This looks very thorough. Could we discuss it in more detail?"

"Of course. Tomorrow will be tricky. What about Wednesday?"

"Over a cup of coffee at about ten-thirty?"

"Good. I'll be there. Bye!" She smiled at them both and strode off to the car. As she went, the sound of her mobile phone rang out and she reached into her bag without changing pace.

"We'll have to remember to put that in the diary," said Mrs Giles.

"I'll go and do it now," said Valerie. "We're busy too and I wouldn't want to forget."

"Well, you know what they say," said the head. "If you want something done, ask a busy woman."

❦   ❦   ❦   ❦

"Won't you come in?" The tall black shape moved aside to let Marnie enter the hall. As the door closed behind her, Marnie stood admiring the elegant curve of the staircase sweeping up to the first floor. "It's wasted on one person living here alone, of course."

"It's beautiful. Were you responsible for the decor?"

"Actually, yes, I was."

"Very daring," said Marnie. "The broad yellow and white stripes ..."

"Would you like to see the rest of the house?"

"I don't want to take up all your time."

"Is that a London way of saying you have better things to do?"

"Not at all. I meant what I said. I always do."

"So do I and it's amazing how often it gets me into trouble. Come and see my bedroom."

"Best offer I've had all day." Marnie laughed. "Sorry. I'm sure that's not the sort of thing one's supposed to say to vicars. I've had a long day."

"Then why don't I show you my bedroom and the rest of the house and then offer you the gin and tonic? That way round, you can't mistake my motives."

"It's a deal." They went up to the first floor. The bedroom and its en-suite bathroom were in dove grey, burgundy and white, cool and masculine. The other bedrooms were co-ordinated in blues and greens.

"Did you have a designer or do it yourself?"

"Have you any idea what a priest earns in a month?" He spoke unlike Marnie's idea of how vicars ought to speak, his cultured voice laced with irony, his expression almost self-mocking.

"This is the dining room," he said, pushing open the door and deliberately waiting a moment before switching on the light. The effect was dramatic. The room was decorated in rich vermilion with gilt wall lights, mahogany furniture and velvet pile carpet in royal blue. Georgian silver candlesticks gleamed on the shining tabletop. The drawn curtains added to the effect of intimacy. The atmosphere was sensual and intense.

"Do you often entertain?" said Marnie.

"Not often enough to justify this, really. But I thought the room deserved special treatment. Do you think it over the top?"

"It depends on what you wanted to achieve. It's certainly powerful."

He steepled his hands together, touching his lips with the tips of his long fingers. "How about that gin and tonic?" he said, leading the way into another room at the front of the house. "This is my study. Very workaday. Have a seat. I'll fetch some ice." He gestured towards a comfortable leather armchair beside a low table opposite an Adam fireplace. This room was lined from ceiling to floor with bookshelves. In the broad bay window stood a Victorian desk on which sat a computer, two piles of books, a vase of roses of various colours and a collection of photographs in silver frames. Within a few moments he returned and went over to a drinks cabinet.

"If everyone had your imagination I'd be out of a job," said Marnie. The vicar dropped ice cubes and chunks of lemon into crystal glasses, poured two good measures of gin and added the tonic.

"The trouble with this place is that everyone, or nearly everyone, thinks they could do my job better than me." He handed Marnie a glass and sat opposite her in a dark green Victorian button-back armchair. "I wish they could just leave me to get on with it. It's not as if most of them have any real belief in the church or religion at all. It's just part of their social fabric."

"Are you always this frank?"

"Sorry. It's my latest preoccupation. The trouble is people in the village think I'd like to be known as Father Randall, waving incense and saying mass. Actually, I try to steer a middle course. People are entitled to their own views. I don't push mine down everybody's throat with the communion wafer."

"There's certainly no shortage of views in these parts," said Marnie.

"I'm as bad as anyone at letting off steam. You're a good listener, Mrs Walker."

"It's Marnie."

"Okay, Marnie. Well, let's get down to business. You said you're not actually an architect."

"I'm an interior designer."

"Right. The problem I have is that part of the church is in danger of falling down."

"You need an architect." They raised their glasses to each other and drank.

"Yes. The other problem is, I don't know any architects. Presumably you do. Perhaps you could advise me on who might be suitable?"

"I'll need to give it some thought. All my contacts are in London."

"Does that matter? I mean, the church's appointed architects are a London firm."

"Why not use them?"

"I want someone I can choose for myself. Do you think that's wrong?"

"Not at all. Most people want to work with someone they can trust, or at least talk to. There is another aspect, though. Architects have different specialisms. They're not all the same."

"I'd need an expert in ancient buildings?"

"Ideally, yes. What sort of project is it?"

"*That*, as they say, is quite a long story."

"*This* is quite a long drink. It's also very good. You've had practice."

"Don't tell the Bishop." He sat back in the chair, stretched his long legs out and crossed his ankles. "I'll keep it brief. You know the church is basically twelfth century, though parts of it are even older. The porch was added in about 1380. Now at that time, of course, the Black Death was prevalent in the area. There were few craftsmen to be found and a lot of work was being done by unskilled labour and apprentices." He spoke as if it was a recent epidemic. Marnie sipped her drink and listened. "The porch was never properly keyed in. Is that the right term?" Marnie nodded. "According to my building file, an architect came up from London and reported that the porch was in danger of 'imminent disastrous collapse'."

"That's pretty serious," said Marnie. "When was that exactly?"

"April … 1937." Their eyes met and they smiled briefly.

"So, you're telling me that part of the building erected 600 years ago and virtually condemned over 50 years ago is worrying you."

"Exactly. It is quite amusing, I grant you. But if it fell down next Sunday morning and injured or killed some people coming out of church, I'd be for the high jump. Can you imagine the headlines? *Negligent Vicar Kills his Flock!* But seriously, from a legal and moral point of view, I can't tolerate the situation."

"Of course not," said Marnie. "I can talk it over with a colleague in London. He'd probably know who could help."

"I have funds in hand," said the vicar, "saved up over the years. That's not the problem. The trouble is my PCC – the Parochial Church Council – they want to use the money for works to the school. They're worried the authority will close it."

"Very public spirited, no doubt," said Marnie.

"That's one way of looking at it. Or you could say they're wanting somewhere for their grandchildren to go. Self interest or genuine concern, it's still my responsibility to care for the church and the local authority's to look after the school."

"I'd need to have some details," said Marnie. "Do you have a copy of the architect's report from 1937 that I could borrow?" The vicar got up and went over to the desk. He picked up a thick file and passed it to her.

"It's all in there. Borrow the whole thing, if you like. As long as you let me have it back some time."

"I'll see what I can do." She finished the gin and tonic and stood up. "This is more like a university library than a study. Sorry, I'm being personal again."

"That's fine. And your comparison is valid. I'm writing a thesis for my doctorate."

"What's your subject?"

"It's on the liturgy. I'll not bore you with the title; it's three lines long." He smiled. "I've been doing it for over five years now. It should be completed by Christmas." He walked over to the desk and picked up a computer disk. "It's all on this. Over 370 pages so far."

"I wonder how many disks it would take to hold your entire library," said Marnie.

"That's it. Everything is changing all around us and some people, *most* people I think, seem to want the church to stand still in the middle of it all. We didn't get on by ignoring what was happening in the world. The founding fathers of the church were revolutionaries in their day. Like them, I'm not a soft touch."

"But you have medieval buildings and are expected to be ossified."

"The Church as Fossil … Jurassic Ark! My first post-doctoral thesis. What a good idea." He laughed heartily. Marnie was struck by the way this man created and changed the atmosphere around him in an instant. She felt quite tempted to go to church herself and hear him preach. No wonder he excited strong reactions, she thought.

❦   ❦   ❦   ❦

Driving into the yard, Marnie spotted Anne coming through the spinney. She blinked the headlamps twice and Anne waved back.

"Hi! How's it been? Not too lonely?"

"No. It's been a good day. I've got quite a lot done. I bet you're tired after all your running around." Marnie realised that she was, a feeling no doubt aided and abetted by the gin and tonic she had just consumed.

"Yes, slightly. I ought to think about supper, I suppose. We can't just pop round the corner for a pizza out here in the sticks."

"No problem," said Anne. "It'll be ready in about fifteen minutes. I've made a salad and there's a quiche in the oven. Why don't you come and relax?"

"Music to my ears," said Marnie.

"There's some of that, too. I've got some of your favourite Bach ready to roll."

"Wonderful. Lead me to it."

Sally Ann looked idyllic, nestling under the trees in her dock, with geraniums in tubs on the roof. The table was laid on the grass beside the boat, with parasol opened and a vase of flowers. Anne had put out small dishes of olives and cashews. Marnie washed and changed while Anne busied herself making vinaigrette in the galley.

"Can I help? I feel much more civilised now."

"No. You have a sit down. I won't be long. There's a magazine to read if you like." Her tone was casual.

"Magazine?"

"Yes. *Residence.*" She bent over the dressing to add mustard powder.

"Okay. Thanks," said Marnie. She opened a bottle of Rioja.

When Anne emerged to put the salad bowl on the table, Marnie was glancing at an article near the front of the magazine. She made as if to close it.

"Oh, you can carry on reading for a bit. I'm not quite ready."

"Fine."

When Anne arrived with the quiche, Marnie put the magazine aside and smiled.

"Anything of interest?" said Anne casually, putting the food on the table.

"I'm only up to page fifty, or thereabouts," said Marnie. "I'll have another go at it tomorrow some time. Or the day after."

They began to eat and Anne told Marnie what she had been doing in the office. Then Marnie related the news from the meeting with Willards. The contract would give them work for some time to come. Marnie looked thoughtful and leaned forward in the chair, her expression serious.

"Anne. Listen. There's been a development. I'm not sure I can afford to keep you on."

Anne looked startled. "But I thought you said there was even more work than you anticipated."

"That was before you were set to become rich and famous." Anne's expression turned to bewilderment. Marnie added: "*Anne Price – Young Designer*, as featured in *Residence* magazine!"

"You beast!" shouted Anne. "You saw it and you didn't say anything. I thought you hadn't noticed. I've been *dying* to tell someone all day. When did you realise?"

"As soon as I saw the magazine. It's not the kind of thing you regularly find in the village shop."

Anne laughed out loud. "I can just see Mr Stubbs rushing into the shop to get it and telling Mrs Appleton all about Colefax and Fowler's new collection."

"I'm sure Albert Fletcher would go ape over Sanderson's latest curtain fabrics," said Marnie.

"We could use them as tarpaulins to keep the rain out of the ruins!" said Anne.

Marnie reached over and poured her some wine. "This is just to celebrate. *Your* fame and *our* contract with Willards." They raised their glasses.

After supper, they had coffee on the aft deck, huddled over the magazine article. Marnie talked about Randall Hughes, his house, his interior design, his work. Anne looked at the thick grey file. It was like a slab of granite.

"Does the file go all the way back to the twelfth century?" she asked.

"No. Only to 1380. Actually, joking aside, I think it does go back to the 1930's."

"It certainly looks like it." Marnie read the article about Anne, while the subject herself half listened to a Brandenburg concerto. The sun was still warm, slanting through the trees that lined the canal and reflecting off the surface of the water.

Anne was thinking about her new life. The room described in the article seemed a long way off in time and space, as if it was no longer part of her, only a pleasant memory. Her home now was a hayloft, with no windows, the probability of leaks when it rained and strange scratching sounds in the night. For all that, she could not have wished for more. Marnie looked up from the article.

"It's a good design and a good article."

"Yes. I've written to thank the editor."

"You're looking rather thoughtful. Everything all right?"

"Oh yes. More than all right. I love our life, Marnie. It's absolutely brilliant."

"Yes ... if you can keep up with it all. I sometimes wonder if I've got the energy for living in the country. London was quite peaceful in comparison."

Part 15

Tuesday 20 June

Just as Marnie was thinking it was time to stop for the day, she heard footsteps outside. Almost seven. She wondered if the vicar was paying them a visit.

Ralph appeared at the door, more tanned than before, in jeans and a navy sweatshirt. "Do you always work this late? I thought you office types worked nine to five."

"In this firm, working a half-day means only twelve hours," said Marnie, kissing him on both cheeks. He went over and gently squeezed Anne's shoulder.

"If you're in the middle of things I won't interrupt. I just wanted to bring back the generator. *Thyrsis* is mended and all is running well."

"I daresay we could take in a passing boatman and provide him with a meal."

"A kind thought, but this passing boatman may have other ideas. When you're ready why not join me on *Thyrsis* and I'll press a gin and tonic into your hand while the casserole is completing its course in the oven."

Less than a quarter of an hour later, Marnie was raising the glass to her lips in the study on *Thyrsis*, with a delicious aroma wafting through from the galley. Anne's drink was sparkling mineral water with ice cubes and a chunk of lemon. Ralph took his seat by the bookcase.

"You know, I could get accustomed to this treatment," said Marnie. "It must be the air round here. Everyone seems to want to ply me with gin and tonic and provide meals for me."

"Do you suspect their motives?" said Ralph. "Who else plies you with gin and tonic?"

"The vicar."

"No wonder the church is the focus of media attention. Gin has replaced the communion wine. And I thought it had something to do with the tension in the village."

"Am I missing something?" said Marnie.

"I heard it on the radio," said Ralph. "Apparently there's been an article in the press on the dispute between the village and the vicar." Anne offered to fetch the paper from the office.

They found a whole page article on the 'unrest' in Knightly St John. It outlined the changes introduced in the past few years with no consultation and referred darkly to the long tradition of animosity between the clergy and the villagers. There had been a pacifist incumbent during the Great War, and at the time of the Reformation a vicar who had preached opposition to King Henry VIII until silenced by the threat of the stake. There had even been rumours that Guy Fawkes and the gunpowder plotters meeting at Ashby St Ledgers in the north of the county had heard prayers said at their meetings by the vicar of Knightly, though this was never proved. Worst of all, was the unsolved mystery of the murder of the vicar 'by person or persons unknown' at the time of the Civil War.

There were photos of the church, the vicar, members of the PCC and the village green. There were quotes from all the parties concerned that had been chosen to make the dispute seem more bitter than Marnie had imagined it to be.

"To judge by this, you'd almost think it was unsafe to walk down the street for fear of getting caught up in a gunfight," she said.

"Newspapers are often out of focus," said Ralph. "But they usually have an element of truth. You know the people. What do you think?"

"I don't know. I've hardly met them, but I thought the vicar seemed quite reasonable. Some people think he's more of a fundamentalist. That's not how he comes over to me."

"You think the villagers are seeing him through rosary-tinted spectacles?" said Ralph.

Part 16

"Sarah, wake up!" It was an urgent whisper. Sarah stirred as her arm was shaken by her sister.

"What is it?" Sarah, her voice hoarse from sleep, blinked in the darkness. A pale grey light fell across the room, a glimpse of moonlight through the window.

"Listen! There are voices." Sarah pulled herself up onto an elbow, yawning.

"I can't hear …," Her sister placed a hand over her mouth. Sarah was starting to shake her head, when they both heard a shuffle from below. A cough. Voices murmuring. Men's voices, deep and gruff, several of them. Sarah was immediately wide awake, pushing back the bedcover, picking up the shawl from the floor beside her bed. The two young women crossed to the window, soundless in bare feet.

"Who is it?" Sarah raised a hand to silence her sister and strained to see down to the lane in front of the house. The moon was nearly full, shining on the church tower beyond the lane, but the shadows from the trees all around were dark and impenetrable. Sarah bit her lip and waited. There was no more sound. She whispered into the ear of her sister.

"Wait here. I shall be quick." Even as she paused at the top of the stairs, she was aware that her sister was following her. They paused again at the front door and Sarah took a deep breath before she pressed down on the latch. The click seemed to echo through the house like a hammer striking the anvil. From outside there was a stirring as she pulled open the door.

"Hush!" A man's voice. In the moonlight Sarah could see the dark shapes of a band of men, a dozen or more. One of them set himself in front of her, a familiar figure, one of the farmers who had not gone to the war.

"What is happening here?" Sarah whispered.

"Nothing. Go back inside. We did not mean to wake you." He spoke in a murmur, his deep voice barely audible.

"But what are you doing?" she insisted.

"No harm. Believe me and go in." He made to take Sarah's arm, but she shook it free. On the ground beside the house she could see farm tools, sickles, a pitchfork, staves.

"I will not go until you tell me what business you have here." She looked towards the church and could see the clock face in the pale light. "It is nearly two o'clock, Mr Pettit." The farmer turned his head as if he too was looking at the clock. Sarah saw that all the men were staring up at the tower.

"Please, Sarah. Go to bed. We may be here a while yet." Sarah strained her eyes to look to the top of the tower. All was still. Without another word she turned and went in, ushering her sister up the stairs to their room. She lay awake, not knowing how long it was until she heard movement from below their window, much later as the men shuffled away into the night.

❦ ❦ ❦ ❦

Wednesday 21 June

"Oh, Mrs Walker. Good morning. You've come to see Mrs Giles."

"Hallo. Yes. Ten-thirty."

Valerie Paxton glanced up at the clock. It was two minutes before the appointed time. "The Head has a parent in with her at the moment. Would you like to have a seat, Mrs Walker?"

"Thanks. Actually, it seems strange hearing my surname used." Marnie smiled. "I don't think of myself as 'Mrs Walker'. Everyone usually calls me 'Marnie'." The secretary looked down at the papers on her desk.

"In schools we get used to surnames, Mrs Walker. I suppose it's because of the children. Or do London children address their teachers by their Christian names?" There was a definite edge to her voice. Marnie felt she was being reminded of her place as an outsider. The use of 'Christian names' also struck her as odd. In her part of London many of the residents were Jewish or Hindu or Moslem. 'Christian name' had faded from use a long time ago, but she thought it wise not to underline the differences between her newly adopted home and herself.

"No. I don't think so." The secretary began opening the mail using her dagger. The silence in the office was almost palpable. At ten-thirty-five Marnie remembered all the things waiting to be done at the office. She really did not need to be sitting here feeling like a sales rep cold-calling with a special offer on double glazing. The minute hand on the clock clicked one notch further. "That's an unusual knife. Is it a replica of some sort?"

"No. It's not a replica, it's real. Actually, it's an SS dagger. It used to belong to my father." Definitely not a good idea to ask if he had been an SS officer, thought Marnie, even in jest, though she thought she detected a certain inherited charm in his daughter.

"He used to say he found it in Hitler's bunker at the end of the war, but it was not quite like that. He really found it in the Chancellery building. The bunker was in the cellar."

"It must have had an interesting history," said Marnie, aware that she had probably not chosen her words very carefully.

"Who knows? Dad was much more interested in the other thing he found there. There was a brand new army motorbike parked in the courtyard. A BMW. It wasn't even scratched, after all that fighting. He tried the starter and it worked first time."

"He would rather have brought that back, no doubt," said Marnie.

"Oh, he did. He rode it round to his lorry and got his mates to lift it into the back."

"And he brought it all the way back to Britain?"

"The following week. The worst thing was having to leave the lorry parked outside Brighton police station for three days before they got orders to report to Weedon depot."

"Weedon on the Grand Union?"

"Yes. Just ten miles up the road. He dropped it off here on his way up."

"Did he keep it?"

"Yes. He painted it black and had it for years. 'Course, he had to keep it hidden for a while. In fact, he kept it in the little barn at Glebe Farm for over a year till he managed to get it registered."

"The little barn? That's probably my office." Valerie frowned and Marnie felt the atmosphere cooling, but the door to the Head's office opened and she emerged with another woman. Both were smiling, one in reassurance, the other with evident relief.

"Don't you worry now. We'll keep an eye on things. Bye." The parent left with a smile at Valerie and the Head held out her hand to Marnie.

"I *am* sorry to make you wait, Mrs Walker. It's a hazard of our job, I'm afraid. Please come in. Mrs Paxton, can we have coffee, please?" The secretary put the dagger carefully into her drawer. "Ah. The famous paperknife. I'm glad to see you putting it out of sight. It has always made me nervous."

"Don't worry, Mrs Giles. It's only used for ceremonial occasions. You're quite safe." The Head took it as a joke. The secretary was not smiling.

"Well, let's get started, shall we? I don't want to take up too much of your time. Your programme looks first class." She closed the door behind them leaving Valerie Paxton making the coffee and wondering why she had taken such a dislike to this newcomer from London.

❦   ❦   ❦   ❦

"Do you take milk, Randall?"

"No thank you, Bishop. Black for me." The Bishop smiled benignly at Rosemary Upton as she left them to their meeting and pulled the great mahogany door silently shut. As the Bishop poured milk from the Wedgwood jug into his cup, Randall Hughes looked over to the tall bay window at the tops of the trees in the palace gardens. Somewhere out there was a city with traffic, pedestrians, a railway, but no sound of it penetrated the inner precincts of the Cathedral Close. He wondered how much the Bishop was in touch with the real world these days and had the feeling that he was about to find out.

"A fine view, isn't it?" The Bishop followed Randall's gaze. "Of course, the danger is that you can get too cloistered in a place like this, protected from the pressures of the world outside. At least, that's what some people think. That's why I like to be involved in so many activities beyond the palace walls."

"You don't approve of the Ivory Tower."

"No. Though I do approve of academic endeavour. I'd like to hear how your thesis is progressing, but that will have to keep for another time. We have other business this morning." He looked Randall straight in the eye. "I was going to ask you to come to see me anyway to discuss an important matter. Then, two days ago I received this letter." He passed it to Randall and sat back sipping coffee while he read it.

"They didn't tell me they were writing to you."

"Does it surprise you?"

"It would've been courteous to tell me about the letter, but its contents don't surprise me."

"On the face of it, Randall, there's been a breakdown in relations caused, among other things, by your unwillingness to spend the church fabric fund on school toilets. Is that a fair assessment?"

"Yes. I've tried to improve the church over the last three years or so and this is the latest cause of friction. It is on the surface a simple matter of my duty versus the desire of some people to protect their personal interests."

"To keep the school in the village without threat of closure."

"Exactly. There *is* no risk of closure. The education authority is quite clear about this, but the school governors are worried that things could change if there are any more cuts in the council's budget. Even if this happened, it would make no difference to my view. The building could become dangerous. It is my responsibility not to let that happen."

"You have my complete support on that matter."

"Thank you, Bishop." Randall waited.

"There is more to this than there seems, isn't there?"

"I suspect there is."

"Is it something you'd like to talk about?" Randall hesitated. "Something of a more … personal nature, perhaps?"

"There is nothing in my personal conduct that is remotely connected with the action of the parishioners who wrote that letter."

"That is what I expected," said the Bishop. "But I wanted to hear you say it. Tell me, if that's the case, *as* that is the case, what do you think is at the back of all this … unrest?"

Randall looked uncomfortable. He looked towards the windows and for the first time noticed the ticking of the long-case clock standing in the corner. "It's almost … I don't quite know how to put this … as if I'm being observed all the time ... watched ... judged ..."

"Not just because you decided to use a different prayerbook or order of service, you mean?"

"No. That may be part of it. But somehow it seems to be more deep-rooted, an animosity bordering on malevolence. I've even heard it said that there's a curse on the church." He looked up sharply "Sorry. This must all sound rather fanciful, as if I'm blaming the shades of the past."

"1645 and all that," said the Bishop with a smile.

Randall's face darkened. "Here," he said, "sitting in this room miles away, it seems totally far-fetched. But I'm telling you, Bishop, that there is in Knightly St John ... an atmosphere ... an undercurrent. There's a very real hostility in the air and it doesn't come only from a group of parishioners who want me to go back to the old prayerbook or spend church funds on the school."

"I thought you liked the village, Randall."

"I do. And I have no desire to leave it. Nor do I believe in ghosts." He smiled. "But I would be misleading you if I pretended that this was a simple matter."

"Yes. We are after all a broad church. I'm no stranger to that kind of controversy myself, as you know." Randall nodded at the recollection of the role played by the Bishop in the debate on the ordination of women. "In my position, Randall, what would you do?"

"I would like to think the Bishop might show support for the vicar, explaining his duty and responsibility to the church. But I suspect it may not be so easy as that."

The Bishop folded his arms and leaned back in the chair. "I must admit I'd like to get to the bottom of this strange atmosphere," he said softly. "It's been going on for too long. The killer of the vicar in the Civil War was never found, which in itself is not surprising. People keep quiet at such times. Reprisals ... recriminations ..." He waved a hand as if swatting a fly.

"The interesting thing," said Randall "is that you can read the transcriptions of evidence and the proceedings of that time. It's all held in the records in the County Archives. Everyone who gave an account seemed genuinely baffled by what had happened. Their words have an air of truth about them. I don't think anybody really *did* know who committed the crime."

"So the murderer was from outside the village? A soldier perhaps? A religious fanatic from an extreme sect?"

"The villagers thoroughly searched the whole building. No-one was found. No weapon. One detail is quite mystifying. It was a rainy night and only one set of footprints was found on the stairs of the tower where the vicar was killed."

"How can that be certain? Think of all the marks as everyone rushed up to catch the person responsible ..."

"It *is* quite certain," said Randall. "Two of the witnesses stated clearly that they waited at the foot of the stairs for a torch to be brought over. When it came, they saw only the one set of prints, those of the dead man. Because of that, they searched the rest of the church first, leaving two men to guard the tower. All the accounts of those who went up referred to them stepping over the splashes of blood. There were no other marks."

"How very curious." The Bishop steepled his fingers and stared ahead of him. "Come to think of it, even more curious is the fact that no-one confessed later to the crime."

"Yes ..."

"That is most odd. In those days death-bed confessions were common. Nobody wanted to die with something so heavy weighing on their conscience. It seems we shall never know." The Bishop looked up at the clock. "Randall, I must talk to you about other matters. I'm sorry to be brusque, but I have to leave in ten minutes to catch a train. Now, this is what I want to do ..." He leaned forward and as he did so, Randall thought he detected a gleam in the Bishop's eye.

❦   ❦   ❦   ❦

"If ever you decide to give up interior design, I'm sure you'd make an excellent teacher." The Head finished her coffee and put the cup down.

"I'll bear it in mind," said Marnie. "For the moment I think I might be able to continue earning an honest crust at the drawing board."

"Are you liking it here? It must be very different after the bright lights of London."

"It *is* different, but I seem to be just as busy. And I seem to be getting involved in things in ways that didn't arise in London."

"Villages can be like that. On the other hand there are some villages where you aren't accepted until you have three generations in the graveyard. Here, you're more likely to be invited to join the church flower rota."

"I've met the vicar," said Marnie. "But he wanted technical advice, not flowers."

"Technical advice?"

"Only about building matters ... the porch. There's a structural problem. I'm sure you know all about it."

"But that isn't *really* your field, is it?"

"No. He just wanted to be put in touch with an architect." The Head looked thoughtful. Marnie continued. "Mrs Giles, I don't normally discuss the affairs of a client with anyone else, but I thought this was common knowledge."

"Yes, of course. Don't worry. You haven't put your foot in it. It's just a slightly sensitive issue. There's a degree of bad feeling and it concerns the school to some extent."

"Well, I wouldn't wish to make matters worse."

"That would be hard to do. Things are bad enough as it is."

"That's a shame, because it *is* a fine old church."

"Yes. It's beautiful. But it has difficult associations."

"The Civil War."

"Among others." The Head drew in a deep breath and smiled. "But that's a long story."

Marnie stood up and held out her hand. "Thanks for coffee. I'll get everything ready for your visit to *Sally Ann*. I'm looking forward to it."

❦   ❦   ❦   ❦

"I'm on your side, Randall."

"The village won't see it that way, I think."

"But you know it."

"Yes. Thank you, Bishop. When do you have in mind for this ... change to take place?"

"For everyone's sake, I want it to go ahead without delay. That would be for the best. Now that I have your agreement, I'll reply to the letter immediately, explaining the first part of my action. I need another meeting with colleagues before I can confirm anything else." He looked up at the clock.

"If that will be all, Bishop, I know you have to be going."

"Thank you for coming to see me, Randall. We must have that talk about your thesis next time. I look forward to hearing about it." The vicar stood up and took the Bishop's hand. As soon as he had left the room, Rosemary Upton came in and gave the Bishop his papers for the London meeting and his rail tickets.

"You should make it to the station in good time, Bishop." She handed him a letter that he quickly read and signed.

"Thank you, Rosemary. I'd like it to go first class, please. I want it to reach Mr Stubbs as soon as possible."

※　※　※　※

Marnie walked from the school to the shop and crossed to the post office counter.

"I'd like to open a savings account."

"Saving up for Christmas?"

"It's not for me, actually, Richard. I shall pay this amount into it each week for the foreseeable future." She slid a note under the partition while the postmaster fished out the appropriate form.

"Very nice. In what name should the account be, then?"

"Anne Price. That's Anne with an 'e'."

Part 17

Thursday 22 June

Thursday 22 June was Midsummer's Day, but at eight-fifteen that morning it was cloudy enough for George Stubbs to wonder if it would be raining by lunchtime. He reversed the Range Rover out of the garage and pulled the door down. He turned to find the postman walking up the drive. They exchanged views on the weather as they had done on countless other mornings and Mr Stubbs asked Alan if he would like coffee. The offer was declined with thanks – "Got a big post today. I'll be on till lunchtime with this lot. Thanks all the same." On the top of the small pile of mail was a plain white envelope, typewritten and franked with an emblem comprising crossed keys and a mitre. Mr Stubbs went through to read his letters in the conservatory.

"Would you like coffee before you go, dear?" He looked up at his wife in the doorway while his thick thumb tore open the first envelope.

"No thanks, Sheila. I'll probably get one when I'm there. I just want to go through this lot to see if there's anything I need to attend to." First, the letter with the diocesan coat of arms. He had certainly not expected a reply so promptly and at once suspected that he would be fobbed off with a few sympathetic noncommittal phrases and a promise to keep an eye on the situation. His surprise increased as he quickly read down the page. He read the letter again, this time more slowly, studying every sentence carefully to make sure he was not missing something, and reached for the phone.

"Albert? It's George. I've had a reply from the Bishop. Listen." He read out the main points and the old man asked him to read it a second time. "I think it's good news," said George. "Better than we could have expected, really."

"Seems like it," said the old farmer. "However the bishop dresses it up, the vicar's been sacked. That's what it amounts to, isn't it?"

"Well, that bit about *'Mr Hughes will now be assuming wider responsibilities that have been under consideration in the diocese for some time'* could mean anything, I suppose."

"That's just to put a brave face on it. He's got the push and I reckon your letter did the trick."

"Thank you, Albert. It's almost too good to be true. Anyway, we've got him off our backs. That's the main thing."

"What's the next step?" said Albert. "Do we have to do anything? Call a meeting of the PCC, maybe?"

"I need to think about that. I'll give you a ring or drop by later. I've got to go to the constituency offices for a meeting this morning. Got to discuss fund raising. Bloody waste of time if you ask me. Get the policies right and we'll attract more members into the party. That's better than having to organise garden fêtes and the like."

"Garden fêtes?"

"Well, you know what I mean. God knows how we'll find the time."

"I'll tell you what," said Albert. "There's something I'd like to celebrate. We could do with a fête to bid good riddance to the vicar. 'Course, we'd not call it that officially, but everyone would know what it was really for."

"That's an idea." George liked the thought that his part in the action would be widely recognised. "I think this calls for a pig roast."

☙ ☙ ☙ ☙

"Walker and Co, good morning." Anne looked round towards Marnie's desk. "Yes, she is. Who's calling, please? ... I'll put you through." She pressed the 'hold' button. "It's Philip from London."

"Philip, hallo."

"You've got a switchboard and staff? This is impressive. Have I got through to the right department?" He chuckled.

"It's Anne. She's working with me for a time. So how are things?"

"Oh, you know, same as usual. Missing you, of course, but Faye's doing a good job. I thought I'd keep you up-to-date on your own contract. The builder can start almost at once. He's been delayed on another project and wants to bring yours forward."

"Excellent. What about building regs?"

"I spoke to the inspector yesterday. They're all happy at the council. We can get things moving."

"Thanks for all that. Actually, Philip, there is something I wanted to talk to you about. How good are you at medieval churches?"

"We haven't built any lately. What do you need?"

"The church here needs some structural work. The porch has never been properly keyed in."

"What do you mean, 'never'?"

"Since it was built, in 1380."

"If it's stood all that time, I shouldn't worry."

"But it was condemned as unsafe in 1937."

"There's a real sense of urgency in your part of the world! I'm impressed again."

"Any ideas?"

"I'll talk to Mike Thomas. Did you know he worked on York Minster? I'll get back to you."

Marnie told Anne about progress on the building works at Glebe Farm and Anne at once reached for a folder. Intrigued, Marnie sat and watched as Anne put a disk in the computer and began typing. She printed a page of text and put it into the folder inside a transparent plastic document holder.

"What's that you've got?" said Marnie. Anne held up the folder to reveal its label: PHASE 1 – COTTAGES 1 AND 2.

"I'm keeping a list of all the details about each part of the work. If you ever need them, you'll find your sketches in here as well." She revealed the contents of the folder. "I keep them on my building projects shelf next to my desk."

"You're amazingly well organised."

"I did a project at school in business studies: planning the efficient office."

"I bet you got an 'A' for the coursework," said Marnie, unable to prevent herself grinning. Anne stuck out her tongue, closed the folder and returned it to its place on the shelf.

❦   ❦   ❦   ❦

At about seven that evening, while supper was cooking, Marnie returned to the office to finish off some jobs. She heard the phone ringing as she approached the barn.

"What's this, knocking off early? Half day is it?"

"No, Philip, we always have a break about now to get the cows in for milking."

"Naturally. Well, I spoke to Mike about your church. He's quite keen, but he's up to his eyeballs in Docklands just now. How urgent is it?"

"I doubt if it's going to collapse overnight."

"That's what I told him. Look, if Mike comes up to see the building, could you keep an eye on the work once it starts? It shouldn't take too much time."

"Sure."

"Good. I'll get Mike to arrange a meeting."

"Tell him I'll put the kettle on."

❦   ❦   ❦   ❦

Friday 23 June

On the Friday morning, soon after eight, the vicar was in his study printing out the notes for his Sunday sermon, when he heard the post drop through the letterbox. He dropped the special offers into the waste paper basket without opening them. Among the remaining letters was the unmistakable Sunday-best stationery of the Bishop. Most of the mail sent out from the palace was in plain white envelopes bought cheaply by the ton. This was the good quality version made of white vellum with the emblem of the diocese on the reverse flap, the kind used only for important communications.

"... *I would therefore like to confirm your appointment as Rural Dean of Brackley with effect from the first of July. In view of the immediate availability of your successor as vicar of Knightly St John, I propose that the new incumbent should commence duties without delay ...*"

The Bishop concluded by wishing him well in his new appointment and also with his doctoral thesis. This would be the first post for the new vicar, who had been ordained a year ago and was currently serving as curate in another part of the diocese. It was an opportunity for a fresh start for all concerned.

Part 18

The men assembled by the front of the house at the end of the lane on other nights. Sarah Anne would hear them and lie restlessly waiting for further movement until they were away. If her sisters heard the sound, they did not leave their beds and only spoke of the incident in the morning when they were alone together. Nothing was said in the presence of their mother. It was the third or fourth time of lying in wait that the commotion happened.

Sarah knew the men were below, huddling for shelter from the rain, and was dozing off when the sudden sound brought her back to consciousness. A tinder striking. Movement. A clatter of tools. By the time she reached the window, the lane was bright with the light of torches crackling and flaring. The men were hurrying away down the path. She saw the shadows changing shape as the torches lit the wall of the churchyard, reflecting in puddles. The whole lane was glowing.

Without a second thought, Sarah hastened as quietly as she could out of the bedroom, pulling on her shoes and shawl, pushing back the hair from her face so that it hung down over her shoulders. Tonight with the rain falling steadily, there was no moon to light the way, but she saw the flickering torches now gathered at the church door, saw them go in ahead of her, heard the clamour of voices, shouting, calling out. Then suddenly hushed. She ran along the church path and in through the open door.

The men were grouped by the altar near the base of the tower, speaking in urgent whispers. Sarah pulled the door shut behind her and began to walk down the centre aisle. Suddenly the men turned, seeing her approach.

"Go out, Sarah!" one of them called and left the group to come towards her. "You should not be here. You must leave now." Behind him, the group split, men hurrying in all directions, searching behind the altar, among the pews, in the vestry, everywhere. One or two remained at the door to the tower, their attention taken with something out of her sight. The man tried to turn her away, back to the door, but Sarah slipped free and ran past him before he could stop her. The men in the doorway did not hear her until she had reached them. She looked beyond them into the tower stairwell and gasped. The men turned towards her, their faces red in the torchlight, desolate.

"You have killed him!" she cried. "You have killed the vicar! Oh my god! What have you done?" She stepped back and slumped against the altar, faint with shock, her hand at her throat.

"Not us, Sarah," said one of the men. "This was not our doing. We found him like this. There has been murder here, but we did not do it." All over the church the men were hunting. As she stood by the altar two of them came down the stairs, each carrying a heavy knife and a torch. They shook their heads, bewildered.

Sarah leaned on the stone altar, her hand resting on the embroidered cloth. She closed her eyes but could not shut out the sight of the vicar sprawled at the foot of the steps, could not shut out the sight of the blood.

"As God is my witness," said the man by the door, coming to support Sarah, "here in His house, I declare we are innocent of this crime!"

"Then who here has done this thing?" said Sarah. "Where is the murderer?"

"It is the work of the Devil," said the man slowly. At the sound of his voice, the men stopped their search and one by one knelt on the stone floor, each man crossing himself in the old way.

☙ ☙ ☙ ☙

Saturday 24 June

Marnie walked up the field track with a spring in her step late on Saturday morning, clutching the vicar's thick building file. Her morning's work in the office was done and she was going to check out the structure of the church before calling in at the pub for lunch. It had already been a busy day. The Glebe Farm rush hour had started at around eight when she drove Anne and Ralph up to the main road to the bus stop. Anne was going home for the weekend, travelling to Dunstable. Ralph had to get back to Oxford and would travel as far as the bus station in Milton Keynes where he would change to a coach. Marnie's offers to take them at least part of the way had been gratefully declined and she found herself with a morning to spend as she chose.

She had rung her sister and suggested that Beth and Paul visit her in the near future. Jane Rutherford had told her the latest gossip in Little Venice and Marnie was surprised at how far away it all seemed. Mrs Jolly had read about the problems at the church in a newspaper article sent to her by an old friend who lived in Towcester. She warned Marnie how easy it was in a small community to be drawn into other people's conflicts.

Marnie wanted no part of the dispute and only wished to have the church repairs put in hand so that she could continue to get on with her own life, which was complicated enough for her liking. That morning she was content to enjoy the firm soil beneath her feet and the smell of the fresh country air that she took in great breaths. She was exultant, stimulated and confident about the present and the future. She wanted to laugh out loud and shout to the breeze that this was *her* time and this was *her* place. Whatever awaited her, she had this moment and she gloried in it.

It was the archetype of an English village church. Built in honey-coloured stone, standing on slightly raised ground, with yews planted in the graveyard, its tall square tower dominated the village and could be seen as a distant landmark for miles around. From the canal it confused and amused the traveller, appearing first on one side, then on the other, staying in view for long before and after passing the village itself. Marnie stood at the gate to take in the general impression. The stonework was merely pointed with thick mortar at the place where the porch joined the main structure. At that moment the door opened and Molly Appleton stepped out, stooping to tuck a bunch of dead flowers into a black plastic bag lying on the floor, she glanced up and caught sight of Marnie.

"I was just on my way to see you to collect the key." Marnie walked down the path.

"My routine's out of joint this week," said Molly. "I usually do the flowers on Friday, but my sister in London's about to have an operation and I've been getting ready to go down there these past few days."

"I'm sorry," said Marnie. "Can I do anything to help?"

"Oh that's all right. I've just got to finish doing these. Did you want to get in?"

"If that's convenient. The vicar wants work done and I need to familiarise myself with the building." Marnie realised she might be saying the wrong thing, but Molly did not react.

"Yes. He did say he'd asked you to find an architect. This is the part that needs attention, isn't it? Looks solid enough to me … but then, I'm no expert."

"Shall I just wander about and let you get on with the flowers? I don't want to hold you up."

"Oh yes," said Molly. "Take your time. I'll be a little while yet." She pushed open the door and went back into the church. Marnie checked the porch inside and out and found herself agreeing with Molly Appleton. It certainly did not appear to be on the brink of collapse. She sat on the bench and read through the papers in the file. It became clear that the vicar himself had been far from convinced of the need for the remedial works. All the pressure seemed to come from the diocesan surveyor, who was being over-scrupulous for fear of contravening the latest health and safety regulations. The vicar had no choice. Marnie read one of the letters written three months earlier.

"... and so I must reluctantly *accept that the porch has to be given priority on the grounds of safety, though my own preference would be to carry out a survey of the tower, which seems to be in greater need of maintenance ..."*

She stood up and went into the church, pushing the door quietly shut behind her and standing still for a few moments, as she always did, to take in the atmosphere. Flowers had been arranged around the altar and the pulpit, roses, delphiniums, irises. The air was fresh with their scent, overlaid with the pale damp smell of foliage. Molly Appleton came out of the vestry at a quick pace, her footsteps resounding in a staccato click-clack, click-clack on the stone floor. Marnie began walking up the centre aisle towards the tower, while Molly knelt down and wiped away the water that had dripped onto the flagstones.

Access to the tower was by a small arched door. It opened easily on smooth hinges to reveal a lobby leading to the stone steps curving away. Marnie imagined the body of the dead vicar lying at the foot of those same steps all those long years ago. There were streaks of brown running down the stairs and in the half-light she could almost mistake them for blood, though she knew they were natural markings in the sandstone and ironstone. Crossing the lobby, she advanced up the first few steps.

The staircase wound round the corner in a steep spiral and Marnie walked up until she came to a window, a source of light not much more than a narrow glazed slit widening out to a deep sill. She was barely tall enough to see through it. All that was visible was the sky and the top branches of a tree. She decided to climb a short way further, treading cautiously on the worn stone. The air smelled musty and the gloom was relieved by another slit. A dozen or so steps later she could see ahead of her a small landing and guessed that it led into the chamber where the bell-ropes hung. Deciding to make this the limit of her climb, she went up, expecting to find a doorway, but it was just a landing. There was no window-slit and it was dark and cramped. The innermost wall was made of wood and Marnie suspected it had something to do with the bell-ropes or perhaps the clock. She could not tell how high she had reached.

As her eyes became accustomed to the half-light, Marnie stepped forward and examined the walls, running her fingers across the stonework to the point where the timber began. It was a close fit, a partition of ancient darkened wood, still sound and firm after centuries. The stonework around the wood was not as smoothly finished as the other walls, though it was too dark to inspect without better light. This was presumably why greater care had not been taken. Few people would ever come to this dark place.

Suddenly Marnie thought she heard a voice or the sigh of the breeze, and she could not tell whether the sound came to her from above or below. She listened. It came again, a faint echo in the air. Marnie decided to go down, carefully treading from step to step. Soon she could see the foot of the staircase and at the bottom she looked up the way she had come. There was something wrong about this place. For a second or two she stood frowning thoughtfully on the last step and as she turned to continue on her way, the tower door was pushed further open and Molly Appleton looked through, her mouth wide, her eyes staring.

"Hallo," said Marnie. "Everything all right? You look as if you'd seen a ghost."

Molly breathed in deeply. "I was calling you. Didn't know where you were."

"I'm sorry. I didn't hear you. Or at least, it wasn't clear. Have I held you up?"

Marnie went over and put a hand on her shoulder. "You've gone quite pale. Why not sit down for a moment? Can I get you some water?"

"No, no thanks. I'm okay. I must get back." She pulled the tower door shut. "Have you seen all you needed to see? I thought you were just going to look at the porch."

"I was, but in the file there was a reference to the tower, so I thought I'd just check it out while I was here."

Outside the church the air was warm. Molly locked the door and fastened the grill to the porch. They walked down the path and turned up the road together.

"Are you sure you're feeling all right?"

"I'm fine now. What did you think to the porch, then?"

"Looked sound enough to me. In fact, it looks as if the vicar thought so, too. All the pressure came from outside."

"Are you sure about that?" said Molly. "I've been in all the PCC meetings and the vicar always insisted the porch had to be done."

"Well, I've read the file. The office gave him no choice." They walked on a few steps in silence and Marnie added: "Do you know anything about the tower?"

Molly stopped abruptly. "What do you mean? I never go near it."

"Just the structure. I mean, had anyone talked about it needing repair?"

Molly thought about it. "Nothing that I can recall." They resumed their walk.

"Is there any reason why you never go near it? It isn't unsafe as far as I can judge."

"Oh, you know what it's like in a village ... superstition ... fairy stories. All my life I've heard things about the tower and the murdered vicar. I just don't like to go anywhere near it. People say it's unlucky."

"What about the bell-ringers? They have to go up to get to the ropes."

"Yes. But there's a crowd of them and they usually take a pack of beer. It would take more than a ghost story to scare that lot!" She laughed. "That reminds me. Are you coming to the pig-roast on Saturday?"

"I didn't know there was one."

"Only just been arranged. A notice went up in the shop this morning. It'll be nice for you and Anne, if you're around next weekend." They separated at the corner and Marnie crossed the road to the pub. A pig-roast, she thought. Anne will love that ...

Marnie read through the file over her ploughman's lunch. Something about the church still bothered her and she stopped at the gate on her way home to look up at the tower. She did not notice someone standing in the churchyard half-hidden by a yew tree until he turned towards her. It was Frank Day.

"Marnie! This is a pleasant surprise."

"Hallo. Visiting your ancestors?"

"No. Just rounding up Cassius and Bruno. They've chased a squirrel round to the other side." He eyed the file that she was clutching. "I suspect the church is locked, but you can get a key from the shop if you want to go in. I'm assuming your visit is professional rather than casual."

"I've already been inside once today. I just wanted to look at the tower in passing."

"It's a fine edifice, though it has a lugubrious past. You know all about that, I expect."

"Do you know the tower, Frank, from the inside?"

He hesitated and glanced round at it. "Yes ... yes, I've been in on one or two occasions." The two black Labradors came bounding up and circled their master, sniffing at the headstones. He snapped his fingers and pointed at the ground and they sprawled out on the grass in the shade of the tree.

"Do you know the landing about halfway up?" said Marnie. "It has a wall of dark timber, probably oak I would say."

"It would be oak in these parts," he said.

"Do you know what purpose it serves?"

"Yes. Or to be accurate, it serves no real purpose. It was put in at the start of the seventeenth century ... a wealthy benefactor paid for a new clock."

"Trying to curry favour with the church?" Marnie suggested.

"Probably. Those were difficult times. Up until then the clock was only a simple mechanism that struck the hour. They took it out and replaced it with the clock you see today, with a face and hands. Very modern for its time."

"And the wooden partition?"

"It covered the place where the old mechanism hung. The new clock was higher up so that the face could be put on the end wall."

"Of course," said Marnie. "There was no need to have access at that level so they boarded it in."

"It would have been a matter of great local pride in its day," said Frank. "No expense spared. The church was the centre of everyone's life."

"Thanks. You've solved my mystery." She smiled.

"A pleasure." He bowed his head.

"You're very knowledgeable about it all. It's funny, there was one thing I couldn't quite put my finger on ..."

"What's that?" said Frank. For a moment he was distracted as one of the dogs leapt up and bounded off. He whistled and it slowed down to turn and jog back, returning to have its ears fondled before flopping down again beside its brother.

"To be honest, I'm not entirely sure," said Marnie. "There's something at the back of my mind that I can't dredge up. You just reminded me of it ..." She frowned and shook her head.

"It'll probably come to light just as you're about to go to sleep."

"Yes. It's frustrating. It's just that there can't be many people who know the sort of detail that you obviously know."

"Probably not. But you see, it was my family ... my *ancestors* as you put it ... who paid to have the work carried out."

"They were the benefactors?"

"That's right." By now the dogs were growing restless, unhappy to remain laid out under the tree. They jumped to their feet and stood expectantly looking up at their master, heads canting to one side and then the other.

"Not much doubt about the message there," said Marnie.

"I'm always being dragged off when I see you," said Frank smiling. "It's nothing personal. You must come over and have a meal with us. It'll be more relaxing."

"Thanks. I'd like that. Perhaps you can finish telling me the story about the gamekeeper's cottage?" Frank looked blank.

"Gamekeeper's cottage?"

"Yes. You started to tell me about it. In the forest near Northampton ... an old couple, worried about 'the visitor' ... remember?"

"Oh that ... yes ... oh, that's nothing much. I shouldn't really go on about such things. Too boring. Sometimes it's better to leave the past behind, I think. We go on too much about that time in these parts. Probably best forgotten."

"If you say so," said Marnie.

"It's just that they had this visitor ... a Cavalier officer, quite old, with a grey beard, bleeding from his wounds. He used to walk through the house some evenings and go upstairs. Rather disconcerting." Frank called the dogs and set off across the churchyard. Marnie watched them, wondering where they were going as they headed towards the hedge on the far side. There was no indication of a break, no door or gateway. Mysteries, murders, ghosts ... so restful, the country life, she thought.

"Now that's no way for a pretty young thing to be spending her time!" The voice came from behind Marnie and she turned to find George Stubbs and Albert Fletcher standing at the gate. She smiled at them and glanced back over her shoulder. Frank Day and the dogs had vanished. "You shouldn't have to loiter all alone in the graveyard, young lady." It was George Stubbs who spoke, with a smile some way down the scale from a leer, but Marnie had to make a determined effort to conceal her irritation.

"It's a kind of professional visit," she said, indicating the thick file. "The porch needs maintenance work doing." The two men narrowed their eyes.

"By order of the vicar?" said Mr Stubbs.

"Not really," said Marnie. "By order of the diocesan surveyor." They looked doubtful.

"And there I was thinking you had a tryst," said Mr Stubbs.

"In the graveyard on a Saturday afternoon?" said Marnie, raising a quizzical eyebrow. They laughed. "Actually, I was talking to someone. Frank Day ... taking his dogs for a walk."

"*Him*," said Albert Fletcher. Marnie wondered if it was safe to talk about anything or anyone without treading on somebody's toes. She had a sudden feeling of sympathy for the vicar and a recollection of Mrs Jolly telling her of the complexities of village life.

"I found his firm very efficient when I moved up from London." She tried to sound matter-of-fact.

"Oh yes ... I've no doubt he runs a good company," said Mr Stubbs.

"I have the impression that half this conversation is eluding me," said Marnie. Her words were uttered more pointedly than she intended. George Stubbs glanced at Albert Fletcher. It was the older man who replied.

"Frank Day is not part of this village and should stop pushing his nose in where it's not welcome." These words were definitely uttered as pointedly as they were intended, causing Mr Stubbs to look uncomfortable. Marnie, on the other hand, was beginning to find it interesting.

"I thought his family *were* locals," she said. "Been here for centuries."

"Depends what you call 'local'," said Mr Fletcher.

"Oh, I know what 'local' means," said Marnie.

"It might mean something different in the country, compared with what you're used to," said the old man, the annoyance gone from his voice.

"I suspect Albert is right," put in George Stubbs with a smile. "We have different ways out in the sticks." He chuckled. "It's not like London."

"No," said Marnie. "In London, 'local' usually means someone who had gone to school in the area. It's not a bad rule-of-thumb definition when you think about it."

"And what do you think it would mean up here?" asked Mr Stubbs.

"That's easy," said Marnie. "Or at least, I always thought it was easy until now. A local is someone who has three generations or more buried in the churchyard." Mr Stubbs guffawed and even Albert Fletcher managed a smile.

"You'll do, young lady, you'll do!" said Mr Stubbs heartily. Marnie tried not to wince. She clutched the file firmly to her chest and stepped towards the gate. Mr Stubbs pushed it open for her, beaming broadly, and the two men stood aside. "Always a pleasure to see you, my dear. You're definitely a local in my book." He chuckled again and Marnie smiled at the compliment, despite her inclination to throw up. "That reminds me," Mr Stubbs added. "Albert and I are organising a celebration on Saturday of next week."

"The pig-roast?" said Marnie.

"So, you're on the old bush telegraph already ... proves you're a local!" said

Mr Stubbs. "I hope that means you're planning to be there."

"I'll check the diary."

"Good. We'll look forward to seeing you then. I'm sure it'll be an evening to remember."

🌹   🌹   🌹   🌹

From force of habit Marnie looked in on the office to check the answerphone when she got back. A two was glowing in the messages box.

"Hi Marnie!" It was Beth. "We were thinking about your invitation. We know you're a workaholic and it would do you good to have a break. So why not give us a ring and we'll fix a date?"

The second message came as a surprise. "Hallo, it's Ralph. Sorry for the short notice, but I've arrived back to find that there's a lunch here tomorrow and I wonder if you'd like to join me. I thought you might like to see All Saints. Could you possibly give me a ring and let me know?" He gave the number of the porter's lodge. "Oh, by the way, it's high table and moderately formal, but quite pleasant. Hope you can make it. Bye now!"

Marnie crossed to the wardrobe that stood concealed at the back of the office. She selected a Liberty print dress in silk and a short fitted linen jacket in natural colour, and sniffed them for any trace of the diesel tang that clung to every item of clothing that had been on *Sally Ann*. All clear. She rang the college and left a message for Ralph.

Next, she dialled a familiar number. "I got your message, Beth. Look, there's a village event next Saturday. Fancy coming up for it?"

"What is it? Human sacrifice on the altar or annual gathering of witches' coven?"

"That sort of thing," said Marnie. "Probably, a bit of both. It's a pig roast."

"How medieval," said Beth. "Will there be an archery contest and jousting?"

"Probably not, just burning a few heretics and virgins, I expect."

"Sounds great! We'll be there."

Part 19

Sarah and her mother finished their work alone. Mrs Lockyer had stayed in the vicarage with much wailing and tears. They had laid the vicar in the side chapel to wash and lay out his body. Neither had spoken while they prepared him, but both had seen the terrible wound in his chest, both had seen the awful expression of shock and agony in his face. Sarah had closed his eyes and mouth, washing the blood from his hair. Too numb to speak, too stunned even to feel, she had held back the nausea with a shudder, knowing that later she would have to give vent to her despair.

Sighing, Sarah's mother set herself down on a bench, elbows resting on her knees, staring at the floor, leaving her daughter to finish covering the body with a linen shroud. Under his head she placed a cushion, not wanting to leave him lying back on the hard table. Finally, Sarah lifted each arm and laid his hands together on his chest on top of the shroud. She silently wished him to rest in peace, asking herself if she would ever know peace again, if the village would ever recover from the horror of this act of murder. She looked down at the body now lying in repose, the face calm and pale, all emotion drained away. She looked down at his hands, crossed flat on his chest, his beautiful hands.

❦ ❦ ❦ ❦

Sunday 25 June

It was just before eleven that Sunday morning in late June that the Reverend Randall Hughes mounted the steps of the pulpit to give his last sermon. There was a stillness in the air, as if the congregation was watching him ascend the scaffold to be executed, having been condemned by their testimony. He placed his notes on the lectern and looked down with a smile at the upturned faces. He let his gaze roam over the whole assembly before speaking, pleased to see how full the church was, recalling the dwindling band of the faithful who had been regulars at the time of his arrival in the village. Nowadays, every service was attended by large numbers, many of them drawn by his magnetism, even if some were suspicious of his views and theology.

"My dear friends, my brothers and sisters, it is with a mixture of joy and sadness that I must tell you that this will be my last celebration of Holy Communion with you as your vicar." A murmur spread among the congregation. "It is three and a half years since I came to be among you." The biblical, almost messianic words, made some feel uncomfortable, as if he had edged close to blasphemy. "Now the time has come for me to move on to another calling and for reasons of which we are all aware, the Bishop has decided that it should take effect immediately. I want to thank you for many kindnesses shown to me throughout my ministry and I will think back with great affection on my days here. I must now leave you and I confess that this move has come sooner than I would have expected. However, the time has come for me to accept new challenges ..."

In the second row, Albert Fletcher leaned forward to whisper in the ear of George Stubbs. "Anyone would think he'd been promoted instead of sacked!" Without turning, Mr Stubbs acknowledged the words with a nod. The vicar noticed the movement below him.

"I spoke of my sadness at leaving Knightly St John, but I also spoke of a sense of joy. This is because I have been asked by our Bishop to assume greater responsibility. He has invited me to become ... the Rural Dean of Brackley and I am sure you will understand how honoured I feel to be asked to take on this role, for it is a great challenge at this stage in my career." A sound resembling a cough, or perhaps a gasp, was heard by everyone in the church. It appeared to come from the second row.

"In asking you to reflect for a moment on the many happy times we have enjoyed together, I would ask you also to look forward to the coming of your new vicar. It is not possible for me to tell you the vicar's name on this occasion, because the Bishop is only now making the necessary arrangements for transfer, but I am sure you will be able to create a good relationship, working together for the benefit of the whole community. For you all, it will be a new beginning and you will be much in my thoughts and prayers in the weeks and months to come ..."

        ❦   ❦   ❦   ❦

While Randall Hughes was addressing the congregation, a dark blue Rover drew up outside. Marnie got out of the car and walked through the gate into the churchyard, taking care not to catch her light linen jacket against the stone wall. She had left time en route to Oxford to stop off and find the gate that Frank Day and his dogs had taken to leave the churchyard the previous afternoon. Marnie looked up at the tower as she picked her way among the graves, its massive bulk seeming to fill the sky above her. She came to the hedge that formed the boundary on the far side and walked along until it gave way to reveal a stone wall about two metres high in which was set a small arched gate. She tried the handle. It opened easily and she stepped through to discover a path in a clump of bushes, leading towards an area of open grass and a small development of a dozen or so modern executive houses. It was the first time she had seen them or even known of their existence. On a sign she read 'Martyrs Close'.

She wondered who the martyr, or martyrs, had been, not trusting the punctuation on a road sign to reveal one or the other. Perhaps it was the patron saint of the church. Was Saint John a martyr? A great many saints had been martyred. It was one of the qualifications for the job, she thought. Or was it a reference to some local person or people, put to the stake in the time of Bloody Mary? Marnie was unsure whether she really wanted to know after all.

In the background she heard the organ start up and she paused, trying to recognise the hymn. Now an agnostic, she had in her childhood attended Sunday school and family services at church and still hummed the more familiar hymns while pottering about on Sunday mornings with the radio playing.

As she stood there, something caught her attention. In among the brambles she noticed what she first took to be part of the wall dislodged from the rest. It was the curved outline of the stone and its lighter colour that led her to it. Almost completely hidden among the bushes, was a headstone marking a grave *outside* the churchyard. Marnie picked her way carefully round the thorny brambles until she could see it plainly. She bent down to pull the brambles aside.

The name surprised her. It seemed to be '*Sally Ann*', but as she inspected the stone more closely, running her fingers over the soft washed away surface, she found it read 'Sarah Anne' and she muttered "Anne with an 'e'," to herself. Little remained of the inscription: "... *memorie of Sarah Anne Day, belov'd daughter of Jonathan* ..." Day! One of Frank's ancestors. Marnie bent forward, trying to feel the almost invisible words through her fingertips. "... *departed this life* ... *45* ..." She ran her hand further down the face of the stone. It was no good. Everything else was worn away. Marnie shook her head and went back to the car. She had no more time to spare.

Marnie wondered how Sarah Anne Day had died. Female mortality was high in those days, especially in childbirth. But if she died with the same name as her parents, she could not have been married. She reached the car and got in. Beside her on the front passenger seat lay the *Observer*, its main headlines proclaiming another explosion in Northern Ireland. Her thoughts returned to the gravestone. A strange coincidence that her name should be virtually the same as the boat's ... and that she had died in the same year as the vicar had been murdered, assuming that the '*45*' referred to 1645.

With that thought, Marnie pulled herself back to the twentieth century, switched on the ignition, pushed a tape into the cassette player and engaged first gear.

🌱　🌱　🌱　🌱

The side access to All Saints took some time to locate in a narrow side street. She discovered a courtyard filled with cars and a single empty space displaying a sign: Reserved – M. Walker.

Ralph was already approaching from a double arched doorway as Marnie got out and took stock of her surroundings. At a distance of about twenty metres, Ralph was confronted by a young man in shirt sleeves and slacks. Marnie walked towards them and caught one or two words in an American accent. "... your views on the 'McDonalds culture' ... its wider relevance to the countries of the Pacific Rim ..." Ralph was nodding thoughtfully and suddenly looked up as if he had noticed Marnie for the first time. The young man turned to look over his shoulder at Marnie.

"Oh, pardon me. I see you have a visitor, Professor Lombard." Ralph smiled. "Well, I look forward to hearing your summing up this evening. I just wanted to say how much I admire your work, sir." With that the young man walked quickly away. Ralph raised his eyebrows and smiled at Marnie.

"Believe me, it's wonderful to see you." He kissed her on both cheeks.

"I take that in the spirit in which it's meant. Thank you. It's nice to be here. I see you have an admirer, Ralph."

"Yes." There was a slight weariness in the tone. "I like America and Americans. They've always been very good to me, but there is a certain style ..."

"Earnest?" suggested Marnie.

"Quite. Let's go to the Common Room and get a glass of something before lunch." They went through the doorway and Ralph guided her across a lobby and along a cloister beside a small lawned courtyard. It was a cross between a stately home and the House of Lords, far removed from Marnie's own experience of college life at art school in London. No messy piles of work being put together for display, no paint-flecked walls. Here all was order and calm, elegance and decorum.

"What was that about 'Professor'? Have you been promoted?"

"No. Every university teacher is called that in America. I'm not likely to get a chair while this government has a say in it."

"Do they have so much influence in such matters?"

"They do *here*. We have a few retired cabinet ministers at this college. No-one is in any doubt about my views."

"I didn't realise you were regarded as such a subversive," said Marnie lightly.

"I'm not. But they regard anyone who has an open mind as not being ideologically sound. 'If you're not with us, you're against us'. They're as bad as the Marxists!" He laughed gently.

"And the ... what was it? ... the 'McDonalds culture'? What's that?"

"Oh, it was just a throw-away comment I made on the emerging free market economies of eastern Europe. You can tell when they've become developed by the arrival of the fast food places on the high streets."

"The old Soviet bloc countries have changed into a strange mixture," said Marnie.

"Very," said Ralph. "I wanted to subtitle this seminar: 'Old McDonalds had a collective farm'!" They went into a book-lined room, large and filled with arm chairs like a London club, with views onto a small garden abundant with pink roses. Groups of men and women were talking in quiet voices, some of them glancing over to acknowledge Ralph, others discreetly appraising Marnie without making it obvious. They were offered sherry and went to sit by a window.

"Very civilised," said Marnie. She sipped the sherry. It was chilled and very dry. "Do you live here all the time?"

"Not all the time. I have a cottage outside Oxford ... place called Murton. It's by the river ... very pretty, a quiet spot. I think of it as home."

"And you have All Saints as well," said Marnie.

"Yes, very privileged," said Ralph. He sipped his sherry. "Lunch will be in the main dining room with all the seminar participants. We'll be sitting on high table with the Master and four other Fellows. I think you'll find it quite agreeable. The Master is looking forward to meeting you."

They were invited to move into the dining room where grace was said in Latin. No-one sat until the Master took his place. Almost immediately Ralph introduced Marnie to the Master who shook her hand warmly. He had a handsome if rather fleshy face, with eyes twinkling behind gold-framed spectacles and a thick mane of white hair. His voice had the gentlest trace of a Welsh accent.

"I believe you are to blame for Ralph's conversion, Mrs Walker." Marnie glanced at Ralph who smiled faintly. "Forgive me. I'm being obtuse. I am referring to his new passion for canals and narrowboats."

"I stand guilty as charged," said Marnie. She sat back in her chair to be served with fresh asparagus and accepted a glass of Sancerre. She was beginning to think she could become accustomed to the academic life. Ralph, seated on her right, inclined his head towards her.

"I chose the menu with you in mind," he said quietly. "I hope you'll find it to your liking."

"You've made a good start." She noticed a printed menu standing in a silver holder in front of her. The main course was poached wild salmon, with fresh raspberries for dessert. She turned to Ralph. "How did you know?"

"That this was your ideal menu? It was mentioned at our first meal together soon after we met ... also in Oxford." Marnie thought back to that evening the previous summer. Ralph continued. "I think you were trying to change the subject to something more agreeable than individual troubles." Marnie smiled and returned her attention to the Master, who raised his glass towards her.

"Welcome to All Saints, Mrs Walker." They sipped the Sancerre. "It's surprising," the Master said. "Everybody in Oxford knows the Isis and the Cherwell, but few ever think of the canal. Ralph describes it as a secret world. I'm sure he's right. Did you know it's only a short walk from here?"

As they started on the asparagus, Ralph said. "I thought we might take a stroll in that direction after lunch, if you agree. It really is just a short step away."

❦   ❦   ❦   ❦

Just a short walk from the Grand Union Canal near Leighton Buzzard, Sunday lunch was in progress under the bower in the garden.

"Mum, this is delicious. My favourite." Anne admired the salmon on her fork before popping it into her mouth.

"Good. I thought it would make a change. Are you able to cook properly on the boat?"

"Oh yes. It's easy in the summer. We just hope at least one of the cottages will be ready before winter sets in." Anne noticed her parents exchanging glances.

"Your mum and I were wanting to speak to you about the future," said Geoff.

Anne looked down to cut through a piece of broccoli before speaking. "I'm not sure I know what to say until the exam results come out."

"No. That's right. But you know we'll do the best we can for you." Anne looked across the table at her brother Richard, two years older and struggling to get a permanent job. Since leaving school he had been on two government schemes, a course at the local college and picked up seasonal work when he could find it. His main hope was to try to get a job with the big car and lorry factories around Luton and Dunstable, but it felt as if there was a queue a mile long for every vacancy.

"If you get good results ..." Jackie began.

"I could carry on working with Marnie for a year, like you agreed with her. And if I don't, ... perhaps I could do evening classes to improve my grades."

"It's working out okay with Marnie?" said Geoff.

"Brilliant. She gives me a small income as well as all my keep. *And* I'm getting good hands-on experience."

"*Hands-on,*" Geoff repeated. "That's good."

"She's all right, your Marnie," said Richard. "A godsend, really." Anne felt her stomach churn. Just let's wait and see what the exam results are like, she thought, pronging a piece of salmon.

❦   ❦   ❦   ❦

After lunch, Marnie and Ralph stood for a few moments in the quadrangle. With the sun washing over the cream stone, the old college buildings looked like a watercolour painting. The scent from a climbing rose mixed in the air with the smell of the freshly trimmed lawn.

Marnie sighed with pleasure. "Cotswold architecture and country house gardens ... that's why Oxford is one of the world's great places."

"I expect you're wondering why anyone would want to have a sabbatical away from all this," said Ralph.

"Fine buildings don't make life easier," said Marnie. "Nobody could understand why I wanted to give up a smart flat in London to live in a ruin. Anyway, you want to come back here, don't you?"

"That's my intention. Unless the book so outrages public opinion, or more likely *private* opinion, that I'm drummed out of the establishment."

"Or drummed out *by* the establishment, as you might put it," said Marnie.

Ralph offered her his arm. "Let's go for that walk."

They walked through the gate of All Saints. The centre of Oxford was thronging with visitors. There were Japanese tourists forming up for photographs and boisterous Italians irreverently clinging to railings. There were families with at least one parent reminiscing about their student days and solitary walkers intently taking photographs of the architecture. Marnie and Ralph left behind the university precincts and made their way through to Jericho, with its small Victorian terraced houses in quiet streets leading down to the canal.

"It's another world, this part of Oxford," said Marnie. "I wonder how many people even know it exists."

"Or the canal, come to that," said Ralph. "The Master was right."

"You seem to have transported your own college onto the canal," said Marnie.

"It's a good place to think. And you are in the process of creating your own world, too, at Glebe Farm. Are you enjoying it as much as you thought you would?"

"It's wonderful. Very satisfying. At least, it will be once we get started on the rebuilding works."

They turned into a small road leading to the gates of the boatyard where they had first met. "Any news of the unsolved murder?" said Ralph.

"Well … it's strange … but there's something odd about the tower. I can't quite work out what it is." They walked through the gates of the boatyard. All was quiet. There were boats moored on their side of the canal and a few drawn up on the opposite bank beside the towpath.

"Odd in what way?" said Ralph. "Is it the atmosphere or something physical?"

"That's just it. I ask myself if I'm reacting to a feeling because I know what happened there. On the other hand, there is definitely something not right about it. I almost identified it the other day, but it slipped away. It probably sounds crazy."

"That's the last word I could think of to describe you, Marnie, especially standing here." They had come to a halt by the edge of the canal. It was almost exactly where they had talked on the morning after Marnie had pulled Ralph out of the water.

"Why have we come here?" said Marnie.

"Just for a walk. Just to see the canal and a few boats … an interest we have in common."

"We all seem to be laying ghosts at the moment," said Marnie. She turned to face him. "Look, Ralph. What happened that night was in the past. Only you and I know about it. I've never brought it up again and I never will. I know you're the great thinker, but my advice to you is to let it go."

"Good God," he muttered. "Do you mean you're *actually* trying to think and you don't even have the basic qualification – a doctorate in philosophy? What ever next?!"

"I'd thump you, if I wasn't a lady," said Marnie wagging a finger under his nose.

"Ah, resorting to violence. The last refuge of the unthinking classes!"

Grinning, Marnie grabbed him by the arms. "It's definitely not too late to throw you back in!"

"There's someone behind you," he muttered between clenched teeth.

"You can't fool me with that old trick." She leant forward and kissed him on the lips.

"Now that could become habit-forming," he said.

"Good afternoon. Hope I'm not interrupting anything." Marnie released Ralph and turned to meet the smiling gaze of the boatyard mechanic. "Oh hallo," he said. "I remember you, miss. We did some work on your boat."

"You sorted out my electrics," said Marnie. "They're still going strong."

"And you were looking for clues on a shoe in the canal," said the mechanic. "You'd make a good detective."

"My reputation's taken a knock lately," said Marnie. "I can't even work out who committed a murder over three hundred years ago."

"Is that your line, then, detective work or history?"

"Neither. Just a bystander." Marnie had no desire to begin the saga of the murdered vicar. "Anyway, it's nice to see you again." The mechanic glanced at Ralph and raised an eyebrow. Marnie looked round in time to see Ralph give the faintest of nods. At that, the mechanic reached into a pocket in his overalls and produced a small, cigar-shaped package wrapped in brown paper.

"I've taken care to keep it clean, Mr Lombard." He handed it to Ralph.

"You two know each other," said Marnie.

"Peter serviced the engine on *Thyrsis*. He keeps me supplied with parts." The two men smiled at each other like conspirators, and the mechanic turned and walked back to his office.

"He seems very reliable," said Marnie.

"Peter's a craftsman," said Ralph. He handed her the package. "A small present to thank you for introducing me to the waterways in general and *Sally Ann* in particular." Marnie took the package. It was heavier than she expected. She pulled open the paper and found two models of working narrowboats in solid brass, a motor and its butty. They had been polished to a brilliant shine.

"Ralph, they're beautiful. Thank you so much." She reached up and kissed him warmly.

"I told you this could become a habit," he said. "I'm glad you like them."

Marnie held them up to admire the detailing. "I shall keep them on my desk so that I can see them every day. I shall use them all the time as paperweights. Narrowboats were made to be practical."

"They've certainly changed my life," said Ralph. "You wouldn't believe the looks of incredulity I had from colleagues when I told them how I was going to spend my sabbatical. Some of them obviously thought I had gone completely mad. One or two came here to see *Thyrsis* and I think they were quite impressed."

"Who knows," said Marnie, "perhaps you'll start a trend and we'll see a whole fleet of scholarly narrowboats on the canals, with satellite dishes linked to the Internet … computer screens glowing through portholes … cries of 'Eureka' echoing across the water!"

Ralph laughed at the image. "The University of Oxford Canal," he mused. "Magdalen Motor and Balliol Butty! A wonderful idea."

They set off in high spirits and looked in on Peter in his office. Ralph thanked him for playing his part.

"No job too big or too small," he said with pride.

"Did you make them shine like that as well?" said Marnie. He nodded. "You did a wonderful job."

"Well, we only have one standard here." He pointed at a boat moored at the bank. "That's my next job. Quite a contrast!" It was rusty and dishevelled, its paintwork faded and peeling.

"Complete renovation?" said Marnie.

"I wish it was. They couldn't afford it. Just a new battery and service the engine."

"How disheartening," said Marnie. "No matter how good your work is, no-one will see it. The boat will still look a mess."

"You have to do your best all the time, even if no-one can see it. *You* know it's been done properly and that's what matters."

Walking back through Jericho arm in arm, Marnie looked at her model boats. "That's what I shall call them," she said. "*Magdalen* and *Balliol* … unless you think it sounds too pretentious?"

"Of course not," said Ralph. "Anyway, no-one's going to know except you and me."

"And Anne," said Marnie.

"And Anne, of course."

❦   ❦   ❦   ❦

Anne and her brother brought coffee out into the garden after lunch. Geoff was in the kitchen stacking dishes beside the sink while Jackie was checking the washing on the line.

"So you're learning a lot from Marnie?" said Richard, putting out the cups.

"Oh yes. All sorts of things."

"Like what?"

"It's hard to think of actual examples ... it's ... well, the way she does things. She gets on with the job and concentrates. She's very ... organised ... methodical."

"Is that Marnie you're talking about?" said Jackie, coming over. "She strikes me as a practical person."

"Yes, mum. Like you. *She* would have got the washing in the machine as soon as I came through the door, just as you did." They laughed.

"But does she teach you about designing?" Richard went on. "That's what you want, isn't it?"

"Yes, she does. She goes over my designs with me, showing me how they're good and how they could be improved."

"That's your 'hands on', is it?" said Geoff, coming out and taking his seat.

"I think ..." Anne chose her words carefully. "I think I'm learning about a lot of things combined. What I've learnt so far is that you have to be *focused* ... that's what Marnie calls it."

"*Focused*," said Richard. "That's good. I like that." He began pouring the coffee.

❦ ❦ ❦ ❦

Randall Hughes was sitting with his coffee in a deckchair in the vicarage garden, reading the *Sunday Times* when he heard the phone ring in his study. He struggled out of the chair.

"Hallo, Randall Hughes." He waited. "Hallo?" He pressed the instrument close to his ear. "I'm afraid I can't hear you." He replaced the receiver and waited in case the caller rang back. Eventually he returned to the garden and was soon immersed in an article on the prospects for peace in Northern Ireland and the attitude of the churches.

❦ ❦ ❦ ❦

At the end of the afternoon, while Ralph was chairing the last session of the seminar at All Saints and Randall Hughes was preparing to say the last good-bye to his congregation at evensong, Marnie swung the car over the canal bridge and round the corner into Anne's street. Half an hour later, after a cup of tea and some home-made shortbread, Anne heaved her bag of freshly cleaned clothes into the boot of the Rover and climbed in beside her friend. The car set off down the street with an arm protruding in a friendly wave on either side.

"They're a very nice lot, your family," said Marnie, pulling out onto the dual carriageway. "They make me feel very welcome."

"You *are* very welcome. They like you."

"Good."

"Especially Richard," added Anne with a cheeky smile.

"Oh yes?"

"Did you see the way he was looking at you when we came out to leave?"

"I think he's impressed by the letters after my name," said Marnie.

Anne gave it some thought. "Marnie Walker, *MA*?"

Marnie shook her head. "Marnie Walker, GT-i." She accelerated to seventy in fourth gear, with a fruity note from the exhaust, and changed up to fifth. They drove on for a few minutes in silence before Anne spoke again.

"My family are thinking about a holiday at the end of July."

"That's good," said Marnie. "I'm hoping to have a holiday at the end of the millennium." She smiled sideways at Anne. "What will it be ... a fortnight?"

"Yes." In the corner of her eye Marnie saw that Anne looked uncomfortable.

"There's no problem. In fact, I can see an advantage. If the school kids sink *Sally Ann* during their visit, I'll be able to sleep in your room while you're away."

"You think I should go with them?"

"Of course. It may be the only chance you get to have a holiday this summer. I'd like to have a break, but with the builders starting, it'll be impossible."

"It's just ... I don't like to leave when there's so much to do."

"There always will be a lot to do, Anne. No, you have a good break. You deserve it."

"Maybe you're right. It may give me the strength to face my exam results."

"Forget about the results. Take one day at a time. They'll come soon enough."

"Yes. I do forget about them most of the time. I'll get on with my work. I shall be focused."

"*Focused*," said Marnie. "That's a good word."

Part 20

Sarah Anne had been the first to see the group of wounded men returning from the war. She had taken her father into the house, shocked at his appearance. He seemed half the man he had been when he left. His right arm had been struck by a musket shot that had broken the bone and torn through the muscle. He had been lucky not to lose it, but it was weakened for ever. At night he slept poorly, plagued by a fever and bad dreams, and Sarah would sit up with him, taking turns with her mother and sisters while he moaned and cried out.

Late one night he sank into a delirium, muttering indistinctly, and Sarah mopped his brow with a damp cloth perfumed with lavender. She gave him a cordial made by her mother from primrose and verbena, and slowly he settled down to a fitful, broken sleep. In the early hours he woke again and asked Sarah to fetch the vicar.

"I cannot do that, father," she said. "We will talk about it in the morning."

"I want to make my confession," he said with infinite tiredness. "Why can you not fetch him? It will soon be light. He would come." Sarah shook her head slowly. Her fathers eyes widened. "Where is he? ... Tell me ... Where is the vicar?" He took hold of Sarah by the arm, his face lined and haggard in the candle light.

"I cannot fetch him. He is ..." She choked on the words and could not continue. Her father stared at her and, with a groan, fell back onto the pillow, his eyes closed. His lips began to move and Sarah had to lean over his face to hear what he said. As he spoke, tears began to fall down her face, she clenched her fists and a great blackness came over her.

❦   ❦   ❦   ❦

Monday 26 June

It seemed to Marnie that she spent most of Monday morning on the phone, the first call coming shortly after eight o'clock. It was Beth, working on the illustrations for a book.

"I'm sitting here at my drawing board searching for inspiration. All I seem to get these days is kids' books on dinosaurs or space creatures. *Now* has gone out of fashion. Today it's dinosaurs."

"I don't think *I* can help you with any original ideas. I can ask Anne if you like." Hearing her name, Anne looked up from the computer where she was busy formatting a box of disks. "Any ideas on dinosaurs for Beth?"

"I did a project on them at school once. I modelled them on the characters of some of the teachers ... they were horrifying."

"Don't you mean 'horrified'?" said Marnie.

"No. 'Horrifying'. You should see our teachers."

Beth could hear this through the receiver. "God, Marnie, she sounds just like you."

"Okay, well, glad to have been of assistance. Time is money, woman. I have to earn an honest crust."

"Aren't you going to tell me about your day with Ralph? Was it nice?"

"It was very nice." End of statement.

"Is that *it*? What about wine, roses, romantic strolls beside the Isis, bondage, flagellation ...?"

"We went for a walk to a canal boatyard that used to be a coal wharf."

"The last of the great romantics! By your standards does that mean you're developing a *relationship*?"

"Beth, I don't have time for anything like that. There's too much to do."

"Will we meet Ralph when we come for the pig roast?"

"We haven't spoken about it."

"Will Anne be there?"

"If she's not gone home for the weekend."

"Good. It'll be nice to meet her. Okay, I'll talk to you in the week to arrange times for coming up. I've got ideas for a dinosaur, a strange one full of mystery … the Marniosaurus."

This call was followed at regular intervals by contractors ringing up about the rebuilding of Glebe Farm, Mrs Giles about the school visit and Willards about the renovation of *The Irish Navigator*. Searching among the papers on her desk for a notepad, Marnie uncovered the church booklet. The photograph on the cover lacked detail, but that only emphasised the silhouette of the tower. Marnie was convinced that if she only had time to think it through, she could work out what was troubling her. Anne came over with coffee.

"Blimey, is it that time already? How are you getting on with your designs?"

"Not bad," said Anne, "but then I don't keep getting interrupted by the phone." She looked down at the clutter on Marnie's desk and spotted the booklet. "Shall I take that out of your way? I can put it in a file."

"No, it's okay there for a while longer. There's something bothering me."

"About the porch?" Anne began putting some of the papers into neat piles.

"About the tower."

"Me too." She collected some of the folders to put away.

"What's bothering *you*?"

"The vicar who was murdered," said Anne. "*I* think the murderer was still there when they found the body. He *must* have been. He couldn't have got out."

"So where was he?"

"In the tower … it's obvious. There's nowhere else he could've been."

"But they searched it and found nothing."

"They didn't search thoroughly enough. Either that or they were in on it."

"So the murderer was still there and whoever searched knew where he was hiding and said nothing to give him away."

"Yes."

"I can see the logic of that, but I'm not sure I understand *why*."

The phone rang. It was Mike Thomas. "Hallo, Marnie. I thought I'd better ring you about this church job. I can do it, only I haven't got a lot of time just now. Perhaps we can work on it together."

"Sure. It's a while since *we* worked on a project. It's nice to hear your Rhondda Valley voice again."

"Marnie, I come from Llanelli."

"I know that. But I can pronounce Rhondda Valley."

"You think so?" He chuckled amiably and Marnie conjured up the image of her colleague. He was over six feet tall, with dark curly hair, a friendly round face and grey eyes that were slightly hooded and seemed perpetually on the verge of a slow smile. One of those Welshmen they quarry in the mountains to make into rugby players.

"Now, I'd better come and have a look at the job as soon as I can, so we can decide how to tackle it. Can you tell the vicar I'll be up in the next few weeks?"

Marnie made a note on the pad that Anne had provided by the phone.

❦   ❦   ❦   ❦

Before lunch Marnie suggested a walk to get some fresh air and a few things from the shop. The weather had turned cooler, and it was more like spring than summer as they walked quickly up the track. At the road, they set off in opposite directions, Anne towards the shop, Marnie to the vicarage.

"This is a surprise. Won't you come in?"

"I should have phoned really, but I wanted a walk and thought I might look in on the off-chance that you'd be here."

"I am, as you see, but not for much longer."

"I'll not hold you up if you're going out." The vicar showed Marnie into his study.

"I'm not sure if the bush telegraph extends as far as Glebe Farm. You may not have heard that I'm leaving Knightly St John. I can tell by your face that you hadn't."

"I had no idea. Isn't this rather sudden?" It just slipped out, not the most tactful thing to say.

"The Bishop has asked me to become Rural Dean of Brackley."

"That has a pleasant ring to it. It sounds rather important. Congratulations."

"Thank you. It *is* a promotion."

"I didn't think church people thought in those terms."

"Well, we're not in it for the money!" He laughed and his face lit up. A happy man. "I suppose that's why we get so concerned with matters of principle and faith. It's more or less all we have."

"Yes, I can see that. Does that mean you're no longer interested in the church porch? Or did you already know this was coming when you spoke to me about it?"

"No, I didn't, actually. As you say, it's all rather sudden. I'm sure my successor will want to pursue it. You've read the file. You know the urgency."

"The urgency in the opinion of the diocesan surveyor," said Marnie.

"They know about these things. It's their job."

"But everyone thinks it was *your* priority."

"I don't have to hide behind somebody else. It was my responsibility."

"And your successor … will he do the same?"

"I don't know. I don't even know who's been appointed. The Bishop's office is sorting it out."

Marnie turned towards the door and remembered why she had come. "Oh, I meant to tell you: my old firm in London has an architect to deal with the porch. He'll come up in the next few weeks. He's something of an expert on churches … did some work on York Minster."

"Good. Thanks. I'm sure the new vicar will want to get things resolved as quickly as possible."

"He can always wash his hands of it and say it's the fault of the diocesan office."

"True, but remember … Pontius Pilate washed *his* hands to get rid of a problem …"

❦   ❦   ❦   ❦

Marnie found Anne waiting for her by the field gate, face turned up to the sky, eyes closed, bag of shopping at her feet.

"What are you doing?"

"Sun bathing." She gathered up the bag and they turned onto the old track.

"You'll be lucky. Looks like rain." Dark clouds were gathering on the horizon. "Was the vicar at home?"

"Yes. I saw him."

"So you know."

"About him leaving? Yes."

"They were talking about it in the shop."

"Of course … the old bush telegraph." Marnie tapped the side of her nose.

❦   ❦   ❦   ❦

The rain came as no surprise in the middle of the afternoon. While Marnie was on the phone, the sky darkened so much that Anne switched on the desk lamps.

She stood in the doorway for a few moments, watching the great drops hitting the dry ground and suddenly thought of *Sally Ann* and *Thyrsis*. She grabbed the boat keys, picked up an umbrella and jogged off through the spinney to check windows and hatches. By the time she returned, the yard was awash and the wind was driving the rain against the windows. Still talking on the phone, Marnie swivelled in her chair and glanced in Anne's direction. Marnie excused herself briefly, put a hand over the mouthpiece.

"Better check the loft. We don't know how secure that roof is." Anne half ran up the wall-ladder. As she stood up and groped for the light switch, a drop of rain hit her on the cheek. There were drips in several places, though the bed was untouched. She moved around the loft, pulling aside the rugs and the few pieces of furniture, already damp.

"How bad is it?" Marnie's head protruded at the top of the ladder.

"Could be worse. I'll get some bowls to catch the water. The bed's dry. What about downstairs?"

"No leaks so far." Marnie surveyed the situation. "We'll need several containers. I'll see if Ralph has any on *Thyrsis*."

Soon they had every leak under control and the floor of the loft looked like an impromptu game of garden draughts. "Back to *Sally Ann* for you till this lot dries out," said Marnie. "We don't want you getting pneumonia."

The rain continued sporadically for the rest of the day. They spent the evening warm and dry on the boat and Marnie prepared a supper of artichokes followed by bean casserole, one of Anne's favourites, and quite a presentable cheese board. Not bad for left-overs, thought Marnie to herself as she reached into the cellar, otherwise known as the cupboard under the sink, for a bottle of Rioja.

When they had finished and cleared away, Anne made coffee, lit a candle and put on a Brandenburg Concerto. They settled in the saloon, Anne reading *Residence* magazine, Marnie looking through the booklet about the church.

"You're not still thinking about that tower are you?" Anne broke into her thoughts.

"Maybe it's all in my imagination. Or maybe I'll work it out just as I'm dropping off to sleep."

But she did not. They drifted off that night to the sound of the rain pounding on *Sally Ann's* roof.

❦   ❦   ❦   ❦

Tuesday 27 June

The early morning was miserable, chilly and wet with drizzle blown about by a stiff breeze. Alan the postman made his rounds in discomfort in semi-twilight, the rain finding its way down his neck. He trekked up the path by the village shop to the Appletons' house and met Richard on the doorstep bringing in the milk.

"What's this, Richard? Had a lie-in?"

"Late breakfast today, Alan. Just seen the paper boys off."

"Oh, 'course. Molly's still down in London?"

"That's right. Her sister's had quite a big operation. She'll be staying a few days. Fancy a cup o' tea?" Alan looked down at his sodden trousers. He had already made a puddle on the quarry tiles.

"Better not," he sighed. "Thanks all the same. I'm behind anyway." He passed Richard a small bundle of letters and squelched off down the path. Richard quickly flicked through the mail: postcard from a friend on holiday in Greece (*lucky blighter*), junk mail (*straight in the bin*) and an impressive envelope with the crest of the Bishop's Palace, addressed to Molly. Bishops did not usually write about special offers or prize draws for subscribing to the church magazine. Recognising its importance, Richard stood the letter on the mantelpiece beside the clock and went to put the kettle on.

❀ ❀ ❀ ❀

"You'd have got mildew if you'd stayed here last night." It was shortly after seven and Marnie was tipping water from the bowls into a bucket. She and Anne had enjoyed the luxury of nearly-hot showers on *Sally Ann* before tramping through the spinney to inspect the barn. While they dealt with the water, rolls were warming in the oven and coffee was filtering in the galley.

"The forecast said it would brighten up later on," said Anne.

"It must have been referring to Syria," Marnie suggested, emptying the contents of a saucepan. "This whole place smells of damp. It'll be some time before you sleep up here, I think."

Anne had no objection to staying on *Sally Ann*, as long as Marnie did not feel crowded. "Marnie, did you see there's a message on the answerphone? I'll empty this if you want to check it." It was Ralph asking her to ring. She dialled his number.

The phone rang once. "Lombard."

"Ralph, it's Marnie. I just got your message. I hope it's not too early."

"No. It's fine. Thanks for ringing. Is that offer of a lift still on?"

"When would you like to come?"

"Ideally today, but tomorrow if that's no good." They agreed on a late afternoon rendezvous at the bus station in Milton Keynes. "Oh, by the way, Marnie, I've been doing some research."

"*That's* news?"

"For you."

"Ah!"

"One of the Fellows here is an expert, possibly *the* expert, on the history of the English Civil War period. A few years ago he did some work on religious factions and he's given me a copy of a paper he wrote. Your part of the world is mentioned and he's quite knowledgeable about what happened."

"Good. Perhaps we can talk about it tonight. Come for supper."

❀ ❀ ❀ ❀

At eight-forty-five the phone rang at the village shop. Richard Appleton was expecting Molly to call before he opened up.

"How's it going, my love?"

"Not too good, really. They said the operation was a success, but when I rang the nurse said she had a comfortable night, but was having breathing difficulties. It's the anaesthetic, apparently."

"Well, she's in good hands. They'll sort it out. This kind of thing probably happens quite often."

"That's what *she* said. It takes a while to get over it. I'm to ring again at lunch time."

Molly's anxiety put all other concerns out of Richard's mind. The last thing he thought of was the letter from the Bishop's Palace propped up against the clock on the mantelpiece.

❀ ❀ ❀ ❀

Marnie looked up from her desk as Anne appeared with mid-morning coffee. The clouds were beginning to part and occasional splashes of sunlight were flitting across the yard.

"You know, Marnie, I'll always look back on this as a wonderful part of my life, whatever happens."

"That's very philosophical for a Tuesday morning. I'm sure you'll have many wonderful times."

"Who knows? But this will be special."

Marnie wanted to tell Anne that everything would work out fine, that she would give her a job, she would go to art school and become a designer with a career ahead of her. Perhaps one day they would be working together in a thriving company. But there were too many unknowns in her own life to be able to make promises about the future to anyone else, least of all to Anne, who believed in her and trusted her. Not to mention the exam results due in August. She looked at Anne standing by the window. There was nothing she could say.

"Good," she said.

❦   ❦   ❦   ❦

"Richard? It's me. I thought I'd catch you before I go out. I'm going shopping."

"How are things, love?"

"They've got Susan's breathing settled and she's sleeping. I can go in this evening for a short visit. Obviously she won't be coming out tomorrow, but she's much better."

"That's great. I've been worried all morning."

"How are you managing? Is Ivy there?"

"Yes. Everything's fine here, don't you fret. Ivy's doing a grand job in the shop."

❦   ❦   ❦   ❦

In the afternoon Anne looked up at the clock and did a quick calculation. "Marnie, can I interrupt you for a moment?" Marnie looked up from the drawing board and refocused her attention towards Anne. "You've got to get that finished before the end of today and collect Ralph this afternoon." Marnie nodded. Anne continued. "You're planning to get some things from the shop on your way."

"Yes."

"If I go up there now, I can post the letters, get the shopping and be back before you set off. That'll give you more time to get the design ready and you won't have to rush."

"Brilliant."

"I'm on my way."

As she reached the road at the top of the track, a Volkswagen beetle chugged past. The vicar was at the wheel, in his black cassock. Walking along the street, Anne wondered whether the vicar was deliberately trying to create an image, or whether he regarded his clothes as a kind of uniform. What sort of person became a vicar? she asked herself. It was hard to imagine anyone wanting to go into the church. Why did they do it?

Ahead, Anne saw children coming out of school. The shop would be busy. She quickened her pace. Even so, her trip took longer than expected. There was a new person serving in the shop and everyone wanted to know about Molly's sister's operation. At last Anne managed to extricate herself and set off back to Glebe Farm even more quickly than she had come.

Passing the church, she stopped suddenly in mid-stride. There was a strange sound in the air. Somewhere, someone was singing. A woman's voice, strong and melodious, a siren call reaching her from a distance. Anne was disoriented, her attention fixed on the voice that seemed to blot out everything else. The singing was beautiful, a trained soprano. It was like hearing the voice of an angel. Anne wanted to go into the church and listen. Instead, she looked at her watch, gasped, and set off reluctantly at full stretch. The music followed her all the way home.

Marnie was reversing the car out from its shelter when Anne arrived back at the farm.

"Sorry, Marnie, I got held up."

The car window slid down. "No problem. Did you get what we wanted at the shop?"

"Yes. It was crowded. Mums and kids from school."

"Of course. Don't worry. I'm in good time. I've got the mobile with me in case you need a word. See you in about an hour."

🌸 🌸 🌸 🌸

"Walker and Co, good afternoon." Anne handled several calls during Marnie's absence and enjoyed being in charge. The best enquiry came from a woman, no a *lady*, with a frightfully-frightfully accent, who asked to be put through to *the department that dealt with Country Houses*. This called for quick thinking, as the only other member of staff present was Dolly, curled up on Marnie's chair. "That would be Mrs *Marnie* Walker." Anne hoped to give the impression that Marnie was only one member of the talented Walker family running the generations-old company in their extensive offices. "Unfortunately, she's in a meeting ..." (no reference to Milton Keynes bus station) "... out of the office ... Oxford University." This seemed to press the right buttons and the tone from the caller was warm and encouraging. "Certainly. I'll ask her to phone you when she gets ... er, when she returns." The name was of course double-barrelled and Anne was wondering how people knew of their existence when the phone rang again. It was Marnie.

"Anne, slight change of plan. Can you go over to *Thyrsis* and open up? Get a bottle of mineral water from our fridge and put it in Ralph's sleeping cabin with a glass. Thanks."

"What's up, Marnie?"

"Ralph has a migraine coming on. I'm going to put him straight to bed. See you soon."

"Marnie?"

"Yes?"

"How long has he had it?"

"Just starting now. Why?"

"Has he been sick?" There was a pause at the other end of the line.

"He says not."

"There'll be two tablets by the water in his cabin. They're soluble. He should take them as soon as he gets back. They may help."

Anne was up in her room over the office checking for damp when she heard the car arrive. Marnie drove past the buildings and on towards *Sally Ann's* mooring. A few minutes later Marnie came in as Anne was putting the list of phone messages on her desk.

"How's Ralph?"

"Rather washed out. I've given him your tablets. What are they? I didn't know you got migraine."

"They're just pain killers, but they're good. My mum takes them if she feels a migraine coming on. If she takes them in time they stop it ... just like that."

🌸 🌸 🌸 🌸

It was quite late in the evening before Molly Appleton was able to ring home. "She's sitting up and she's managed a little soup, but she's still weak."

"At least she's showing signs of improvement," said Richard encouragingly.

"Yes, but she's so pale. I never thought she'd be like this."

"What do the doctors say?"

"*Making satisfactory progress*, whatever that's supposed to mean."

"Cheer up, love. I'm sure she'll be much better tomorrow." Richard was upset to hear his wife sounding so downcast. Not a word was said about the shop or the village, such was their concern. After hanging up, Richard made his way slowly and thoughtfully upstairs to bed.

In the darkened living room the letter from the Bishop's Palace leant against the clock on the mantelpiece.

※　※　※　※

"I suppose we could get a de-humidifier," said Marnie, thinking out loud as she cut two slices of water melon in the galley. Anne was going in and out, laying the table on the bank beside *Sally Ann*. "Some of them can take out more than a litre of water a day."

"That might play havoc with the tagliatelle," said Anne, looking in the saucepan boiling on the stove.

"Has anyone told you, you get more like my sister every day?"

"I thought she said I was getting to be like *you*."

"Let that be a lesson to you! I was thinking about the damp in your loft. I don't want you going down with a *chest* or something."

Anne struck a pose that emphasised her slender outline. "No danger of that with me, I think!"

Over the meal Anne told Marnie about the singing she had heard at the church that afternoon. "It really was like the voice of an angel."

"It could hardly be choir practice at that time of day," said Marnie. "I can't think who it would be. Did you recognise the music?"

Anne shook her head. "I couldn't put a name to it."

"We always seem to be puzzling over that church one way or another. There must be some simple, logical reason for the singing."

"Someone using the church to practise?" suggested Anne.

"Could be. The acoustics would be good, I imagine. Practising for a solo or a concert."

"Perhaps just someone full of the joys of spring," said Anne. "Someone with something to celebrate."

"We'd better book *you* in for a session in August when the exam results come out."

"Oh, don't," said Anne with a weary sigh. "It'll be a dirge in my case, I expect."

"One way to solve the mystery is to ask the vicar. He'll know who's singing in his church."

"Don't bet on it. I saw him driving off as I got to the road."

"Molly Appleton, then. She's bound to know."

"She's in London," said Anne, "Her sister's had an operation. Village shop. Bush telegraph."

"I give up," said Marnie. "Another mystery."

"You've got quite a lot of choral music, haven't you, Marnie? Perhaps I'll go through your tapes after supper and see if I can find it."

It was later that evening, while Anne was screwing up her eyes to read the tiny print on the box of a cassette that she was playing, that Ralph appeared in the hatchway in his dressing gown. He looked drawn, but not desperate.

"Palestrina, *Missa Papae Marcelli*," he said softly, his voice huskier than usual.

Anne smiled at him. "I can't make out the name of the group singing."

"It sounds like Pro Cantione Antiqua," said Ralph. "Very distinctive."

"How are you feeling?" said Marnie standing to pull up a chair.

"Surprisingly human. I've just come over to thank you for bringing me back. Sorry to be such a nuisance." He brushed aside their protests. "Also, I wanted to thank my guardian angel. Your tablets were marvellous, Anne. They made a tremendous difference."

"My mum swears by them."

"So will I from now on. Anyway, I'd better get back to bed."

"Is there anything I can get you?" said Marnie, touching his arm. "Something to drink, perhaps?"

"No thanks. I just need some sleep. I'll be fine by morning." Ralph put an arm round Marnie's shoulder and squeezed gently. He smiled at Anne before leaving, and she sat lost in her thoughts.

"Are you okay?" said Marnie, noticing the change in her mood.

Anne hesitated before replying. "Marnie?"

"Something bothering you?"

"Will Ralph be all right, do you think?"

"Yes, of course he will. Especially after your tablets."

"No, I mean ... will he be all right over on *Thyrsis* ... by himself?"

"He'll be fine. No problem."

"I wouldn't want to be in the way," said Anne.

Marnie sat beside her. "I know. And you're not. It's nice of you to be so considerate. Right now he just needs to sleep."

While Marnie washed up, Anne dried and put things away. The music played softly in the background. "Marnie, were you surprised when Ralph recognised the Palestrina, and the group, Pro Cantione Whatsit?"

"Not really, though offhand I can't think of anyone else I know who could have done that. Nothing about Ralph would really surprise me, I suppose." She put the last plate in the drying rack and Anne looked at her speculatively as she picked it up.

That night, after Marnie had put out the light, she lay awake in the darkness for some time. There was so much waiting to be done and she had promised herself that she would devote all her energies to her career. At least until she had become established. And then what?

Anne, reasonably comfortable on the camp bed in the saloon, slipped easily into a contented sleep, her mind filled with the sound of angels singing. Guardian angels.

❦ ❦ ❦ ❦

Wednesday was a Good Day. Anne worked happily while Marnie talked to the builders outside in the yard. They had started two weeks earlier than expected. The weather had returned to full summer and in the old gardens at the back of the farmhouse and cottages, flowers had appeared in profusion. Delphiniums, hollyhocks and sweet peas had thrust themselves up through the undergrowth. Nasturtiums that had seeded themselves added bright splashes of orange and gold along the edges of forgotten paths, and roses were blooming.

Returning from a morning coffee run to the builders, Anne discovered a vase of honeysuckle on her desk with a card: *For Anne, with love and thanks. Ralph.* She guessed that he had found them growing in one of the old gardens, and the gesture touched her deeply. Marnie came into the office and Anne saw that there were no flowers on her desk. Marnie began searching among her papers, picking up a set of notes that she had made at the meeting with the builders earlier that morning.

"At this rate we should be in the first cottage ahead of schedule and have the second one ready well before Christmas." She finished reading the notes and looked up, noticing the flowers.

"They're lovely," she said.

"They're from Ralph."

"A nice thought," said Marnie. "He was very pleased about your tablets. You really saved him from a migraine." Anne said nothing and looked awkwardly down at the honeysuckle. Marnie walked over to her. "Don't you like them?"

"Of course, it's just that …" Her voice trailed away.

"Did you think I'd be jealous?"

"Oh, no! Well, I suppose … I'm not sure what I thought."

"I'm delighted that Ralph has thanked you. I couldn't possibly be anything but pleased."

"That's good," said Anne. Her voice was matter-of-fact. "No-one's ever given me flowers before." Marnie put an arm round her friend, unable to remember the first time she had been given flowers but sure that Anne would always remember this.

"You're sure you don't mind?"

"Anne, who do you think lent him the vase?" They smiled at each other and went back to work.

"I must thank Ralph as soon as I can."

"He's working on his book this morning, but you'll see him this evening. I've invited him to supper."

❦ ❦ ❦ ❦

Ivy Matthews spent her morning in the shop stacking the shelves and pricing tins. She was happy in her work, especially as Richard had offered her a part-time job, and she went from rack to rack humming a tune that only she recognised. The atmosphere in the shop had improved greatly since Monday, with Richard silent and thoughtful in his glass booth. Now, things were better. Molly had phoned to say that her sister was making a rapid recovery, walking around the ward, some of the colour returned to her cheeks. They were talking about letting her go home very soon.

❦ ❦ ❦ ❦

"How's your loft coming along?" Ralph enquired, sipping a Pimm's on the aft deck of *Sally Ann* that evening.

"Almost dry enough to move back," said Anne, holding up her glass to admire the deep burnt orange colour of the drink. Another first. It was a memorable day. "A few days yet, I think."

"The tarpaulin adds a touch of insouciant elegance to the barn," Ralph observed as Marnie appeared from the cabin and picked up her glass.

"I see you've made a full recovery," she said. "And you're right. Electric blue is so discreet."

"Blends in so well with the countryside," said Anne. "At least it will stop any more rain getting in. Is the soup ready?" Marnie nodded and Anne rose to fetch it. "You two sit down and I'll serve."

She had just placed the bowls of chilled gazpacho around the table and set out the side dishes, when from inside the cabin the mobile phone began to ring. Marnie, muttering under her breath, excused herself and left Anne and Ralph with their Pimm's, promising to be as quick as she could.

"Marnie says you're very busy at the moment," said Anne.

"Yes. I want to get this book written."

"Will you be able to stay for the pig-roast?" She wrinkled her nose at the thought of it.

"Tell me about it."

Anne began to explain when Marnie emerged from the boat. Ralph called across to her. "Come on Marnie, your soup's getting warm!"

"Sorry about that. It was Beth, of course, confirming arrangements for the weekend. They're coming for the pig-roast."

"Anne was just telling me about it. Sounds splendidly medieval."

"That's what Beth said. Will you be here for it?"

"I could be. It would be interesting to see the locals … This gazpacho is delicious. Just the right balance. I think I sometimes put in too much garlic."

"Talking of locals, you said one of your colleagues had done some work on the Civil War in these parts," said Marnie.

"Ah, yes. Very strange. Do you know Hanford?"

"Not exactly. I know where it is. A few miles up the road."

"And Yore?"

"That's a bit nearer and it's on the road further up the canal."

"Do you know that to this day the people of Yore will have nothing to do with Hanford? It seems that there were *incidents* during the Civil War that have left their mark on these communities. Yore was a centre of Puritanism, Anabaptists apparently. Before the battle of Naseby, a squadron of royalist cavalry passed through Hanford and heard about the puritans who were for Parliament. They rode over, knocked the folk about and burned their thatch. Nothing too nasty, I gather, no killings, but it left Yore in a sorry state. After the battle, units from Cromwell's army came by and saw what had happened. A group set off and burned half of Hanford to the ground."

"What about Knightly?" said Marnie.

"Also raided, apparently, but it doesn't seem to have been so bad here. The people kept their heads down, though it was known that they were a divided community. A number of volunteers went off to join the Parliamentary army, but on balance neither side was really welcomed."

"*A plague on both your houses,*" said Anne. "There must have been a horrible atmosphere in the village."

"Undoubtedly," said Ralph. He passed Anne a dish of diced cucumber. "Everyone in the area knew about the murder of the vicar and the village was regarded with suspicion, if not actual dread."

"A place to be avoided," said Marnie.

"Like the plague," said Anne, and shivered.

"That was a very long time ago," said Ralph, spooning croutons into his gazpacho.

"Three hundred and fifty years next summer," said Anne. "I checked the dates in the booklet."

"Then it's high time the whole business was laid to rest," said Marnie. "It's one thing to do a project in the classroom. But life has to go on. I was wondering about the organisations that perform Civil War battles … whether in centuries to come there'll be re-enactments of the Troubles in Ireland. Will they be remembered for all the horrors, or will people think of them just as a colourful pageant?"

"I don't think the re-enactments are meant to glamorise," said Ralph. "I think the Sealed Knot and the English Civil War Society look at it in a serious, historical way."

"Don't they just like playing at war?" said Marnie.

"I expect some of them like that aspect, but many want to understand the complexities, the religious tensions and factions."

"Sounds just like Knightly," said Marnie.

"Certainly does," said Ralph. "Perhaps the place has never quite recovered from it."

"Do you think the vicar's glad to be leaving?" said Anne. Ralph raised an inquisitive eyebrow.

"He's going to be the Rural Dean of Brackley," Marnie explained. "He told me it's a promotion, but half the village wanted him out. They wrote to the Bishop and the next minute the vicar leaves. Do you think it looks as if he's been pushed out?"

Ralph frowned. "Either the Bishop is weak and bowed to public pressure or he was going to promote the vicar anyway and the time had come. A variant on the theme of 'church outing'."

"I can't make up my mind about it," said Marnie.

"Of course the Bishop may have his own agenda."

"What do you mean?" said Marnie.

"I'm not sure, but we may soon find out."

❦   ❦   ❦   ❦

As the week wore on, a buzz of activity settled over the village. Outwardly it seemed much the same as usual, basking in the warm summer weather. The estate agent's brochure had described Knightly St John as a 'sleepy English village', but Marnie thought this was too superficial. As far as she was concerned, there was nothing sleepy about her way of life. She was as busy as ever.

The change in tempo brought the occasional delivery van heading towards the parish hall with supplies for the pig-roast. George Stubbs and Albert Fletcher would be seen in the village field pacing out the distance for lighting cables, supervising the positions for stalls and the area for children's sports. Contractors' vans trundled each day down the rough field track towards the cluster of ruins at Glebe Farm. Already skiploads of rubbish were being cleared away and sections of scaffolding revealed where rebuilding was in progress. Marnie made forays out to suppliers of decorating materials and fabrics for the renovation of *The Irish Navigator*. Anne crossed items off her lists and added new ones, moving discreetly among the builders to keep a watchful eye on developments while supplying mugs of tea and coffee. In the study on board *Thyrsis*, Ralph sifted and analysed his way through source material, typing drafts on the laptop, updating his list of further data required.

Meanwhile down in London, Molly Appleton's sister was up and about in the hospital, gaining strength every day. She would be able to go home on Friday morning and it was agreed that Molly would return to Knightly St John on Saturday afternoon in time to help on the WI stall at the pig-roast.

Saturday morning was bright and sunny, with a gentle breeze and light clouds, all that was best of an English summer day. Beth and Paul arrived at eleven, impressed by the progress on the resurrection of Glebe Farm, taking Anne arm-in-arm as if they were old friends and meeting Ralph when he was encouraged to emerge from his study. Marnie had collected an armful of flowers growing untended in the old cottage gardens and presented these to her sister as they began their tour of the domain. Paul and Ralph chatted about university matters, while Marnie, Beth and Anne walked round the buildings and looked in at windows to see how things were coming on. When she was sure they were out of earshot of the two men, Beth leaned towards her sister and spoke in a low voice. "You didn't tell me he was like *that,* Marnie." Anne glanced at Marnie to see her reaction.

"Like what?" said Marnie in a neutral tone. They came to a halt among builder's materials.

"So *distinguished-looking* ... so *handsome.*"

"Well, he's not exactly a bit of rough, is he?" said Marnie. "I mean, he is a Fellow at an Oxford college."

"Sure," said Beth. "But I know academics and they're not all like him. He's like a sort of ... thoroughbred in the stable." Anne spluttered and Beth turned to her. "I suppose Dr Lombard seems old to you, Anne, but really, he's quite something."

"I think Ralph's super," said Anne with an impish smile.

Marnie had prepared lunch and the table was laid on the bank beside *Sally Ann* under the broad cream parasol. Anne put out smoked salmon while Beth and Ralph chatted at the table. Paul came through to the galley clutching a carrier bag that clinked.

"Marnie, we brought some wine. It's been in the fridge overnight and I wrapped it in newspaper, so it should be cold if you want to use it."

"That's great. Thanks. Is it one of your Ozzie Chardonnays?"

"Two, actually."

"Perfect. I've made an asparagus soufflé. These are just right. Can you open one of them and stand it in the cooler? There should be room for the other one in the fridge."

Paul set about his tasks. "So, that's Ralph Lombard. He's much nicer than I expected."

"What did you expect?" Marnie began tossing a salad.

"Oh, you know … these eminent types who write books that make them famous. A lot of them become very aware of their own importance. He seems very natural."

"Like an ordinary person?" suggested Marnie.

"No, not ordinary. He's very authoritative. Sometimes the heavyweights seem almost bored with anything or anyone outside their field, as if they can't be bothered to talk to you. I get the impression with him that he has a sense of … well, modesty."

"Modesty." Marnie repeated the word. She knew he had taken some knocks in his time, but she kept the thought to herself.

"He's absolutely churning out the work at the moment," said Paul. "Did you know that? He's published a series of papers over the past six months that have sparked off a good deal of correspondence in the *Times*."

"I knew he was writing a book," said Marnie. "The thoughts of leading economists aren't widely discussed in the village shop."

"Well, he's advancing some very interesting ideas and the word is that he's much in demand in high places. I mean *very* high places."

"Perhaps that's why he's taken to the canals to write his book," said Marnie, rinsing her hands.

"It wouldn't surprise me," said Paul.

After lunch they decided to have a trip on *Sally Ann,* as the great event of the day was to take place in the evening. *Sally Ann,* to her credit, started at the first touch of the button and burbled happily along while her passengers drank coffee on the aft deck.

"I like the look of your boat, Ralph," Paul had said as they reversed past *Thyrsis.*

"It's a floating research library," said Marnie. "Probably the first narrowboat to be connected to the Internet via satellite link." Beth and Paul raised their eyebrows in comic unison.

"It's true," said Ralph. "I can't deny it." He seemed glad at being teased. Beth gave her sister a knowing look.

"Talking of libraries," said Paul. "Did you know this area's in the papers today? There's an article in the *Independent* about the last battles of the Civil War. Some papers have been found in the library at Winton Hall. Apparently some of the very last actions took place hereabouts after Naseby."

"We never seem to get away from it," said Marnie. "They'll still be talking about the four hundredth anniversary and the five hundredth after that …"

❦   ❦   ❦   ❦

"It really does look medieval," said Ralph. The group of them stopped at the gate to the village field to buy their tickets.

"This is my treat," said Marnie in a firm voice.

"Admission is one pound each," said the woman at the desk over the top of half-moon specs.

"Is that all?" said Marnie.

"That's right. The pork has been provided by George Stubbs and Albert Fletcher, as well as salads and jacket potatoes. All free of charge. The entry fee is just a contribution to church funds." They walked into the field to the accompaniment of folk music playing over loudspeakers.

It was still bright in the early evening, but a faint twilight was already advancing as clouds in the west obscured the sun. The effect was to cast a theatrical glow over the scene in front of them, with torches burning along the perimeter of the playing field, separating the festivities from the roped-off cricket square. Coloured lights shone in the trees and on the opposite side swirls of smoke could be seen where the pig was roasting on a spit, drops of fat splashing down onto the hot coals. A small crowd watched George Stubbs in boater and striped apron, basting the carcass. Nearby a steam traction engine was emitting a plume of smoke from its chimney and occasional shrill calls from its whistle. The warm smell of the pig-meat wafted across the field. Ralph moved closer to Anne.

"Does this disturb you?" he said under his breath, nodding in the direction of the barbecue.

"No, it's all right, thanks. Provided I don't get too close it won't bother me. Actually, I was just wondering if this was your sort of thing. I couldn't have imagined you being here."

"That's true," said Ralph. "Although I was thinking of suggesting to the Master that we might organise one of these events in the Fellows Garden at All Saints." Anne laughed and Marnie, who had overheard part of the conversation joined in.

"No doubt Ralph would run the home-made jam stall for the WI," she said. "It's an important part of any village fête."

"I must say," said Ralph, "I half expected it to be a fête worse than death, but this is impressive."

They made their way from stall to stall and became a focus of interest. Everyone had heard of the new 'young woman from London' who had moved into the ruins and was doing amazing things. Several of the stall-holders asked if she really was living on a 'barge' and Marnie suspected that they had built her up to be some kind of eccentric. The sight of her family and friends seemed to reassure village opinion that she was quite 'normal'. At the Tombola the woman running the stall enticed them all to have a go, including Marnie's 'gentleman-friend'. Ralph said it made him feel like a travelling salesman or a bookie's runner. He attracted a good deal of attention, cutting an elegant figure in navy blue silk shirt and cream slacks, compared with the jeans that most people were wearing.

Gradually clouds covered the sky, bringing a premature dusk that made the scene more colourful. The smell of the roast was now everywhere and George Stubbs was wielding his carving knife, cutting slices of juicy flesh from the carcass and laying them in a neat pile on a huge platter beside the spit. The music stopped and a voice came over the loudspeakers inviting everyone to be served with pork generously provided by Mr Stubbs and Mr Fletcher. There was a ragged salvo of applause and a general movement towards the fire. The music began again and, in tune with the holiday atmosphere, the traction engine gave out a long low call.

The queue was efficiently served by the helpers from the WI and soon there were clusters of villagers sitting on hay bales or sprawling on the grass. The few vegetarians, including Anne, were provided with huge potatoes baked crisp in their jackets, oozing butter and covered with a mound of grated cheddar and home-made chutney. Mr Stubbs and Mr Fletcher continued carving meat in the warm glow of public good will and burning coals.

Ralph picked his way across the obstacle course of reclining bodies, carrying a tray of chilled lager from the beer stall. Looking up, Marnie noticed a bustling movement at the far edge of the field by the entrance gate and recognised a familiar shape hurrying towards the grill. It was Molly Appleton, arriving late from London. In her hand she clutched an envelope, and seemed seriously agitated.

"George!" she called out. He frowned when he saw the expression on her face. Breathless, she came to a halt beside the revolving carcass and put a hand to her chest.

"What is it, Molly?" Everyone now fixed their gaze on what she was carrying.

"This letter's from the Bishop," she gasped. "It came to me as clerk of the PCC, but I think you should really have it as Chairman of the Parish Council."

Mr Stubbs shook his head, revealing hands that were greasy from carving the pork. "Can't it wait, Molly? Come and have some of this pork. It's best middle white."

"It's important, George. It affects the whole village. You should have had it before."

"If it's *that* important, perhaps you'd better read it out." He placed the carving knife on the bench and wiped his hands on his apron front. Molly pulled out the letter and began to read in a voice still unsteady from her exertions. The fairground music came to an abrupt stop. From where they were sitting, Marnie's group could hear every word.

"*... and consequently I have acted as quickly as possible to appoint a successor. I am pleased to be able to confirm that your new vicar will be available with immediate effect, so that the parish will not be left untended. It is a great joy to me to name the Reverend Toni Petrie as the new vicar of Knightly St John.*" A murmur of polite interest passed around the assembled villagers, only a few of whom noticed the abbreviated Christian name. "*Toni will be moving to her new post in the next few days and I know you will make her welcome. She is currently curate at ...*" Molly's voice died away and she looked up to see the bewildered expressions of those around her. There was a silence lasting several seconds as the news sank in. Mr Stubbs became pensive, the perspiration on his bald head shining in the light from the coals. Beside him, Albert Fletcher stared at Molly, his face reddened by the fire like a martyr burning at the stake.

"*She!* Did you say '*she*'?" Molly nodded. The old farmer let out a howl of pain and rage. "*She*, just like that? No consultation, not a single word? Must it always be *change, change, change*? Can't we ever have peace in this village? *Never?*" He seized the heavy carving knife from the bench where George Stubbs had laid it and raised it high above his head before plunging it into the pig, almost to the hilt. Everyone backed away and the old man stormed off, leaving a shocked silence behind him. Calmly, George Stubbs withdrew his knife from the carcass and wiped the blade on a cloth, staring thoughtfully after the old man as he vanished from the field into the darkness.

Part 21

Sunday 2 July

"I thought *Sally Ann* had turned into the *Marie Celeste*." To the sound of church bells carrying down from the village, Ralph stood in the doorway of the barn. "Coffee pot still warm in the galley, washing pegged out on the line, but no crew in sight."

Marnie looked up from her desk. "Have you had breakfast?"

"Long forgotten. I see I'm not the only one who starts work early, even on Sundays."

"Just tidying up some loose ends, nearly finished. Will you join us for lunch, Ralph?"

"Thank you, but no. I have other plans. I intend to go to the Manoir aux Quat' Saisons near Oxford. However ... do you think it's only academics who begin sentences with *however?* ... well, anyway, to get there I need a chauffeur and a navigator. I'm interviewing candidates for both jobs."

"But you'll never get a table, surely, at such short notice?"

"I booked last week but forgot to mention it." Seeing Marnie's doubting expression, Ralph added: "I've known the owner since he first opened back in the seventies. Say you'll join me?"

"An offer no-one could refuse. Thank you on behalf of both candidates."

At that moment Anne breezed in with an armful of newspapers. "Thank goodness you didn't want the *Sunday Times* as well as the *Observer*. I'd have needed a wheelbarrow!"

"Do you have any dresses or smart skirts in your cupboard, Anne?"

The girl stopped in her tracks. "I've got the things you bought me in Oxford Street."

"Good. I think you're going to need them. How good is your French?"

"We'll know the answer to that question on the twentieth of August."

"I'm taking you both to lunch, or rather you're taking me," said Ralph, relieving her of the papers.

"Great!" Anne turned her head towards the door. "Do you know those bells have been ringing for over an hour? And there are loads of people swarming around the church."

"The new vicar," said Marnie. "The bush telegraph."

❦ ❦ ❦ ❦

Every eye was on Toni Petrie as she crossed the nave and mounted the steps to the pulpit. She paused briefly, before speaking. The parishioners saw a woman in her early thirties, with shoulder-length brown hair and a fresh clean complexion. Her enthusiasm was bordering on exultation.

"Ladies and gentlemen ... it must be strange for you to hear me address you like that. I would rather begin by calling you 'my friends', but I would not presume to do that when we don't yet know each other. Like most of you I am a country person and I believe it takes time to build a friendship." A faint murmur of approval. "I was born and brought up in the Cotswolds, near Cirencester, though I've spent much of my life working in deprived areas in the Midlands. Let me say that whatever problems and misunderstandings there may have been in the past, my only wish is that we should work together to create a renewed sense of community, sharing our lives together in the service of God, here in this beautiful village." A lump came to her throat as she saw heads nodding all round the church. She wanted to rush down and embrace the people, *her people*, to seize them in her arms and tell them it would be all right. "I hope, ladies and gentlemen, that you will come to accept me so that we can work together. But I must not personalise things. The church is not about me. It's about service. It's about worship. It's about the glory of God and His creation. I give you my promise that I will do everything in my power to make this a ministry of joy."

She looked out from the pulpit. Every face was upturned. It was a new beginning, a chance to put aside centuries of strife. Almost every seat in the church was taken. Only in the second row was there a gap. The seat behind George Stubbs was unoccupied for the first time in living memory.

❦ ❦ ❦ ❦

"I wonder how the new vicar's getting on," said Ralph. He opened the parasol on the deck of *Sally Ann* and set out three safari chairs.

"I've just thought of something!" said Anne, as came up the steps from the cabin carrying a tray. "The singing in the church the other day ... perhaps that was the vicar. It was a woman."

"*And then my soul, like to the lark at break of day arising,*
Sings psalms at heaven's gate ..." Ralph quoted.

"Sounds possible," said Marnie, unfolding the table. "Mind you, I thought Shakespeare was writing about a different kind of joy."

"But the same sense of excitement," said Ralph.

"That was beautiful," said Anne. "It was just like that. If I'd had my wishes granted I'd feel like singing at heaven's gate. Well, I ... I do ..." She reached forward to pour coffee into the cups.

"So do I," said Ralph, passing a cup to Marnie.

They settled back with coffee and the newspapers to enjoy the warm Sunday morning. For once, Ralph did not take himself off to work on his book; Marnie did not settle down at her desk; Anne's list of tasks was nowhere in sight. A boat went by. Ralph read the political commentaries. Anne read the colour magazine. Marnie studied the main news pages, apparently engrossed in the same article for some time, studying Ralph over the top of her paper. It was true, what Beth had said. Ralph *was* distinguished. She had admitted as much to Beth when they found themselves alone together.

"I'd say he was quite a catch," Beth had said. "And he's very keen on *you*. You're keen on him too, aren't you?" Marnie had merely smiled indulgently at her sister. But Beth was not one to be put off so easily. "Okay, so it's none of my business. I can take a hint." The pause lasted nearly three seconds. "But you are keen. I can tell, Marnie. I can read you like a book."

"Then you don't need to ask me so many questions, do you?"

"I want to see you happy. Ralph could ..." Marnie had walked away, round the pottery stall, picking up the odd item. Beth followed and, just as she was thinking the conversation was at an end, Marnie looked up.

"This is more complicated than just any relationship," she said. "And we hardly know each other."

"But I've seen the way Ralph looks at you. You don't even seem to notice."

Marnie sighed. "I don't want Ralph to feel he has to be nice to me."

Beth looked puzzled. "Why *should* he?" Beth knew nothing of his attempted suicide.

"Look, Ralph is a very special sort of person ... he's very eminent in his field. I'm not in his league. I know nothing of his world. I'm not sure I'm the right sort of person for someone like him. Also, to be quite frank, I don't feel ready for a relationship ..."

"Are you serious? After nearly three years!" Her voice was getting louder. "Are you planning to turn Glebe Farm into a nunnery?" The woman running the pottery stall jerked her head up at them.

"Why not make an announcement over the tannoy?" said Marnie under her breath. Smiling light-heartedly in the direction of the stallholder, she pulled Beth to one side. "And I'm not in the market for a casual lover. I've had all that sort of thing and it's not for me."

"Or for Ralph, I would've thought," said Beth. "I bet you could have him eating out of your hand."

"I wouldn't *want* him eating out of my hand."

"It's only a manner of speaking. You see? You're getting as pedantic as an academic yourself."

"Let's say no more about it," said Marnie. "Not a single word. Agreed?"

"Okay. Agreed."

"Good," said Marnie. "That's good." She picked up a small vase.

"Sounds to me like you're just the sort of person he needs," said Beth.

"I said ... there's some hope of things improving in Ulster." It was Ralph speaking, looking over the top of his paper. Marnie quickly composed her thoughts.

"Oh, sorry ... I was concentrating. Does it? There's nothing in the main news section."

"It's in the business review. The banks are feeling more optimistic about the future and some industrialists are talking about increasing investment in the province." He looked thoughtful.

"Do you think that's significant?" said Marnie. "It's all bombs and bullets on the front page." Ralph stared for a few seconds into the middle distance.

"Hm ... hard to tell, really. Something could be in the air. That's the trouble with newspapers. They tend to print only what they think they can report. I sometimes think I only understand what's going on when I've had dinner with a minister the night before." Marnie felt completely out of her depth and rather depressed at the thought.

"Do you really have dinner with ministers?" said Anne.

"Sometimes ... or shadow ministers. We get quite a few at All Saints." He returned to the paper and Anne looked over at Marnie. Ralph turned the paper down. "Sorry. I shouldn't do that. It's like name-dropping. It's just that I'm in that line of business in a way ... on the sidelines, of course."

"Paul mentioned you'd been offered a chair in the States," said Marnie. She felt deflated, as if she was groping to try to keep up with the conversation and she knew Ralph was sensitive enough to realise how little she understood of his world. Strangely, it was Ralph who looked uncomfortable.

"Yes ... at Yale, actually."

"Oh," said Anne disappointed. "Does that mean you'll be going away?"

"Well, not necessarily. They've asked me to consider it and ... I am."

"Are you tempted?" said Marnie.

"The terms are very generous. Good facilities, research staff ... beautiful house."

"It sounds too good to miss," said Marnie. "Of course, it's not the same as Oxford, I suppose."

"That's right. It all depends on what one has to sacrifice. I like to think life is more than just a large research budget and a well-stocked library." He smiled across at Anne. "There are certain things I would be loth to give up."

"What's going on over there?" said Anne suddenly standing up. On the opposite bank a commotion had broken out. There was a blur of white, the sound of splashing and raised voices. Marnie and Ralph leapt to their feet in time to see a man run off down the towpath, leaving behind another man who appeared to be wrestling with a swan.

"It's Frank – Frank Day," said Marnie. She called across the canal. "Frank!

What's happened?" The reply came in gasps as he fought to gain control of the bird, battling against the beating wings. Marnie recalled reading somewhere that a swan's wings could break a person's arm.

"Bloody fool with a fishing rod!" he cried. He and the swan fell to the ground still writhing. It was hard to tell who was winning the struggle.

"Can we get across?" said Ralph. Without replying, Marnie leapt to the hatchway and switched on *Sally's* engine. Ralph ran to cast off at the bows and Anne followed his example, pulling the stern rope free from the mooring ring. In a few seconds they had reversed across the canal and found Frank securely holding the swan, both wings pinioned to its sides. He struggled to his feet as they approached, and Marnie pushed the lever into forward gear to avoid ramming the bank.

"Good morning. Nice day," he said in the most casual of tones, his clothes dusty and dishevelled. The swan made no effort to struggle free.

"What was all that about?" said Marnie over the noise of the engine. She pulled the lever into neutral and looked quickly up and down the canal. *Sally Ann* was blocking the whole channel.

"Damn fool of an angler got his line caught round the swan. It would have torn itself to pieces, and he just stood there gawping." He shook his head in disbelief.

"It seems all right now," said Marnie.

"Oh yes, for the moment. I need to cut her free. Do you have a sharp knife on board?"

"In the galley," said Anne and turned to go into the cabin.

"It'll have to be good. This line is really strong stuff."

"In the locker," said Marnie. "You know the one. It has a handle with rope bound round it."

"You had quite a battle just then," said Marnie.

"You've got to treat these things with caution."

Anne bounded up from the cabin holding the knife carefully away from her. In her haste she tripped on the top step and pitched forward. She tried to steady herself against the side of the boat, but lost her grip on the handle and groaned as the knife bounced on the gunwale and dropped into the water. Ralph stopped her from falling, but the knife was lost.

"Are you okay?" said Marnie.

Anne pulled a face. "I'm sorry. How stupid!"

"Don't worry. It could've been worse." She turned to Frank. "Will a kitchen knife do?"

"I've got a better idea. There's a knife in my car. It's just parked under the trees over there."

"I'll get it for you," said Anne. They all looked at her, including the swan. "To redeem myself." She jumped from the stern to the bank, retrieved the car keys from Frank's jacket pocket and jogged towards the car. This time she made no mistake.

"Here, Anne. Cut the line by her feet." Anne sawed carefully and the line came loose. "Can you pull it gently free? That's it. Good. Well done!" He set the swan down at the edge of the canal and she shook herself, standing upright to flap her wings. They watched as she settled herself in the water and slid away from the bank without looking back.

"I haven't introduced you," said Marnie. "Ralph, this is Frank Day. His firm handled my move from London. Frank, this is Ralph Lombard, a friend from Oxford." The men raised their hands in greeting. "Can you join us for coffee, Frank?"

"It's kind of you, but I've got the dogs here somewhere." He dusted himself down. "I ought to try and find them. Perhaps another time?"

"Of course. You'll have to tell me about handling swans in case I need to learn the trick."

"There's nothing to it. It's just a case of being determined. You can have them eating out of your hand. No problem."

After Frank had gone on his way, they guided *Sally* back to her mooring. Anne promised to rescue the knife and as soon as they docked, she went below to find the magnet. Marnie and Ralph resumed their places.

"You know, Marnie, when I'm with you I often have the strangest feeling."

"You make me sound like indigestion!"

"Yes. I could have chosen my words better. What I meant was ... well, you often make me feel ... inadequate."

"*Inadequate?*" said Marnie.

"Yes. You're very decisive. You always seem to know what to do in any situation. You must think me very pedestrian."

"I'm sure the ministers who dine with you don't find you pedestrian, Ralph."

"Anyone who reads the newspapers can have ideas. You make things happen. You're a very special person, Marnie. Well, I never thought I'd ever see *you* blush!"

"It's the sunshine," said Marnie, feeling the glow spread from her cheeks. Just then Anne came up on deck, shaking her head.

"It's no use. I can't find it anywhere."

"What?" said Marnie.

"The magnet. I need it to get the knife back."

"Don't worry for now. We ought to be setting off. We don't want to be late for lunch."

"I'll change, then," said Anne. "Won't be a minute." She hesitated before going down the cabin steps. "Marnie, you ought to put some cream on your face. You look as if you've caught the sun."

"Get a move on!" said Marnie. "We've got to go and eat." Anne grinned as she went below and Ralph went over to *Thyrsis*, promising to be ready in five minutes.

"*... eating out of your hand ...*" Twice she had heard that expression in as many days. *All a question of being determined*, she recalled. No. That was not her style. Even so, she would set off for lunch with a spring in her step. *Inadequate.* Amazing!

❦   ❦   ❦   ❦

The Range Rover pulled up in the yard of Rooks Farm and George Stubbs climbed out. He walked over to the kitchen door, the top half of which was open, and stuck his head inside.

"Good morning!" Across the tiled floor he saw Maureen Fletcher kneeling in front of the dark blue Aga, basting a joint in the top oven. He breathed in the aroma of the joint of beef and freshly cut vegetables on the chopping board. Maureen slid the tray back into the depths of the oven and came over to the door, wiping her hands on her apron. "That's what I like to see," said George, "A fine piece of sirloin with roast potatoes. It's what Sunday morning is all about ... and church, of course."

"Some of us have to dash back to see to the joint in the oven, while others can call in somewhere for a swift half," Maureen said with a smile.

"Well, there you'd be mistaken, my dear. I went home to take Sheila back. Then I just thought I'd nip round to see how Albert was. I didn't get a chance to see him in church this morning."

Maureen smoothed her apron. "And you'll not get a chance to see him here, either. He's out."

"*Gone out? On a Sunday morning?*"

"That's right. Took himself off early. Said he wanted some air. Had his boots on." She invested the statement with symbolic meaning.

"Do you know where he went?"

"Over the fields, I suppose. No doubt he'll be back for lunch. I'll tell him you called."

George climbed back into the Range Rover and started the engine. *He had his boots on* ... And on Sunday morning, too.

❦ ❦ ❦ ❦

The vicar of Knightly St John dropped a note in through the letterbox of the vicarage to let Randall Hughes know that his suggested arrangements for moving out were fine. Randall seemed to be adopting a low profile, giving her scope to move into the village without his shadow hanging over her. For some seconds she stood with her back to the front door and listened. There was a heavy droning from the bees in the honeysuckle and the sound of birds singing all around. *And the sound of birds singing all around.* Toni Petrie wanted to join in with her own chorus, just as she had done on the day she received the phone call from the Bishop's office.

From the doorway she could not see the road because of the bend in the drive. She waited, wishing that she could go in and take possession of the vicarage there and then. But she would not impose herself on the village, would not come unbidden like an intruder. She would be patient, even though that was not her style. In time they would get to know her. But for now, she would hold back. She turned to look up at the eighteenth century façade of the house. The kitchen and the rooms above it were said to be fifteenth century and the cellars even older. What a difference from the modest semi she shared with two other women curates in Wellingborough!

The warmth, the humming and the birdsong made her drowsy. She walked slowly round the house. Randall Hughes was no gardener. The lawn was neat enough, but the flowerbeds were unkempt with weeds sprouting everywhere and branches tangled together. Toni began pulling up the nearest groundsel, leaving small piles at the edge of the grass. She sat down on a bench in the sunshine and planned how the garden would take shape under her care, overwhelmed at the thought that all this was her domain, all this and the parish of Knightly St John!

❦ ❦ ❦ ❦

"I don't think they taught us this kind of French at school," said Anne.

"You'd have enjoyed the coursework, though," said Marnie, whose French was above average, honed by practice on numerous holidays.

"I'd have gone all out for an 'A' in the practical."

"What practical?"

"Eating," said Anne. Ralph chuckled without taking his eyes from the menu. They sat at a table near the window overlooking the gardens, with a white cloth, a bowl of roses and silver candlestick. The restaurant was all restrained elegance, an English country house transformed into a small château set down in the countryside outside Oxford.

The head waiter approached across the room, a discreet smile at the corner of his mouth. Marnie was surprised that they had been given so little time to study the menu. In her experience of French restaurants they took food seriously and always allowed the customer to choose at leisure.

"*Monsieur Lombard.*" He pronounced the name in the French way, the 'o' long, the 'r' rolled, the 'd' mute. "It is such a pleasure to see you again. And it is the first time you have come with your charming family." He shook hands with Marnie. "*Madame Lombard, enchanté.*" Marnie murmured "*Monsieur,*" in a very passable accent. "*Et mademoiselle.*"

"*Monsieur.*" Anne smiled charmingly and the waiter was delighted. He turned to Ralph.

"*Mes compliments, monsieur. Elles sont ravissantes!*" At that point any explanation would be embarrassing. Before Ralph could speak, the waiter continued. "Excuse my interruption. I will leave you in peace to choose. But I am sure the *patron* will want to see you later." He departed as quickly as he had come.

"*Madame Lombard,*" said Anne in an exaggerated stage French accent. "Oh, Ralph, I could get used to this. I like being *mademoiselle.*"

"I'm so glad," said Ralph. He turned to Marnie. "I could ask if you liked being *madame*, but I might get a shirty answer."

"You might, if you come between me and the menu."

"Fair enough," said Ralph. "It's not easy to choose. Everything they do here is very good."

"Do they have restaurants like this in Yale?" said Anne.

"Well … Yale is in New Haven, that's Connecticut on the eastern seaboard. There's a restaurant I know just along the coast heading towards Cape Cod where they do the most *superb* clam bake, served with a dry white wine from a small family-run vineyard in California."

"Sounds like you've already made up your mind," said Anne.

"Yes, I rather think I have."

🌸   🌸   🌸   🌸

That night, on board *Sally Ann*, Dolly jumped down from Marnie's bed and wandered over to her basket in the saloon. It was her custom at the end of every day to sit on the bed, while Marnie sat up reading until it was time to turn off the light. She curled round and round in the basket and settled into the hollow she had formed in her blanket.

"Okay if I put the light out?" said Marnie.

"Fine by me," said Anne from her camp bed in the saloon. "And I don't think Dolly will object."

"No. She seems to have adjusted very well to country life." Marnie reached up to the light switch.

"I hear her purring every night when I'm dropping off to sleep," said Anne. "It's very soothing. In fact, I feel like purring myself tonight."

"You've enjoyed today?"

"I enjoy *every* day," said Anne. "But today was special. I loved the restaurant. It was marvellous."

"Yes, it was," said Marnie.

"Is Ralph really going to go?"

"Tomorrow morning," said Marnie.

"No, I mean to America, to Yale."

"I don't know."

"I'd miss Ralph," said Anne. "So would you." There was no reply, only the faint sound of Dolly, softly purring in her basket. "The best part was when the owner came out to see us. *Please come back soon, monsieur,*" Anne grossly exaggerated the owner's French accent. "*Your colleagues are nice but they are not as charming as your beautiful ladies!*" They laughed together in the darkness.

"Bonne nuit, *mademoiselle,*" said Marnie.

"Bonne nuit, *madame.*"

🌸   🌸   🌸   🌸

The vicar's first full week in office was not marked by disasters, natural or manmade. No bolt of lightning struck the church. No plague of locusts descended on the ripening crops. No-one became deranged and ran round the village attacking the inhabitants with a chain-saw. Everyone went about their usual business and, while there was much talk about the *woman vicar* in the shop, outside the school and on street corners, comment was mainly favourable or at least open-minded.

Ralph set off towards the south on the next leg of his journey aboard *Thyrsis*, promising to keep in touch when he could. Building works continued to make good progress at Glebe Farm.

Toni Petrie began her rounds of the village without delay, clutching a large blue notebook and a filofax. Someone commented that the village was being taken over by yuppie women, but it was said without malice. She arrived at the school by appointment on Tuesday morning and was shown into the Head's office by Valerie Paxton, who for some days had been withdrawn, camouflaging her silence by immersing herself in assessments and reports, the countless jobs to be done before the end of the school year. While the Head and the vicar drank coffee and talked about the monthly service held in the school hall, confirmation classes and the board of governors, Valerie sat at her desk opening the post, pondering the changes that had happened in her world, absent-mindedly fingering her dagger. After the first few letters, she forgot about the rest and sank into her thoughts. A child came into the office and put a class register on her desk, but she did not look up.

The sudden laughter as the head's office door opened nearly rocked Valerie from her seat. To cover her surprise she turned quickly back to the post, but as she reached for the letters she jerked the hand holding the dagger and dug the point into the side of her thumb. The sharp pain rushed like lightning to her head, making her feel sick and draining all colour from her face. The Head and the vicar stood silenced in the doorway before reacting. Blood ran down Valerie's wrist and dripped onto her skirt.

The Head rushed forward, producing a paper tissue from her sleeve. "Valerie!" she cried, reaching for her arm. At last Valerie realised what was happening. Abruptly she stood up and rushed out of the room, leaving splashes of blood on the desk and on the floor.

🌹   🌹   🌹   🌹

The wound was still painful when Valerie stood at the sink in the kitchen that evening, putting a fresh plaster on her thumb after doing the washing-up. Her husband came in from emptying the waste bin and looked at the old plaster lying on the draining board.

"That's a *nasty* cut, love," he said. "Don't you think you ought to see the doctor? You might need stitches in that."

"I'll see how it is in the morning."

"You don't want to get an infection."

"I've put Savlon on it. It'll be all right, I expect. It was a stupid accident. Mrs G probably thinks I had it coming. She's always going on about my paperknife."

"Looks like she's got a point, love. Can't you get one of those plastic letter-openers? Safer."

"All right, all right! Don't you go on as well. It's bad enough knowing what the Head thinks. The two of them must have had a right old gossip about me when I was in the loo with my hand under the tap. It was because of them bursting into my office that I stuck the knife in my thumb ... making me jump like that ..."

"So you've met Rev Petrie, then," he said, trying to change the subject.

"*Rev Petrie*," repeated Valerie.

"What's she like? Nice?"

"Euphoric."

"What?"

"That's what she's like … *euphoric*. Full of herself. She's like a child at a party that's just won pass-the-parcel." Her husband began pulling off his shoes, the usual prelude to putting his boots on before going out to do 'a bit in the garden'.

"Probably excited at having her own parish," he said. Valerie did not reply and stood staring out of the window, remembering how it used to be. Her husband stepped into his boots and pulled open the back door. He looked at the plaster on the draining board, with its thick brown stain. "First blood to the new vicar," he said without spite and went out shaking his head. Valerie stared after him, wondering what on earth he had meant, what on earth he knew.

❦ ❦ ❦ ❦

Wednesday 5 July

"Good morning, Mrs Walker. The Head won't be long. She's on the phone at the moment. Would you like a seat?" Valerie indicated a chair in the opposite corner of her office. The room was filled with the unmistakable school smell, a compound of chalk, bookshelves, children and plasticine.

"Thank you," said Marnie. "That must make typing difficult." Valerie looked at her thumb, encased in a fingerstall.

"I keep hitting three keys at once." Marnie gave her a sympathetic smile. There was the sound of footsteps in the corridor outside, hurried and business-like. Valerie looked towards the door and Marnie noticed her expression cloud over for a brief second before resuming its impassive stare. A soft tap on the open door and in came Toni Petrie, smart and brisk in clerical black.

"Sorry to interrupt, Valerie. I thought I'd just pop in to see how you were." Valerie flushed and glanced over to where Marnie was sitting. The vicar noticed her for the first time. "Oh, good morning. Didn't see you there." Marnie stood up and sensed that the vicar was torn between her concern for Valerie and meeting a parishioner. Toni leaned forward and lightly touched Valerie's wrist. The effect was startling. Valerie stiffened and rose awkwardly to her feet.

"Would you excuse me a moment." She picked up a bundle of registers from her desk and left the room. The two women looked at each other and the vicar held out her hand.

"Toni Petrie. I don't think we've met."

"We haven't, but we were about to. My name's Marnie Walker." They shook hands. "Your predecessor asked me to help him with the porch."

"You're an architect, Marnie?"

"I'm an interior designer, but I have links with my old firm and one of the partners deals with churches. Of course, you may decide that you want someone else to handle it. No problem."

"Perhaps we can get together to talk about it," said Toni. "Is your architect local?"

"No, London, but he could come up at the weekend if you'd like to see him."

"Bring him to the church open day on Saturday," said Toni. "Let's get it done."

"Don't you want to think about it first?"

"No. Let's get on with it. I don't like things hanging round. Life's too short."

"Fine. Saturday it is." The vicar turned to leave.

"What was that about an accident?" said Marnie.

"I'm afraid it was partly my fault. The Head and I surprised Valerie and she stabbed herself with the paperknife. Sounds funny, I know, but it's quite a vicious thing."

"I've seen it," said Marnie. "I think it's rather a bone of contention in the office."

"What you might call a sore point!" Toni guffawed at her own joke and stopped abruptly. "Sorry. I ought not to laugh. It was a nasty wound. Bled all over the place. Nice to meet you. See you on Saturday." Marnie walked over to the window. The vicar was striding across the playground. Literally a woman with a mission. *Focused.* One of the modern breed of women. Marnie wondered if that was how people saw her. In her line of business women were on equal terms. But what did people want in a vicar? Was the argument about women priests all over now, or did it still simmer below the surface? I bet I can guess, thought Marnie. The inner door clicked open behind her.

"Mrs Walker! Please forgive me. I always seem to be keeping you waiting." The Head looked around the office. "And no-one to look after you. I'm *so* sorry. Have you been here long?"

"No. And I've just met the new vicar and arranged a meeting, so my time has been well spent."

"Good. Come in, come in. Coffee's all ready." Just then, Valerie returned. Her expression made it clear that she knew the vicar had gone and was ready for any criticism of her absence from the office. "Ah, Valerie. Will you hold any calls, please, while I'm talking to Mrs Walker."

"Right."

"I gather the vicar was here." It was a statement that expected a reply.

"Yes, she came to see me."

"To see *you*?"

"Yes. Aren't I a lucky girl? She came to ask how my hand was." There was a prickly silence. "It makes a change, doesn't it, for someone to come to see *me*."

"In a way, I suppose," said the Head. "A pleasant change, I hope. It was a kind thought."

"Yes." Valerie breathed the word out like a long sigh. "We've had a lot of changes lately, not all of them for the better." She walked round the desk and sat down, pulling the keyboard of her computer towards her to mark the end of the conversation. The Head turned towards her office and Marnie made to follow. "Our vicar ..." Valerie began again. "Our *real* vicar was a wonderful man ... whatever people may say behind his back. He was an inspiration to us all." She looked down to concentrate on hitting the right keys.

🌷 🌷 🌷 🌷

Saturday 8 July

"What are you up to, young lady?" Marnie looked in through the open door of the office barn.

"Just tidying up," said Anne, crawling out from under her desk. "I'm rearranging the plugs on my computer. I've been wanting to do it all week, but we've been so busy, I didn't get a chance."

"You're a bigger workaholic than I am. Eight o'clock on a Saturday morning is a time when most people are glad to take things easy. Are you coming for breakfast?"

"I'll be over in five minutes. Promise. I want to give your friend a good impression, so he'll tell everybody in your old office what a smart outfit you have up here."

"And what a great team," added Marnie. For ten minutes they knocked the office into shape before walking back through the spinney. "Well, he'll be impressed with that," she said. "Mike's one of those artistic types who always works in a mess. He has a sort of curly, unkempt charm, I suppose, but his drawings are wonderful and his handwriting's a work of art."

"When's he coming?"

"About noon, in time for a chat and a bite before the big event."

"I think the vicar's very brave to have an open day so soon after arriving," said Anne. They stepped on board *Sally Ann* and walked through to the galley.

"It was already arranged," said Marnie. She relit the gas under the kettle and took the croissants out of the oven.

"She could have put it back to another day," said Anne, loading crockery onto the tray.

"Yes ... she could have, but I don't think it's in her nature. *Life's too short,* she said. She strikes me as rather impulsive. The sort who likes to rush in."

"Where angels fear to tread?" said Anne. Marnie smiled and measured ground coffee into the cafetière. Anne picked up the tray.

"I expect she knows more about angels than I do," said Marnie. "It is part of her business after all. No, I'm not suggesting she's a fool. But she makes you feel there's something bubbling away inside her ... loads of energy bursting to come out."

"The same goes for that kettle, I think," said Anne indicating the steam billowing from the spout.

"Right on cue. Let's go for it."

❦ ❦ ❦ ❦

Anne was taking photographs in the middle of the yard when the Sierra estate pulled up by the barn. She was making a record of the conversion of Glebe Farm. The man who climbed out of the car, removing his sunglasses, was just as she imagined him from Marnie's description. He wore putty-coloured slacks with a country check shirt of blue and green and a petrel blue sweatshirt slung casually over his shoulders.

"Hiya! You from the tabloids?" An unmistakable Welsh accent.

"I'm Anne. I'm from the firm."

"Me too. Mike Thomas."

"Have you come alone? I thought your family were coming too?"

"That was the plan. Unfortunately Zoë – she's two and a half – is running a temperature, so Stephie's had to stay at home with her."

Anne led the visitor towards *Sally Ann*, but not before he had given the buildings a quick inspection. Anne insisted that he saw the office barn and, pronouncing himself impressed with the whole set-up, they made their way chatting easily together through the spinney. Over lunch Marnie outlined the problems with the porch and they decided to visit the church before Mike met the vicar.

Armed with clipboard and notepad, Mike inspected the porch at close range, running his hand over the stonework, peering at the pointing where it abutted the main structure, examining it inside and out.

"What do you think?" said Marnie. Mike shook his head.

"I don't know what all the fuss was about, really." He pointed at the base of the porch. "Look at this. It's built on solid rock and they've done a good job. I know loads of so-called builders who couldn't touch this. If this was done by apprentices, they had a pretty good idea what they were about."

"Then why was the diocesan surveyor so worried?" said Marnie.

Mike shrugged his broad shoulders. "Hard to say. Probably covering his own back. Trouble with other buildings, maybe ... wanting to show he was taking action."

"Have you seen enough for now?"

"Yes. I've got the picture. It's a lovely church ... beautiful stone."

"Come inside. There's something I want to show you." Marnie led the way into the church. Anne put a coin in the box, took a history booklet and gave it to Mike. They crossed the nave to the tower door at the foot of the sanctuary steps and Marnie tried the handle. It slid open noiselessly.

"In the Civil War the vicar was murdered in this tower," said Anne. "You can read about it in the booklet. They never found out who did it."

"How was he killed?" said Mike.

"I'm not really sure. He fell to the bottom of the steps."

"I don't think the booklet tells *how* he died," said Marnie. "I thought perhaps he'd been shot. I don't know why." They began to climb the narrow steps. At the first window, Marnie turned to Mike. "What do you think of the mullions here?" Mike stood on tiptoe to inspect the detailing.

"Nice work. You're not going to tell me the apprentices built the tower, are you?"

"Is it possible?"

Mike shook his head. "This is real craftsmanship. People just take old churches for granted, part of the landscape. But men built them with fairly simple tools and they've stood for centuries. Look at this stonework." Lovingly, he ran his broad palm down the wall. "They took extra care with churches, you know. A matter of pride. Only the best was good enough."

"That's what I thought," said Marnie. She resumed the climb, leading the way up to the ledge with the wooden partition. It was in shadow and Marnie leaned to one side to let Mike take a closer look.

"It's very dark," he muttered. Craning forward, he touched the surface. "What is it ... oak?"

"How do you know that?" said Anne.

"That's what they used round here." He passed his hand over the stonework. "That's odd ..."

"What's odd?" said Marnie.

"Not sure," said Mike. "You find a lot of strange things in ancient buildings." He thumped twice with his fist on the wood as if it was a door. The hollow sound was loud in the confined space.

"Hallo!" The voice, a woman's voice, echoed all around them in the tower, an unexpected reply to Mike's banging on the screen. Anne gasped. Mike turned in a split second and caught her wrist as she slipped from the step, bracing himself against the stone wall and dropping his clipboard so that he could grasp her shoulder. The board clattered down the steps into the gloom below.

"Hallo! Hallo! Who's up there?" The voice was louder now and Marnie, who had reached forward to put an arm round Anne's back, called out in reply.

"It's me, Molly ... Marnie Walker. We're coming down." She turned to Mike and Anne. "All okay?" They groped their way carefully down the steps, Mike leading, with Anne in the middle. The clipboard had fallen all the way to the bottom. Molly Appleton was waiting for them by the door.

"I didn't know it was you," she said. "I heard a banging and thought it might be kids. It can be dangerous in the tower – easy to fall." Marnie made the introductions and explained Mike's presence. She noticed that Anne was quite pale.

"Don't tell me the new vicar wants to rebuild the tower as well," said Molly.

"No. no. I'm just getting the feel of the place," said Mike.

"Mike's a specialist in this sort of building," Marnie explained. "He worked on the restoration of York Minster."

"Oh, I hope we can afford you," said Molly with a smile.

Mike looked at Marnie. "I expect we'll do this on a ... friendly basis," he said. "A sort of favour to Marnie to help her settle in to the village." All around them people were arranging flowers under the direction of an elderly lady with a plan in one hand, leaving the other free to command.

"We always used to have a Flower Festival in the summer," said Molly. "Then it grew into an open day, but flowers still play a big part. Mrs Grainger has been in charge of it for as long as I can remember. You'll have to excuse me now. I'm helping her and she doesn't like it if things don't go according to plan. I'll just lock the tower door. Don't want anyone else going up. You never know what might happen to them up there."

The three of them walked slowly down the aisle and Marnie put her arm round Anne's shoulder.

"Sorry about that," said Anne. "Thanks for catching me, Mike."

"How are you feeling?" said Marnie.

"Okay. Not bad. I just got such a shock."

"Me too," said Mike. "I should have warned you I was going to bang on the partition. I wanted to see how solid it was. I didn't expect an answer."

"What shall we do now?" said Marnie, changing the subject. "It's about an hour before the opening."

"Well, it's a warm day," Mike began. "We could go over the ..."

Before he could finish, Marnie interrupted him. "I think there's the answer to our question." Toni Petrie, in a light grey cassock, neat brown hair shining in the sunlight, stood in the entrance waiting for them to emerge. She was wearing a silver chain and cross, in the style of a Celtic wheel cross, the size of a child's fist, with matching ear-rings.

"Good god," muttered Mike under his breath. "You've only been here five minutes, Marnie, and you've installed a designer vicar!" Anne nearly choked trying not to laugh.

Marnie smiled sweetly at Mike and spoke through clenched teeth. "You wait till I get you outside."

As it happened, Mike's idea was precisely what the vicar suggested. Sitting round a table in the pub garden, they pored over the plans of the church while Mike outlined his views. The most important task was to find a reliable stone mason who had a sympathy for old structures.

"Any bloody fool – oh, sorry, Vicar – anyone ... can chop out the stone, shove in another bit and slap mortar over the join."

"Even *I* could do it," said the vicar.

"Quite," said Mike. "Oh sorry, no ... I mean ... well ..."

"I know what you mean. By the way, please call me Toni. So, how do we find our builder? What about your chaps, Marnie?"

"They seem to be okay. You've seen their work, Mike. What do you think?"

"They're fine."

"And Anne keeps them well lubricated," said Marnie.

"I'll have to get a bike if I've got to come up here as well," said Anne. "I'll be like meals on wheels."

"That's a snag, of course. They're not a big firm and they're going to be down with us for some months to come."

"Well, the porch isn't dangerous," said Mike. "But you're still under pressure to get the work done."

Toni looked at her watch and drained her glass. "So we may have to find another firm," she said.

"The council will probably help," said Mike.

"Good idea," said Toni. "We'll find the best we can. After all, we don't want it to be a bloody mess, do we?"

It turned out to be one of those golden days that people remember years later. The sun shone, children behaved themselves, dogs lay in the shade under yew trees in the churchyard and not one discordant note was sounded all afternoon.

The whole scene looked like the setting for a television commercial depicting village England. It was to be the only golden day that summer.

Marnie could not fully disengage her thoughts from the tower. But she was determined not to unsettle Anne and did not mention the murder of the vicar again. One of the displays was called *All Our Yesterdays* and Marnie wandered across to see if it contained anything about the Civil War. There were boards covered in photographs and a large table of memorabilia dedicated to the two world wars. Marnie was drawn to a collection of pictures showing the canal, one of which had Glebe Farm faint and shadowy in the background. She strained to pick out some details. The roofline was clear, but most of the buildings were hidden behind one of the crew of the boat in the foreground. As she squinted with her nose only inches from the photo, Marnie felt sure the crew member was a woman in trousers. She was putting all her weight on a pole, pushing the boat away from the bank.

"You'll strain your eyes doing that," said a voice from behind her. Marnie turned to find a man in the dark blue uniform of a fire warden, with a tin helmet bearing the letter 'W'. He was about sixty with a pleasant, unremarkable face and not much taller than Marnie.

"I'm interested in the canals," she said pointing at the photo. "And I think that's where I live in the background." The man peered at the picture.

"That's Glebe Farm all right. I was born on it. Ron Fletcher's my name." He stuck out a hand. "And you're Mrs Walker."

"Marnie."

"Marnie," he repeated. "That's nice. I've never met a Marnie before."

"And you're a relative of Albert Fletcher, of course."

"Younger brother. I'm the youngest of seven. Lived here all my life ... well, so far, anyway." He grinned at her.

"Do you have any other pictures showing the farm? I'd love to see what it used to look like."

"Bound to have some somewhere. Boxes of them in the loft, I think."

"And the canal?" said Marnie.

"I'm not so sure about *that*. Maybe in the background. We used to take photos of outings and parties, family snaps. The canal was just everyday work. We took it for granted."

"But someone took these pictures," said Marnie.

"That's because they were women and got stuck in the mud. Trainees, they were. Took them ages to get off."

"Did you see them yourself ... or were you too little, perhaps?"

"I was there. I was about ten at the time. One of the women was on the bank. She had this rickety old bike and wanted to push from the edge of the water, but couldn't get near enough. My granddad came down to have a look and sent me back to get a pitchfork handle."

"Did it work?"

"Oh yes. But I felt sorry for the woman with the bike."

"She fell in?"

"No. She left her beret behind. I found it later in the grass long after they'd gone."

"Did you ever see her again?"

"No. They didn't do regular runs." He looked thoughtful. "Just a minute." He bent down and rummaged under the table, producing an old biscuit tin. "Do you know what people used to call them, those women trainees?"

"'Idle women'," said Marnie.

"That's right. And this is why." He picked a small round badge out of the box. It was made of plastic and bore the letters 'IW' standing on two wavy lines under the inscription 'National Service'.

"Did *they* tell you that?" said Marnie. "The letters really stood for Inland Waterways. 'Idle Women' was just their joke."

"They never spoke to me," he said. "I saw a television programme about them a few years ago. That's when I remembered the badge. It was on the beret ... just lying in the tin all those years. I used to wear it to play soldiers for a while." Marnie handed it back.

"I met one of them myself last year," she said. "Tough as old boots. They had to be, I suppose."

"It's no use to me," Ron Fletcher said. "Why don't you have it? Take it back to Glebe Farm. Better than lying in that tin."

Marnie shook her head. "Oh, I couldn't ..."

"Go on. You were meant to have it."

"I don't really believe in fate," said Marnie. "But thank you, if you're sure. I'd love to have it."

She found Anne and Mike engrossed in conversation with Frank Day. As she approached, Frank half turned towards her.

"Ah, Marnie. Hallo. Have you met Janet?" Frank's wife was not what Marnie had expected. She seemed older, matronly and comfortable, with a countrywoman's ruddy complexion and grey hair swept back in a bun.

"I feel as if I know you already," she said. "Frank has told me all about your plans for Glebe Farm. I gather work is really coming on."

"So far so good," said Marnie. "Still a long way to go."

"It's all change in Knightly at the moment," said Janet. "Have you met the new vicar?"

"Yes. We've just been talking to her. Mike's going to sort out the problems with the porch."

"Is that her over there talking to Molly Appleton?" Janet pointed to the far side of the churchyard. There was an open area where stalls were set out in a semi-circle.

"Yes. Brown hair, grey dress ... only it's a cassock."

"Very tasteful," said Janet thoughtfully.

Anne leaned forward to examine the IW badge that Marnie had attached to the lapel of her jacket. "I'll tell you about it later," she said to Anne. "I'd rather like to see a few more stalls. Perhaps the WI will provide us with a cake for tea. Shall we see?"

For the rest of the afternoon they wandered round the stalls. Mike insisted on buying a cake, as well as some scones and home-made raspberry jam. The doyennes of the WI stall told Marnie that she could bring him back any time.

Marnie's thoughts kept returning to the tower and the unsolved murder. She made up her mind to talk it over with Ralph, but not mention it to Anne.

"Come on, Marnie." Mike was standing beside her. She had not noticed him approach. "Time to switch off. Relax." She gave him a puzzled look. "You're staring up at the tower. You can think about work tomorrow. This is fun time."

"Is it fun for you, Mike?"

"Oh yes. But then I'm not a workaholic like you."

"Can I just ask you something, while we're alone?"

"Good god, you're not going to propose are you? I don't know how I'll tell Stephie. She'll definitely want custody of the parrot."

"Mike, be serious! Listen." Marnie glanced over her shoulder and saw Anne studying the old photos. "This morning, in the tower, you were starting to say there was something odd about it."

"Was I?"

"Just before Anne slipped off the step. Can you remember what it was?"

He concentrated. "Something about the partition, I think. It just flashed into my mind suddenly."

"What was it? And why did you bang on it?"

"To see, how solid it was. Did you think there was something strange, Marnie?"

"Yes I did, but I can't put my finger on it."

"Nor me. Anyway, it's the porch we're supposed to be worrying about ... which reminds me: if I do the spec and the working drawings, will you keep an eye on it? It's a pretty straightforward job."

"Yes, of course. Mike, I really want you to think what was odd about the tower."

"Okay. I'll try to remember."

"Good, but let's change the subject now. Anne's coming over. She gets nervous."

"Right. You're determined about this, aren't you?"

"Definitely. I'm going to get to the bottom of this business if it kills me." She smiled as Anne came up. "Do I take it you've worked out where I got the badge?"

"Yes." Anne looked rueful. "Some people can't take a hint."

"I hope you didn't try to suggest that he gave you something from his collection," said Marnie.

"Not so he noticed apparently," said Anne. She reached forward and touched the badge. "Is it a genuine 'Idle Women' badge?"

"The real thing."

Part 22

Sarah Anne sat alone on a bale of straw under a beam in the cool of her uncle's barn in the heat of the day. Her eyes staring, her mind was filled with words and images. The words were war and guilt, bigotry and hatred.

"... forgive us our trespasses ... lead us not into temptation ... forgive ... forgive ..."

She recited her prayers over and over, her lips moving but no sound coming from them.

"... pray for us sinners now and at the hour of our death ..."

Words flooded into her mind, sin and shame, dishonour and sacrifice.

"I believe in God, the Father Almighty, maker of Heaven and Earth ..."

The images were flames and smoke.

"... the forgiveness of sins, the resurrection of the body and the life everlasting ... the forgiveness of sins ..."

The images were blood and death.

"Vengeance is mine; I will repay, saith the Lord ..."

In her hands, hands that had known hard work all her young life, hands that tended her father and had laid out the body of the vicar, she held a length of rope. It was good strong hemp, twelve feet of it, the kind they used on the farm for binding hay and tethering animals. As she murmured her prayers, Sarah Anne twisted the rope, round and round in her fingers. She twisted it like a rosary.

Monday 10 July

Fact: the vicar was killed in the tower one night in 1645, thought Marnie. She was walking more slowly than usual up the field track towards the village.

Question: how was he killed? She had re-read the church history booklet the evening before, after Anne had gone back to her loft. There was no mention of any murder weapon.

Fact: the murderer, or possibly murderers, had never been found.

Question: was someone covering up for the murderer? If so, who? Why?

Question: what wounds did the vicar have? Could he have died from falling, or being thrown, down the steps? This detecting business was more complicated than it seemed, thought Marnie. In the books she had read, a brilliant sleuth would be presented with a whole array of clues, all of them baffling and after much thought, plus a few helpful coincidences thrown in, would arrive at a dazzlingly clever solution to the whole thing. What did she have? An incomplete description of the event in a booklet costing twenty pence!

She reached the top of the field and hesitated before turning right towards the school and the main street. She had a few minutes in hand before her meeting with Margaret Giles. The road was deserted. People were at work. The week was just beginning. *All over the village it was a normal day.* Marnie looked back to where Glebe Farm was nestling below her, where Anne was happily engrossed with the computer.

Some movement away to her right caught Marnie's eye. Coming across the field on the top path was Albert Fletcher. Marnie fingered the IW badge on her lapel and waited as he drew near. At first she thought he had not seen her by the gate and might even walk by without a word, but at the last moment he looked up and stopped. His face seemed more drawn than she remembered and he gave her an almost grudging smile, just this side of courtesy. Marnie showed him the badge his brother had given her. He glanced at it with little interest. It occurred to Marnie that farmers are interested in the larger things in life, harvests, seasons, herds, the land passing from generation to generation. It was scholars like Ralph who interpreted the world through detail. Mr Fletcher asked how the works were going and seemed pleased at their progress. At that there was little more to be said between them and they went their separate ways.

Albert Fletcher had gone barely ten metres when a Range Rover came by and stopped beside him. The driver's window slid noiselessly down.

"Well, Albert," said George Stubbs. "Was that the delightful Mrs Walker you were talking to?"

"It was."

"I see you're not yet opposed to all women, then." George had a twinkle in his eye.

"I would like to think she'll restore the farm so that it has a useful purpose again," Albert said slowly. "I can't make out what she's going to do with it, but I expect she has her own ideas."

"We're not seeing much of you just now," said George. Albert remained silent. "We're coming for lunch on Sunday. Will we see you in church?"

"I'm giving church a miss for a while."

"In protest at the new vicar?"

"I'm not protesting. No use in that. I don't believe the village will be happy with a woman priest, that's all. I'm just giving her enough rope to hang herself."

❦   ❦   ❦   ❦

"I think this is a very good programme, Mrs Walker – Marnie. Would you like another cup of coffee?" She was surprised when Marnie accepted, surprised and pleased. Margaret Giles found Marnie's company highly agreeable. It made a pleasant change to meet someone so full of creative ideas, so full of energy.

"Mrs Giles … Margaret, there's something I'd like to ask you about the church. It may seem an odd question, but do you know how the vicar was murdered in 1645?"

"That's rather a strange question. You'll appreciate it's not the kind of subject that we'd choose for a school project on local history." She chuckled. "I think the honest answer is that I don't really know."

"What *do* you know?" said Marnie. The Head pondered this. In her position it was unusual to find herself admitting to ignorance.

"Only what's written in the church booklet. I don't think it says *how* he was murdered, does it?" She smiled. "Most of my thoughts about murder concern some of the more difficult parents."

"Of course," said Marnie. "It was just a thought. I can't imagine the Civil War impinges much on your daily life."

"Oh, I didn't say that," said Margaret. "In fact, I'm in correspondence with the education office about it at the moment."

"Really?"

Before replying, Margaret reached down to the bottom drawer of her desk and brought out a small, well-thumbed booklet. "This is the County Education Plan of 1947. Every authority had to produce one as part of the implementation of the 1944 Education Act. Sorry, I'm starting to sound like a teacher … force of habit. Anyway, in here you'll find a proposal to close the school in Knightly St John and send the children to Saint Luke's Primary School, Hanford, along with the children from Yore."

"I thought all the children from those villages came here," said Marnie.

"They do," said Margaret. "They always have. The idea was fiercely opposed and never implemented. The people of Yore said they would never send their children to Hanford. It was unthinkable so they closed it and sent them all here." There was a knock on the door and Valerie Paxton walked in.

"The chairman of governors has arrived, Mrs Giles, and Mr Hutton and Mrs Kemp."

"Thank you, Valerie."

Marnie heard the door click shut behind her. "I'm sorry I'm taking up your time."

"Not at all. It was good of you to come." She stood up and came round the desk. They crossed to the door.

"Just briefly," said Marnie. "Why did the plan propose sending the children to Hanford?"

"Simple ... because there were more children in that village. There still are. Always have been."

"So why did the parents object?"

"You might not believe this, Marnie. It was because of something that happened in the Civil War, right at the end ... at the time of Naseby."

"I could believe anything," said Marnie. "Perhaps we can talk about it again?"

"Of course. But if you were one of my pupils, I'd encourage you to research the subject properly."

"In the library?" said Marnie.

"Better still, in the County Archives ... source materials."

"When I can find the time," said Marnie. "Thanks for the idea."

"See you Friday. Prepare *Sally Ann* to receive boarders!"

🎺 🎺 🎺 🎺

When Marnie walked into the office barn, Anne was just putting the phone down. She paused for a few moments before speaking. "Hi, Marnie. Would you like some coffee?" The tone of her voice had none of Anne's usual spark.

"No thanks. I had some with Margaret." Anne sat reading a file. "Everything all right?"

"Oh, yes."

"Who was that on the phone? And, before you answer, let me say that I am quite happy for you to use the phone at any time. In which case it may have been personal and none of my business."

"What made you ask about the phone?" said Anne.

"Just a little detail. Normally after a phone call one of those yellow sticky notes hits my desk within three seconds accompanied by a list of jobs for me to do. I notice these things." A faint smile crossed Anne's face. "Was it Willards telling us they've given the contract to somebody else?"

Anne's expression changed to horror. "They couldn't do that, could they?"

"They could, but I don't think they would."

Anne sighed with relief. "Marnie?"

"Ye-e-s?"

"That was Mum on the phone."

"Right." Marnie thought a question like *All well at home?* would be out of order. She waited. It was odds-on that her father had lost his job again, or her mother, perhaps ... or both.

"They've arranged the holiday at the end of the month." Anne sounded like a doctor giving a patient a diagnosis of athlete's foot. "To Scotland." In both feet. "They definitely want me to go with them." A terminal case.

"Anne, on a scale of disaster marked one to ten, that ranks about minus something. What's the problem?"

"There's so much to do here."

"Oh great! So it's my fault. The wicked employer who won't let you go. I knew I should have chained you to the desk."

Anne laughed silently. "I know it seems silly ..."

"Correct. Got it in one. We've been over this before."

"... but I'm really enjoying it here and we're just getting things right."

"I know. How long are you going for?"

"*Two weeks!* Mum said we could talk about it when I go home this weekend."

"Fine. Put it in the diary. Two weeks holiday with pay, or in your case, with pittance, and I'll give you a holiday bonus. How's that?"

"Oh Marnie, I couldn't let you do that ..."

"No arguing. Now, tell me something. What do you know about the battle of Naseby?"

The sudden change of tack threw Anne off balance. "Mm. 1645 ... other end of the county ... Prince Rupert and his dog 'Boy' ... King captured ... last big battle of the war ..."

"That's more than I knew."

"Thinking of going on *Mastermind*?"

❦   ❦   ❦   ❦

"Is it Thursday already?" Marnie looked at the timetable for the schoolchildren's visit that Anne put on her desk. "This is really good." Anne had used the graphics program on the computer to decorate the paper with scrolls and roses. It was the nearest she could find to traditional canalboat style.

"What about these, Marnie?" She pointed to a pile of folders. "There are two dozen of them. I got them from the stationery cupboard. We never use these ... I hope it's all right."

"Sure. They can put their papers in them. I suppose they'll have notebooks, won't they?"

Anne smiled at her. It was a smile bordering on the smug. She opened one of the folders. Inside was a question-and-answer worksheet, a notebook bearing the logo of the National Canal museum, a pencil with the inscription of the Inland Waterways Association and a round coloured badge carrying the title: 'CREW'. "If the programme's okay, I'll print them off and put one in each folder."

"Anne, they're brilliant! The kids'll love them. How did you manage to do all this?"

"Easy. I went to the chandler's in Leighton Buzzard when I was home for the weekend."

"You must let me pay for them," said Marnie. Another smile from Anne, this time conspiratorial.

"I told the man in the shop about the school visit. I knew him from when I was doing my GCSE project on the canals, and he let me have them at cost. He gave me all the pencils for nothing. And I wrote the worksheets last week." Marnie hugged her.

"Thank goodness you're here. We've been so busy, I haven't had time to think about it properly this week. I'd better do some baking this evening. I've promised them a picnic tea tomorrow."

"Would you welcome any suggestions about that?" said Anne.

❦   ❦   ❦   ❦

"What do you think of them?" Marnie pulled a tray out of the oven. "For such a small oven this doesn't do a bad job." She put the tray of gingerbread men on a cooling rack on the workbench.

"They're wonderful," said Anne. "Mine usually fall apart or end up like concrete. One for every child?"

"Yes. Twenty-three are coming, so there's one for you, too." Anne was not quite sure how to take this, but Marnie's wink was re-assuring.

"Can I do mine now?"

Marnie put both trays out in the cratch and left Anne to her 'creation' while she went back to the office barn. She cleared space for the children and set up her slide projector and video player. Anne had put vases of field flowers around the office to make it welcoming. The phone rang. It was Ralph. They chatted about the school visit, their work and the hazards they both understood about running a narrowboat single-handed.

"Marnie, there was something I wanted to tell you. I've been reading some notes from Guy Fellheimer. You remember, he's the colleague at All Saints working on the Civil Wars."

"Yes, of course. And there's something odd *I've* found out, too. You go first."

"I'd rather not talk about it on the phone. I was wondering if I could come up and see you."

"That sounds serious ... I mean, the part about not talking on the phone. You can come up and see me any time. When do you have in mind?"

"I can probably get a coach from Berkhamsted. Could I come this weekend?"

"Sure ... assuming Anne and I survive the visit here tomorrow. We're turning the place into Glebe Farm University and *Sally Ann* College." The joke was feeble, she realised that, but Marnie was surprised that Ralph did not react to it at all. Perhaps he was too much of a heavyweight for her after all. Or perhaps what was on his mind was more serious than she imagined.

❦   ❦   ❦   ❦

"I had no idea the canals were so interesting," said Margaret. The children were taking off their life jackets and dumping them in a pile beside the docking area. Anne was organising the children for a picnic tea. "I think the teaching profession has missed two people of outstanding potential, Marnie."

"I hope the interior design profession has gained two such people," said Marnie. The children were forming themselves into small groups around tablecloths laid out on the grass beside *Sally Ann*. "They seem to be enjoying themselves, anyway." The two women sat on safari chairs up by *Sally's* bows, under the large cream parasol.

"And I'm sure they've learnt so much from your excellent programme."

Marnie had to admit to herself that it had gone well. At first, the group had been quietly curious and respectful during the conducted tour of the boat. They had all giggled at the heads and laughed when told it was called a *Porta Potti*. They took notes about the parts of a boat – *cratch ... gunwale ... anodes* – and answered the questions on their worksheets. It had taken all Anne's charisma to drag them away from *Sally Ann* to go into the barn for the slide and video show and Marnie's talk. They gasped at the images of aqueducts, tunnels and bridges, especially the slide of the Pontcysyllte Aqueduct, and made suitable noises at the sight of old film footage on video of horses drawing boats along the Shropshire Union.

The main surprise for Marnie was the children's behaviour during their trip on *Sally Ann*. She had told Anne beforehand that this was the part that worried her. But they did exactly as they were told, even when their natural exuberance made them cheer loudly when rising and descending in the lock chamber on each leg of their voyage. The trip lasted about an hour and they conscientiously looked out for the plants, animals and trees on their worksheets, spotted the old canal stables and pumping station and wrote down the distance to Braunston from the mile-post that they passed.

Anne had by now organised a team of helpers to serve gingerbreadmen and orange juice to the chattering groups. Marnie felt superfluous and was happy to leave Anne in charge.

"They are so *mature*," she said to Margaret Giles.

"Oh yes, at this age they're wonderful to work with … sensible and responsible, with a child's enthusiasm for practically everything." At that moment, a girl and a boy came over to them with cups of coffee. "Your Anne is an absolute godsend."

"Yes. I'd be lost without her." They sipped the coffee while the children concentrated on their biscuits. Anne was sitting on the grass, helping a group of them to draw trees. "Margaret, there was something you were going to tell me about the Civil War … an incident, I think you called it, towards the end of the war." The Head sipped her coffee. "It was something that happened round here, I think you said. We were interrupted when your governors arrived."

"I'll try and remember what it was," said Margaret. "It's slipped my mind for the moment." A sudden cheer rang out. The children were on their feet clapping as Anne stepped carefully from *Sally Ann's* aft deck, carrying a large steel platter. Margaret and Marnie went over to look. On a folding table, Anne set down the platter, and the children crowded round to see. She had made a cake in the shape of a working narrowboat, with Smarties for portholes and coloured icing for livery.

"What sort of boat is it?" Anne called out. With one voice they cried: "*A Josher!*" It looked too good to eat, but no-one protested when Anne cut it into slices. Everyone's attention was on the sponge filled with jam and cream under the icing. Nearly everyone's attention. Marnie was wondering what it was that Margaret Giles had been going to tell her, and that she was now concealing.

❦ ❦ ❦ ❦

They set off like a column of infantry across the yard, Anne leading the way surrounded by a clutch of admirers, chatting happily. She had organised them to pile up their life jackets in the office barn, while a platoon dumped the black plastic rubbish bags in the builder's skip. At the end of the line, Margaret and Marnie walked along together. There were no stragglers. Before going up the field track, Marnie had made a final tour of inspection. Not a trace remained behind of their visit. Not a trace remained of the cake or the gingerbread men, either.

"The van from the education office will come down some time on Monday morning to pick up the lifejackets. I hope they'll not be in your way till then."

"They'll be fine, but are you sure you wouldn't prefer me to bring them up in the car? This track is so rutted the van may find it difficult. I think it's got worse since the builders started working here."

"You're lucky the weather's dry," said Margaret. "I've known this field look like the battle of the Somme after a spell of rain."

"Even so, I remember the removals van swaying all over the place the day we moved in."

"You used Days, didn't you?" said Margaret. "Some people in the village were surprised you used a firm from Yore. Did you have a particular reason for choosing them?"

"Not really. I just bumped into Frank Day by chance. He ran a local firm … seemed pleasant … they did a good job. Is there a problem? Surely we don't live in a no-go area?"

"Marnie, strictly between you and me, Frank Day is not well liked in the village. His wife comes from Yore and she wouldn't move here. Frank is viewed with suspicion for doing that. He'd rather live in Knightly, of course, but he can't. You know the background. It must seem very silly to someone from outside, especially coming from London, but it can be like that sometimes."

"Bigotry, hatred, suspicion, going back over hundreds of years," said Marnie.

"Hard to believe, but it can happen," said Margaret.

"I know," said Marnie. "Ever heard of Northern Ireland?"

🌻   🌻   🌻   🌻

Saturday 15 July

"Shall we have a cup of coffee while it's like this?" Marnie and Ralph peered out at the driving rain from the booking hall of Milton Keynes central bus station. It was mid-morning on Saturday, the day after the school visit.

"It might be preferable to get wet on the inside," said Ralph. "I'm sorry to drag you out here in this."

"That's okay, I had to come anyway. I've just put Anne on the bus. She's gone home for the weekend."

They headed for the café. The place smelled of damp clothes, the atmosphere stoically cheerful and the coffee drinkable. Ralph stuffed his weekend bag in dark blue trimmed with tan leather under the table that they shared with an elderly couple. Marnie was amused to see Ralph trying to look as if he sat in bus station cafés as a regular occurrence. It was not the place for a private conversation.

"It's odd," said Marnie. "The forecast was for bright spells. This looks as if it's in for the day."

"When did Anne decide to go home for the weekend?"

"Monday, I think." She smiled. "It was nothing personal, I'm sure."

"She didn't get flooded out by the rain in the night?"

"No. The roof is sound. Not a drip in sight."

The old lady sitting beside Ralph began taking a transparent plastic mac out of its pouch. She shook it open and smiled at Ralph.

"I was hoping I wouldn't be needing this, me dook," she said. Her accent was homely Northamptonshire with a country flavour. "Still, you never know when it might come in handy."

"Quite right," said Ralph. "I never go anywhere without mine." His timing was unfortunate. Marnie was just raising the cup to her lips. She jerked convulsively, splashing coffee over the table, catching the saucer with her elbow. People stared. In a deft movement, Ralph reached forward and laid a paper napkin over the puddle.

"Your wife all right?" said the old man.

"Hiccups," said Ralph. "She's always been prone to them." Marnie fought to control her features, giving all her attention to mopping the table and muttering apologies.

"Oh look," she said. "It's stopped raining. We'd better escape – I mean leave – while we can."

"So it has," said Ralph. He turned to the elderly couple. "Goodbye. Have a good journey. It looks as if I shan't need my Pacamac after all."

The rain held off long enough for them to reach the car. By the time they were pulling onto the northbound A5 it was scudding down again.

"Have you recovered?" said Ralph.

"From my *hiccups*? Huh! Perfectly, thank you. *Pacamac!*" She flicked the wiper switch to the fast position and craned her head forward.

"Sorry," said Ralph. "I'd no idea my harmless remark would have such consequences."

"Talking of which," said Marnie. "I was intrigued … *concerned,* about what you wanted to tell me that you couldn't say on the phone. I wouldn't normally describe you as melodramatic."

"No. It was a question of choosing the best time to talk."

"Driving through heavy rain is probably not quite right, either, is it?" They slowed for a roundabout.

"I've brought the papers with me," said Ralph. "We could look at them together this morning. Then I'll take you to lunch."

When they reached the village the downpour was fierce, lashing across the road and sending torrents of water and mud down the field track. The car bumped and slithered through the quagmire.

"I've never seen it like this," said Marnie. "The wipers can hardly cope." She steered round a deep rut that had become a small river.

"It's like the battlefield of Wipers," said Ralph. "Or should I pronounce it 'Ypres'?"

"The Headteacher from the school was right. She said it reminded her of the battle of the Somme down here in bad weather."

"This place has had battles of its own," said Ralph.

❦   ❦   ❦   ❦

Marnie sat at the table in the saloon on *Sally Ann*. It was covered in documents, papers and photocopies and she was concentrating hard. Ralph sat opposite. The rain was now a steady drumming on the steel roof. It filled the silence in the cabin. Eventually Marnie spoke.

"You think it was here, don't you?"

"When I read these, I didn't know what to do for the best. As a researcher, I just wanted to get at the truth. In this instance, there was another dimension … you, Marnie."

"Were you going to keep this from me?"

"I admit I thought about it. You've made your life here. This has been your new start. I know how valuable a new start can be. I learnt that from you."

"You didn't want to spoil it for me."

"Of course not. But then I realised that Fellheimer found these papers in his research. Sooner or later you might find them, too. Apart from that, there could well be people in the village who knew what had happened. You could have found out from a variety of sources."

"Better to find out from you."

"Truth is always better than rumour," Ralph said. "Knowledge is better than speculation. Even so, it was a difficult choice. In the end I decided to tell you like this."

Marnie re-arranged the papers on the table, lining them up in chronological order. "You did the right thing, Ralph. Can I just make sure I've got it straight?" She pulled one group of documents towards her. "These reports show that the vicar supported the King … was very High Church. But many people in this area were for Parliament. Why was he so different?"

"Fellheimer says this wasn't uncommon. The clergy often came from outside the local community … many were younger sons of landed gentry with High Church leanings."

"But the booklet says he wanted to unite the whole community and will be remembered for his good works in the parish."

"That's not inconsistent. He wanted to unite them behind the King. That's why he preached strongly against the Puritan Anabaptists in the area. Local opinion was divided, but nobody wanted to force confrontation. That could be very dangerous with army units wandering about the country."

"Yes. That was how the villages were attacked, of course. The Royalist cavalry came looking for supplies … someone – perhaps the vicar – told them about Puritan support in Yore. Cavalry rode off … burnt thatch, as we know. After Naseby, victorious Ironsides took revenge."

"That's right. Now this is where Fellheimer's research is interesting." Ralph picked out one of the documents. "This is from the archives of the Northampton Grand Committee. Royalist sympathisers were strictly controlled for long after the war ended. Here we see that the Knightly vicar was allowed to stay with the rector of Great Hanford while repairs were carried out to the vicarage."

"So the vicarage was attacked by the Ironsides too," said Marnie.

"Presumably ... which suggests a degree of animosity."

"But why murder the vicar when the war was virtually over?"

"Did you know," said Ralph, "that two million Germans were killed in genocide – *after* the last war?"

"Killed by the *allies*?" said Marnie incredulously.

"Not directly. Revenge killings," said Ralph. "Old enemies ... scores to settle ..."

"But what harm could the vicar do?" said Marnie.

Ralph drew out another paper from the pile. "These are troop movements after Naseby. Cromwell ran the New Model Army very efficiently. It was well documented. Now look at this. A squadron of light cavalry was deployed in this area to flush out remnants of the King's army. Here's the officer in charge, Captain Thomas Flaxman. His unit was operating for months afterwards."

"Did they fear the Royalists might regroup and try to free the King?"

"That's *exactly* what they expected. The King's supporters were active for years and, of course, in the end they regained power. It was a real danger that Cromwell took very seriously."

"And you think the vicar might have been helping them?"

"Someone must have been helping them," said Ralph, "someone who knew where they were hiding. Remember, it was much more wooded here in those days."

Marnie read from the army papers: "... *horse movement between Great Hanford and Watling Street. No contact was made but detachment sent to Knightly St John to secure route to south ...*"

"They had their eye on this village," said Ralph. "No doubt about it. But there was no record of any trouble from this community at any time. Everyone was war-weary and wanted to get on with their lives. It was fanatics like the vicar who were causing the trouble."

"And inspiring one or two individuals by their charisma and personality," said Marnie. She thought of her conversation with Randall Hughes. "*I'm not a soft touch.*"

"Sorry?"

"Oh, that's what the vicar said to me about his own problems with the parish. The school secretary said he was an inspiration to us all. Anyway, in Flaxman's report for the third of August 1645 he states that on a patrol in the area he was summoned to the village and informed that the vicar had been killed three days earlier. '*It had been seen ... that lights were showing from the church tower. There was reported sighting of unknown cavalry in woods to north. Vicar was suspected of giving succour to the enemy. A force of villagers stormed the church ...*' We know the rest."

"Look at how the report ends, Marnie. Flaxman was sure no-one in the village knew who had committed the crime. They were obviously shocked at having a killer in their midst."

"So we come to this enquiry about the woman." Marnie scanned a collection of papers.

"That was later the same year," said Ralph. "The Prosecutor General ordered an investigation into the death of a daughter of the village blacksmith."

"I haven't read this properly," said Marnie. "She went into some sort of decline a few weeks after the vicar was killed."

"Yes. The account is incomplete; the records were partly destroyed in the Great Fire of Northampton in 1675. She was dead before the end of September, but Fellheimer points out there was no record of her burial in the church register. He wondered if she came from another village. Then he decided to look at wills and property deeds and he came across this." Ralph pushed a bundle of photocopies across the table.

"Do researchers always have to go into this much detail?" said Marnie.

"Oh yes. The historians love this sort of thing, Marnie. They thrive on it! A nice pile of dusty old papers keeps them amused for hours."

"But what was he researching?"

"Changes in property ownership, the impact of the Commonwealth on the economic structure of this area in the period up to the Restoration of the Monarchy, or something like that. It's for a book."

"Enthralling," said Marnie. "Bound to be a best-seller. So he came across this by chance."

"Yes. He realised that something strange was going on and just followed it up out of curiosity. Research is like that sometimes. You'll see he found a mention of *'my poor beloved daughter'* in the will of Jonathan Day dated 1662. It mentions how she had died a *'sorry death by her own hand out of sorrow at her family's part in the death of the lamented vicar'*. The will included money to provide a decent headstone for her grave. It says she hanged herself in the cow byre of Beech Farm but really died *'out of shame for what had been done by her own kin'*."

"And Fellheimer thinks this is Beech Farm?" In reply, Ralph turned over a copy of an old field plan, dated 1793. It showed the route of the proposed new canal, following a contour line as it looped round the village. Beech Farm nestled in the crook of the watercourse, where Glebe Farm now stood.

"It looks like the only clue to who committed the murder," said Ralph. "Jonathan Day's 'poor beloved daughter' knew and took the secret to her grave."

"Was her name Sarah Anne?" said Marnie.

Ralph sifted through the papers. "Yes, it was. How on earth did you know that?"

"Elementary," said Marnie.

"Really? And I suppose you know where she's buried, too?" said Ralph.

"As a matter of fact, I can show you," said Marnie. "She was buried outside the church wall ... and she hanged herself in our office barn."

"How can you be sure?"

"It's the only one that was here in those days."

❦   ❦   ❦   ❦

Lunch was a more subdued affair than usual. The pub was half empty thanks to the storm. Marnie and Ralph sat at the table near the window, Ralph beginning to doubt the wisdom of telling Marnie what had happened. He had only done so because he could not think of concealing something so important. He also believed that if anyone could cope with the situation, it was Marnie. He watched her from across the table, her clean, intelligent features, smooth complexion, shining, dark wavy hair. It pained him to think he might have spoiled her dream of a new life and her own company. She looked up suddenly and found him staring. He thought she knew what he was thinking.

"Right," she said. "So now we know. I'm glad you told me about the research, Ralph. It doesn't help me find out who murdered the vicar, but it fills in part of the story."

"Is that what you want to do ... identify the murderer?"

"I had thought of doing that, yes. Of course, I also have to earn a living and I have plans for Glebe Farm. There's a lot to do, and nothing is going to spoil it. The people who lived in the past have had their time. This is *our* time and we have to get on with it. As the vicar said – the new one I mean, Toni – life's too short. Is there any wine left in that carafe?"

Ralph poured a glass each. "I don't think I tasted the first glass at all," he said.

"Often advisable with house red," said Marnie. She raised her glass.

"To the new life – *la vita nuova*," said Ralph. They clinked glasses and sipped. The wine had not greatly improved in flavour, but the atmosphere was better.

"This quiche isn't bad," said Marnie. "Home made."

Ralph agreed. "Tell me, the new vicar: what's she like?"

"Youngish ... thirtyish ... friendly ... very excited at having her own parish ... quite stylish."

"How well is she being accepted, or is it too early to tell?"

"Some like the *idea*, some don't ... as you'd expect, really. I think everyone would like her as a *person*."

The sunlight was now shining in through the window. After being enclosed for most of the day so far, they decided to postpone coffee and take the air while they could.

"Do you feel like meeting Sarah Anne Day?" said Marnie.

Minutes later, they pushed through the gate on the far side of the churchyard, out into the executive housing estate, along the path and across the wet grass.

"She's tucked away out of sight in that clump of brambles over there," said Marnie. "It was probably wooded in those days."

"Just outside the consecrated ground," said Ralph. "Her family obviously cared for her a great deal. They kept her as close to the church as they dared."

"She got her headstone," said Marnie. "Look. You can just see the top of it among the bushes." They had to walk round to the other side of the clump before it came into view. "Oh!" Marnie stopped suddenly and Ralph almost collided with her back.

"What is it?" he said. Marnie stood aside for him to see. The undergrowth had been cut back and the face of the headstone had been cleaned. Little of the inscription was legible, but it no longer looked neglected and abandoned. At the foot of the stone someone had laid a bunch of bright, blue cornflowers, tied with a white ribbon.

"How strange," said Marnie. "The other day, the stone was almost concealed by the bushes."

Ralph stooped to read the markings. "This certainly seems to be her grave."

"But how different it looks," said Marnie. "It's nice to think someone has taken the trouble to clean her up after all these years."

"Yes. Yes, it is," said Ralph, but his mind was pondering a different question. If the grave was so well concealed, how did anyone know where to find it ... unless they had been watching Marnie, or even following her? Marnie knelt down beside the flowers.

"There's no card. Nothing to show who sent them." She ran her fingers across the surface of the stone. "Someone has used a stiff brush on this. You can see the scour marks. I wonder if the idea was to make the stone cleaner, or to try to reveal the inscription." She swivelled round, still crouching, and looked up at Ralph. "Whatever the motive, it hasn't made ..." Her voice stopped in mid-sentence. She stood up, staring over Ralph's head. He turned and followed the direction of her gaze. A small figure could be seen at the top of the tower, watching them. Against the skyline, it seemed to wave.

"Shall we go and see who our guardian angel is?" said Ralph. Marnie was already on the move. He set off behind her and was still trailing when they crossed the churchyard and turned past the west front. He wondered if they both had the same thought. This was how it must have been that night when the vicar was killed. Someone spotted on the tower; a signal being made; the rush into the church; the finding of the body. Ralph caught up with Marnie as she slowed to open the grille to the porch. They entered the building together. It was empty. Silent. The faint smell of old stone and wood polish. Light falling across the nave from the stained glass windows.

They made for the door to the tower without a word said between them. It swung open at Marnie's touch. They began to climb the steps at a steady pace. The afternoon sun dazzled them as they passed the first window and moved on and up into the shadows. The landing with the wooden partition came and went. Breathing more heavily, they came to the second window. Through the bell chamber they climbed up to a small landing. They had reached the highest point. Marnie pushed open the door and the sunlight poured in. At first the roof of the tower seemed deserted. Then they saw the vicar, standing in the corner, looking out over the crenellations. She turned to face them.

"You got up here a lot quicker than I did!" She came over, smiling. "Isn't this fantastic?"

"Wonderful," said Marnie, breathless. She made the introductions. Ralph and Toni shook hands, Ralph trying to look as if he had not just run up the equivalent of six floors.

"Come and see," said Toni. She pointed to the south. "I think that's Buckinghamshire over there. And on the horizon that dark patch might be the Cotswolds." A few miles off, another church tower could be seen, poking up between the trees. "Do you see the trace of silver over by Hanford? I think that must be the canal. And there's your farm, Marnie. You can see the rooftops."

"If there were any rooftops," said Marnie, still breathing heavily.

"There will be soon. Have faith," said the vicar with an encouraging smile.

"It all looks so much more wooded from up here," Ralph observed. "You wouldn't think there were busy roads and houses down there. And once it was thick forest."

"Oh yes," said Toni. "You could've hidden an army between the villages."

"Quite," said Marnie. "Toni, did you recognise me when you looked down?"

"I thought I did. It was rather an inspired guess. I wondered what you were doing down there, actually. Had you lost something?"

"We were looking at an old gravestone. It was odd to find it outside the churchyard."

"*Very* odd," said Toni. She frowned. "Of course, there always has been a place where ... certain types of burial were conducted."

"A place of sanctuary for lost souls," said Ralph.

"In times past," said Toni, "there were special circumstances: witches, the excommunicated, heretics ..."

"Suicides?" suggested Marnie.

"Yes."

"So they were excluded from society even in death," said Ralph.

"The church had strict rules about certain categories of sin," said Toni.

"But isn't it unusual for her – it was a woman from Knightly – to have had a headstone?" said Marnie. "And be buried almost on church land?"

"She may have been an offender against the rules of the day," said Toni, "but she was still part of somebody's family. Someone cared about her."

"Is it unfair to ask what you would have done in those days as vicar?" Ralph said quietly.

"I wouldn't have had a say in it in those days, would I? Some might say that it was just as well ..."

The air was warm even at the top of the tower and Marnie thought how peaceful it all seemed. She strained to see through the top branches of the spinney for a glimpse of *Sally Ann* or the canal. The voice of old Albert Fletcher came into her mind. *The place is cursed!* Did he mean the village or just Glebe Farm? She became aware of Ralph close beside her. She felt him reach for her hand, as if he had been reading her thoughts again. She squeezed gently.

Gradually the clouds were clearing, but there was still a haze hanging over the countryside. Far off, at the edge of their vision, they could make out the traces of a rainbow. Toni took a deep breath and turned to face them.

"Why not come back and have tea at the vicarage?"

"That's kind of you," said Marnie.

"Not at all." Toni grinned broadly. "I've been dying to say that ever since I got the job."

❦ ❦ ❦ ❦

The sun was lower in the sky by the time Marnie and Ralph walked hand in hand through the spinney back to *Sally Ann*. Under the trees the ground was wet and the air smelled of vegetation.

"What would you like to do this evening?" said Ralph.

"After the pub lunch and tea at the vicarage, I don't need much. What about you?"

"The same."

"Suppose I prepare something light, open a bottle of wine, put a tape on? We could sit out and eat on deck ... drier than the ground."

"Marnie, I think you've just described my idea of paradise."

"Ralph, there's something on my mind about Sarah Anne. In Fellheimer's papers ... that bit about her sorrow at her family's part in the death of the vicar. What do you make of that?"

"It implies that she knew who'd committed the murder," said Ralph. "I can't think of any other explanation. Can you?"

"It took her a while to make up her mind," said Marnie.

"Months of torment that she couldn't bear any longer, perhaps?"

"It's possible. Ralph, do you think it could have been her own father?"

"If it was, presumably some of the other villagers would've known."

"Unless they were hiding the fact," said Marnie. "They could have been covering up."

"I have two comments on that. Oh god, I'm sounding like an academic again, sorry. Anyway, the first is: why did they go through the charade of searching the church on the night of the killing if they knew all along who'd done it?"

"They were lying, perhaps?"

"Well, the story has the ring of truth about it. They were in shock. For all their anger, I don't believe they wanted to *kill* the vicar, just capture him and turn him over to the authorities. These weren't evil people. They wanted to get back to normal life. They'd had enough of war."

"Yes. What's your second point?"

"That officer, Flaxman, he was convinced no-one knew what had happened. From reading his reports I get the impression he was nobody's fool. He patrolled the area for months and eventually flushed out all the Royalists. He was respected in these parts for his judgement and his fairness."

"Where does that get us?" said Marnie.

Ralph breathed out with a sigh. "I'm no detective, but I would've thought something must have happened between the murder and her suicide, that revealed who'd done it. That was what she couldn't bear." They walked on in silence and Marnie unlocked *Sally Ann*. Dolly, who had been dozing on the hatch, jumped down and wound herself round Ralph's ankles. He stooped to stroke her.

"It does all make sense," said Marnie, "but only up to a point."

"You've found a weakness in the argument?" said Ralph. Marnie remembered what it was like to be a student.

"Not so much a weakness as a gap. Look. The vicar is killed. Everyone is shocked. Weeks later a villager discovers somehow that a member of her family was the murderer. A dreadful discovery, okay, but why did she commit suicide?"

"Go on," said Ralph.

"The will mentions her sorrow," said Marnie. "You don't go and hang yourself in a barn out of *sorrow*. Even allowing for her father using the wrong word, this is a major understatement."

"I'm not quite sure what point you're making."

"It would all make sense to me only if Sarah Anne was in love with the vicar. She would've been distraught at his death, but to find out one of her own family was responsible would make her life unbearable."

"Ye-e-s," said Ralph slowly. "I can see the logic there."

"Of course, I've no evidence," said Marnie, getting the point in first. "And I don't see how we can check the facts."

"We have the accounts of the raid on the church," said Ralph. They spread the documents over the table in the saloon and he began making notes as he sifted from one paper to another. "That's interesting," he said eventually. "I've checked the names of all the men who were present that night. There was no-one called Day or Wise in the party at all – her mother's maiden name was Wise."

Marnie tut-tutted. "Please, sir, does that knock my theory on the head?"

"It doesn't support it. But it doesn't invalidate it, either. Something else might have intervened. Perhaps we should sleep on it."

"Good idea. That's enough theorising for one day. Shall we have a drink before supper?"

"Excellent. What shall I do with my bag?"

"Oh, put it on the bed for now," said Marnie. "You can unpack later ... unless you'd prefer to sleep in Anne's bed in the barn?"

"Of course not," said Ralph. "I'm sure she'd be horrified at the very idea."

"Well, it's an academic question," said Marnie. "She's not likely to find out, is she?"

❦   ❦   ❦   ❦

Marnie was convinced she was becoming obsessive about the whole thing. It did not bother her that she had nearly an hour to wait after seeing Ralph off before Anne was due at the bus station on Sunday evening. She simply installed herself in the café and re-read the notes Ralph had left with her. The more she read, the more convinced she became that he was right. The men who entered the church on the fateful night did not know who had committed the murder either then or later, and they could not have fooled a hard-bitten army officer like Captain Flaxman, whose life depended on his judgement. Sooner or later someone would have made a deathbed confession to receive absolution. But there was no record of this ever happening. Fellheimer had checked all the possibilities.

Only the will of Jonathan Day gave a clue to the identity of the murderer. But who could it have been? There was no-one hiding in the church. No-one from the family was present. What did Sarah Anne find out that made her kill herself? Strangest of all, how was the deed committed when there was no weapon and no-one to wield it? The same old story. Marnie felt frustrated. She had the feeling the answer was staring her in the face. She let out a long sigh and looked at her watch.

"Don't worry, love. It may never happen." She had not noticed the man sitting diagonally across the table. His voice was deep with a faint country burr. Marnie half smiled and glanced at him. It was the T-shirt that held her attention. "I don't suppose you've been stood up."

"No," she said. "I'm just bored with waiting." She excused the lie because the truth was too complicated. "You have a boat?"

The man seemed surprised by the question. "A *boat*? Yes, I do."

Marnie nodded at his T-shirt. It was a faded red, well worn and past its best, but bearing an unmistakable coat-of-arms. "Grand Union Canal, isn't it?"

"Not many people would know that," he said.

"I have a narrowboat," said Marnie. "Where do you keep yours?"

"Just up from the Iron Trunk. *Thor*. Pete Malan." He held his hand out over the table and Marnie wondered fleetingly which name was his. His grip was firm, of course, but not uncomfortable. Not young, he had a young man's body, lean with powerful shoulders, his forearms muscular and tattooed. He had the face of an Old Testament prophet, though his beard was shorter and his hair, surrounding a balding top, was long, grey and wispy. Even seated, he looked tall.

"Marnie Walker. *Sally Ann*. I'm Marnie," she added, for the sake of clarity.

Pete thought for a few seconds. "Up Knightly way? By Fletcher's farm?"

"Yes, that's us. Glebe Farm."

"Nice spot. Cryin' shame about the farm." Marnie found it hard to imagine Pete Malan crying about anything. "Builders there, I think. That right?"

"Yes. We're aiming to restore it. It's a long job."

"You'll do it, my love. That's just what the place needs. A nice family to bring it back to life." His voice was friendly and somehow re-assuring. He made it all seem possible. He looked over her head and unfolded himself from the chair. "Talking of families, here's my youngest."

Marnie turned to see a young man approaching. He had the same sharp features as his father. They were both very tall, perhaps six foot five or six and Pete put an affectionate arm round his son's shoulder. "This is my Raymond, and this is Marnie from *Sally Ann*." Marnie stood up, partly out of politeness and partly so that she could see faces that were so far from the ground. Raymond grinned and said hallo in a similarly deep voice, but Marnie's attention was most drawn by the hat that he held at his side. It was wide-brimmed, made of light brown felt, with black braiding and a long feather.

"Good job the bus wasn't full," said Raymond. "Or I'd have had to pay for a seat for the hat." The two giants chuckled.

"It's quite unusual," said Marnie. "They're not very fashionable round here these days, probably for that reason." The men laughed. "What is it, actually, if you don't mind me asking?"

"Part of my uniform. I'm a captain in the Sealed Knot. We do re-enactments."

"The Sealed Knot," Marnie repeated. "Ah, yes. Are you re-enacting a battle?"

"We don't do many actual *battles*," said Raymond. "We're doing what we call a muster, followed by a skirmish. It's for a charity appeal, for the local hospital. Should be quite a big event."

"In Northampton?"

"Over by Hanford, next weekend. Worth a visit if you've got time. Should be fun. I like it, anyway. Get's me out in the fresh air."

"Raymond's studying to be an accountant," said Pete. Marnie could imagine Raymond wrestling with figures. She had little doubt who would win. With expressions of good will and the hope that they would meet again on the canal some time, father and son took their leave and Marnie wandered over to the newspaper kiosk.

She still had half an hour to wait and sat down with a boating magazine. Nothing had changed. There were projects to restore forgotten waterways; trials of three new boat designs; a photographic section featuring a boat in London that was famous for its flowers and towpath garden. The owner, resplendent in shorts and Panama hat, stood smiling at the camera, surrounded by his handiwork. Time for another sigh from Marnie. She wondered when she would be able to stand in gardens packed with flowers and shrubs at Glebe Farm. Or was it Beech Farm? Or Fletcher's Farm?

❦   ❦   ❦   ❦

"Oh, it's nice to be back!" Anne dropped her bag in the office barn and they made their way through the spinney to *Sally Ann* for supper.

"You've only been away since yesterday morning," said Marnie.

"I know, but this feels like home to me now. You know what I mean. *My* place. It was lovely to see my room and think I lived there."

Marnie felt her stomach tighten. "Good. It's nice to have you back. But I'm sure you had a good weekend ... nice to see your parents and your brother."

"It was, yes. How about you? Not too lonely?"

"Too busy to be lonely," said Marnie, unlocking the doors. "After one of your mum's Sunday lunches, I don't suppose you're very hungry. I've made some *tapas*. Is that okay?"

"Terrific," said Anne. "I'll put the table out, shall I? I must just wash my hands. I always feel sticky after a journey."

They ate out in the warm evening air. High, thin clouds shielded the sun making a pleasant opaque light. Marnie said nothing of Ralph's visit, partly because she did not want the conversation to turn again to the subject of the vicar's death. More than anything, she never wanted Anne to find out about Sarah Anne Day's suicide in the office barn. Also, Marnie wanted to keep her relationship with Ralph private. She was unsure where it would lead or how long it would last. They were like two working boats, plying the same canal, meeting at intervals, but essentially going their own ways.

Anne chattered on about her family, the plans for the holiday in Scotland – *camping! I mean, camping, Marnie! Can you imagine it? We'll probably die of hypothermia!* – simple domestic routines of everyday life – *oh, Mum washed those sheets I took back, so they should be aired enough to use ... I've got two big jars of home-made jam for you as a present ... nearly broke my back carrying them!* She told Marnie about some ideas she had had for a restaurant colour scheme.

Once or twice, she asked Marnie again if she had not been lonely. Marnie reassured her and Anne seemed glad. They sat out talking until the light faded and Anne said she wanted an early night so as to be fresh for Monday. They strolled back through the spinney together and said goodnight at the door to the barn. Marnie had just reached the edge of the trees when Anne called after her.

"Oh, by the way, Marnie, you ought to call Ralph and tell him he left his toothpaste in the shower-room on *Sally*. I hope he's got a spare. Good night!" The door closed quickly behind her and Marnie thought she heard laughter.

❦   ❦   ❦   ❦

"What a coincidence," said Beth. "I was just going to ring *you*. So, how are things?"

"Okay. Busy. Lots to do." Marnie wanted to talk about the murder and Fellheimer's research. With Anne settled in the barn, she could speak freely.

"What sort of weekend have you had?" said Beth.

"Fine. Anne's been home for the weekend and I've been thinking over one or two things. In fact, there's something I wanted to talk to you about."

"I thought so. Tell me all about it. How are things going with Ralph?" Oh god, thought Marnie, she's doing it again. Why is my one and only sister a mind-reader?

"He's okay. Anyway, I wanted to ask your opinion about something."

"Just *okay*? Is that all? Have you seen him lately?"

"Yes, but that isn't what I wanted to talk about, Beth ..."

"How recently? *Very* recently? Or just some time ago recently?"

"Recently. I've seen him *recently*, as in ... recently."

"So you know about his news?"

"*News?* I don't think he mentioned any news." Marnie searched her memory.

"He didn't tell you about his decision: that he's turned down the chair at Yale?"

"No. He didn't tell me that," said Marnie. I didn't give him a chance to, she thought. I was too busy going on about people who have been dead for three hundred and fifty years.

"Apart from that, the relationship is developing well?"

I wonder how Ralph would answer that, thought Marnie. "Relationship?" She was definitely not going to let Beth push her into talking about that. She knew that as long as she kept clear of any details, there was nothing Beth could do to elicit anything from her. "Who said anything about a relationship?"

"I guessed as much," said Beth. "How do you see it shaping up from this point on?"

"From what point on?"

"You tell *me*," said Beth. "How can I tell, stuck down here in London?"

"I haven't the remotest idea what you're talking about," said Marnie.

"So there *is* a relationship ..."

"Beth, I think you're exaggerating things."

"Goodness ... I didn't realise it had gone *that* far already. So it's serious, then?"

"Beth, having you for a sister is like being related to the Spanish Inquisition."

After they had hung up, Marnie decided to shower and go to bed. In the tiny cubicle, she let the warm water splash over her as she turned slowly under the nozzle. It was the only movement possible. Ralph's toothpaste stood on the shelf, looking as if it belonged there. She put the research papers firmly away for the night and changed the sheets. Lying in the fresh smelling cotton, she put out the light and listened to the darkness. There were the usual sounds of the waterway. Leaves rustled. There was a *plop* as a fish jumped nearby. She heard the owl in the trees on the opposite side of the canal. Last of all, she heard Anne's voice drifting towards her from the barn ... *this feels like home to me now ... my place. It was lovely to see my room and think I lived there ...*

Part 23

Monday 17 July

Marnie put down the phone after a long discussion with one of her suppliers in London.

"Why does everyone in London ask me how I'm finding it in the country with nothing going on and no-one around to talk to?"

"Townies!" said Alan, the postman good-humouredly. He stood up and smiled at Anne. "Thanks for the tea, my love. Time to be off." In the yard outside, the builders were extending the scaffolding on the row of cottages. They had surprised even themselves with their rate of progress. A combination of Marnie, *the guv'nor,* working on site, plus the ministrations of Anne who just *popped out* at intervals to see if there was anything they wanted – especially tea – encouraged a healthy level of activity.

Marnie looked at the clock. "I could really use some of that peace and quiet everyone keeps talking about if I'm to get this design finished on time." There was a tap on the open door.

"Remember me, Mrs Walker? Tony Dyson from the estate agents."

Marnie sat back and barely suppressed a sigh. "How could I forget? Good morning, Mr Dyson. What can I do for you?"

He scanned the office, noting the computer, the drawing-board, the air of efficiency, nodding at Anne who seemed absorbed in her thoughts. "Not calling at an inconvenient moment, am I?"

"That depends on what you have in mind," said Marnie, indicating a chair.

"I was just passing and I thought I'd look in and see how things were progressing."

"I think," said Anne, looking through the window, "the concrete lorry has just poured its load over a car parked by the main house ... a red one ..." Mr Dyson started in panic. Marnie raised a hand and he sat down.

"Oh yes," he said with relief, "I see ... it was a joke. Well, I must say you're certainly pressing on." Anne gave him a disarming smile, swung her bag over her shoulder and went out on her rounds. "Are you in a position to know when you might be putting anything on the market, Mrs Walker?"

"To tell you the truth, Mr Dyson, I've not had much time to think about that side of things. I wanted to see how the works shaped up."

"Yes, of course. I think you'll find our terms very favourable. Perhaps I could let you have some samples of brochures we've produced for similar types of country property. A lot depends on presentation, you know. I'm sure we could guarantee the highest possible price ..." Marnie nodded, appearing to find this all very fascinating. In reality she was hoping a thunderbolt from heaven would come through the door – without damaging the rest of the building – and reduce Mr Dyson to a glowing pile of charcoal on the floor. The phone rang. She excused herself.

"The managing director? Yes, certainly, though I do have someone with me just at the moment ... urgent? I see ... a crisis. I'm sure we can sort it out. By all means put him through. I'll deal with it at once." She put her hand over the receiver, waiting to be connected. "I'm sorry about this." Dyson stood up. He knew that if he stayed any longer, he could be sitting around for half an hour. He held up his business card and put it on Anne's desk, miming good-bye and promising to be in touch. Narrowly avoiding decapitation by a builder's ladder, he successfully crossed the yard and got into his car. Anne came back into the office and saw Marnie on the phone. She sat down and glanced at Mr Dyson's card while reaching into her bag. She pulled out the mobile.

"Ah, Mrs Walker," she said. "The problem seems to have solved itself after all. Sorry to have bothered you." They cackled like fishwives and put down their phones.

"If anyone comes in without being invited in the next half hour," said Marnie ominously, "I kill." She returned to the scheme she was trying to finish.

Luckily for Margaret Giles and the group of children who appeared in the doorway, over an hour had passed since Marnie issued her threat. The Headteacher tapped on the open door, looking fresh in cream shirt and dark blue skirt, flanked by four children, two girls, two boys, each carrying a bunch of flowers.

"I know we must be disturbing you, Mrs Walker," she was in school-speak mode, "... but we just wanted to give you and Anne a little something to thank you for the marvellous visit to *Sally Ann*."

"Oh, there was really no need. It was a pleasure having you. Thank you, they're lovely. Would you like coffee? Anne, do we have some orange juice?"

"No, no, thank you. We're definitely not staying. You have work to do and this is just a flying visit."

"Well, thank you," said Marnie. She turned to the children. "Thank you very much for coming. It was nice of you to take the trouble."

"Take the trouble?" said Margaret. "We had to draw lots to decide who would come. These were the winners." She turned and spoke softly into Marnie's ear. "I expect we'll find there have been riots in the playground when we get back. Everyone wanted to come." Marnie and Anne accompanied their visitors across the yard and up as far as the track, Margaret and Marnie walking together, while Anne shepherded the children past the building operations.

"Sorry for the intrusion, Marnie. I was going to ask Valerie to pop them in so as not to disrupt your work, but she's gone very strange these days."

"What's the matter? Has her thumb gone septic or something?"

"She's just very peculiar. Hardly says a word. She's even abrupt to the children."

"How old is she?"

"No, it can't be that. She's only late thirties. If I went peculiar that would have to be *my* excuse! You know, I have a feeling that it has something to do with the vicar."

"You think she doesn't approve of women priests?" said Marnie.

"I mean the one before: Mr Hughes." Margaret stopped walking. "Between you and me, Marnie, I've started to wonder if she wasn't more attached to him than anyone imagined. I think she's taken his departure rather badly." *An inspiration to us all;* Marnie remembered the words. Margaret put a hand on Marnie's sleeve. "Sorry. I haven't mentioned this to anyone else. But I am getting worried about her."

"Probably just a temporary state of mind," said Marnie. "Or do you think she needs help, counselling or something like that?"

"She needs something, I think, but it's almost impossible to talk to her. She just avoids me the whole time. The more I think about it, the more concerned I become. I'm not sure what she might do. Anyway, I'd better get the children back. I shouldn't be wittering on like this."

"I wish I could do something to help. Does she have a close friend you could discuss it with?"

"Not that I know. She has a brother, but he lives in the north of England. And I don't really know her husband ..." Anne came bounding up. Margaret smiled, a bright, encouraging teacher's smile. "I must remove these children and let you get back to work. Thank you again. Bye!"

The children were skipping up the field track with their Headteacher following close behind. Birds were singing in the sunlight and the trees were rustling in the breeze. The girls were wearing blue gingham dresses, the boys were in white shirts and dark shorts. It was a happy village scene. Halfway up the track they turned and waved. Marnie and Anne waved back. Everyone was smiling.

❦ ❦ ❦ ❦

Over the next few days the village settled into its summer rhythm. The school term approached its end. Conversation in the shop turned to holiday plans. Yellow signs sprang up advertising gardens open to the public for charity. The honey stone of the houses glowed in the sun, and cottage gardens provided a free show to passers-by. Down at Glebe Farm, building works rolled steadily on. Anne made her daily trip to the post at five and returned with fresh provisions. At the centre of her world, Marnie strove to meet her deadlines, organised suppliers, directed her projects, advised her clients.

On Tuesday Anne was leaving the shop when she met George Stubbs posting letters. "Good afternoon." His well-padded voice almost caressed her. Even on a summer's day he wore a tweed jacket and a hat, which he raised in gallant fashion. "And how is the lovely lady of Glebe Farm today?"

"Marnie's fine, thank you, Mr Stubbs." Anne adopted her most inscrutable face. Her skilful parry was recognised and admired.

"I hear work is in full swing, my dear. Perhaps I might look in some time … offer a word of encouragement … and perhaps a warning."

"A *warning?*" said Anne.

"The dangers of over-working. Long hours, a punishing schedule. These things can take their toll, believe me, even when you're young and healthy." He looked her up and down.

"Oh, I don't think we're overdoing it all that much," said Anne. "Anyway, it's fun. We love our work. In fact, I'd better get back, if you'll excuse me."

"Of course, of course. But tell Marnie what I said. What would happen if she couldn't keep up the work? You must judge the pace to suit the race."

❦ ❦ ❦ ❦

Thursday 20 July
A day or two later, Marnie stopped off at the village shop on her way back from a site meeting at *The Irish Navigator*. While she was hesitating over her choice of cat food for Dolly, Richard Appleton called across from the post office booth.

"I've got something here for you, Marnie," said Richard. "One parcel. Alan brought it in this afternoon. He was going to drop it off, but you can have it now, if you don't mind carrying it." The parcel bore the familiar franking mark of the office in London.

"These will be the structural drawings from Mike," said Marnie. "The church porch." She took out her wallet and the pass book for Anne's savings account. By the time Anne went to college next year, she should have a fair amount to help her on her way. It would be a surprise present. "Put this in Anne's account, please. Usual amount."

"How's the church job coming on?" said Richard, writing up the pass book.

"Just starting really," said Marnie. "I think these will give the vicar an idea of what's needed."

"If you want to see her, you should catch her in the church," said Molly. "She was in here not ten minutes ago and said she was going to do some clearing out in the vestry."

"There's the woman's touch for you," said Richard. "I can't imagine Randall Hughes spring cleaning the pews with a feather duster." They laughed good-naturedly. "Or you," said Molly to her husband.

Marnie spotted Toni Petrie by the church gate as she drove down the road and pulled up beside her. The vicar was carrying a bulging, black plastic rubbish bag that was evidently heavy.

"Hi Marnie. You would not *believe* how much rubbish there is in that vestry. I think some of it must go back to Norman times."

"I can give you the name of a firm that hires out skips," said Marnie. "I don't want to hold you up, but I've just got a parcel from London. Probably the drawings from Mike. I'll be in touch."

"Fine. I'm ready when you are. Any time. Pop round for coffee. Give me a ring."

❦ ❦ ❦ ❦

Marnie pressed the doorbell at the vicarage for the second time and waited. It made a hollow sound that seemed to echo in empty space. She had a strong feeling that there was no-one at home. Just after ten-thirty. That was the time they had agreed on the phone. It occurred to her that the vicar might be in the garden and she followed the path round the house to explore. There was no vicar, but the garden bore all the signs of hard work. The lawn was mown in stripes with neatly trimmed edges. The flower beds had been weeded and mulched. Roses were the main source of colour, but they had support from straggling delphiniums and foxgloves. There were clumps of marguerites and drooping peonies in deep red. Some evening primroses were trying to join in and here and there Lakeland poppies swayed on tall stalks. In gaps where the cutting back had been most severe stood pots of brilliant geraniums in red and pink. *By their works shall ye know them* ... The old familiar words came into Marnie's mind as she looked at Toni's handiwork.

The faint sound of a door closing reached Marnie and she made her way round to the front of the house and pressed the bell once again. The response was immediate.

"Marnie! Excellent timing. I've only just arrived myself. Come in. I've been over at the school." Still talking, Toni led Marnie into the kitchen, gestured her to a stool and switched on the kettle. "End of term service. Lovely kids. I always feel on a high after a service. Sorry, I'm babbling."

"I understand," said Marnie. "It is a nice school."

"Yes. I gather you had a group on your boat last week. They're all talking about it. The place is full of pictures and models of canals, bridges and an amazing aqueduct with a weird name."

"Pontcysyllte," said Marnie with a passable pronunciation.

"I'll take your word for it. Everyone has spelt it differently, but Mrs Giles hasn't corrected any of them. I don't think she can spell it either. You and Anne are certainly big stars."

They spread Mike's drawings out on the kitchen table and Marnie explained what had to be done.

"I'll check with the surveyor's office what I'm supposed to do about this," said Toni, "but I'd be grateful if you could contact some builders for a price in the meantime. Am I right in thinking there's no actual danger of the porch collapsing?"

"None at all, according to Mike. He thinks the diocesan surveyor is just sticking to the rules to cover his own back."

"Good. I hate to think anyone might come to harm, in the church of all places. Do you have any plans of the building as a whole?"

"Only these sketches that Mike drew. Nothing more accurate. The surveyor will have some, I expect. Do you want me to find out?"

"No, no. You've done enough already. I just want to get to know every inch of my church. It's very kind of you to take all this trouble. Will you let me have an invoice for your fees, and Mike's of course, including his travel expenses for the visit."

"There's no charge, Toni. We're just doing it to help out. That's okay."

"That's very generous of you. Are you sure it's all right?"

"Of course."

"Thank you. And you're not even a churchgoer, are you? Sorry, that sounds like a reproach."

"I went to church when I was young … Sunday school, brownies, you know … but I'm very lapsed now. In fact I'm so lapsed I think I'm even a lapsed agnostic." Toni laughed. "Actually," said Marnie, "since my marriage broke up a few years ago, I've been trying to find a new identity for myself. It's been enough to cope with doing that."

"You started from inside," said Toni. "Rather than looking for support from outside."

"I've tried to rebuild, so I know who I am again."

"That's not easy," said Toni. "I gather you work very hard."

"So do lots of people. But I have compensations … family, friendships and of course *Sally*."

"I have the impression the boat is more than just a hobby," said Toni.

"*Sally Ann* has really helped me to make sense of my life again."

"A boat can do *that*?" Toni was trying hard to understand.

"*Sally* gave me a new start. I know others who've had much the same kind of experience."

"I suppose we all have to come to terms with life in our own ways," said Toni. "It was the Sermon on the Mount for me."

"Well, I don't deal in absolutes," said Marnie. "But I know that what I do is interesting, I believe it's worthwhile and I hope it may be of use to people. And it has nothing to do with money."

"It sounds as if you have a vocation, Marnie, and I'm sure it's no less valid than mine. Good old *Sally Ann*." She began gathering up the plans. "But I'll tell you what. If ever you think of going into the church, I could use a really good Sunday school teacher who can inspire the kids like you do."

❀ ❀ ❀ ❀

"Hallo. I'd like to speak to the surveyor who deals with Knightly St John, please." Toni waited to be connected, humming along with the *Eine kleine Nachtmusik* that played on the phone. It was an up-beat version. *Eine kleine Nachtmuzak*, she thought. It stopped abruptly.

"Maxwell."

"Hallo. This is Toni Petrie at Knightly St John. We're having work done on our porch. I need to check that I'm going about things the right way." She explained the current state of affairs, and took notes of all she had to do. She repeated her understanding of the procedures back to the surveyor. "I think I've got that. Thanks. Oh, one last thing. Do you have any detailed drawings of the church as a whole? There are just a few sketch plans in the files here."

"Have you got other problems with the fabric, then?"

"I don't know. I don't think so. I just wanted to get to know the church and I thought a set of plans would be a good start. Is there anything you could let me have?"

"There's not much, only some Victorian survey drawings. The older plans were lost in the fire."

"Oh, I didn't know you had a fire. I'm sorry."

"In 1675, The Great Fire of Northampton. The plans were held there for a survey of church property. They never sent them back, so many of the old records were lost."

"What a pity. Never mind. I'll just have to explore the church myself."

"Try not to find any dry rot," he said.

In the diocesan office, Mr Maxwell closed his file. Whatever you thought of women priests – and he was not at all sure about the idea – they did listen properly and they tried to learn. Not like some of the men, her predecessor being one of them, who did what *they* thought and told *you* afterwards. You had to be firm with that sort.

In the vicarage, Toni read her notes and made a list of jobs to do. Even the prospect of arranging a meeting with the surveyor thrilled her. Everything about her work was a source of excitement. She looked forward to exploring the church and getting to know every corner of the building.

❦ ❦ ❦ ❦

Marnie was rummaging under the desk for a swatch of curtain materials when the phone rang later that afternoon. Anne, immersed in some designs of her own, picked up the receiver.

"Walker and Co, good afternoon." It still made Marnie smile to hear Anne use that formula when taking calls. She half listened, expecting Anne to announce the caller's name and was surprised when Anne turned her head away. This had the effect of making Marnie listen all the more. She could just make out what Anne was saying. "Hallo. Yes, it's me ... Look, I thought I told you not to call me at work ... it's embarrassing, that's why ... you know why ... yes ... of course I do ... don't be silly ... me too ..." Marnie sat up on her chair, looking across at the back of Anne's head. Suddenly Anne turned round and Marnie was caught staring. "Marnie?" said Anne. "It's for you."

"*What?*"

"It's Ralph." Marnie picked up her phone.

Ralph was laughing. "I feel like the straight man in a double act," he said.

"Yes, well after this call I'm going to take Anne down to the boat and make her walk the plank into the shark-infested Grand Union Canal."

"Sorry to be the cause of so much disaster."

"Ralph, I'm glad you phoned. When you were here, I'm afraid I went on so much the history of the place that I didn't give you time to talk about you."

"What about me?"

"Your decision about the chair in America."

"Oh, *that*."

"Beth told me you'd turned it down. You probably wanted to talk about it, but I never gave you the chance."

"Not at all. I decided that I was making a new start here, with a new book, a new boat and ... perhaps even a few other things. I just thought I'd give you a ring to say hallo and see how you were."

"But I told you not to call me at work ... you know why ..." The sound of a loud raspberry coming from the phone could be heard clearly right across the office.

❦ ❦ ❦ ❦

Saturday 22 July

"If I look at another lot of curtain material or a colour chart this week, my eyes are going to fall out," said Marnie over breakfast on Saturday. "Why don't we go off for a picnic somewhere? We could visit one of those gardens."

"Great," said Anne. "Or there's some sort of fair on in Hanford. I saw a poster in the shop window." They decided to check the details when they went up to buy food. It was another fine day and they met the vicar coming out of the church gate. She was as effervescent as ever.

"Do you know, I nearly swore in the church when the battery gave up in my torch just now." Marnie laughed and Anne feigned deep shock. "Anyway, I'm having a grand time exploring everywhere. I thought I'd start with the crypt and work up to the belfry."

"The crypt," said Marnie. "Isn't that a bit creepy?"

"That's what you'd expect, but actually, it's just like a coal cellar. There's a few hundredweight of it down there, left over from when there was a solid-fuel boiler. I'm going to see if any old people burn coal and distribute it round the village for the winter."

"The crypt," said Marnie again. "Is it possible to get down there from inside the church?"

"From inside? No, I don't think so. There are steps round the back, some of them crumbly. You take your life in your hands going down there. Talking of which, I must go round and see *your* grave outside the wall."

Marnie felt her face tingle. "Unfortunate choice of words," she said in a light tone.

"What grave?" said Anne.

"Oh, it's just an old tombstone I came across by the wall of the churchyard. That's all."

"It may only be a village church," said Toni, "but it's absolutely full of history. I never cease to wonder at it. I'm going to get to know it thoroughly from top to bottom … at least, I will do when I've got new batteries in the torch." They had only walked a short way when Anne suddenly stopped.

"What's the matter?" said Marnie.

Anne cocked her head to one side."Can't you feel it?" she said. "The ground. Listen." They did as she asked.

"I can't feel anything …" Marnie began.

"Yes," said Toni. "There is something." Now, the trembling in the ground became a vibration in the air. Rounding the corner about fifty metres away came a group of riders, their harness clinking, stirring up a small cloud of dust under their hooves. They were dressed in Civil War uniforms, and reined in outside the pub. One of their number, evidently the officer in charge, spoke rapidly to his men and broke away from the group, riding towards the three onlookers. Marnie stepped forward as he approached.

"I'd know that hat anywhere," she said, "even if I can't see the face under it. Hallo, Raymond."

"I thought I recognised you," said the rider. He sat tall in the saddle.

"Is this a raid, or are your intentions peaceful?" said Marnie.

"We're doing a tour to publicise the fair in Hanford."

"The tour involves visiting the pubs in the nearby villages, no doubt."

"By coincidence it does." Marnie turned to introduce Raymond to Toni and Anne. "Perhaps we'll see you at the fair," he added. He grinned amiably at the vicar and her dog-collar. "We can always do with some wenches."

"Thank you, kind sir," said Marnie, with a curtsy that contrasted interestingly with her jeans and slip-on shoes. Raymond raised his hat, wheeled round and rejoined his troop.

"How do you know him?" said Anne.

"Would you believe we met at Milton Keynes bus station?"

"There's more history about than you might ever imagine," said Toni. "Now, where were we? Ah yes, torch batteries. What was it you were wanting, Marnie?"

"Just a few things for a picnic. I think we'll visit a garden today. You can have too much history. What do you say, Anne?"

"Suits me."

Part 24

Monday 24 July
No wonder people make a fuss about Monday mornings, Anne thought, as she wrote her fourth message for Marnie and it was still only just after nine. She wondered what it must be like for people who did not love their work as she did. Three of the messages were from Willards, even though Anne had told the same person that Marnie had set off for the meeting over half an hour ago. Why did people have to panic? Marnie had organised everything down to the smallest detail and she had allowed two weeks for slippage. It was an odd state of affairs, she thought, when a sixteen year-old was making reassuring noises to a major company worth millions. The phone rang again.

She pulled the message pad towards her. "Walker and Co, good morning."

"Oh, er, yes ..." The voice was familiar, very agitated. Certainly not the woman from Willards.

"Hallo. It's Anne here, Anne Price. Who's calling, please?"

"Oh, sorry Anne. I was expecting it to be Marnie. It's Toni here."

"I'm afraid Marnie's out this morning, at a meeting. She won't be back till lunch-time at the earliest. Can I help?"

"Er, I don't think so ... thank you."

"Is something the matter? If it's urgent I can get her on the mobile." Anne had a vision of the porch fallen down, a pile of dusty rubble.

"No, it'll keep, but could you ask her to ring me urgently when she comes back?"

"Would you like me to tell her what it's about? Unless it's confidential. I'll just say you want her to contact you as soon as possible, shall I?"

"Thanks, Anne. You could tell her it's ... it's about her grave."

"Her grave?"

"I'll be back at the vicarage from about twelve onwards. Thanks a lot. Bye!"

Well, thought Anne. The world's going mad. I'm the only sane one left. And I haven't even got my GCSE results yet. There must be someone sensible to talk to.

"Hi Anne, it's me. There's no-one here. The place is deserted. Any messages from Willards?"

"They're on their way. Should be with you any time now. They've been panicking about the timing for the re-opening. I've told them everything's under control, but they seem to be in a tizzy."

"So what's new?" said Marnie. "Ah, here comes a car. They've made it. See you later."

"Before you go ... the vicar rang up. She was in a bit of a state, too. Wants you to be in touch as soon as poss."

"They're all at it. Must be an attack of the Mondays. That porch has been standing for six hundred years. It can manage a few more weeks."

"It's not about the porch, Marnie. She wants to talk to you about ... your grave, she said."

"My *grave?* Blimey. Things aren't that bad, are they? My nervous breakdown now, that could be imminent, but the grave can wait a little longer, I hope. Okay. I'd better sort this lot out. I'll talk to her later. Everybody's gone mad except for us. See you!"

And *we're* heading that way, thought Anne as she put the phone down.

🌷   🌷   🌷   🌷

"Just collecting the empties," Anne called up the ladder to Bob, the foreman.

"Righto, me dook." He liked Anne. All the builders liked her friendly manner, the way she was always around with tea and coffee. Not like some people. Marnie and Anne looked after you, especially Anne. She really spoiled them. In fact, they would be quite sad to leave when the job was completed. There were some jobs where everything fitted into place. The foreman put it down to luck.

Anne picked up the empty mugs and looked up at the foreman, who was fixing a new window. "Shall I bring some more in about an hour?" she called up.

"Ta very much, love."

"It looks great. Nice window."

"Yeah."

"Is that tarpaulin okay?"

"Tarpaulin?"

"From down here, it looks a little bit loose at the corner. Probably my imagination, I expect." Without another word she turned and walked back to the office. She did not look back.

When she was out of sight, Bob made his way to the end of the scaffold and examined the tarpaulin, pulling it back into position and making it secure again. It would have been a nuisance if the wind got up and lifted it off. He was glad the girl had spotted that, especially as the guv'nor drove into the yard a moment later. He liked Marnie too, but differently. Quite differently. She waved as she strode over to the office, but left him to get on with the job. They were okay, those two. They knew when to leave things alone. Leave men's work to the men.

Marnie was glad to see that Anne was already putting the kettle on. "Phew! What a morning! How are things?"

"Not bad. Coffee?"

"Lead me to it."

"I've put your messages by the phone. Nothing urgent ... oh, except the one from Toni. You can ignore the Willards ones, I expect."

Marnie quickly read the list. "I don't know why they're flapping. We're ahead of schedule."

"That woman this morning," said Anne. "She kept phoning to ask me things."

"Mobile phone-itis," said Marnie. "It's a well known syndrome. How's *our* work coming on?"

"Fine. You were right about the tarpaulin. I dropped it casually into the conversation. Bob's fixed it already." Anne poured coffee and took it over to Marnie, who was pressing buttons on the phone.

"I suppose I'd better ring Toni and see what's bothering her."

"Have you had anything to eat, Marnie?"

She shook her head. "Toni, hallo, it's Marnie. Problem?" Marnie listened. "I see ... first thing this morning ... right ... I'd better come and look ... okay, I'll see you there."

Marnie was already slipping her jacket off as she walked to the back of the office where the wardrobe stood. She quickly changed out of her business clothes into a sweatshirt and a pair of jeans.

"You can't go round like this without eating," said Anne. "It's not good for you."

"No, mummy."

"I'm serious. Have a banana. It'll keep you going till I can make you a sandwich."

"Yes, mummy." She took a bite on her way to the door and winked over her shoulder.

"It really is good of you to come, Marnie. I felt so upset when I got here this morning and found it."

"I can understand why," said Marnie, kneeling down to examine what remained of the headstone. "What do you think did this ... a sledgehammer?"

"I suppose so. It must have been a terrific blow to break it like this."

The headstone had fallen in three large pieces. Fragments and smaller chips of stone lay all about. The grave had been trampled and the flowers trodden into the ground. Marnie looked up at Toni, who was obviously still distressed at the sight of the desecration.

"Any idea when it could've happened?" said Marnie.

"Yesterday? Last night perhaps? Who knows? It's horrible to think someone might have done such a thing at any time, but on a Sunday ..."

Marnie stood up. "Someone must have heard something. Those houses aren't all that far away. Although there was the fair at Hanford and it was a nice weekend. People would have been out, I suppose."

"Do you think ..." Toni began. "Do you think someone was watching? Waiting until people had gone out, before doing this?"

"I don't know," said Marnie. "We've got to decide what to do about it. Sorry, I mean it's *your* decision, of course, but we can't leave it like this, can we?"

Toni seemed to pull herself together. "No," she said firmly. "No, we can't. I don't care what she may have done that made them bury her out here. She belonged to the village and has a right to a decent grave. I'm going to see she gets it."

"Toni ..." Marnie spoke softly. "I believe there's evidence that she committed suicide, hanged herself. You need to be aware of that."

"That's what I figured. That's what you hinted at, when we were looking out from the tower. Apart from witchcraft, it's the obvious reason. Do you know why or how?"

"She appears to have been mixed up somehow in the murder of the vicar in the Civil War."

"You don't mean she could have been the one who did it?"

"No. There's no evidence that she was anywhere near the church that night. She may have found out who did it. Perhaps someone in her own family. Who knows?"

"How do you know all this, Marnie?"

"Her father's will ... a bequest that paid for this headstone. I've been following it up and a colleague of Ralph's came across some papers dealing with the period. I can show you the evidence."

"And you're sure she could not have been the murderer or an accomplice?"

"Quite the opposite, I think."

"Then I'm going to give her sanctuary. Can you help me shift these pieces of stone?"

❦ ❦ ❦ ❦

They stood in the semi-dark, stretching their backs, breathing heavily in the dusty air that smelled of damp, old stone, mouse droppings, coal. At their feet lay two pieces of headstone.

"They were heavier than I imagined," said Toni between breaths. "I shouldn't have asked you to help me."

"Don't worry," said Marnie, gasping. "We can probably manage the other piece between us."

Toni shook her head. "No-one's going to run off with it," she said. "It's pretty well hidden by the undergrowth. I'll come over later on with the wheelbarrow. That'll make it easier."

"Okay," said Marnie. "Take care on the steps. They're more dangerous than the tower. I've never been in a crypt before. What's it used for?"

"Not a lot, really," said Toni. "Mostly for coal, as you see … or nearly see. They used to bury people in them. Or keep relics if they had them … saints, martyrs. They sometimes used them as chapels for private prayer, or even places of pilgrimage. This is rather a sad, dark place, I think. Pity, really. I'm going to clear it out and clean it up. But not today."

"No," said Marnie. "Not today."

At the top of the steps Toni pulled the door shut. "I'm going to have to get a lock for this door," she said. "Sad, isn't it? I've always been opposed to locking churches and here I am in my first church as vicar planning to put a lock on the bloody crypt! I'm sure nobody's set foot in it for years."

"What are you going to do now?" said Marnie. "You said you wanted to give her sanctuary."

"I'm going to begin proceedings to have the grave relocated inside the churchyard."

"Do the authorities have to give permission?"

"I won't give them any choice."

"Toni, I can't imagine you doing a grave-robbing job under cover of darkness!"

"They won't have any choice *morally,* not after I've told them what has to be done and why."

"Is that wise, do you think?"

"Probably not, but then I don't think I've ever been a particularly wise person. I'm not leaving her out there for her grave to be desecrated again. If they'll do this, who knows what else they might do?"

"But if you just remove the headstone pieces for now, you can deal with the grave itself when the whole matter has died down. If I were you, I'd be cautious for a while."

"I know … I know. But this business is upsetting and I want to get it sorted now. It's not in my nature to be cautious. In any case, what harm can it do, after all these years?"

Marnie went back to the car full of misgivings. These vicars could be a determined lot, she thought. Toni reminded her of Randall. *I'm not a soft touch.* That could just as easily have been said by Toni as by him. She sighed. Their lives were dominated by principles, faith, beliefs. Take them away and what was left? She sat for a while looking through the windscreen at nothing.

With a sigh, she leaned over and opened the glove compartment in the dashboard. She always kept a torch there …

The door to the crypt was patched and peeling, dusty and neglected. The hinges were rusty, as was the clasp that once must have held a padlock. It felt rough and dirty as Marnie pushed it to open the door. The creaking echoed in the void beyond.

❦   ❦   ❦   ❦

"Hallo, I'd like to speak to the Bishop, please. It's Toni Petrie, Knightly St John." She waited while the *Eine kleine Nachtmusik* came down the line.

"Bishop's secretary."

"Is the Bishop available, please? I need an urgent word, if possible."

"I'm afraid the Bishop's away till Friday. If it's urgent perhaps the Archdeacon can help." *That old woman,* thought Toni. Then she mentally corrected herself. It was wrong to be prejudiced against old women, even if they *were* men. Judging Toni's silence to be indecision, the secretary continued. "Unless you think it might be a matter that the Rural Dean could help you with?"

"The Rural Dean?"

"Well, he does know the parish as well as anyone."

"That's true. Thanks for the suggestion. I'll give him a ring."

The number was on the list she kept by the phone. She pressed the buttons, knowing it was likely to be the answerphone. The ringing stopped almost immediately.

"Randall Hughes."

"It's Toni, Randall. I want to ask your advice about something. Have you got a minute?"

❧ ❧ ❧ ❧

In the office Anne had a list of six phone messages waiting for Marnie. More important, she had a cheese and pickle sandwich wrapped in cling film sitting patiently on the desk with a bottle of Perrier water. Anne looked at her watch. Where *was* she? She sighed and rang the mobile.

"Sorry. The mobile number you are calling is unavailable at the moment. Please try again later."

❧ ❧ ❧ ❧

Even with a powerful torch and the door left half open, the crypt was a sad and gloomy hole. It was about half the floor area of the church, with a vaulted ceiling. Now it seemed to hold nothing but junk, tea chests, old brooms and a cupboard with one door missing. To keep her mind from pondering the creepiness of the place, she tried to imagine what it could become, given some renovation work. Although the ceiling was low, the vaulting was impressive, with stout columns supporting arches that were well proportioned. Willards would pay a fortune for a setting like this in the cellar of one of their restaurants. With the right kind of lighting it would be much less frightening. Marnie remembered when she was a child, her mother talking about her to friends, telling them *nothing seems to frighten her.* Just keep believing it, Marnie.

Systematically, she made her way round the walls, searching for the outline of a staircase that might once have existed there. It was not easy to make out the surface of the stone under the accumulated dust and cobwebs. Why had they let it get into this state? Generations of vicars had their minds on higher things, obviously. Don't think about tombs, Marnie, just concentrate on the task in hand. Don't think about skeletons. They're only bones anyway. *Dem bones, dem bones, dem dry bones!* Now what's this? The wall was straight, clear of the vaulting but marked as if something had been removed. She tracked the line of the marking in the torch-beam: just a horizontal line in the wall. About six feet long. Above it she found another mark and above that another. Could this have been a staircase? But it was too wide and the distance between the 'steps' too great. Nearly two feet. If not a staircase, then what? The answer presented itself without difficulty: a stacking place for coffins. Marnie shivered. Well, at least they were long gone. There was no mark in the ceiling to show where a trap door might have been. The trail had gone cold … *cold as the grave wherein my love was laid.*

She tried to recall where the quote came from, and just then struck something with her foot. It clinked. In the torch-beam she saw a cluster of old tools. She squatted down. Two cold chisels, but they were not covered in dust like everything else down there. Three clout hammers with short stubby handles no longer than their heads. Beside them, a fourth wooden handle, extending off into the darkness. She shone the torch along it, but already knew what she would see. It was a sledgehammer, old but serviceable, the handle smooth from years of use, some of it possibly recent.

The torch light faltered briefly as if someone had turned a dimmer switch. Damn and blast! Rechargeable batteries lasted for years and were less heavy than conventional ones, but when they lost their power the decline was sudden and swift. In seconds the light was weaker than a single candle. Marnie stood up, prepared to grope her way out if necessary. She turned towards the steps at the far end of the crypt, grateful for the daylight seeping through the half-open door. Blinking in the unaccustomed dimness, she could almost persuade herself that the daylight too was fading. She opened her eyes wide and blinked again. There was no mistake. The light was vanishing as quickly as her torch had done. *Someone was closing the door!* Marnie dashed forward, opening her mouth to call out, stumbling over something solid on the ground and sprawling in the dust. Before she could regain her control, the door had shut and she was in total darkness.

It took some minutes to feel her way to the foot of the stairs. Perhaps it had been just as well that the pieces of headstone had tripped her. Otherwise she might have come face to face with the person who had smashed the headstone. *Thank you, Sarah Anne, for intervening.* Marnie pulled the door gently to open it without making a noise. It would not move. She tugged firmly. No change. She heaved on it with all her weight. Locked.

This is where I'm supposed to make a plan for fighting my way out, she thought. There were weapons enough, hammers, chisels, the sledgehammer. Visions of the god Thor crossed her mind. Now, someone like Pete Malan, *he* could handle a sledgehammer. *I* could barely lift it. Be practical, Marnie. She felt the weight of the torch in her hand. It was better than nothing. Just about. She squeezed it for reassurance. The casing was made of rubber. I hope he bruises easily, she thought.

❦ ❦ ❦ ❦

"Toni, hallo, it's Anne here. Glebe Farm."

"Hi! What can I do for you?"

"Is Marnie with you?"

"Marnie? 'Fraid not. Haven't seen her for ages."

"That's very odd. She hasn't come back yet. She did come to see you?"

"Yes, but it's over an hour since she left."

"I wonder where she could've gone," said Anne. "Did she mention where she was going?"

"No. She just got in her car and drove off. No, wait a minute. I saw her go towards the car and get in. I don't think I actually heard it start and drive away."

"And you just met at the vicarage and talked over this problem you had ..."

"Not quite. We met by the church and then went to the crypt."

"*The crypt?* What for?"

"We needed to put something there. Actually, Marnie seemed quite interested in it. You know how keen she is on history ... oh, my God ..."

❦ ❦ ❦ ❦

"You are *very* lucky not to be suffering severe rubber battering right now," said Marnie. "If you hadn't called my name, I was going to unleash an attack the like of which has not been seen in these parts since ..."

"1645?" suggested Anne.

"Something like that."

"Marnie," said Toni. "I am just *so sorry*. I had no idea you were down there when I came back with the padlock. Why didn't you call out?"

"It's a long story."

Toni attempted to brush some of the dust from Marnie's clothes. "In the circumstances, there's only one thing for it. We go back to the vicarage. It's got to be a bath for you while I make tea."

"And I'll fetch some clean clothes," said Anne.

"Sounds good to me," said Marnie. Toni replaced the padlock on the door and snapped it shut. She fumbled with the key-ring and held out her hand to Marnie.

"Why don't you keep the spare?" she said. "Then you'll be able to get in if you need to. And take a church key as well for the porch works. I've got another at home."

They set off across the churchyard. "Can someone please tell me what all this is about?" said Anne. "I mean, what were you doing in the crypt anyway?"

"Well," said Marnie, "we found an old broken headstone and Toni wanted to bring it into the church for safekeeping ..."

"For sanctuary," said Toni.

"Yes. I helped her carry the pieces. I thought the crypt looked interesting ... the vaulting's very good ... and accidentally got locked in while I was down at the far end." That should do the trick, thought Marnie. She was confident that Anne would accept that and be satisfied.

"Fair enough," said Anne. "I understand now." Marnie nodded. Anne went on: "I can quite see why moving some old bits of stone was so important you had to drop everything and rush over before you even had time to eat anything."

🌷 🌷 🌷 🌷

"And you thought you'd been trapped by the same person who destroyed the headstone?"

"Of course. What else should I have thought?"

Ralph sounded worried. "Marnie, I'm not sure it was wise in the circumstances to go down there alone without telling anyone."

"That's just what Beth said. I phoned her a few minutes ago. Actually, that's not quite true. Her actual words were: *was I an utter bloody cretin.*"

"Sister's privilege. She's known you longer than I have." He still sounded worried. "You must be careful, Marnie. I have misgivings about this whole business."

"So have I, but Toni won't be put off. She's determined to get the grave relocated straight away. She's even thinking of having a special service to consecrate the burial."

"Frankly, I think that's asking for trouble after the vandalism. Try to dissuade her if you can. She might listen to you. You don't know what you're stirring up."

"I *do* know. You should've seen the headstone ... and the flowers ... totally destroyed."

"Sorry. I shouldn't be going on like this. You don't need me to tell you what to do. I ought to be making encouraging noises, re-assuring you."

"Don't worry. It's a comfort just talking to you."

"Good. What about Anne ... is she aware of all this?"

"Not really, but she's no fool and may be working it out for herself. I'm doing my best to keep things from her so as not to worry her too much."

"I take it she's not with you just now."

"No. She's in her room in the office barn. I'm ringing from *Sally Ann*. Actually, I'm in bed now."

"Marnie, you shouldn't say things like that to me on the phone. It'll bring on my palpitations ..."

🌷 🌷 🌷 🌷

Tuesday 25 July

"Just *some* of the truth will do," said Anne next morning over breakfast. They were sitting in the saloon on board *Sally Ann*. It had rained in the night and the ground was still wet.

"I *have* told you some of ... I *have* told you the truth," Marnie insisted. Anne gave her a pointed stare. "All right ... all right ... I came across an old headstone outside the church wall, over by the executive housing estate. ... It marked the grave of Sarah Anne Day ... and we know she committed suicide in 1645. That's why she wasn't allowed to be buried in the churchyard."

"*We?* Who's *we?*"

"Ralph did some research and found out."

"I see. This headstone ... it was in pieces?"

"Not when we first found it last week."

"How did it get broken?"

"Vandals, I expect."

"Why did Toni want to move it into the crypt if it was already broken?"

"She said she wanted to give it sanctuary in the church."

"Sanctuary? If this Sarah Anne committed suicide, can Toni do that without special permission?"

"I do enjoy entertaining the Spanish Inquisition for breakfast," said Marnie. "Such a nice change from the *Today* programme on Radio Four. Although, on second thoughts ..."

"It's the only way I can find out what's going on round here," said Anne in a reasonable tone.

Marnie sighed. "I seem to be sighing a lot these days," she said. "Look. I know you find the church creepy. I do, too, sometimes. If you aren't keen on the *tower*, you should try poking around in the *crypt* ... and getting locked in when your torch batteries are running out ..."

"I'll put 'recharge batteries' on your list," Anne interjected quickly.

"Thanks. As I was saying ... something made me want to find out who killed the vicar. I don't know why, but I had the strangest feeling there was something obvious staring me in the face."

"But we've already talked about this," said Anne. "You don't have to keep it secret from *me* ... unless there's something I don't know about ..."

"I didn't want to keep going on about it," said Marnie, hoping Anne would not detect the evasion. "It *is* rather morbid, after all. In fact, I decided to drop the whole thing. Then this business with the headstone came along and I gave Toni a hand."

Anne looked at her thoughtfully. "Right. I suppose that'll do for now." She dunked her croissant in her bowl of coffee. "I think you're right about it staring you in the face. I've said it before: the murderer *was* there in the tower that night ... he *had* to be to commit the murder. How else could it have happened? And he couldn't have run out." She dunked the remaining part of her croissant. Marnie could not fault Anne's logic. "Ah, that's why you went back to the crypt, Marnie. You were looking for a way in from the church ... some steps or something. Is that right? Did you find any?"

"No," said Marnie. Another sigh. "Definitely no way down there from inside the church."

"Then you do agree with me."

"Logically, yes," said Marnie. "But *where* was he hiding?"

Anne drank some coffee. "He was hiding behind the wooden panel on the landing."

"That's what I thought," said Marnie. "But it's solid. You saw how Mike banged on it."

"I suppose so," said Anne. She pulled out a pad and a pen, scribbled 'batteries' at the top and wrote a few notes. "There's the roof of the tower."

"They went up and searched it," said Marnie.

Anne put a line through one of the items. "In the belfry?"

"There's no room, only bells, and no floor," said Marnie. Another line through.

"Could he have hung on the bells?"

"You can put Quasimodo down as a suspect if you want. You know who he was, don't you?"

"Of course," said Anne.

"I know," said Marnie. "You did a project on Victor Hugo ... got an 'A' in the coursework."

"No. I saw the film on TV. *The Hunchback of Notre Dame ... The bells! The bells!*"

"Anyway," said Marnie, "they would've made a noise."

"I give up," said Anne. "Anyway, there's nothing we can do about it. It's all in the past."

Is it? thought Marnie.

✿ ✿ ✿ ✿

Wednesday 26 July

It was late morning the following day when Anne suddenly looked up from her computer. "You know, we ought to be on the Internet," she said.

Marnie only managed to climb halfway out of the depths of concentration. "Right," she muttered. "We can use the fax machine as an ornament." She immersed herself again in planning atmospheric lighting for the reception area of Willards' largest hotel.

"This Sarah Anne Day," Anne continued. "You're assuming she was a relative of Frank Day ..."

Marnie climbed out again briefly. "Seems logical. Same village, same name."

"Then why not ask him if *he* knows anything. After all, he is always hanging round here. Perhaps he has some views on what happened. It's worth a try. You've got nothing to lose."

✿ ✿ ✿ ✿

Marnie watched Anne head up the field track to catch the five o'clock post. It would be at least twenty minutes before she returned. She dialled Frank Day's office number. The answerphone cut in. She hung up and looked in the address book for his mobile. No luck, but his home number was there.

"Hallo, Knightly 639." A woman's voice. *Damn!* thought Marnie ... what's his wife's name?

"Oh, hallo, it's Marnie Walker here. Is that ..."

"Hallo, Marnie. Yes it's Janet."

"Janet, hi! Is it possible to have a word with Frank? I've tried the office but got the machine."

"I'm afraid not, Marnie. He's out on business at the moment. I'm not sure what time he'll be back, but I can give him a message. Or perhaps I can help?"

"Thanks, but I think I really need to talk to Frank. It's about something in Knightly. I know he'll be concerned because ... well, I know how much he loves the village."

"*Loves the village?*" said Janet. There was incredulity, even scorn in her voice. "Knightly St John? He hates the village. It has only ever brought him trouble." Marnie felt her cheeks redden.

"Oh, I see. How silly of me ... I didn't realise ..."

"You've been listening to the people in Knightly, Marnie. They seem to think there's only one village in England and that everyone else is interested in their comings and goings. Don't get me wrong. I wish you well with your business, but remember there are other points of view."

"Of course. It was something concerning Frank's family that I wanted to talk to him about."

There was a pause. "Frank's family?" This time the tone was wary, bordering on suspicion. "I didn't realise you knew his family."

Marnie's brain went into overdrive. She was already regretting what she had said so far and was determined not to repeat the mistake. "It was just something I came across the other day. I thought I'd mention it to him out of interest. I could leave a message, if that's okay."

"I think you'd better talk to him direct. I'll ask him to ring you."

"Thanks." Marnie thought for a second. "Janet, it isn't my wish to stir up any problems ..."

"That's all right. Don't worry."

"But if there's any ill feeling ... any awkwardness ..."

"There can't be any ill feeling, Marnie. You see, Frank hasn't got any family. None living, at any rate. Unless you count me, of course, and they never did."

❦ ❦ ❦ ❦

Frank Day rang back soon after Anne returned from the shop. Whether by chance or from a sense of discretion, Anne put the call through and immediately left the office to stow food away on *Sally Ann*. Frank's voice sounded strained, not the usual easy-going banter.

"Frank, I need to talk to you, but I can't easily do it just now. Can we meet?"

"I think we should. Soon."

"Are you free tomorrow? Perhaps in the morning?"

"Sure. Do you want me to come over?"

"No. Let's have coffee somewhere. Say ten-thirty?"

❦ ❦ ❦ ❦

It was a pleasant hotel and restaurant that had once been a coaching inn. The car park was laid out with cobbled bays and planting, and the interior was newly redecorated, but Marnie had other things on her mind. She saw Frank sitting in the lounge. He stood up as she approached, his smile barely camouflaging the serious expression underneath.

"I've ordered coffee. Is that all right?"

"Fine. Am I late?"

"No. I was early." He gestured to a seat beside him. It felt like a conspiracy.

"Frank, if I said the wrong thing to Janet on the phone yesterday ..."

"I've seen the grave, Marnie. I know the headstone is gone."

"I'm sorry about what happened, Frank."

"It was an injustice to my family ... at least that's how I see it. Okay, so the church was right not to let her be buried in the graveyard, but it was all so long ago. Surely the church can forgive at last."

"Was it you who put the flowers there?" said Marnie.

"Of course. I found the headstone quite by chance. The dogs chased a rabbit into the bushes and there she was. I hope your message means you know where it is."

"It's in the crypt."

"How did it get there?"

"The vicar and I did it between us."

Frank looked incredulous. "Two women could never *lift* it. It's *much* too heavy."

"It was in pieces," said Marnie softly.

"So that explains the state of the flowers," said Frank. "I take it you didn't trample on them when you moved the stone." A cheerful waitress bustled over with a tray of coffee and biscuits.

"Frank, I ought to tell you that I know about the will that paid for the headstone."

He looked at Marnie in amazement. "How could you *possibly* know about that?"

"Completely by chance, actually. Rather like your dogs chasing the rabbit. It was a colleague of Ralph's from Oxford doing research who happened to find it in the archives. I was just curious about the unsolved murder of the vicar and this turned up unexpectedly."

"What else did you find out?" said Frank. He looked wary. What else *was* there to find out? Marnie thought.

"That was it, really. She killed herself shortly after the murder. No-one believes there's any connection between Sarah Anne and the deed itself, of course."

"No," said Frank. They sipped their coffee.

"I don't want to pry, but if there is anything you think the vicar ought to know, you should tell her."

"The vicar?"

"She's going to begin proceedings to have Sarah Anne re-interred in the churchyard." Frank frowned. "That would be your wish too, wouldn't it, Frank?"

"It *was,* but now I'm not so sure. At least, not at the moment ..."

"Why not?"

"You saw what happened to the headstone and the flowers. Someone did that. Someone in the community. The hatred is still there, still alive. I'm not sure now's the time to stir up more trouble."

"Perhaps it was just vandals," said Marnie. "Coincidence."

"No. Definitely not." Frank bit his lip. "I can't tell you why it's important, Marnie. I have to think about it. It's a private family matter. I'm sure you understand."

"There's nothing more to say, then," said Marnie.

"I'll try and explain some time. But not just yet. I don't want to be the cause of any trouble for you. It's a pity the vicar's got involved, really ... a great pity."

❦ ❦ ❦ ❦

Thursday 27 July
"A second mobile phone for me would be handy," said Anne, without looking up from her desk. She was writing a list. Marnie, sitting at her desk, a few metres away, looked over at her friend.

"If you can't hear me I can raise my voice. If I get a sore throat I can ring you from here."

"I meant for Scotland," said Anne. "While I'm away on this holiday."

"The last thing you'll want is phone calls about work when you're on holiday. That's the point."

"But you might need to check something with me ... ask me something."

"I won't have time," said Marnie. "It'll take me the best part of a fortnight just to read through all the things on that list. Scott had fewer notes to follow when he went to the South Pole."

"He didn't get there, did he?" said Anne ominously. "There's no way you'll be able to reach me if there *is* something you want. We're going to be miles from anywhere. I can't even pronounce the name of the place. I think there was a battle nearby."

"That describes most of Scotland," said Marnie.

"I bet *you've* never been on a camping holiday in the Highlands of Scotland. The Greek islands ... Tuscany ... Provence ... they're more your scene."

"My husband and I ... that sounds funny, doesn't it? Like the Queen. Anyway, we had a holiday in Scotland. We went to the Trossachs, the Isle of Skye ... we even had a day on Muck. That rather sums up much of my marriage!"

Anne giggled. "Was it nice? The holiday, I mean."

"Very. Two days visiting the galleries in Glasgow. And we discovered the Borders, Melrose Abbey, Peebleshire. You're going to have a lovely time, so just enjoy it. Don't think about work at all."

Anne returned to organising Marnie's life for the next two weeks. "Bet you weren't camping in a tent," she muttered.

❦   ❦   ❦   ❦

Marnie was halfway up a ladder talking to Bob the foreman when Anne came jogging across the yard from the office barn. "Fax from Willards!" she called.

The machine was still pouring out paper when they reached the office. Marnie frowned.

"... *in the circumstances we are holding an extraordinary meeting of the Board of Directors to discuss the major projects to which we are currently committed. These include the refurbishment programme of our Canalside Inns, Traveller Hotels and Trencherman Restaurants, plus the renovation of head office. The meeting is scheduled for ...*"

"Oh damn," said Marnie. "They want me to go to a special board meeting tomorrow." She read the list of all the information they wanted her to bring. She was to give a 'short presentation', on each scheme, with individual statements of cost and a situation report on the whole programme. They wanted material samples, colour charts and sketches. "This is going to take all afternoon," she sighed.

"You don't think they might stop the contract?" said Anne. "They couldn't do that, could they?"

"Well, they could ... but I don't think they will." Marnie read down to the bottom of the page.

"... *and we hope this will not cause you any inconvenience. We look forward to seeing you on Friday at 10.30 am.*"

"Right," said Anne. "I'd better phone my parents and tell them I can't go on holiday. This is an emergency. Our whole contract might depend on this meeting."

"Don't worry," said Marnie. "I can handle it. You go on your holiday and have a nice time."

"Okay," said Anne reluctantly. "I'll try not to worry myself sick in my tent halfway up a mountain ..." She quickly read the rest of the fax. "You're invited to stay on for a buffet lunch. Oh, what's this? ... *as some of the directors are concerned that the recession is not yet over ... may be prudent to rephase the programme ... the green shoots of recovery.* I've heard that somewhere."

"Something the Chancellor said. I think it was in the budget speech."

"Are they getting cold feet?"

"Some of them. But don't worry. Now is actually a good time to get ready for when the market picks up. At times like this you've got to make more of an effort, and they're a profitable company."

"Marnie, do you think it's possible you might not get back in time to get me to the bus station?"

"If I'm late, I'll just run you home myself. It's not far."

"You've got enough to do. I'll make a contingency plan. Just in case."

❦   ❦   ❦   ❦

"Anne!" The voice came from behind and stopped Anne on her way to the shop. She turned to see Toni Petrie struggling through the church gate, with a pile of books, rolls of plans under her arm and a briefcase in her free hand. "Are you in a hurry?"

"I don't want to miss the post. I'm getting everything tidied up before I go on holiday tomorrow afternoon. Can I help you carry those?"

"No, I'm all right, thanks. Where are you off to?"

"Scotland, with my parents. Camping on the top of Ben Nevis."

"Really?" said Toni. "That sounds like fun."

"Well, not actually on the top ... more nearby."

"I rather thought as much. Let me not hold you up, but can you give Marnie a message for me?" At that moment, one of the books fell to the ground. Anne picked it up: a battered paperback Bible.

"Have you been to a meeting?"

"No," said Toni. "Just tidying the vestry. You can keep that, if you like. My good deed for the day."

"Converting the pagan natives?" said Anne.

"That's the idea."

"Thanks. You said you had a message for Marnie?"

"Oh, just that I've shifted the rest of the headstone into the crypt and I've spoken to Randall Hughes about proceedings for the re-interment."

"No probs," said Anne.

"How are your building works coming along?"

"Fine. Our main problem's an unexpected meeting tomorrow that could make Marnie late back. She's taking me to the bus station and if she's late she'll want to take me all the way home. I don't want her to have any more to do. She works so hard already."

"I'll be here all day," said Toni. "If Marnie's late, give me a ring and I'll run you to the bus."

"That's really kind of you."

"As you might say, no probs!"

❦ ❦ ❦ ❦

"I used to think the whole world smelled of diesel," said Marnie, sniffing one of Anne's shirts as she helped her pack that evening. "When I was living on *Sally Ann* last summer, I mean."

Anne sniffed it before laying it in the suitcase. "Keeping all the clothes over here, away from the engine, was a good idea," she said. "It doesn't matter so much for me. I've only got some of my things here anyway."

Marnie folded a pair of jeans and passed them over. "Yes," she said. "You don't have a lot to pack. I suppose most of the things you'll need on holiday are at home."

"Yes. I'll do my real packing tomorrow night. My summer holiday things will all be there for me. Thermal vests, snow shoes, survival kit, ice pick, elephant gun ..."

"*Elephant gun?*" said Marnie.

"You know me," said Anne. "Be prepared. You never know ..."

❦ ❦ ❦ ❦

It was after ten that evening by the time Marnie finished checking all her materials for the board meeting in Leicester. She had taken them over to *Sally Ann* so that she could go through her presentation without disturbing Anne. She was going to ring Beth, but it was her sister who rang first.

"I don't know where the weeks have gone," said Beth wearily. "We seem to have been going non-stop for ever."

"You need a holiday," said Marnie.

"So do you."

"No. I'm fine. Remember I had all last summer off. Now, I just want to press on with the new life and get Glebe Farm sorted out."

"Well, don't overdo it. Actually, we are going on holiday. I've told Paul we have to get right away, otherwise it's no break. He's got a research student doing a doctorate who's always pestering him."

"So where are you going?"

"Mum said she wanted us to visit them ... said some Spanish sunshine would do us good. But staying with family isn't the same as a real break, so I've booked us a package to the Greek islands."

"You shouldn't tell me that," said Marnie. "Now I *will* be jealous."

"It was thinking of your holidays there that gave us the idea. Do you remember that time you and Simon came round for dinner after a sailing holiday in the Aegean?"

"The time Paul's visiting professor was there?"

"Yes. The pompous twit! He kept saying how *wonderful* you looked with your *beautiful* tan."

"Yes," said Marnie. "I remember. He went on and on about how vibrant the spirit of the islands was, the essence of culture and purity."

"And then he asked you which islands you'd liked best, and you said Lesbos and Syphilos!" Beth guffawed.

"Anne's off on holiday tomorrow," said Marnie. "Her family are going to Scotland."

"Nice," said Beth.

"They're going camping in the Highlands."

"I hope the weather stays fine," said Beth. "Does that mean you'll be on your own or have you made plans to have visitors ... or one visitor at least?"

"No. I'll be here working. I've got a lot to do."

"Come for lunch on Saturday," said Beth.

"Okay. Thanks."

"Will you be all right by yourself?"

"Of course," said Marnie. "I'll have Dolly for company and plenty to do."

"You won't mind being alone at Glebe Farm?"

"The builders are here all day. Anyway, this is the country. Nothing happens here."

Marnie was looking up Ralph's number when the phone rang again. "I hope it's not too late to ring, Marnie? I've tried your number for the last half hour and it's been engaged."

Marnie closed her address book. "Talking to Beth," she said. "How are you, Ralph?"

"Fine. But I'm concerned about this headstone business. Any news about that?"

"I gather Toni's going to have the grave shifted inside the churchyard. She told Anne. The headstone is now safely tucked away in the crypt."

"You must be very careful about everything connected with the church, Marnie. It worries me. Any ideas about who might have been responsible for the damage?"

"Not a clue. Nor has Toni. It's not the sort of thing you can casually ask about. *Oh, by the way, have you vandalised any gravestones lately?*"

"Quite. Whoever it was and for whatever reason, obviously someone there doesn't like Sarah Anne and what she stood for. It could be dangerous for the vicar ... and for you, too."

❦ ❦ ❦ ❦

Friday 28 July

The clock in the oak-panelled boardroom at Willards had looked down on meetings for almost a hundred and fifty years. Nowadays only the exterior of the clock was the original, the workings inside having been replaced by an electric mechanism a few years previously. The company liked to see itself in a similar light, traditional on the outside, modern below the surface. Marnie glanced up at the Roman numerals. She had been in the meeting since ten-thirty and now it was a quarter to twelve.

"I think we have to use our own judgement," said the deputy chairman. "It's true that sales aren't as buoyant as we hoped, but they're still at a reasonable level given the overall market conditions."

"Depends what you mean by *reasonable*," said one of the older directors. "If you look at Bass Charrington, they're increasing their market share throughout the Midlands and we can't match them. They've got the resources behind them. We're a small concern in comparison."

"My point precisely," said Cawdrey, the deputy chairman. "They are *expanding* because they're *investing* in their existing pubs and restaurants and people want to use them. They're attractive places. People are choosy about where they spend their leisure time." He looked to Henry Willard, the chairman, for support, but Willard seemed determined to be impartial in the debate.

"Well," he said. "I think we've given that discussion a good airing." *A good airing*, thought Marnie. They had been going over the same ground almost from the start of the meeting.

The chairman raised a hand in Marnie's direction. "I think we've kept Mrs Walker waiting long enough to bring us up-to-date on progress with *The Irish Navigator* and the other projects she's been working on." Marnie stood and went over to the table where an overhead projector and a slide projector had been set up for her. The chairman continued. "Most of you know Marnie. She's done a number of projects for us over the past two or three years when she was in London. Now she has her own company. You're very welcome here, Marnie. Please regard yourself as among friends. Perhaps you could start with *The Irish Navigator* and then we'll see how things go from there. We may have a break for lunch before you deal with the rest of the programme, if everyone's in agreement."

"Thank you, chairman. *The Irish Navigator* is a good starting point because it embodies many of the principles on which my other designs are based." She clicked the button and the first slide appeared, an early 19th century water colour of the inn, a pastoral scene with sheep grazing in fields in the background, men sitting outside on benches smoking pipes and a horse-drawn barge laden with barrels, going by on the canal. "Much has changed since the inn was first built in 1793, but the atmosphere of the canals still appeals to us today." She clicked the button a second time and the slide changed to a view of the inn as it appeared before the bomb. "My design aims to invoke that age, but with all the comforts and facilities that we now expect ..."

❦ ❦ ❦ ❦

"We'll miss you when you're off on your holidays, me dook," said Bob the foreman, taking his steaming mug of tea from Anne's tray.

"Marnie will be here to look after you, don't worry," she said.

"But who'll be looking after Marnie? I don't like her being all by herself. It's not right."

"She'll be okay." Anne turned back to the office, convinced that Bob was right. Even now, she wished she could find some excuse for not going. And yet, she could not quite explain her misgivings. Why should Marnie not be perfectly fine? It had always been her plan to live and work here alone. She put the empty tray down by the sink at the back of the office and went to go over her list again. Two o'clock. When the phone rang ten minutes later she was not surprised at what Marnie said.

"We're only just resuming and I've barely described one job so far. I have a feeling I'm going to be on for at least an hour."

"How's it going?"

"Fine." The flat tone of Marnie's voice told Anne that there was someone else in earshot.

"Are you persuading them?"

"Probably. Anne, about your lift to the bus station. I think the best thing to do is for me to take you home when I get back."

"Don't worry. Toni said she'll take me."

"Oh, right. Well, let's see how it goes. I don't want *you* to worry. I want you to get off to a good start and have a really nice holiday. Anyway, I have to go now. Talk to you soon."

Anne gave it half an hour before ringing Toni.

❦   ❦   ❦   ❦

"If there are no more questions ..." The chairman looked around the boardroom table. He knew he had been right to give his fellow directors a brief taste of Marnie's work, followed by a good lunch and a session with Marnie weaving her magic. By the end of the presentation he could sense that they not only wanted the programme to continue, but were impatient for it to be implemented at once. He indicated Marnie's chair and she switched off the equipment and returned to her place. "Thank you, Marnie, for a most interesting and inspiring exposition of the programme." To his, and Marnie's, surprise, the directors applauded. She acknowledged with a smile and sat down, wondering if she could leave or whether she had to wait to be invited to withdraw. She wondered what the founding fathers of Willards Brewery would make of it if they could see the board of directors being lectured by, a young woman (well, youngish), playing her part in the running and future of their company.

❦   ❦   ❦   ❦

"I'm afraid the car's a bit of a mess," said Toni, heaving books off the front passenger seat to let Anne climb in. "I'd apologise for its unusual state, but it's always like this with me. I never seem to get around to sorting it out."

"Don't worry," said Anne. She trod on something soft in the foot-well and reached down to pick it up. It was an old brown teddy bear.

"Oh, *there* he is!" said Toni. "I wondered where he'd got to. That's Augustine."

"Hallo, Augustine," said Anne. "Shall I put him on the back seat?" She pulled the door shut and Toni eased the elderly Austin Allegro out of the yard towards the field track. The builders, who were just clearing up for the weekend, waved her off.

"This must be a far cry from that stylish car of Marnie's," said Toni. "She's a very smart lady." Her voice stopped abruptly as she hit a rut in the dry soil and they bounced in their seats.

"It's very good of you to take me," said Anne breathlessly. Looking back at the farm, she caught a glimpse of Dolly crossing the yard, her tail held high.

❦   ❦   ❦   ❦

At that moment, Marnie was standing in the brewery's car park in Leicester listening to the ringing tone on her mobile. After several rings the answerphone cut in and she heard her own voice telling her there was no-one available to take her call, but she could leave a message after the tone.

"Anne, hallo, it's me, Marnie." She waited to give Anne time to pick up the phone. "Have you gone? If you've gone, please pick up the receiver and let me know ..." She half expected at any moment that Anne would reply and laugh at her feeble joke. With a feeling of disappointment and anti-climax she finally hung up. She had not meant it to be like this. It felt as if Anne had disappeared like the boats that tie up on the canal at night and slip away in silence in the early hours.

❀ ❀ ❀ ❀

It was strange arriving back at Glebe Farm to find everything shut up and silent. Marnie realised how she had come to rely on Anne always being there, a cheerful word at every homecoming. On her desk she found her lists but no message. The office was neat and tidy, everything in its place. Not only was Anne the organiser and the unobtrusive supervisor of the builders, but also the cleaner and washer-up, the emptier of bins, the tidier of shelves. Marnie suddenly recognised that she, the enlightened, liberated, pinko-liberal, took her friend for granted. It made her feel even more guilty that she had not taken Anne to the bus station or driven her home. For an irrational moment she felt annoyed with Anne for going like this. It's not as if Marnie begrudged taking her home. But of course, Anne was only trying as always, to lighten her load. Marnie sighed and locked up.

Walking through the spinney, she found Dolly at her side and reached down to stroke her head. She told her about the meeting, enquired whether she had seen any good mice lately and asked what she would like for tea. It was a predictable conversation.

Putting the key in the lock on *Sally Ann*, Marnie noticed the corner of a piece of paper tucked into the door. She pulled it out, expecting Anne's handwriting, but this was typewritten and unsigned.

"I've got a problem.There's something very strange. You're the only person here that I can talk to. If you'll look in at the vicarage I'll put you in the picture. Thanks."

Several possibilities flashed through Marnie's mind: more vandalism, a threatening letter, a break-in in the crypt, a hostile reaction to moving the grave. She reread the note and picked up the phone.

"Hallo. This is Toni Petrie at the vicarage. Sorry to miss you, but please keep in touch by leaving a message after the tone. God bless."

"Toni, it's Marnie. I've got your note. I'll call round. See you soon. Bye!"

❀ ❀ ❀ ❀

Marnie prepared supper for one: a Greek salad with olives and feta cheese in a warm pitta and a glass of red wine. Outside, it was clouding over, breezy and cool. She ate in the saloon, listening to Radio 4. Something was happening in Northern Ireland, statements, activity behind the scenes, intrigue, accusations, denials. She glanced at the note from Toni and sighed. Old conflicts.

Over coffee, she rang Anne's number. "I'm sorry I missed you. The meeting dragged on and on."

"No, *I'm* sorry to leave like that, but I didn't want you to have to do all that extra driving after your long day. How did it go? Do I sign on at the Jobcentre?"

"No." Marnie laughed. "No. They approved the whole programme. We carry on as before. Don't worry about it. You can enjoy your holiday. Have a good time."

Moments after putting the phone down, Marnie heard the raindrops on the roof. With the hatch shut, the doors closed and a baroque tape in the cassette player, she poured another glass of wine, opened the latest edition of a boat magazine and put her feet up. She was ready for an early night.

❦ ❦ ❦ ❦

Saturday 29 June

Marnie showered before breakfast on Saturday morning and slipped into jeans and sweatshirt. Her first glimpse of the day revealed clouds breaking up to let the sun through, but everywhere was sodden and she had heard heavy rain in the night. She pushed open the doors and almost fell over Dolly who leapt in on route to the galley, leaving damp marks on Marnie's jeans. Feeling guilty at leaving her out all night, Marnie fed her at once and rubbed her down with an old towel.

It was one of those summer mornings when the air is steamy and cool, promising warmth for the rest of the day. Marnie stood on deck, enjoying the birdsong and the watery smell from the canal. She wanted to shout in pleasure and understood Toni's excitement. *Oh god, I'm so lucky!* Probably the same words that Toni uttered, thought Marnie. Capital G in Toni's case, of course.

She brought a chair out onto the deck and fetched her coffee. Dolly followed her out, rubbing her nose against the chair leg.

"You poor bedraggled thing. Stay there. I'm going to brush you."

Dolly settled down on Marnie's lap, her purring in rhythm with the brush strokes. Soon, the black fur was sleek and smooth, though some of it came out in the brushing. It clung to Marnie's jeans and she swished it away as best she could. Programmed as she was by Anne, Marnie knew she could not plan the day without checking the Saturday list. It included a trip to the shop that she would combine with a visit to the vicarage, anxious to deal at once with the 'problem' that was bothering Toni.

❦ ❦ ❦ ❦

"I don't suppose you've seen the vicar this morning?" said Marnie in the shop.

"She was in here not ten minutes ago," said Molly Appleton.

"That explains why she wasn't at home when I called in just now. Any idea where she's gone?"

"You could try the church."

"Sounds logical," said Marnie. "When she came in, did she seem all right?"

"I thought so," said Molly. She glanced sideways at Richard sitting in his post office cubby hole.

"I thought she was a bit, sort of, subdued," said Richard. "I said so to you, didn't I Molly?"

"I didn't notice," said Molly. "But it's funny you should ask, after Richard thought that too. But you said you hadn't seen her."

"No, I haven't. But I need to have a word. I'll go round to the church. If you see her, could you tell her I'm looking for her?"

"Will you be in this afternoon?"

"No, actually. I'm going to see my sister in London. How's *your* sister getting on? Is she better now?" It was a bad move. Molly's answer was biological, graphic and comprehensive. It was several minutes before Marnie could extricate herself.

The church door yielded when Marnie leaned on it and she stepped inside. Perhaps it was her imagination, but the church seemed brighter, fresher, more cared for than it used to be, as if the spirit of the new vicar had swept everything clean. All was silent and Marnie had the unmistakeable feeling that the building was empty. She walked down the centre aisle as far as the altar. Why was the church open? Someone must be here. She tried the door to the tower and it swung open.

"Hallo!" Her voice echoed up the stairs. No reply. She returned to the main door via the aisle on the far side. There was nowhere Toni could be without Marnie seeing her. It was just like that night in the Civil War. No-one could conceal themselves in this church.

She went back to the vicarage and rang the bell. There was no reply. No-one in the garden. No car in the garage.

"You've missed her, I'm afraid." Marnie turned to see George Stubbs in Harris tweed and polished brogues standing on the drive, raising his hat. "I saw her drive out of the village a few minutes ago."

"I seem to be chasing her shadow," said Marnie.

"A well-turned phrase, my dear." Marnie tried not to cringe. A sudden vision came into her head of George Stubbs writhing on the ground clutching his groin. She suppressed an involuntary laugh, but could not prevent it from becoming a smile. George looked delighted and beamed back at her. He knew how to please a woman, he thought. They all like a little flattery, bless 'em.

"Well, I'm out of luck today. Unless she returns soon."

"I wouldn't count on it, Marnie. She was going very fast, and she looked deadly serious."

Marnie frowned. "Thank you, George. I'll have to catch her when I can." He watched her walking down the road in her designer jeans. Everything about Marnie Walker was well-turned, he thought.

🌸 🌸 🌸 🌸

"I've had an idea," said Beth over lunch.

"Well done," said Marnie.

"The weather forecast's fine. Why don't we go to the open-air concert on Hampstead Heath this evening? It's the LSO and the programme looks good." She passed the local newspaper to Marnie.

"Debussy, *Prélude à l'après-midi d'un faune*, Tchaikovsky, *Midsummer Night's Dream*, Vaughan Williams, *Fantasia on a Theme of Tallis* ... All very pastoral ... good idea. Let's go for it."

"It shouldn't make you too late getting back," said Beth. "There's no reason for you to rush off is there?" Marnie thought of Toni's note.

"Well, there is something I have to sort out ... but one more day won't make any difference."

🌸 🌸 🌸 🌸

Marnie slowed down going past the vicarage on her way home. Lights were showing in two of its windows, and she pulled up on the opposite side of the road. *I've got a problem ... something very strange ...* She looked at the clock. Eleven forty-two. Probably too late to call, even on Toni.

Marnie hesitated. Perhaps Toni had left another message. She reached for the mobile and rang her own number to check the answerphone. Waiting for the machine to cut in, she saw a curtain move in the house where she had stopped. She turned off the engine. If the phone rang more than twice, it meant there were no messages. Four rings. She hung up. Too late to go knocking someone up. *The only person I can talk to ...* But not at nearly midnight, perhaps. She started the engine and drove home. One more day would not make any difference.

🌸 🌸 🌸 🌸

Sunday 30 July

Sunday was like old times. Marnie pottered about on *Sally Ann*, cleaning, tidying, coiling ropes. She was surprised at how much pleasure she derived from swabbing her over. The paintwork gleamed in the pale sunlight and she settled down mid-morning with coffee on the deck to polish the brass mushrooms. Anne and her family would be halfway up the motorway by now, she thought. She screwed the mushrooms back into place and set off to the shop to buy a paper.

"I thought you were a churchgoer, Molly." Marnie placed her paper on the counter. "How do you manage with opening the shop on Sunday mornings?"

"Easy," said Molly. "We go to communion first thing. It just gives me time to change before opening up. Sometimes we go to evensong as well. That's my favourite."

"So there are services throughout the day?"

"Vicar does matins, communion and evensong, plus The Grange and Autumn Lodge after lunch."

"What are they?"

"Old people's homes. She does communion for folk who can't get about very easily."

"She's a busy lady," said Marnie.

"Well, Randall started at The Grange and Toni's added Autumn Lodge. *And* she's added the junior choir. Village Cathedral Choristers, she calls them. She got the choir master at the cathedral to let her have the choristers' old cassocks when they got new ones. She coaches the children herself. She's a very good singer." Marnie remembered what Anne had said: *the voice of an angel.*

"Very enterprising," said Marnie.

"*And* she's started a new Sunday School group," said Molly. She lowered her voice. "You know there are some in this village who don't agree with women priests, but I must say I think Toni's done wonders. And everyone likes her. Well, *nearly* everyone, if you get my meaning ..."

Sunday was obviously not the best day to go calling on a vicar, especially this one. Marnie walked back past the church, past the cars parked up and down both sides of the road, while their passengers filled the ancient building. The gate was freshly painted. The sign board had been rewritten: Revd Toni R Petrie, BD, LRAM. In the churchyard the grass was mown short and the path had new gravel. The church was wearing its Sunday best. Sunday, the day of rest. But not for Toni Petrie.

Part 25

Monday 31 July

Monday morning felt like Monday morning without Anne around. Although, in a sense, she *was* around. Her influence was everywhere. She had left a list of the times she made coffee or tea for the builders and a note of jobs to be done, including any follow-up from Friday's meeting at Willards and a reminder about an appointment with the accountant in Northampton (street map attached). Finally, there was yet another list of phone calls to be made, mostly the names of suppliers. At the bottom Anne had added Mrs Jolly and Jane in Little Venice, followed by a cryptic note: *I don't suppose you'll feel like ringing Ralph ... That girl!*

Marnie dutifully attended to her tasks and by mid-morning, after giving the builders their refreshments to the accompaniment of stage whispers – *Look busy, 'ere cooms the guv'nor!* – she was ready to set off to see the accountant. First stop vicarage, to let Toni know what time she would be back. She would suggest lunch on *Sally Ann*.

Arriving at the top of the field track, Marnie was surprised to have to wait for traffic to pass. Not much ever came that way. She turned towards the centre of the village and passed a sign: Road Ahead Closed. Roadworks? That was odd. They were not on Anne's list. Pulling round the bend, she found her way blocked by blue and white tape stretched across the whole street. Beyond it, cars were drawn up on both sides of the road, one of them in police livery. Marnie stopped, thinking she should call in on Toni on her way back. Perhaps there had been trouble at the pub. She tried to think of other possibilities. *I've got a problem ... something very strange ...* She caught sight of movement in the churchyard. Oh god, she thought, more vandalism? What can it be this time?

She got out of the car and walked quickly towards the barrier. As she reached it, a policeman stepped forward and confronted her across the tape. "Morning, miss."

"Hallo. I just need to have a quick word with the vicar. Can I come through?"

"I'm afraid not. Nobody's allowed through."

"But I just have to look in at the vicarage. It's that house over there. It won't take a minute."

"I'm sorry, miss." He shook his head gravely. "Excuse me," and walked to the other side of the road to open the barrier. An ambulance drove through, heading towards the church. She heard voices call out and the ambulance reversed up to the gate. A feeling of dread came over her. The tower swayed before her eyes. She raised a hand to her forehead and took a deep breath.

"Are you all right, miss?"

"What's happened?" Marnie heard her voice, dull and distant, and saw paramedics getting out of the ambulance. They were in light green uniforms like the tunics of racing drivers. Their movements were purposeful, but unhurried. "What's happened?" she repeated.

"I'm sorry, miss. There's nothing I can tell you."

"But I only want a quick word with Toni Petrie. She's the vicar. She needs my help."

"She needs your help, miss? I think you ought to have a sit down. You've gone very pale. Why don't you sit in your car and I'll get a WPC to have a word with you."

"Why won't you tell me anything?"

"There's nothing I'm allowed to tell anyone, miss. Believe me."

"Okay." Feeling suddenly weary, Marnie turned to go.

"Do you live in the village, miss?"

"At Glebe Farm."

"And your name?"

"Marnie Walker." She found herself sitting in the driving seat with no recollection of opening the car door. In the rear-view mirror she saw that he had been right. Her face had a pale sheen like marble. She pressed the button to open her window and began breathing slowly and deeply, trying to collect her thoughts. All she could remember was Toni's message. What could have happened?

The policeman left his post and walked across to the cars parked by the pub. Marnie could feel her self-possession returning. She tried to think logically. Obviously something serious had happened. but there was nothing she could do at this stage. Preferring action to waiting, she started the engine and reversed from the barrier, making a U-turn and setting off to her meeting.

❦ ❦ ❦ ❦

The meeting with the accountant went by in a dream. Marnie took notes, drank coffee, answered questions, produced documents. Inside, she was somewhere else. The accountant spoke in encouraging terms about her business plan, suggested she diversify her client base and set out a timetable for presenting the first year's accounts. He explained about allowances, tax concessions, VAT registration and schedule D.

At around one o'clock she drove out of town, switching on the radio to catch the lunchtime news. She was on auto-pilot, vaguely aware of fierce political debates, kidnappings in Kashmir, street protests in Ulster. Marnie noticed that cars were overtaking her, an unusual phenomenon.

Just before the final summary, the presenter hesitated briefly. "Ah ... a report is just coming in of a serious injury to a woman vicar in Northamptonshire. We have no further details at present, but we'll bring you an update on the PM programme at five o'clock. And the closing headlines this Monday lunchtime ..." Marnie heard nothing else. *Serious injury ... a woman vicar ...*

That afternoon Marnie sat at her desk as if paralysed. At three, she switched on the radio. A bomb had exploded in a suburb of Belfast. Eighteen people had been injured, shops damaged and a bus destroyed. One of the paramilitary groups was suspected. She did not hear which one. A priest appealed for calm on all sides. She switched to a local radio station, unsure of the wavelengths, and found she was listening to a farming report from Bedford.

Restless, unable to settle to anything, Marnie walked up the field track. It was warm and overcast. There could be thunder. She shivered. The tape across the road had been taken down, but the church was cordoned off and a constable stood at the gate. The street was deserted as if the village was holding its breath. She turned and walked back. At four she listened to the bulletin.

"The Northamptonshire vicar who was injured in an incident earlier today has been named as Miss Toni Petrie, one of the first women to be ordained in the diocese. No details are yet available of the cause of her injuries, but she is undergoing treatment in the intensive care unit of Northampton General Hospital. Her condition is described as 'critical' and the police are treating the case as suspicious."

The afternoon dragged on. Marnie wondered whether she should phone the hospital, but they would probably tell her nothing. Anne's lists lay abandoned. She tried to fathom what could have happened. An *incident*. What did that mean? And the police regarded it as suspicious. Someone must have attacked Toni. Even at this minute she was fighting for her life.

Marnie would have to tell the police about the vandalism. But what could she tell them? She had no idea who had done it or why. What would they make of a story about bigotry going back more than three centuries? Was it really about which prayerbook should be used? Did any of that matter? Was it about the scriptures? Marnie was stirred from her thoughts by the blast of electronic music at the start of the five o'clock news programme.

"The news read by Charlotte Green. Nine people are still undergoing treatment in hospital following the bomb blast that shook Belfast at the height of the rush hour this morning. Police chiefs say that only a miracle prevented a massacre. Minutes before the explosion, a crowded bus full of commuters had stood at the stop where the device had been left in a holdall. Police in Northamptonshire are investigating the death of woman vicar Toni Petrie. She died of injuries following an undisclosed incident this morning in the village of Knightly St John, where she had been vicar for less than a month. The prime minister has called for party unity. In a speech given at the ..."

Marnie put her head in her hands, her elbows on the desk and felt the hot tears flow down her cheeks. She sat for several minutes, her mind adrift, unable to come to terms with what she had heard, unable to believe she would never again hear the cheerful voice, never again see the ready smile. She opened the drawer and pulled out a paper tissue to wipe her face. Worst of all, she knew that she had failed to answer Toni's call for help. Days had passed and she had not spoken to her, even though there was a clear urgency in her message. Of course there were reasons why she had not contacted her, and it had not been through lack of effort. Could she have prevented this from happening if she had only knocked on the vicarage door on Saturday night? And what was it that had happened? *An undisclosed incident* ... What the hell was that supposed to mean? She jumped as the phone rang beside her in the silent office.

"Marnie? It's me. I've just heard about Toni on the news. God, how dreadful."

"Beth. Hallo, yes. I don't know what to say ... I think I'm in a state of shock."

"Do you know what actually happened? They didn't say on the news."

"No. I've no idea. There's no-one to ask, no-one to talk to. I'm just glad Anne isn't here."

"Yes, but it means you're there alone. Why not come and stay with us for a few days?"

"Thanks, but I've got a lot on just now."

"Marnie, I'm worried for you. I don't want to sound alarmist, but you're there by yourself ... I'm not sure it's a good idea ..."

"Don't worry. I'll be all right. I'll be careful. I always lock up ..."

True to her word, Marnie began to close the office, picked up her bag and tried not to think of the other tragedy that had befallen the village centuries earlier in that very barn. She remembered to glance at the answerphone as she passed. Four messages. She pressed the button. The first message was confirmation of a site meeting from Willards; the second was from Sandersons about material; the third was from Toni ...

"Hi, Marnie, it's Toni. Molly said you were trying to contact me. Thanks ever so much. Sorry to pester you, but I really do need your advice. I don't want to talk about it on the phone. You'll understand why when I see you. Anyway, let's keep trying. See you soon. Oh, by the way, I'll not be at home Monday morning. If you want me, I'll probably be in the church. Bye! God bless!"

Marnie did not listen to the fourth message. She opened the machine and took the cassette out, holding it in her hand like a talisman, while she stood, head bowed in grief and pain.

❦ ❦ ❦ ❦

Tuesday 1 August

A restless night, followed by a tiredness that overcame her around dawn. Marnie woke feeling exhausted at eight to find Dolly asleep at the foot of the bed. Dimly aware of hearing the workmen's van arrive, she got ready and had a quick coffee, willing herself to start the day, telling herself she must press on. Opening the last tin of cat food, she made a shopping list and thought of Anne.

As she came out of the spinney, there were two cars drawn up by the farmhouse and a group of men standing in a huddle in the middle of the yard, one in police uniform. She walked steadily towards the group as they turned to face her. One of the men stepped forward and introduced himself as Inspector Bartlett, a tall, solid-looking man of about forty, with thinning dark hair. Marnie opened the office and went in with Bartlett and his sergeant, an older man whose name was Marriner.

"Sorry to disturb you, Miss Walker, but I'm conducting enquiries and I'd be grateful for your help."

"Of course. I understand." Marnie had to struggle to keep her attention focused on the men. She had the feeling she was going to speak in clichés.

"I believe you tried to see the Reverend Petrie yesterday morning. Is that correct?"

"Yes. I needed to have a word."

"Would you mind telling me why you wanted to see her?"

"I'm handling the repairs to the church porch. There was something we had to discuss."

"Can you tell me exactly what that was, please?" Marnie hesitated. It was difficult to think straight. "It must have been quite urgent, miss. You seemed to be very agitated when you spoke to my officer."

"I was surprised to see the police cars and the tape blocking the road."

"Yes. And the matter that you needed to speak with her about? The urgent matter?"

"Well, I'm not sure exactly." Marnie tried to force herself to concentrate. The inspector began to speak, but she made a supreme effort to be coherent. "I'm sorry. I haven't slept very well. Toni was a friend, you see. She sent me a note asking me to see her about something urgent. She said she needed my help on a matter that was bothering her. That's why I was anxious to see her and why I'm not sure what the exact matter was."

"She sent you a note on Monday morning? How did she do that?"

"No. It wasn't on Monday. It was, er, Friday. She left it when she called round, while I was out."

"She left an urgent note and you waited three days before going to see her. Is that right, miss?"

"I tried to contact her several times. Molly Appleton in the shop will tell you that."

The sergeant made a note. "You said the vicar was your friend," he said. "How long had you known her?"

"Just a few weeks."

"And you were doing some work for her." He looked over his shoulder. The scaffolding and cement mixer were framed in the window. "Do you work for a builder?"

"I'm an interior designer. I was looking after a project for an architect I used to work with."

"And you got on well with Reverend Petrie." Marnie nodded. She was finding his way of putting questions irritating, simple statements based on what she had already told them. He seemed to invest her words with hidden meanings. "She was a close friend?"

"She was a friend. We'd only known each other a short time."

The inspector took up the questions. "So your *friend* left you an *urgent* note on *Friday* and you went round to her house on *Monday morning* in a state of some *anxiety*. Why were you anxious on Monday morning but not on Friday or Saturday or Sunday? What was in the note that made you feel anxious? Do you have the note?"

"I'm not sure, I mean about the note. There was something she wanted to discuss. Something was bothering her. I tried to contact her, but never managed to. That's why I was anxious ... *concerned*, on Monday. I wanted to get it sorted out. That's all it was."

"And you destroyed the note?"

"*Destroyed?* It was just a note. I may still have it somewhere. I don't know."

"Can you remember exactly what the note said, miss?"

Marnie drew a deep breath. "It was something like she had a problem and wanted to talk to me about it."

"Did it refer to the porch directly?"

"No. It just said a problem."

"And you assumed it meant the building work." The statement was simple enough, but Marnie knew the note had nothing at all to do with the porch and could not understand how she had fallen into the hole of telling the police a story that she knew, and that *they* would find out, was false.

"It didn't mention the building work. It might have been something else ... something more personal. She was new to the village and may have turned to me as a personal friend. I didn't turn out to be a very good friend after all, did I?"

"Do you live on the premises, Miss Walker?"

"Yes. Well, at the moment I'm living on the boat. It's moored by the canal through the spinney."

"Do you live here alone?"

"I have an assistant."

"Where is your assistant at the present time?"

"She's away on holiday. She left on Friday. Toni took her to the bus station while I was out. That's when she left the note for me. She'll be away for two weeks. She's in Scotland with her parents and her brother. Her name is Anne Price, and she's sixteen."

"Do you know how we can get in touch with her? Where she is at the moment?"

"No. They're camping somewhere in the Highlands."

The detectives stood up. "That's all for now, thank you. I'd like to see the note if you come across it. I may have further questions in due course."

In due course turned out to be later that afternoon. Bartlett arrived with Marriner while Marnie was finalising a design for Willards' head office. She had gone over the same area on the plans three times when Bartlett knocked on the open door and came in without waiting for an invitation.

"Good afternoon, Mrs Walker. Sorry to trouble you again so soon. I don't suppose you've come across that note? We really would like to see it." Marnie noticed the change in title.

"It could be on the boat. I honestly don't recall what I did with it." She reached down to the waste paper basket and looked in.

"Would it be convenient for us to take a look now?"

Dolly was curled up on the roof of *Sally Ann* and raised her head as Marnie and the policemen came aboard. The sergeant stroked her head.

"This is your cat, Mrs Walker?"

"Yes. Dolly."

"And your boat?"

"Yes. Well, no, actually. *Sally* belongs to my sister and brother-in-law. They don't use it much."

"Obviously not," said Bartlett. Marnie showed the detectives into the cabin. The note was on the workbench in the galley. Bartlett read it and passed it to Marriner without comment. They exchanged glances. "This is rather more than just a routine note about some building repairs, wouldn't you say, Mrs Walker? Or are you suggesting that the reference to you being the only person she is able to talk to relates to your professional expertise?"

"I thought it would be on a more personal matter," said Marnie.

"A more likely assumption," said Bartlett.

"The problems of women vicars," said the sergeant softly. He was wiping his hands together. Marnie found the gesture almost threatening and wondered if they could become aggressive. She suddenly felt uncomfortable, alone in the boat with the two men. She stepped back and bumped into a chair.

"Do you remember what shoes you were wearing at the weekend?" said Bartlett.

Marnie looked down at her feet. "Not these. I had on some casual flat shoes on Saturday ... and a pair of sandals on Sunday."

"Could you show them to me, please." Marnie had to squeeze past the men to open the cupboard at the head of the bed. She produced both pairs.

"Not a lot of room for your clothes," Bartlett observed. "I'm always surprised how many things ladies have. So many different pairs of shoes, for example."

"I keep most of my things in a wardrobe at the back of the office barn." Bartlett raised an eyebrow. "Because if you keep them on the boat, they start to smell of the engine. It's just behind those steps, and the smell of diesel seeps through after a while." The policemen sniffed the air.

"I see what you mean. Do you remember what were you wearing on Saturday?"

Marnie thought back. "A sweatshirt and a pair of jeans."

"Have they been washed since you wore them?" Marnie felt uncomfortable again, as if they were making a judgement on her personal habits, as if they were mentally undressing her. They seemed to be holding her life up for examination and finding fault with her feminine foibles.

"Not yet. I only wore them that one day."

"So they're in the wardrobe in the office?" said the sergeant.

"Yes."

"We'd like to borrow them for a day or two, if you have no objection. And your shoes and sandals." He looked down at his hands, spreading out his fingers. "Would you mind if I washed my hands? I seem to have fur on them."

Marnie showed him the heads. "Sorry. Dolly moults in warm weather. I'm always having to clean up after her. You can use the navy blue towel." She turned to Bartlett. "Can you tell me what happened to Toni?"

"I'm afraid it's early days, Mrs Walker. We're still making routine enquiries. Tell me something. Do you approve of women priests?" The question took Marnie by surprise.

"I don't really have a view on the matter. I'm not religious, not a churchgoer. I don't see any reason why women shouldn't be priests."

"You're not religious and you don't attend the church, but you were the vicar's friend, the one she turned to ... the only person she could talk to about a mysterious problem. Are you telling us you really don't know what was worrying her?"

"She was concerned at some vandalism in the churchyard. That may have been the problem."

"Nothing about this has been reported to us," said Sergeant Marriner standing in the doorway of the heads, drying his hands. "What kind of vandalism? Do you know when it happened?"

"Damage to a gravestone. A week or so ago."

"Do you know why it wasn't reported?"

"I suppose because Toni didn't regard it as sufficiently serious."

"Not sufficiently serious," said Bartlett slowly. "Mrs Walker, she was killed shortly afterwards. We regard vandalism as a serious matter. One violent crime can lead to another."

"I expect Toni hoped it might be an isolated incident and wouldn't happen again. She'd only just settled into the parish. You must understand that she wouldn't want to bring in the police as soon as she arrived. For all she knew it was just a freak incident."

"Mrs Walker," Bartlett's face was close to hers in the cramped space at the foot of the steps. He spoke softly. "I once heard an Irish story about a man who died. Someone asked his neighbour what he had died of and the neighbour said he thought it wasn't anything serious. I shall want full details of this *vandalism*, all the facts, and I don't want you to withhold *anything*. Now let's fetch those clothes."

Marnie watched their car bumping up the track, trying to understand how she had made such a mess of their interviews. She knew she should be giving the police all the help she could, but something in their manner put her on the defensive. The suspicion with which they approached her made her actions seem questionable, made her want them to go away and leave her alone. At this very moment she knew she should, drive to the police station and give them a complete statement of everything she knew. They would think her wish to find the unknown killer of the vicar in the Civil War utterly silly, the schoolgirl fantasy of a woman who had made a mess of her private life, now lived alone on a boat with a cat and worked in a makeshift office in a creaking barn. None of this was important. Only the finding of Toni's killer should matter. And yet, niggling at the back of her mind was the thought that whatever she said, they would interpret it in some other way. She knew they did not trust her or believe her. Bartlett had made that much clear. From now on, she would be more direct with them, sharing all she knew, doing everything possible to work with them for Toni's sake.

It was only when she turned and found herself standing alone in the silence of the deserted yard, that it occurred to her how isolated she was.

🌷   🌷   🌷   🌷

"She's hiding something," said Marriner as the car bumped and lurched up the field track. "Does she farm all this?"

"No. She just owns the farm buildings. She's doing them up to sell. Probably make a quick buck and get out before the punters find the roof leaks and the windows don't fit. You know these flash London types. Ouch!" Bartlett's head made contact with the roof as Marriner failed to miss a deep rut.

"Sorry, guv. She'll have to do something about this road, too."

"Well, that's *her* worry. In the meantime, *you* could try slowing down." He rubbed his head and braced himself in the seat. "But you're right. There's definitely something she's keeping back. My guess is she knows what that note means and it isn't about repairing the church. Most likely it's connected with the vandalism. Anyway, we'll get forensic to have a look at it."

"We ought to have some reports from the house to house enquiries by now," said Marriner.

"Always assuming you manage to get us back in one piece."

🌷   🌷   🌷   🌷

Marnie was locking the barn door when the phone called her back to the office. She was hoping it might be Ralph. But it was Molly Appleton. She sounded agitated.

"Marnie, I thought I'd let you know you're going to have a visitor. The vicar's coming to see you."

Marnie's vision clouded over as the floor moved under her feet. "The vicar?" For a second she wondered whether it had all been a horrible dream caused by something she had eaten.

"Randall Hughes. He's very upset … not himself at all. I heard him telling George Stubbs in the shop he was coming to talk to you."

"That's very thoughtful of you, Molly."

"That's all right. Are you okay down there? We know Anne's gone on holiday. She was telling us about it the other day. Not keen to go, was she?"

"No. But I'm glad she's out of all this."

"So you're by yourself, then."

"Yes. Though I seem to have the police for company at frequent intervals."

"Same up here. They've been knocking on every door in the village. Richard and I have been questioned three times already. Did we see anything suspicious … did we have any reason to suspect anyone … any strange goings on …"

"They've got to do that, I'm sure," said Marnie.

"Don't take it the wrong way, Marnie, but they wanted to know about you and we did mention that you'd been asking for Toni on Saturday. I hope you don't mind."

"Of course not."

"They wanted to know all about you and what you were doing. We only said what everyone knows, you know: your work at Glebe Farm, living on your boat, Anne working for you. Of course, there's nothing else to tell …"

"You did the right thing, Molly. As far as I'm concerned you can tell them anything you know."

"Well, don't feel alone down there. If you get nervous, you can always come and stay in our spare room till … you know …"

"Yes, I know. And thank you for the offer. I'm all right at the moment, though it's been a terrible shock. It was good of you to phone, Molly. And please don't worry about talking to the police."

"Now there's a funny thing," said Molly. "It was really odd. Do you know what they asked us? Did we know if you had any pets?"

"Pets?"

"Yes. Naturally, we told them about Dolly. Anne's always telling us stories about her. Why should they want to know about a cat?" In the background Marnie heard a car pulling into the yard and ended the conversation. She went to meet Randall Hughes, still thinking of the police asking about Dolly, recalling the bulky shape of Sergeant Marriner rubbing his hands together in the cabin.

Seeing Randall coming towards her, it almost seemed as if Toni had never existed, that this had always been the vicar, in his long black cassock, coming to call on routine church business. But as he came nearer, Marnie saw a different man. His face was lined and gaunt. He smiled but it vanished instantly. Marnie ushered him into the office, sat him in Anne's chair and put the kettle on.

"Marnie, have the police been to see you?"

"Twice so far and I expect they'll be back soon."

"Did they give you any indication of what happened? How Toni was …?"

"None at all. They didn't tell me anything, just asked questions."

"You know about the gravestone, don't you?" said Randall. "You know what happened."

"I was the one who found it and told Toni about it, yes."

"And you helped move it."

"Into the crypt," said Marnie. "I haven't told the police about that. I mentioned there had been vandalism and they asked why Toni hadn't reported it. Do you know why?"

He stared at the floor for a few seconds. "We talked about it. I should have urged her to report it at once. Instead, I suggested we waited to see what would happen. Now we know. Dear God ..."

Marnie got up and made coffee. "I told the police I thought she probably didn't want to involve them in anything so soon after moving here. It would be an unhappy start to her ministry."

"It turned out to be an unhappy end," said Randall. "I blame myself, of course."

"You can't do that ... you mustn't. Why should you? Reporting something to the police wouldn't have solved anything. We don't know who did this or why. The police don't know, either."

"Toni agreed not to go the police, Marnie, on *my* advice. You may be right about her reasons. But I should have insisted. I knew about the tensions here ... about the atmosphere."

"You couldn't know what would happen, Randall."

"That's not the point. It *did* happen. And I know the real reason I urged her not to report the situation was because I didn't want there to be any trouble in *my* patch. There was someone out there prepared to do violence and I wanted to hush it up. And now Toni's dead."

"Randall, I think you should try to see things objectively. You're upset. We're *all* upset. I feel quite desolate about it. I didn't tell them *everything* about the vandalism because I thought it would seem foolish. Toni wanted a good start and so did you. None of this has anything to do with what happened."

"I can't expect you to understand, Marnie. There's a depth of feeling below the surface here. I've lived with it. It's buried deep in this community."

"I've lived with it, too. Only in the last month or two, I agree, but I found the gravestone, I saw the destruction and I know about Sarah Anne Day and what happened to her ..."

"What *did* happen to her?" said Randall.

Marnie looked up at the beamed ceiling. "She hanged herself in here. I'm sure that's why she wasn't allowed a church burial." Randall picked up the mug and sipped the coffee, staring ahead of him, hollow-eyed, far away in his thoughts. He put down the coffee and stood up.

"Thank you for talking to me, Marnie. I'm sorry you've been drawn into all this." He paused on the threshold. "You know, I have the strangest feeling ... as if the murderer was the same person both times. It was the same hatred." He walked over to his car and drove away.

🌸 🌸 🌸 🌸

That night, when Marnie turned out the light in bed, her last thought was to be glad that Anne had not phoned. With any luck all this would be over by the time she returned.

🌸 🌸 🌸 🌸

Wednesday 2 August

Bartlett and Marriner drove into the yard shortly before nine the next morning while Marnie was talking with the builders in cottage number one. It was already beginning to feel like a house again.

"If it was me ..." the foreman began. Marnie waited. "Your visitors are back, seems like."

"Go on, Bob. What were you saying?"

"Well, if it was me, I'd be keen on making a dogtooth pattern in the brickwork under the eaves. It used to be used a lot in these parts. You can see it on the front of the farm house." Outside, the car doors were slamming in the yard. Marnie walked with Bob to the front door of the cottage and nodded to the police. She looked up at the eaves of the main farm house and turned back to the foreman.

"Good idea, Bob. Let's go for it. Will it add to the cost?"

The foreman shook his head. "No. But it'll make a nice job of it."

"Yes, it will. Thank you."

In the office barn the detectives declined coffee and remained standing. Bartlett began the questioning. "Can you tell us why you were parked opposite the vicarage on Saturday just before midnight? You were seen by some neighbours, Mrs Walker. Who were you phoning?"

"Phoning? Oh, yes. I was ringing my answerphone to see if there were any messages."

"But you were only two minutes from home. Or were you planning to be out much longer?"

"I'd just come back from London and I saw a light on in the vicarage. If there'd been an urgent message from Toni I would've knocked on the door. There was no message. I decided it was too late to call on her and continued home. I hope that answers your question."

"Do you have a typewriter, Mrs Walker?" This time it was Marriner.

"Of course. Though strictly speaking, it's not a typewriter as such. We have a shared computer that we use for word-processing, among other things."

Marriner produced Toni's note from his pocket. It was in a cellophane envelope. "You recognise this note. Did you type it, Mrs Walker?"

"Of course not. That's Toni's note. *She* wrote it to *me*."

"You're quite sure about that?"

"You know I am. Anne would confirm that if she was here."

"But you say she's in Scotland with her family. And you have no idea where they're staying. Do you know the make or number of their car, Mrs Walker?"

"I've no idea. Probably a Vauxhall of some kind. Her father used to work in one of the car plants."

Marriner held up the note. "Do you notice anything about this note?"

Marnie studied it through the cellophane. "Do you expect to find a chip in the 't' and the lower case 'o' out of alignment?" she said wearily. She was saddened to think they were talking as if all this was some kind of whodunit, rather than the death of a friend.

"Do you notice anything?" he repeated.

"There's no spacing between the sentences," said Marnie. "Looks like it was typed in a hurry."

"Yes. Good. And the paper?"

Marnie strained to see if there was anything remarkable about it. "Plain white copying paper. It seems ordinary enough to me. The sort you find everywhere."

"What about the typeface?"

She peered at it closely. "No serifs. Arial?"

"Very good!" said Bartlett. "Or is it very familiar?" He turned to the computer on Marnie's desk. The monitor glowed blue with goldfish swimming across it. He pressed one of the keys and it changed to a screen of text, a specification listing colours and materials. In a blue band at the top was the title: *Microsoft Word – WILNAV07.DOC*. Above the text in the font box was the name *Arial*. "Would you mind typing something for me, Mrs Walker? Would you please copy the note." She quickly opened a new file on the computer and typed. "Can you print it, please?" She pressed the buttons and the printer by Anne's desk whirred into life. Bartlett took the sheet of paper from the tray. "You did that very well, Mrs Walker. I noticed you're not a *trained* typist, but you were quite fast, and accurate." Once again Marnie felt as if they were judging a child who was asked to perform.

"It's part of my job to write documents. And I see what you're getting at. But a lot of people have word-processors and use this kind of paper." Bartlett held it up to the light.

"The vicar had an old dot-matrix printer and an ancient Amstrad. Her only font had serifs." He stepped towards her and this time she did not move back. "What would you say, Mrs Walker?"

She looked him straight in the eye. "I'd guess that note was probably typed on *my* machine, printed on *my* printer using *my* paper."

"So would I. And to make sure, we're going to take away both notes for comparison."

"Mr Bartlett, it seems obvious that Toni dashed off a quick note when she came to take Anne to the bus station. It's no mystery."

"While we're here," said Marriner, "I'd also like to borrow the black hairbrush you keep on the boat."

"That's only used for brushing the cat," said Marnie.

❦   ❦   ❦   ❦

Village life had begun to settle back into its usual routine, though the sense of shock hung in the air like an autumn mist. In the shop and on street corners people spoke about Toni's death in hushed voices, partly out of respect, partly out of horror at what had happened and partly from the unspoken thought that someone in their midst had committed murder. The attention that Marnie was receiving from the police was noticed by everyone, but nobody had speculated openly about her being directly involved. The gossip for which village life is infamous was curiously absent, as if people knew that the truth would be harmful enough to their community without any extra help to speed it on its way.

Toni's body had been discovered by Pauline Fairbrother, a woman in her mid-fifties who was responsible for the flower rota. She had gone to the church on Monday morning to change the water in the vases and had been surprised to find the door unlocked. There was no reply to her call as she went in. On her way to the vestry she came across the body lying sprawled face down at the foot of the tower steps. She had rushed forward to help, thinking that Toni had fallen, but saw blood everywhere and knew at once that Toni was dead. She had hurried to the shop and phoned the emergency services before returning to be with the vicar until they arrived. The police questioned her for half an hour, praising her for acting quickly and decisively, and asked her not to reveal anything she had seen or done to a single person.

Mrs Fairbrother was only too glad not to talk about the horrific incident, and in view of the respect with which she was held in the village, nobody even attempted to draw out of her an account of the events of that Monday morning.

Molly Appleton told her customers she felt like a traitor for telling the police that Marnie had been asking for Toni on Saturday. Mrs Ingram, who lived opposite the vicarage and had seen Marnie pull up on Saturday night, felt the same. George Stubbs was in the shop at the time. He had told the police he had talked to Marnie at the vicarage that morning. He had two abiding memories from his interview. One was of Marnie walking away from him in her close-fitting designer jeans, which he kept to himself. The other was that the police were far from certain what they were looking for.

"They couldn't fool me," he said. "I've been around too long. I think they're groping in the dark."

"What do you mean?" said Molly. "Don't they always ask a lot of questions?"

"It wasn't so much their questions," said George. "It was the way they asked them. Too general. They weren't trying to pin down *my* movements. It was as if they were trying to pick my brains. Too much *did she have any enemies?* Not enough *where were you on the morning in question?*"

"Perhaps that's just part of their method," said Mrs Ingram. "Anyway, I'm sure they wouldn't suspect *you*, George."

"Why not? It could be *anyone* in theory. Mind you, I'm quite sure they're wasting their time pestering Marnie Walker. If I'm any judge of character, it's got absolutely nothing to do with her."

"I'm sure we'd all agree with that," said Molly.

George picked up his cigars and turned to leave. "There's been trouble in this village from long before Marnie Walker ever set foot in the place ..."

❦   ❦   ❦   ❦

Speculation as to exactly how Toni had died was still featuring prominently in the local press, though it had disappeared from the national media except as a postscript.

The police presence in the village was unrelenting. By now, two days after the death of the vicar, almost every member of the community had been questioned at least once and for all they took seriously the police advice to keep calm, the initial sense of unease that followed the shock of the death had now given way to a guarded tension in the air. The village was learning to live with the presence of violent death that touched all their lives in one sense or another. Care was taken to lock doors that had never been locked before. Children were kept at home to play in gardens with invited friends, while fishing streams and ponds went neglected and bicycles gathered dust in sheds and garages. Bunches of flowers had been laid against the church gate in sympathy by people who had seen the custom on television. The village watched and waited. Some prayed.

The Bishop rang the Chief Constable to ask what progress had been made and received only the same answer as that given to the media. Enquiries were proceeding. Leads were being followed. These things took time. Meanwhile, the Archdeacon was arranging for a neighbouring vicar to take services until a new appointment could be made. He did not ask Randall Hughes to step in.

❦   ❦   ❦   ❦

"This is getting to be a habit," said Marnie. She was standing outside the cottages with the foreman when the police car pulled into the yard. "What were you going to say, Bob?"

"If it was me – "

"I know. Apart from that."

"Well, I think it would be good if we used old reclaimed slates for the roofs of the cottages. It would make them blend in with the roof of the farm house and not look like a new roof."

"It's a good idea," said Marnie. "Can you get some? We've not planned for this."

"That's why I'm saying it now, me dook. A mate o' mine's taking down an old barn over by Charwelton. He'd let us have the slates if we wanted them. Many as we want."

"Would it add much to the cost?"

"No dearer than buying new ones. I could send two of the lads over in the van."

"Sounds good to me," said Marnie. "You're sure they match the existing ones here?"

"Yes, I had a look last night. Welsh blues just like these. Not as old, but no different to look at."

"You take a lot of trouble, Bob."

"Nice to make a good job of it." Behind her, Marnie heard a discreet cough and turned to see Bartlett standing beside his car, accompanied by a woman neatly dressed in a dark grey jacket and skirt. She had shoulder length blonde hair and would have had a pleasant face if it had worn a smile.

In the office the police refused coffee as usual. Bartlett introduced his colleague as Detective Constable Lamb and she positioned herself, still unsmiling, near the door. Marnie wondered if they thought she might try to make a run for it.

"I'll come straight to the point, Mrs Walker. How do you explain the vicar's note being identical in every respect to the one you typed for us yesterday? Can you explain why your cat's fur was found on the door of the church? Can you tell us why your footprints were found all round the tower? And where exactly is your assistant, Mrs Walker?"

"I don't know ... exactly," said Marnie.

"You can't answer any of my questions?" said Bartlett.

"Of course. I meant I don't know where Anne is, apart from Scotland. To tell you the truth, I'm glad she's not here. I was rather hoping you'd have sorted it all out before she came back."

"I'm sorry if we're not working fast enough for you, Mrs Walker." Bartlett's voice had taken on an edge. "How we get on often depends on how much information we're given." Marnie wondered about the pressure he was facing. If they were pursuing her, seriously trying to attach blame to *her*, they were making a big mistake. She sensed that now was not the best time to make the point.

"Okay. I don't know the exact location of my assistant at this moment. Also I don't really see why it's such an issue." Bartlett opened his mouth to speak, but Marnie continued. "The answers to your questions are that the note was typed on my machine. At least, I guess it was. It seems logical. Dolly's fur on the church door must have come from me, I suppose. I've been to the church a few times. I remind you that I'm working on a project there. My footprints round the tower are no great surprise. I've been in the churchyard recently. Now those are straight answers to your questions."

When he spoke, his tone was quieter. "Consider the evidence and your answers, Mrs Walker. Do you find them satisfactory?"

"Yes, of course I do. Completely."

"That may be one of the problems."

"Do you *really* regard *me* as a suspect?"

"We know you're not telling us everything. You're concealing something. It's a pity your assistant isn't here to corroborate your story."

"It doesn't need corroborating. It's simply the truth. And while you're spending time with me, the real murderer is out there."

"Do you have any suspicions about who that person might be, Mrs Walker?" Marnie thought about all the possibilities, but her mind kept straying to the other murder all those years ago. It was somehow impossible to disentangle the two events and they merged in her brain every time she thought about them. *As if the murderer was the same person both times*, Randall Hughes had said. She wished desperately that Ralph was there and suddenly jerked back, realising that Bartlett and Lamb were standing in her office, watching her, waiting for an answer.

"S-sorry," she stammered. "No, I don't know who it could have been, I really don't. No idea."

"How tall are you, Mrs Walker?"

"About five foot seven. One metre sixty-one, if you prefer metric."

"Thank you. However you measure, that's quite tall for a woman, I'd say. Would you describe yourself as strong?"

Marnie had never really considered this. "For a woman, probably yes."

"Fit?"

"Reasonably, I suppose. Look, I don't understand where all this is ..."

"Do you like cooking?"

"*Cooking?* Well, yes. It's a relaxation. I really don't follow ..."

"May we visit your kitchen?"

"For the time being I'm using the galley on *Sally Ann*. It's small, but adequate for our needs."

On board, Bartlett and Lamb both came down into the cabin, the woman standing in the saloon while the inspector examined the cooker and the shelves and touched the jars of herbs on their rack over the workbench.

"Very neat and well organised, Mrs Walker."

"You have to be on a boat. Everything has to have a place."

"And where's the place for the cutlery? Will you show me?" Marnie pulled open the drawer. "Are these your cooking implements at the side?"

"Most of them. I have a set of kitchen knives and some other tools on hooks by the stove."

"Where are the knives?" Marnie opened the drawer further and showed Bartlett the box of knives, each one resting in its own slot, every slot occupied.

"And your tools?"

"They're in crates in the cratch and there's a small box of screwdrivers and spanners under the top step ... handy for the engine."

"What's the cratch? Can I see the crates?"

"The cratch is the bows. I'll show you." She opened the cratch doors and stepped in, lifting up the cover from the bench on the left. Bartlett followed her, stooping slightly under the lower ceiling. The crate was made of strong red plastic, designed for stacking. There were six identical red crates in all and one of the top ones contained tools, several standing in tins. One tin was empty.

"What goes in there?" said Bartlett pointing at it.

"I'm not sure, to be honest. I don't use the tools very often these days. I mainly use *Sally* as living accommodation." She looked through the collection.

"When was the last time you used the tools?" said Bartlett. "Can you remember?" He peered into the tin without touching it. Marnie tried to think. When could it be? "Is this where a knife is kept?" said Bartlett.

"Good lord! Yes it is. How did you know that?" said Marnie in astonishment. She leaned forward to look at the tin. It was empty. "It was when Frank Day was on the towpath with a swan caught in fishing line. He wanted a knife to cut it free."

"And you were able to oblige ..."

"No, not actually. The knife fell over the side. Anne had to fetch Frank's own knife from his car."

"Anne being your assistant who isn't here," said Bartlett. "Why not use a kitchen knife?"

"We could have, I suppose, but I'd rather not use them for something like that. Anyway the line was tough nylon and the boat knife would be better ... heavy and sharp."

"And now yours is lost in the canal. What a shame."

"I'll get it back," said Marnie. She was finding his questioning even more irritating than usual.

"How? How will you get it back?"

"With the magnet. We keep a heavy duty magnet on board for this kind of eventuality."

"Let's try," said Bartlett.

The search was not easy. Marnie edged *Sally Ann* across the channel and began trawling with the magnet. Ten minutes is a long time pulling a line through the opaque water of a canal. Several times the magnet clanged against the hull and had to be yanked clear. She was about to give up when she felt the line stiffen with contact. She pulled gently but firmly, keeping it well away from the side of the boat and hauled in. The magnet broke clear from the water, locked on to the lost knife.

"There!" said Marnie in triumph. "I told you." She reached forward to grasp the handle, but Bartlett took it first, holding it in a handkerchief. It shone faintly in the afternoon light, its wide thick blade and chunky handle partly covered in mud and weeds, staining the clean white cotton. Marnie stared at the knife and at Bartlett. "A knife," she said. That's what you've been looking for all along ..." She drew in a deep breath. "I thought ... I mean, I didn't realise ..."

"What didn't you realise?" said Bartlett.

"About the knife. I thought ... at least, I just supposed ..."

"Go on, Mrs Walker."

"It's just come home to me ... what this means. Toni was ... killed with a knife. Is that right?"

"What did *you* think had happened?" The detectives studied her closely.

"I don't know. On the radio they just said you were treating it as suspicious. I had the idea she'd died falling down the steps."

"Why did you think that?"

"Because they're worn and dangerous and the tower's very tall. A vicar was killed here once before, you know. That was in the tower."

"When was that exactly?" The two police officers exchanged puzzled glances.

"In the summer of 1645 at the end of the Civil War. The murder weapon was never found."

"Who committed the murder?" said Bartlett. Marnie sensed his professional interest, even in a crime of such antiquity.

"They never found that out, either."

"What about *this* crime?" said Bartlett. "Who are we going to get for *this*?" Marnie shook her head. It was one thing to hear about it on the radio, but quite different to see the kind of weapon that could have killed someone, even if her own knife was just a tool. "Do you have a solicitor, Mrs Walker?" Bartlett was speaking softly, his voice reaching her as if from a distance.

"Not really, only the one who did the work on moving house." Marnie realised what she had said before she fully registered the question. "Why should I need a solicitor?"

"I advise you to contact him."

"Whatever for?"

"Tell him the situation and he'll explain why."

"But this has nothing at all to do with me, inspector. That knife couldn't have killed Toni."

"Shall we go back now?" Marnie automatically went through the motions of bringing the boat in. Was she going to be arrested? Were they going to charge her with something? This was ridiculous! She moved purposefully about the boat, guiding her in and making her secure before shutting down the engine. They stepped onto the ground and walked back through the trees. No-one spoke. It was a still, peaceful afternoon, warm and bright, the sun making patterns on the floor of the spinney. None of them noticed. As they approached the complex of farm buildings, a ringing could be heard and Marnie jogged ahead to answer the phone. She reached it as it stopped ringing.

"No answerphone today, Mrs Walker?"

"They must have hung up. A lot of people don't like talking to machines."

"But surely it would have cut in? I didn't hear the message, just the ringing." He walked to Anne's desk and opened the lid of the answerphone. "Didn't you realise there was no tape in the machine?"

Marnie look surprised. "No tape? *Surely* there must be ... Oh!" She put a hand to her mouth, remembering Toni's last message, the tape taken from the machine. What had she done with it?

"Oh what, Mrs Walker?"

"I took the tape out. I'd forgotten. Sorry."

"Why did you do that?"

"It's hard to explain."

"Where's the tape now?"

"I'm not sure. I think I put it in my pocket." There was a waistcoat hung over the back of her chair. She reached into the pocket and pulled out the micro-cassette. Bartlett took it from her and slotted it into the machine. The messages rolled and Marnie felt a lump in her throat as Toni's voice came on. She tried not to listen, not wanting to embarrass herself in front of the two detectives.

"*... See you soon. Oh, by the way, I'll not be at home Monday morning. If you want me, I'll probably be in the church. Bye! God bless!*"

Marnie swallowed, retaining her self-control. "Now you know why ..." Bartlett raised a hand to stop her speaking. The machine peeped and another message began.

"Hi, Marnie, it's me. Anne with an 'e'. Just thought I'd let you know we have a phone number if you need to contact me while we're away. You see, you can't get rid of me as easily as that. We've found a really nice spot on a farm near Balquidder. There are just a few other families camping here and we get fresh eggs and things from the farm. It's great. Hope the meeting went off OK. Mum and Dad send their regards. This is the number. Ring any time and I'll get a message." Bartlett nodded to his colleague and she took down the number. The machine peeped again and stopped, before the hiss as the tape rewound. Bartlett removed the cassette. "I'll need to keep this. That was presumably your assistant? Why did you tell us you had no means of contacting her?"

"Because it was true."

"Are you telling me you didn't listen to the messages?"

"Of course I did. If you must know, I was very upset by Toni's message and I stopped the machine. Now you know where Anne can be reached, you can check everything I've told you."

"Oh, we will, Mrs Walker. You can count on it."

❦   ❦   ❦   ❦

Bartlett was glad that Cathy Lamb managed to drive round the bumps on the field track more successfully than Ted Marriner. Whatever you thought of women police officers, and Bartlett on the whole shared the general view, they were not without some qualities, and a few, like Constable Lamb, were attractive to have around, though she was not in the same class as Marnie Walker. But you knew where you were with her, unlike Walker, who seemed able to make up excuses to fit any situation.

"Some points to follow up there," said Bartlett.

"Yes, sir." She kept her eyes on the rough track and concentrated on reaching the top without upset. Bartlett considered it part of his role to help her understand the complexities of the job.

"I think we're going to be able to break down Mrs Walker's story from this point on." He glanced sideways at Constable Lamb as she manoeuvred carefully around a deep rut. "So far, she's been able to tell us anything she pleased. Now, we can get hold of her assistant and start to get at the truth."

"Yes sir."

Sometimes, Bartlett thought it could be hard going with these new officers, even when you tried your best to help them. "What do you make of it all, constable?"

"I'm not really sure what truth you mean, to be honest, sir." She kept her attention on the track.

Bartlett breathed in deeply and realised he would have to be very patient. "About the facts," he said gently. "The evidence, you know. The cat's fur, the footprints, why she was waiting outside the vicarage at midnight, concealing the answerphone tape, the missing knife, the missing assistant, the typewritten note ... The facts in the case."

"Yes sir."

"Well, don't you have a view? Don't you have some ideas on all these matters?" Constable Lamb brought the car to a halt at the top of the track inside the field gate. She pulled on the handbrake.

"Well, I thought ... in a way ..."

"Go on," said Bartlett.

"What she said seemed to be consistent."

"*Consistent?*"

"She was doing a job for the vicar at the church, so all that side seemed reasonable to me. I mean, she had to go there in connection with the work. Also, they could be friends. They were the same age, both new to the village, professional women. Why not? The message sounded friendly."

"You're satisfied with her story then, are you?"

"I don't see why it shouldn't be true, sir." Lamb looked uncomfortable.

"And the tape taken from the machine? What about that? Isn't *that* suspicious?"

"I had the feeling she was telling the truth ..."

"*Feeling?* What's this, feminine intuition?"

"Not really. I can understand her taking the tape out after hearing the message from her friend who'd just been killed. I mean, it's a big thing, one of your friends being murdered. A terrible shock."

"All right, all right. What about the knife?"

"She had no idea a knife had been used in the murder. That was obvious, sir."

"You mean she looked convincing."

"Yes, sir."

"With all those sharp kitchen knives she just had to get the heavy knife from the tool box and it just accidentally happened to go over the side. You don't think that's a strange coincidence?"

"Possibly, yes. But I can understand why she didn't want to use one of the kitchen knives to cut something tough. It might have got damaged."

"Are you serious?"

"Yes sir. I saw those knives in the drawer. They were top quality chef's knives. Do you know what they cost? Someone like Walker, someone with her kind of taste, would never think of using one of those like a boy scout's jack knife."

"So you think she's being level with us and telling the truth? Everything is just as she says?"

"Not really, sir. No."

Bartlett was baffled by this. "What do you mean?"

"When she answers your questions, I think she's telling the truth as far as it goes. But she's not telling us everything, is she? There's something she's keeping back."

Bartlett would have called this intuition too if the same idea had not already been clear to him. "And I suppose you have a theory about that?"

Constable Lamb frowned. "I'm not sure. I was wondering about the vandalism. What was that all about?"

"We'll soon find out."

❦   ❦   ❦   ❦

"I'm afraid Mr Broadbent is out of the office. Can anyone else help?"

"No, it's all right, thanks," said Marnie. "I'll catch him at home."

"He's not at home at the moment. He's away attending a court hearing."

"Oh ... Will he be away long?"

"We expect him back possibly late tomorrow afternoon. It depends on the traffic on the M1."

"Could you pass on a message?"

"Certainly. He phones in every day."

❦   ❦   ❦   ❦

Ted Marriner was beginning to wonder where the enquiries were leading. He had been on a few murder cases in his time and usually they were very different from the popular idea gained from whodunits. Most murders were sorted out quite quickly. Often it was someone from the victim's family, and there were few doubts about the facts almost from the start. After a few sessions of questioning, the murderer was only too relieved to confess to everything. Then it was just a matter of collecting the evidence to make a case that would stand up in court.

This case, on the other hand, was what he called a 'messy one'. For a start, there was no murder weapon. He was never comfortable about not having the weapon. It usually pointed to one of the suspects. Then there was the question of motive. He never liked to rely on motive. In his experience, people frequently did things for the strangest of reasons, and murderers were no exception. But in the case of Toni Petrie, the only apparent source of hostility to her was that she was a woman.

As for opportunity, that was even more complicated. The murder had taken place first thing on a Monday morning in the church, a building always kept locked. There was no evidence of a fight or even a scuffle; no trace of an intruder, a vandal or a tramp seeking shelter. The only clear signs were some cat's hairs on the door and footprints outside by the tower, both pointing to Marnie Walker. Marriner was far from happy with her story, but loose ends were one thing and evidence, facts and sheer common sense were a different matter. He could think of no reason why she should want to kill Toni Petrie. If he was any judge of character, she was genuinely shocked and upset by the murder. Bartlett did not trust her, but he drew back from actual suspicion, at least for the time being.

Top of Marriner's list that afternoon was George Stubbs, and he pulled into the drive beside the fine stone house, complete with dark green Range Rover outside the converted stable/garage block. It looked like a still from a tourist brochure. He asked if he could talk in private with Mr Stubbs and they went round to sit on a bench in the garden. Mrs Stubbs made tea.

"I'm sorry to have to bother you again, sir. You see, there are several matters that aren't yet clear and we have to eliminate everything that isn't relevant to our enquiry."

"Of course, of course. How can I help you, sergeant?"

"I believe you hold a key to the church."

"Correct, but I haven't used it since I don't know when."

"Do you know where the key is at this moment?"

"It's on its usual hook in the key cupboard in the hall."

"Could we check that before I leave, sir?"

"Certainly."

"Has anyone borrowed it for any purpose at all in the last few weeks?"

"No."

"Do you remember the last time anyone used it?"

"Pauline Fairbrother used it some time last year. She was round here having lunch with my wife – they're on the WI committee together – and she wanted to look in with the flower rota. She used my key to save her going home to fetch her own. That was the only time I can remember it being used in years."

"For what reason do you keep a key, then, sir?"

"I'm just a keyholder in case of emergency."

"And you didn't need it when the recent vandalism took place?"

"*Vandalism?* What vandalism? We don't have vandalism in Knightly St John, sergeant."

"You've had a murder in Knightly St John, sir," Marriner said quietly. "The recent case of vandalism in the church is what I mean."

"*In the church?* What *are* you talking about? I can assure you there's been no vandalism in our church." Mr Stubbs began to sound indignant.

Marriner flicked back through his note book and found the notes he had made of Marnie Walker's testimony. "In the church *yard* to be precise, sir. Damage to a gravestone."

"No. That can't be right. I supervise the maintenance of the churchyard. In fact, I pay a man from the village to mow it and keep it tidy. I'd be the first to know if anything of that sort had taken place."

"We have a witness, sir. Someone who was informed of it by the vicar."

Mr Stubbs frowned. "When was this vandalism supposed to have happened?"

"Within the last two weeks."

"No. Impossible. That can't be true." He got up suddenly and walked briskly to the house. Marriner, unaccustomed to being abandoned in the middle of his questioning, trailed after him. He arrived at the back door to find Mr Stubbs in the kitchen, pressing buttons on the phone attached to the wall.

"Henry? It's Mr Stubbs. Do you know anything about vandalism in the churchyard? ... Yes, recently, last week or two ... a gravestone, apparently ... Yes, I know you would. I just wanted to make sure ... Of course. Listen. The police will want to ask you about it. Sergeant Marriner. I'll give him your name and address. All right? ... That's right, yes ... Thanks, Henry." He turned to Marriner waiting in the doorway. "As I told you, sergeant. Definitely no vandalism in the churchyard, not in the last two weeks or any other time. That's final and you have a witness to prove it."

The two men sat down for tea in the conservatory, Marriner still puzzled by this new development. Why should Marnie Walker invent a story like that? She must realise it would be easy to disprove. There would be evidence, the actual damage, possibly witnesses.

"You have a lot to do with the church, sir."

"I'm a churchwarden, member of the PCC and a benefactor. The family has been in this village for generations. This place has been good to us and we've tried to be good for the village."

"Are you still in business here, sir?"

"I have business interests all around here. And, yes, I still keep a small butchery, though it's really only to serve the immediate community."

"Could I see it?"

"Certainly." He led the way to the annexe. Marriner stepped inside and found himself confronted by the well-scrubbed butcher's block, the tiled walls and floor and the rack holding a collection of knives, cleavers and choppers. Everything was shining and immaculate, especially the knives that Marriner inspected closely. They were honed to the peak of sharpness.

❦ ❦ ❦ ❦

"You don't have an appointment, do you?" Valerie Paxton looked up in confusion at the two police officers and checked the desk diary. Beside it stood a small vase of white roses.

"No. We don't usually make appointments. We tend to think murder enquiries take priority over everyday matters." Cathy Lamb watched her senior officer in action from the back of the office and saw the effect he had on people. She wondered if Bartlett deliberately behaved like that to put them off balance or if he just liked throwing his weight around.

"The Head has some parents with her at the moment. I don't think I can interrupt them just like that. If I'd known you were coming I could have altered the time of their meeting."

"Then perhaps we'll talk to you while we wait. It's Mrs Paxton, isn't it?"

On hearing her name, Valerie gave a start. "Yes, it is. Why do you want to talk to me?"

"Just routine, as they say." He smiled reassuringly, but Valerie did not look reassured. "Did you know the vicar?"

"Yes."

"Are you a regular churchgoer?"

"Yes."

"Are you on any of the church committees, the PCC, anything like that?"

"I'm on the PCC."

"And do you have any other role in the church?" Valerie hesitated.

"Do you help with the flowers, perhaps?" It was Cathy Lamb who spoke in a quiet voice and Bartlett was momentarily taken by surprise.

"I do sometimes. My husband's a keen gardener. Chrysanthemums. I helped with the harvest festival." Cathy nodded encouragement. "That's all, really. Oh, and I have a key to the church."

"How long have you had it?" said Bartlett.

"For a year or two. It was the vicar's idea. In case we wanted to go in the church for any reason."

"Where do you keep the key?"

"Here in my desk."

"Has anybody used it recently? Borrowed it?"

"No. No-one."

"When was the last time it was used?"

"I don't remember." Valerie was becoming agitated, frowning and biting her lip.

"Can you show us where you keep it, please." She pulled open the top drawer and took out the key. It was strangely antique, heavy and ornate, in contrast to the modern office fitments.

"We'll need to borrow this for a while. Will that cause any problems?" Valerie shook her head and went to close the drawer. "Just a minute." Bartlett walked round the desk. "Is that your knife?"

"Yes."

"What do you keep it for?"

"Only as a paperknife. It was my father's ... a souvenir from the war."

"I'd like to borrow that, too, please."

"Why?" She stared up at Bartlett, and Cathy Lamb thought she was going to shut the drawer.

"Just to help our enquiries, Mrs Paxton." With both hands he picked up the knife in its scabbard with a finger at each end. Cathy produced a transparent envelope and Bartlett dropped it in.

Valerie watched this with her mouth half open. "What do you want it for?" She stood up.

"Tell me," said Bartlett. "How did you feel about the vicar?" His voice was quieter now.

"How did I feel?" Valerie began breathing quickly as if her throat was constricted, her eyes widening, her head jerking from side to side. With both fists clenched she pressed down on the blotter on her desk and leaned forward. "How did I feel? How would *you* understand what I felt? Nobody understood the vicar ..." Her voice rose to screaming pitch. "Nobody but me! I was the only one ... *the only one!*" She was swaying backwards and forwards, wild-eyed, almost spitting out the words in fury. Bartlett, shocked by the outburst, stepped back, pushing Cathy Lamb off-balance so that she stumbled and dropped the envelope containing the knife. Valerie was still screaming, incoherent with emotion, as the words spilled out. "He only wanted the good of the parish ... for the people ... everything was for the people ..."

At that moment, the door to the head's office flew open and Margaret Giles rushed in. "What on *earth* is going on?" She took in the scene before her at a glance and rushed towards Valerie Paxton. Bartlett, regaining his self-control, raised a hand in warning, but Mrs Giles put an arm round her secretary and made her sit down. "Valerie, Valerie, calm down. It's all right, it's me ... it's all right." Valerie slumped forward across the desk, breathing heavily, sobbing.

"I loved him!" she cried. "Don't you understand? *I loved him!* There's *nothing* I wouldn't do to keep him in the village ... *nothing, nothing, nothing!*" Her voice faded away, leaving her sobbing and shaking, great teardrops splashing the blotting paper on the desk. Margaret Giles, her arm still round Valerie's shoulders, looked down at her in amazement. Bartlett stared and Cathy Lamb squatted to pick up the knife in its envelope. Margaret Giles looked at it and her eyes widened. From the doorway the two parents stared out with shocked white faces.

"I'll take Valerie home," said Mrs Giles. "I think it would be better if you continued your ... conversation some other time. Valerie is obviously upset. The whole village is feeling the strain."

" '*Him*,' " Bartlett muttered. "When she spoke about the vicar she said '*him*'. I don't understand."

"Women have no right to be vicars," said Valerie in a weary voice, without looking up. "They should keep out where they're not wanted. They have no place interfering in the work of the church."

"That will do, Valerie," said the head. "Come on. I'll take you home."

❦   ❦   ❦   ❦

Sergeant Marriner turned into the long drive of Rooks Farm, past oak and ash trees standing knee-deep in cow parsley, and pulled up by the handsome stone farmhouse. He rang the doorbell. Turning to look around him, he discovered a border collie, evidently now in retirement, that had strolled across from its kennel to stand in amiable silence, tail gently wagging, beside the stranger at the door.

"Did you want eggs?" A man's voice called out from one of the barns. "My wife's probably in the garden." Marriner walked over. He found a tall, lean man of about forty holding a spanner. Behind him in the barn stood a tractor with parts of its engine laid out on a plastic sheet on the floor.

"Good afternoon, sir. I'm looking for Mr Fletcher." He showed his warrant card.

"Which one? I'm Leonard and my father's, Albert."

"It would be Mr *Albert* Fletcher. I'm Detective Sergeant Marriner from the county CID."

"In connection with the death of the vicar," said the farmer. It was a statement, not a question, and Marriner noticed that the son seemed not to be surprised at his arrival.

"Quite so. Can you tell me where I can find him, sir?"

"He's here somewhere, but I haven't seen him for a while, not since lunchtime in fact."

"Have you no idea?" said Marriner.

The farmer indicated the tractor with a toss of his head. "I've been sorting out the fuel pump for the last half hour or more. This is a big place, sergeant. We farm six hundred and fifty acres. You'll probably find him in the old stone barn over there, or in that forty-acre field, checking the fences."

"Thank you very much, sir. If you don't mind, I'll look round till I find him."

"That's fine by me. You just go ahead."

Marriner stopped at the open door and peered in. At first it was difficult to see anything, as there were no windows, only thin slits that grudgingly let in pale shafts of daylight. "Hallo! Mr Fletcher?" Silence. Marriner stepped forward. Standing in the middle of the barn, beside the old tractor, he waited a few seconds while his eyes adjusted to the conditions. He turned to scan the interior until his gaze came to rest on the end wall.

"*Christ!*" he muttered under his breath.

❦   ❦   ❦   ❦

They had agreed to meet back at the incident room at four-thirty. *Incident room* was a rather grand description of what, in normal circumstances, was the old church room, a small brick building tacked onto the church in the middle of the last century to serve as schoolroom. Now it was only used for the Sunday school and as a convenient scullery where tea could be prepared. It was here that Pauline Fairbrother fetched water for the flower arrangements. The police had rigged up a temporary phone line and brought in two desks, there being no room for more. Bartlett perched on the corner of one of these, while Marriner stood and Cathy Lamb sat in one of the two chairs.

Bartlett was summarising. "One of them has to be lying," he said. "Or mistaken, I suppose."

"It's difficult to *be* mistaken about vandalism, I would've thought," said Marriner. "I had a look round the churchyard and I couldn't see any damage. And Stubbs would surely have known."

"He ought to have known," said Bartlett. "He pays the groundsman and does a lot for the church."

"Thinks he owns the place, I reckon. I got the impression he resented the vicar interfering in it."

"Ted, I want you and Cathy to check out this gardener, Henry Tutt. Get his story. If he backs up what Stubbs told you, we'll confront Walker with it and see what she has to say for herself."

"That seems clear enough, then," said Marriner.

Bartlett frowned. "Clear enough?" he said.

"Well, if there is no vandalism, Stubbs must be right. It stands to reason."

"Yes, but why invent something so easy to disprove?" said Bartlett. "There's no sense in that."

"So you believe Walker?" said Marriner.

"Look, Ted, she's not stupid. Why make up a story she can't prove? It's not logical."

"No. I see what you mean. I'll go round straight away and see this Tutt character."

"You could have another go at finding old Fletcher as well."

"Now there's a queer business," said Marriner. The phone rang and Cathy Lamb picked it up. He went on. "One wall of the barn was covered in farm implements, all very old, but kept like new. Some had blades, sickles, scythes and the like, and every one was shining like they'd been polished. They were all razor-sharp." In the background Cathy spoke quietly into the receiver, taking notes on a pad.

"Did his son think it strange he couldn't be found?" said Bartlett.

"Not a bit. Apparently the old boy often goes off on his own. In the last few weeks he's been out for most of the day, just coming home for supper. The son just said he goes for long walks. I couldn't get any more out of him, but I'm sure he's not telling us all he knows … or thinks."

Cathy hung up. "That was forensic, sir. They've been over every inch of the tower. It's clean. No prints … the surfaces are too rough. No trace of a struggle. Nothing."

"There must be *something*," said Bartlett, exasperated. "A woman was murdered there, for Chrissake! Killing someone isn't like shaking hands."

Cathy looked down at her notes. "… *bloodstains indicate the murder took place by the landing halfway up the tower …*"

"We *know* that." He looked in desperation at Marriner. "You'd think they'd have found *something*."

"They don't seem to have, sir," said Cathy. It was her first murder case since transferring to CID and she had soon learnt about the, the increased pressure felt by all the officers involved.

"Cathy, a murderer doesn't come to the scene of the crime in a sterile envelope. They bring things with them and leave things behind them … things a microscope can see. We're looking for a footprint, a scuff mark …"

"A trace of cat's fur," added Marriner.

"Something like that," said Bartlett. "The surfaces are too rough for a fingerprint. We *knew* that. So we're looking for a thread of cloth, something that might rub off. Let me see your notes."

"They're in shorthand, sir."

"That's OK. I can read it … usually." He studied the notes. "Was this everything they said? What's this here?"

Cathy deciphered her hieroglyphs. "Just some notes about the tower itself, sir. *The stone walls are in good condition, steps worn, some quite badly … the top step on the landing is wobbly …*"

"I don't remember that," said Bartlett.

"I do, sir," said Cathy. "I stood on it and it did wobble slightly."

"Well we know she didn't die by slipping off a wobbly step. Is that it, then?"

"That's all they said, sir."

"Have you got your notes about the murder weapon there?"

Cathy flicked back through her pad and read hesitantly. "*The weapon was broad-bladed with one edge only sharpened ... sharp point ... thickness of approximately three millimetres on unsharpened edge ... one blow only entering between fourth and fifth rib to a depth of approx eleven centimetres piercing the ...*" She paused, trying to decipher the medical term.

"Eleven centimetres," muttered Bartlett. Marriner joined him in the calculation of what that was in real measurements. Although they had grown accustomed to working in metric, both men were of an age that only felt comfortable in feet and inches. "That's about four inches, isn't it, Ted?"

"'Bout that."

"That's a hard blow, going that deep."

"Or a lucky one," said Marriner. "Going between the ribs like that."

"And a big instrument," said Bartlett. "How wide was the blade, Cathy?"

"Er ... *at its widest point the wound was approximately five centimetres ...*" She held up her thumb and forefinger as a guide, having been educated entirely in metric.

"That's quite a blade," said Bartlett. "Too broad to be Mrs Paxton's dagger."

"Not too broad to be a butcher's knife. Or a sickle or scythe," said Marriner.

"What about a boatman's knife?" said Bartlett. "Or a boatwoman's ..."

❦ ❦ ❦ ❦

It was the third time Marnie had rung that number without reply. She was not even sure why she was ringing, apart from a vague sense of anxiety, a feeling that below the surface there was a real need for understanding, an intense pain that had to be released.

"Hallo?" It was a tentative voice, unexpected, the voice of someone who gave the impression they had never seen a telephone before, let alone knew how to use one. A woman's voice.

"Oh, hallo, I was ... I was trying to get in touch with Randall Hughes ..."

"Are you from the Bishop's office? Only I told you before when you rang that he isn't here. He *still* isn't here."

"No." said Marnie. "I'm not from the Bishop's office. I'm a ... well, I'm a sort of friend of Randall's." Now was not the time for lengthy explanations. "Are you a ... relative, perhaps?"

"Relative ...? No. I'm Mrs Partridge. I do his cleaning, twice a week, Mondays and Thursdays."

"I see. Do you know when he'll be back?"

"I don't."

"Does he normally come home for lunch, do you know?"

"That's just it. He's always so regular. Always here for lunch at twelve-thirty, or he leaves me a note with my money."

"And there was no note today?"

"That's right. Nothing. And I'll tell you something else. His bed hasn't been slept in."

"You don't think he just made it before he went out?"

"No. I'm quite sure. He always makes his bed, does Mr Hughes. He's very particular, very tidy. You see, he always changes his sheets on Wednesday and does them in the machine on the cheap electricity overnight. I put them out to dry first thing and iron them when they're ready."

"Is there anything missing from the house? An overnight bag? Things from the bathroom?" There was a silence: Mrs Partridge thinking, Marnie wondering. "What do you think, Mrs Partridge? Could he just have gone off for a few days and forgotten to tell you? A sudden change of plans?"

"It's hard to say," came the reply. "He always puts things away. I never have to clear up after him, so I can't see if anything's missing. But I do know he hasn't slept here. I'm quite sure of that."

"Thank you. I'm sorry to have bothered you."

"When he comes back, do you want me to give him a message?"

"You could just say Marnie phoned, if you would. You're not normally there at this time, are you, Mrs Partridge?" Marnie could see by the office clock that it was after five.

"Of course not. I come at eight o'clock sharp. I just popped back to see if he was all right."

"Yes, I understand. Well, between us I'm sure we'll soon be seeing him." Marnie tried to sound cheerful and positive.

"But where is he? What do I tell the Bishop's office? What should I do?"

"I think all you *can* do is tell them what you've told me. Perhaps they'll be able to get in touch with his relatives." Marnie assured her that everything would be all right. There was some perfectly simple explanation for his absence. After putting the phone down, she realised that neither of them believed that and, if it was true, it was unlikely to be a source of comfort.

🌼 🌼 🌼 🌼

The three detectives emerged from the cool, damp-smelling church room into a warm summer's evening. From the other side of the church they could hear a scraping sound, rhythmic and slow, and their instincts led them to investigate. They discovered a stocky man of about sixty in shirtsleeves and dungarees raking the gravel path. He paid no attention to the arrival of the strangers and continued his work without looking up.

"Good evening," said Marriner.

"Evenin'."

"Would you be Henry Tutt, by any chance?"

"That's me. And you must be the police. You want to know about this *vandalism*. That right?"

"So you know about it?" said Marriner.

"I know it never 'appened."

Bartlett stepped forward. "Mr Tutt, I am Detective Chief Inspector Bartlett. We know from what Mr Stubbs has told us, that you believe no vandalism has taken place."

"'s right."

"You seem quite sure of this."

"Look around you. Do you see any?"

"What if I said we had a statement from a witness that there had been such an incident recently?"

"Vandalism means damage, don't it?"

"Of course."

"Where is it then? What damage?"

"You've not tidied anything up, anything broken? Something that might have looked at the time like an accident, perhaps?"

"There's been nothin'." He shook his head firmly.

"Mr Tutt. I remind you we have a witness. Are you saying that person is lying? Has there been no sign of any disturbance of any kind in the last few weeks?"

The gardener thought hard, staring down his rake handle at the ground. "Everything's been just like always," he said quietly. "Been no *vandalism*, no actual damage, unless ... no, can't be ..."

"What can't be?" said Marriner.

"Nothin', really. It's just that ... well, there was the scrapin' on the path. That's not *vandalism*."

"When was this?" said Marriner.

"Last week some time. But it were nothin', just the path was scuffed. You know, like someone'd been draggin' their feet along. The gravel was all scraped."

"This path?" said Bartlett. "Where exactly?"

Henry pointed towards the wall. "All along this bit," he said. "Up to the church."

"You didn't mention this to anyone?" Henry gave him a funny look.

"I can't see Mr Stubbs bein' that interested in me tellin' 'im the path needed rakin', can you?"

"When *exactly* did this happen?" said Bartlett. "Can you remember what day?"

"One day last week. This time o' year I come in an' out regular. There's always summat to do ... cuttin' the grass, strimmin' the gravestones, takin' off the dead flowers ... I can't be sure what day."

"It wasn't Sunday, was it? Or early Monday morning?"

"'C o u r s e not. No-one works in a church on a Sunday ... apart from Vicar, that is." Henry grinned at his joke and stopped smiling abruptly.

"Right. We'll need to get a statement from you. Please try to remember what day it was that you found the path like that. In the meantime, don't touch the path or the grounds until we tell you."

"If you say so," said Henry. It all seemed a lot of fuss for a few scrapings of gravel.

Standing by the car, Bartlett ordered another examination of the grounds. Cathy Lamb was to set the search in motion, while Marriner would make further enquiries in the executive estate and Bartlett himself would be heading back to HQ to report on progress to the Head of CID.

"I want a thorough examination of every inch of the path to find out what was dragged along it. I want no stone left unturned ... and that isn't a joke."

🌼 🌼 🌼 🌼

Marriner's last call of the day was to the shop. He waited discreetly while Molly served the few customers making hasty purchases before closing time and Richard checked the takings of the post office. Conversation was muted and artificial in Marriner's presence and Molly saw the last customer to the door like a hostess saying goodnight to guests at a dinner party. She flicked the sign to *Closed*.

"I won't keep you long," said Marriner.

"That's all right. How can we help?"

"Are you aware of any damage in the churchyard in the last week or two?"

"Damage?" Molly and Richard exchanged puzzled glances and shook their heads. "To what?"

"Anything at all," said Marriner.

"No-one's mentioned it to *me*," said Richard. "The bloke you ought to ask is Henry Tutt. He looks after the grounds. He'd know. Larks Lane. April Cottage."

"But you're quite sure the vicar didn't say anything about vandalism?"

"No," said Molly. "Definitely not."

"Have you seen Mr Fletcher lately, Mr Albert Fletcher?"

"He was in this morning, soon as we opened. First customer."

"You don't suspect him of vandalism, do you?" said Richard smiling.

"We don't suspect him of anything," said Marriner. "I'd just like a word. You could mention it next time you see him, if you wouldn't mind."

"We don't see much of him these days," said Molly. "He's been keeping to himself lately."

"Oh? Why's that? Not been well?"

Molly wondered if she'd said something she should have kept to herself. "No, it's just that … well, he wasn't too happy about having a woman vicar. He's a bit old-fashioned about that sort of thing. There's plenty of people who feel like that … women as well as men …"

"Interesting," said Marriner. "So Mr Fletcher was a supporter of Mr Hughes?"

"Well, no, not really." Molly looked at her husband for help.

"Go on, Mrs Appleton. You were explaining about Mr Fletcher's views on the vicar."

"He didn't like some of the things Mr Hughes was doing, that's all. He's a traditionalist. He likes things to stay as they are."

"Was he involved in having Mr Hughes replaced as vicar?"

"He wrote the letter," said Richard. "He and Mr Stubbs sent it on behalf of the PCC."

"*Some* members of the PCC," added Molly. "But it was nothing personal. He only wanted things to be nice and stay the same as they've always been. He likes old ways and old things."

"Like his collection of blades," said Marriner conversationally, turning towards the door.

"*Blades?*" said Richard. Molly looked doubtful.

"Yes, you know, his collection of old farm implements, sickles and scythes."

"I didn't know he had any," said Richard.

"You *do* surprise me. I would've thought everyone would know about them. Very proud of them, he must be. Some of those tools must be a hundred years old and he keeps them cleaned and sharpened like new. I'll see myself out. Thanks for your time."

🌲 🌲 🌲 🌲

Marnie was leaving the office that evening when she noticed how untidy it was. In these past few days the lack of Anne's influence was showing. She put down her bag and began to tidy up, tut-tutting to herself. Anne's desk was a model of neatness, while her own lay hidden under a mass of papers, notes, lists and files. She began picking up scraps of paper from the floor and imagined Anne spending part of each day cleaning up. Conflicting thoughts welled up in her as she moved about the office. Part of her wished that Anne could be there, helping to cope with the police enquiries, while part of her was glad that Anne was away from it all, away from the horror that lay below the surface, away from the strained tense atmosphere in the community. She gave a start as the phone rang.

"Hallo, Marnie Walker."

"Marnie, it's Ralph. How are you?" The anxiety in his voice was clear.

"Fine." She was confused for a few seconds. The line was as clear as if Ralph was in the next room. "Are you back? I thought it was some time next week."

"It is … it was. I'm in Seattle. Marnie, I've heard about Toni. I found out yesterday. I've been trying to ring you on and off, but your answerphone doesn't seem to be working. Are you okay?"

"I'm all right, apart from the fact that the police have me down as a suspect …"

"*What?* Good god! Look, I'm trying to get my return flight brought forward to the weekend. I hope to be back by Monday."

"What about your visit to Harvard?"

"I'll go some other time. Marnie, you're not alone at Glebe Farm, are you?"

"It's okay here, really it is."

"I don't want to be alarming, but you ought to think of having a break at the moment."

"If I skipped town, the police would put out the dragnet."

"They can't *seriously* suspect you of anything, surely?"

"It's partly my own fault, Ralph. I seem to say the wrong thing when they're here. They sort of antagonise me and I haven't always been frank with them about Toni. It would all seem silly, so I've just told them part of the truth. Now, it would seem sillier than ever."

"You must judge what's best, Marnie. But please don't take any risks."

"No. Honestly, I'm okay. I'll make sure the answerphone's on. Is the conference going well?"

"Oh, it's fine, but if I could get a flight today, I'd come back immediately. Easier said than done, I'm afraid. I'll get back as quickly as I can. See you soon, darling. Take care."

"Thanks, Ralph. But I'm all right ... honestly. Don't worry."

Satisfied that Anne, if not entirely proud of the office after its tidy-up, would at least find it acceptable, Marnie locked the door and walked back to *Sally Ann*. A cool breeze was riffling through the branches. Strangely, she did not feel threatened or in danger, even though she was alone, well out of ear-shot of the village. Her mind was still coming to terms with the depression she had felt constantly since Toni's death, like the aftermath of a migraine. A shadow moved in the undergrowth and Dolly appeared, calling out for supper, falling into step with Marnie as they strolled on together. It was warm and close in the cabin, and Marnie opened the hatch and all the windows to air the boat. She switched on the radio to catch the seven o'clock news bulletin while pouring herself a spritzer.

"*... giving way to more prolonged outbreaks of rain, some of it heavy in places throughout the night. And finally, the outlook into the weekend. Warmer, drier weather returning to the south and west including Wales, a less settled pattern in the north of England and the borders, and heavy cloud over the rest of Scotland and Northern Ireland, bringing more rain. Now back to the studio.*"

"I wonder how Anne's getting on, Dolly." Marnie put down a bowl of cat food. Dolly gave her full attention to salmon and tuna in jelly.

It was soon after nine when the phone rang. "Oh Marnie! I saw a newspaper. It was Tuesday's. I read about Toni. I've been crying all afternoon. It's dreadful. Are you all right?"

"Yes. Yes. Everything's okay here. It's a terrible business. What can I say?"

"Have they found out who did it?"

"Not yet. The police are questioning everybody in the village."

"Do they think it has something to do with the smashed gravestone?"

"Er, no. I haven't spoken to them much about that."

"I expect they haven't got down to Glebe Farm yet."

"Oh, yes ... they're practically tenants. Actually, I'll tell them when I next see them. What about you? How's the holiday?"

"It's fine ... fine. Lovely place ... weather's been nice so far. Only today it's got colder and looks like rain."

Marnie made herself eat supper and took her coffee outside, but the first drops of rain came down and she sat in the saloon going over the events that had brought tragedy to this tranquil place. Too indolent to turn on the cassette player or even put on a light, she sat in silence, looking out across the rippling water as the shower fell. She recalled some words from a poem she had read at school, something about '... *the lachrymose pane* ...' and thought of Anne far away up in Scotland, weeping all afternoon at the loss of their friend, suffering her own lachrymose pain. She stood up to draw the curtains and caught sight of her reflection in the window, her face streaked with the rain.

❦ ❦ ❦ ❦

Friday morning and a drive to Northampton to see her accountant again. A grey, damp road under a grey sky. Would it make it any better if the sun was out? Probably. But today the poppies lining the road were drooping and the fields awash all around.

Passing her in the opposite direction, she did not notice the grey Vauxhall Cavalier, but Detective Sergeant Marriner recognised the dark blue Rover as it swept past. What was it about that woman, he wondered? *Dashing*. That seemed to sum her up, in many ways. There was a time when only men could be thought of as dashing. Things had changed. Marnie Walker always looked as if she knew where she was going. One of these new women, the professionals, always in a hurry. He wondered if she had ever been caught speeding. He wondered why she did not tell them what she knew.

❦ ❦ ❦ ❦

Too early for lunch after her meeting ended, Marnie decided to check out a shoe shop before returning home. Absorbed by the display, she did not see the person standing beside her.

"I don't know how they dream up some of these prices, really I don't. Hand lasted, I suppose."

Marnie at first failed to find the name to go with the face. "Janet," she said. "Sorry. I was ..."

"I understand," said Janet Day. "You were lost in thought."

"I need a new pair of shoes for the office."

"Flat and comfortable. What my mother calls *sensible shoes*. Have you thought of cabbage?"

"Pardon me?" Marnie smiled at the idea. It was her first smile for ages.

"Cabbage. Ends of lines. Clearance stock. Surplus orders, you know."

"In the market?" said Marnie.

"No. Discount shoe shops. I could show you where to go, if you like."

Marnie looked at her watch. "Is it far? I don't want to seem ungrateful, but I'm the only one in the office this week."

"What about a quick cup of coffee, then? I can tell you where to go next time you're in town. That's another good thing about Northampton. It has a really good coffee shop just along here."

"You've persuaded me. My accountant's a nice man, but his coffee ..."

The café was full, run by mumsy ladies in brown gingham dresses and little hats perched on top like tiaras. A friendly, old-fashioned atmosphere, and the cakes and sandwiches looked home-made.

They found a table in the no-smoking section. "I hope this is all right for you," said Janet. "There isn't a seat in the smoking area. It's usually pretty crowded in here."

"That's fine. I don't smoke."

"Oh, I imagined you did. I could picture you smoking those very long cigarettes with the gold band near the filter." Marnie wondered what kind of impression she had given Janet.

"Actually, I used to smoke, but I gave up last year. Your description makes me want to try again. In fact, I've been wanting a cigarette from time to time just recently. This coffee is excellent."

"Good," said Janet. "I think we've all needed a cigarette, or a stiff drink, these last few days."

"Yes. The whole village seems quite stunned. It's like a bad dream."

"Not just Knightly," said Janet. "Yore is in a state of shock."

"Yes, of course. I didn't mean ..."

"And Frank's very distressed, as you can imagine, history seeming to repeat itself all over again."

"Sorry. I'm not with you."

"Well, it's like the other vicar who was killed," said Janet, lowering her voice. "Frank's family were closely involved in the death of the vicar in the Civil War."

"I didn't know that. I thought nobody knew exactly what happened."

"Strictly speaking, nobody does," said Janet. "But that's how the trouble started. Frank's family supported Parliament and had relatives who were Baptists living in Yore. The vicar and some of the families in Knightly were high church. Staunch royalists."

"But that isn't a reason for suspecting they were to blame for the murder," said Marnie. "Nor should Frank feel involved in what's happened now."

"Oh, but he does, you know. His family were suspected of complicity in a plot to kill the vicar, but nothing was ever proved. The knife was never found."

In the car on the way back to Knightly, Marnie kept hearing voices in her head. Randall, wondering if the same person could be responsible for both murders. What on earth had he meant? Another voice that she could not recognise, a woman's voice, was whispering that nowhere had it ever been written that the vicar of Knightly St John long ago had been murdered by stabbing.

❦   ❦   ❦   ❦

Valerie Paxton looked up as Marriner entered her office. She blushed deeply and began rearranging the papers on her desk.

"Sorry to disturb you," said Marriner. Valerie stood up.

"I'll tell the Head you're here."

"It's not Mrs Giles I've come to see, actually. It's you."

"Then you've got both of us." Marriner turned to see Margaret Giles standing in the doorway of her office, cardigan draped over her shoulders, clutching the inevitable file of papers. "Sergeant, I know you are accustomed to walking in wherever and whenever you wish, but in a school there may be times when we simply cannot abandon what we are doing and give you our full attention. I'd appreciate it if you would in future let us have some advance warning of your visits."

"I hear what you say," said Marriner in an even tone. "But we have a job to do as well and we can't always choose our timing."

"Even so. We want to help you, of course, but the children are our first responsibility, and your investigation obviously has nothing to do with any of us. Please just bear in mind what I said."

"Actually, I only came to return this." He produced a packet, took out the SS dagger and handed it to Valerie. "We've finished our tests. We're no longer concerned with it. You will remember to keep it safely. Technically, it's an offensive weapon." The two women stared at the dagger lying in Valerie's hands as if she were Lady Macbeth. Their expressions were almost as horrified.

"You couldn't have thought for one moment that the murder had anything to do with Valerie, surely!" said Mrs Giles slowly and deliberately.

"We have to think about a lot of things in our work, madam. You'd be surprised." Valerie put the knife in the desk drawer and closed it.

"The vicar was stabbed?" said Margaret quietly. "There's been no mention of it in the news."

"We don't give out details unless we have to," said Marriner.

"I'm shocked that you could *possibly* have thought my secretary was in any way implicated ..."

"Like I say, madam, we have to consider all sorts of things, none of them pleasant. We also have responsibilities." Outside in the corridor a line of children walked past, chattering in subdued voices. "Just something to remember as you go about your business. Good morning."

❦　❦　❦　❦

"I didn't realise you were going to come here," said Marnie. "Your message was quite a surprise. If I'd known you were coming ..."

"You'd have baked a cake," said Roger Broadbent. "Don't worry, Marnie. I'm trying to cut down."

"But seriously ... I wouldn't want to drag you out just for a quick word of advice." Marnie poured Roger a cup of his favourite Earl Grey. It had already occurred to her that he obviously did not regard it as a trivial matter, otherwise he would not have called in on his way back from Nottingham.

"It's no trouble. I was almost passing your door." He looked around him at the spinney, the canal and *Sally Ann.* "Well, *almost* almost." He took a sip. "Delicious. Just what I needed. So, ... from what you've told me so far, the police haven't indicated that they're going to charge you with anything?"

"No. They keep making veiled threats, talking about evidence, acting as if they don't believe me."

Roger drank some more tea and sat for a moment looking at his cup. "Marnie ... I'm not quite sure how to put this to a friend. The police go on facts of course, but experienced officers, like your Bartlett and his sergeant, develop an instinct for what's going on. They often know when things aren't quite what they seem and when what they're told isn't the whole picture."

"You think I'm not telling the truth?" Marnie felt annoyed that Roger seemed to be siding with the police. She waited for his rebuttal of the suggestion. It did not come.

"Well, as far as it goes ..." They sat in silence, drinking tea.

"I don't know how it happened," Marnie sighed. "I think it was the shock. I said the first thing that came into my head and then got caught up in a story that only touched on the whole truth."

"What is the whole truth, Marnie?"

"It sounds so ridiculous. That's what held me back in the first place. I found a gravestone outside the churchyard wall. It marked the grave of someone who may have been implicated somehow in the murder of the vicar here at the time of the Civil War. She committed suicide in the barn that we now use as our office ... that's why she was buried in unconsecrated ground."

"I'm not sure I see the connection with the murder of Toni Petrie," said Roger softly.

"That's just it ... I know it all sounds silly. Anyway, the stone was vandalised the week before Toni's death. That's the connection. I should have told Bartlett about it, but I thought at first it wasn't connected and in any case I felt stupid."

"Why should you feel stupid?"

"Oh, I don't know. I kept getting the murders mixed up in my mind. I had this strange idea going round in my head that it could have been the same murderer both times ... totally absurd ..."

"You're losing me, Marnie." He was looking intently at her face, his own expression a frown.

"Sorry. I find it complicated and confusing … everything gets mixed up. You see, I *did* tell them about the vandalism, but they made it seem as if *I'd* been guilty of something."

"They probably thought you were concealing material facts, Marnie. They have to explore all the circumstances."

"Do they have to try and antagonise me all the time?"

"I see your problem. Look, the best thing to do is to make a fresh start, tell them everything you know and just keep to the facts. There's no need to go back over past history." Marnie poured more tea. She wondered if any old packets of cigarettes were lurking at the back of a drawer in her desk.

"I'm sure you're right. Mind you, I'm equally sure Bartlett will try and twist what I say into something else."

"If it would help, I could be there when you talk to them."

"Thanks, but wouldn't it make it seem as if I had some reason for needing legal representation?"

"You think you don't?"

🌵 🌵 🌵 🌵

"You cannot be serious!"

"I am," said Marnie, chewing a biro in the saloon on *Sally Ann* that evening. "Roger said they could get awkward if they thought I was withholding evidence that was important to their enquiry."

"Are you smoking, Marnie?"

"No, Beth. I'm just chewing a pen … really."

"But what could they do … charge you with something?"

"Bartlett could take the line that I've been obstructing their enquiries by withholding information. It's bad enough dealing with them at all. If he thought I was deliberately hampering their work, he'd go ballistic. The atmosphere here is not good."

"But you have told them everything you know, haven't you? Why would you want to keep things from them? She was your friend, for goodness sake!"

"I suppose I got used to being secretive to protect Anne. She was so nervous about the tower, I tried to keep the vandalism secret. I never did tell her about Sarah Anne hanging herself in the barn."

"Not nice to think about as you climb up to bed, I suppose," said Beth. "But she's bound to find out the whole story sooner or later."

"I suppose so. I wish I'd never heard about the murder of the first vicar, or Sarah Anne Day."

"You know what I think?" said Beth. "I think you've got to tell Anne what you know. You don't have to say *where* Sarah Anne hanged herself. Just talk it over and put it behind you."

"We'll never be able to put Toni's death behind us. And there's the question of who did it. That person is still here somewhere."

"Yes. And that means you've got to see Bartlett and tell him everything, too. Forget about what he might think. Just tell him the whole story as you know it. Your solicitor friend is right."

"Roger said he'd come up after the weekend and arrange an interview with them."

"Probably a good idea. One thing's certain. Ignoring the problem won't make it go away."

🌵 🌵 🌵 🌵

When the mobile phone rang at eight o'clock the next morning, Marnie was sure who it would be. "Hallo … hallo …" She waited, wondering if the battery was low on charge. "Beth, is that you? I can't hear you." She pressed her ear close to the phone. Several seconds went by but no-one spoke. She put the phone down, returning to her toast and coffee. She had the distinct impression that someone had been at the other end. She dismissed it as probably just a fault on the line.

Five minutes later it rang again. "Marnie, it's me. Can you hear me all right?"

"Anne, hi! Yes, I can. Have you got a problem?"

"You're not kidding! We're flooded out. What's it like where you are?"

"Cloudy at the moment. I think the forecast is okay. What's happened?"

"A *terrific* storm here in the night. Where we camped is like a *river*. We nearly got washed away."

"That's terrible. Are you all right?"

"We are, but everything's soaked and it's *still* pouring down. We have to come back today. We've packed as best we can and we're setting off now. Can Mum and Dad drop me off on the way down?"

"Of course they can. What time will you be here, roughly?"

"Dad thinks early afternoon." Anne was having to raise her voice over the sound of the storm.

"Stay for tea. I'll make a cake. Anne, tell me something. Did you try and ring a few minutes ago?"

"Yes." An engine was revving in the background.

"I couldn't hear you at all. Could you hear me speaking?"

"No. Your line was engaged, so I gave it five minutes before trying again."

"Engaged?"

"Marnie, I've got to go. My money's run out …" The line went dead.

❦ ❦ ❦ ❦

"Got visitors, have you?" Molly Appleton loaded the flour, butter and apples into a carrier bag.

"Anne's coming back a week early. Bad weather in the Highlands."

"So you're baking something to cheer her up?"

"They're coming to tea. I'm making Dutch apple cake. Do you have any whipping cream, Molly?"

"I don't stock it as a rule, but the ordinary double will whip. Don't take the extra thick by mistake. It clots if you so much as stir it."

"That's all for now, I think," said Marnie. "No sign of the boys in blue today?" Molly began adding the items on the till. "They won't be here today."

"How can you be sure? I was thinking of having car park tickets printed, they're so often down at my place."

"Oh no. They'll be over at Buckingham. The Queen's opening the County Show. They have a lot of security these days. She likes to do a walkabout. Cathy Lamb – she's the woman PC – said they all get nervous when she does that. I think we've got the weekend off."

"You haven't seen Randall Hughes lately have you, Molly?"

"Funny you should say that. Three pounds twenty, please. Mrs Ingram said she thought she saw him just recently at the vicarage."

"That was probably Tuesday," said Marnie. "You remember he came down to talk to me. You saw him that day."

"No. This was since then. Thursday or Friday, I think. She said he looked really rough."

Without thinking of it, Marnie found herself walking down the road towards the vicarage. It was the first time she had approached the house since the

Saturday before Toni's death. Just one week ago. She put her shopping bag down by the front door and rang the bell. It echoed emptily. Marnie was glad Bartlett and Marriner were away. She had no idea what she would say if they asked why she was there. She walked round to the rear of the house. Already the lawn looked unkempt. The sense of order had gone in just a week of neglect. Nature had started to take over. Weeds were visible in the flower beds. There were deadheads on the roses. Marnie wondered if there was anything more melancholy than dead flowers. Away in the far corner stood an old apple tree, its boughs bent and twisted but still full of life. Through its branches a honeysuckle had insinuated itself, weighing the tree down with a mass of flowers, cream and pink. Toni would never see them again.

Marnie shuddered at the thought of Toni lying under a shroud in the mortuary, reassembled after the autopsy. In a week she had become history, no longer a person. Soon she would be laid in her grave and a stone would be erected at her head, like Sarah Anne Day. Perhaps someone would come along with a sledgehammer and destroy her tombstone, too. The hatred would go on for ever and for ever. And *why*? Who cared so much about what had happened centuries ago?

In fact, thought Marnie, *that* was the question. Who *did* care and *why* did they care? In that moment she began to doubt that anything that had happened in recent times had led to Toni's death. She could not believe it had anything to do with the ordination of women or Randall's changes. Whoever had carried out the crime must have felt all the ancient hatred as if it was still alive. What sort of person could harbour such grudges after so long? She realised that the flaw in her argument was the vandalism to Sarah Anne's headstone. And there was the strange non-phone call of that morning. But smashing a stone was one thing. Stabbing someone to death in cold blood, with a steel blade, on a Monday morning was a different matter. She could not imagine a passion so strong it could rise up and kill an innocent woman who had been in the village for only a few weeks.

She sat on the old bench facing the lawn and closed her eyes in the pale morning sunshine. In this peaceful place she could almost believe there had been no murder, now or in the past. There was only the quiet of the new day, the warmth on her face, the sound of a blackbird singing in an apple tree in a walled vicarage garden. Nearby, she could hear the humming of bees in the lavender border and for a moment she felt drowsy. She breathed in deeply, taking in the sounds of the morning. The bird had stopped singing, but there was no silence. Far off was the sound of a small aeroplane, nearby the bees, somewhere in the village a car was going by. If only she could ...

What was that? Another sound, a footfall on the gravel. She opened her eyes and turned in the direction of the path. There was no doubt that someone was walking very quietly and carefully beside the house. "Randall?" she said softly. The footsteps faltered. A face looked round the corner. George Stubbs.

"Oh, Marnie! It's you."

"Hallo ... er, I was wondering about the garden ... what was happening to it."

"Were you expecting to find Randall Hughes here?" He sat beside her on the bench, his thick fingers resting on his knees.

"I don't know. It was the first person I could think of."

"I saw the shopping bag by the door and thought I'd better come and investigate."

"You thought perhaps a hit-squad of commandos from the WI armed with pink striped carrier bags had moved in to take possession?"

He smiled at her and reached forward to pat her knee. "You know, I admire you, Marnie. Not just, of course, because you are a very lovely lady. A lot of women would be frightened of living where you live in *normal* circumstances, let alone after what's happened here. And you can still joke about things. Tell me. What is your secret?" Marnie held his gaze and he moved his hand from her knee.

"I suppose because I can take care of myself in any situation." She hoped her meaning was clear.

"I'm sure you can, my dear, but you must be careful. Somewhere here there's a murderer at large. If ever you become anxious about anything, just give me a ring. Please. I'll be happy to give you any help I can. I hope you look upon me as a friend." He was leaning towards her. She could see small beads of perspiration on his face and the shirt collar tight against his thick neck.

"That's very kind of you. Thank you." She stood up. "Now, I think I ought to get on with my baking. I have visitors for tea."

"Marnie, you mentioned the garden ... your concern about it."

"Yes."

"I'll get Henry to mow the lawn and keep the beds tidy. Keep it in shape, you know. Sad to let a nice garden go to seed."

"Yes. That would be nice. Goodbye." She set off round the house and passed the garage on her way to the front door. It was an old timber structure like a large garden shed, coated with creosote, with a window in the side. She looked in, wondering what would become of Toni's ancient Allegro, unaware that the police had taken it away for examination. Presumably she had a family somewhere who would come and sort out her things. A sad business. Strangely, the car she saw looked different than she remembered it, probably a trick of the light. She pressed her face close to the dusty pane. This car *was* different, not even the same make. Behind her, she heard George's footsteps. She hurried to the front door, collected the carrier bag and walked briskly down the drive.

🌷　🌷　🌷　🌷

"Well, I must say, Marnie, I'm relieved to know you'll have company again." Just the sound of Mrs Jolly's voice comforted her with the thought that somewhere life could be normal.

"It'll be good to have her back of course, but I had hoped she'd be spared the investigations."

"The young are more resilient than we sometimes think, my dear." It was the second time that morning she had been called *my dear,* but what a difference. "We have to let people live their own lives and find things out for themselves. It's called experience. Anyway, you don't want to listen to me prattling on. Coming back to your question, I think it all depends on getting the right amount of cinnamon. Too much and you take away all the other flavours. Too little and you might as well not bother. I would tend to use *slightly* less than your recipe contains. Some of these modern cookery writers go a bit overboard ... and that would never do on *Sally Ann*, would it?" She laughed gently.

"Not at all," said Marnie.

"Of course, I'm assuming you *did* just want to ask my advice on your apple cake. Or perhaps there's something else you had in mind. A chat about things in general?"

"You know, Mrs Jolly, you're almost the only person who hasn't tried to persuade me to get away from here. Nearly everyone else seems to think I'm taking unnecessary risks by staying."

"Ah, but you don't think that, do you?"

"I'm not *absolutely* sure what I think, to be honest."

"A lot depends on your own nature. I'm sorry to hark back to the Dark Ages, but during the war we learnt that sometimes the only way to cope with a situation was just to see it through."

"I have to admit the situation here could be risky. I suppose I'm starting to think like this because of Anne coming back."

"That's understandable. But you know, everything depends on how you look at it. One person will be overwhelmed by a situation, another will see it as a challenge. We none of us know how we'll react under fire. It's all a matter of character. I would say you have to trust your own judgement. And that rather goes for the cinnamon in the cake, too ..."

♣ ♣ ♣ ♣

"Hallo, Anne! It's nice to see you back. Sorry to hear about the holiday."

"Hallo, Mrs Appleton. It's nice to *be* back ... sort of. Yes, the holiday was a wash-out, I'm afraid." She introduced her parents and her brother.

"Have you seen Marnie yet?" said Molly. "She was in here this morning."

"No. We're on our way down to Glebe Farm just now. Mum wants to buy a box of chocolates for her as a thank-you. She's invited us to tea."

"I know," said Molly. "I think you're in for a treat, but I'll say no more." She pointed to a display along the counter. "We've got some of those mints in dark chocolate that Marnie likes."

"Marnie's all right, then?" said Jackie Price. "I was worried about imposing on her."

"Life goes on," said Molly. "What's done is done. It's all very tragic. We're all trying not to sit around moping. Especially Marnie. You know what she's like ... never stops ..."

"So things are settling down?" said Jackie.

"Well, they're going to allow the church to be used tomorrow, so normal life is returning, I suppose ... apart from the newspaper reporters, the occasional television crew and of course the police in and out the whole time ..."

"The police are here a lot?"

"Oh yes. They're usually around."

"I hadn't thought of that. I kind of imagined the village empty and quiet."

"Oh no, it's busier than Piccadilly Circus in Knightly at the moment. You can't move for strangers. They're all over the place. Mind you, there's only a group of reporters from the local papers today and a couple of PCs tidying up ... the rest are in Buckingham for the Queen's visit."

Outside in the car, Anne's mother noticed two policemen winding up the tape barrier by the church gate and a group of men sitting at a table in the pub garden on the opposite side of the road.

"Do you think they're from the press?" she asked her husband.

"No doubt about it," said Geoff. He started the engine. "I'll tell you something. The police could save a lot of time in their investigation. No need to question everybody about what happened. They just have to ask that Mrs Appleton. She seems to know everything."

♣ ♣ ♣ ♣

"This is delicious, Marnie. Do you think I could have your recipe, or is it a family secret?"

"Sure. It's one I cut out of a magazine ages ago. You've been my excuse to try it."

"I can do a photocopy of it," said Anne to her mother.

"This is how I imagined our holiday," said her father, looking round at the sunlight reflecting off the surface of the canal. "It's so peaceful here, and the water stays where it's meant to be."

"Yes," said Marnie. "The rush hour here is when two boats go by within ten minutes of each other. Actually, we do see quite a few boats in the holidays, but that only adds to the interest."

"I imagine it's very quiet here at night," said Anne's mother, moving gently towards a subject they all knew would have to be discussed.

"It doesn't disturb me at all, Jackie. I like the peace and quiet."

"Even after ... you know ... what happened?" said Richard, accepting a second slice of cake.

"I can't pretend things are the same, but I don't feel afraid, if that's what you mean."

"Naturally, we're thinking about Anne," said Jackie. "Geoff and I thought it might be better if she came home for a while, until after they've found whoever did it."

"Yes." Marnie glanced at Anne, sitting tense and still, looking vulnerable, her pale skin washed out after a night with little sleep and a long car journey. "You must do what you think is right."

"I must say ..." Jackie began, "the village seems ... sort of normal. Do you know what I mean?"

"It doesn't feel like a serial killer is prowling around and we're all huddling together at night behind barricaded doors?" said Marnie.

"That's right," said Anne's father. "I get the impression you really aren't afraid, are you Marnie?"

"No. I'm just sad about Toni."

"And you don't feel in danger?" said Richard.

"There's no reason why anyone would want to do *me* any harm. If there was conflict here, it was centred on the church. As far as my life is concerned, Knightly hasn't changed."

"Well," said Jackie, "it certainly seems peaceful enough." Dolly came out of the spinney and sat beside Anne, who reached down to stroke her head. She took her saucer, poured some milk and set it down. They listened to the sound of the lapping of milk and the cat purring.

"I'm very sorry about your holiday," said Marnie. "Look, why don't you borrow *Sally Ann* for a break some time? If you were able to take a week in September, I could sleep in the office barn and by then we'll have all the services laid on."

"Oh, we couldn't do that," said Jackie. "How would you cook?"

"No problem. I've got a barbecue and a camping gaz cooker. It'd be easy."

"But you'd have nowhere to wash."

"The first cottage will have a bathroom four weeks from now. It's a serious offer. I wouldn't say it if I didn't mean it. Think it over."

"That's very generous of you, Marnie," said Geoff. "It would be great fun. Meantime, what do we do about Anne?" They were all aware that Anne had not spoken for some time.

Marnie smiled at her. "Perhaps you need a good night's sleep before deciding anything," she said. "There's no rush. I'd rather not influence you one way or the other."

"But you're really not nervous about being here?" said Jackie. Marnie shook her head.

"In the car coming down ..." They all looked at Anne as she began to speak. "You said you were wondering about asking Marnie if she'd like to come and stay with us for a while ..."

"Good idea," said Richard.

"That was before we'd seen how things were," said Jackie.

"So you're not thinking of suggesting that now?" said Anne.

"Well, I wasn't going to ... unless you think it's a good idea, Marnie? You're very welcome." But Marnie had understood Anne's line of thought at once. She smiled and shook her head again.

"So, now that you've seen what it's like here, you don't think it's dangerous any more," said Anne.

"Well … I'm not sure I'd go as far as that …" Jackie realised where this was leading.

"You mean you want to stay," said Geoff.

"I'd be company for Marnie … if she didn't mind, of course." Marnie had to admire the way Anne tried to pull her into the conversation as an ally. Jackie and Geoff looked at her expectantly.

"I can only speak for myself and you know how I feel about the situation."

"Well, if it isn't dangerous for Marnie, I don't see how it can be for *me*," said Anne. "Nobody would want to do *me* any harm." She stood up. "I'll make another pot of tea, shall I?"

"We're not really sure what to do for the best," said Jackie, after Anne had gone.

"It all seemed different from reality somehow," added Geoff. "In the car we were convinced this wasn't a safe place for Anne to be, or for you either. Now …"

"It just seems ordinary," said Marnie.

"Yes."

"You couldn't imagine anywhere nicer," said Jackie. "I can understand why you fell in love with the place. This is really beautiful."

"Brilliant," said Richard.

"And the farm's going to be lovely when you've renovated it all," said Geoff. "It's idyllic."

"What are we going to do about Anne?" said Jackie.

Geoff looked at Marnie. "Do you really want her here at the moment?" he said. "Nobody's asked what *you* want."

"At first I was glad that Anne was away. Now …"

"I expect you've got a lot of work on," said Jackie. "Anne's been telling us about your projects. It all sounds very interesting."

"Yes. There's plenty to do."

"Suppose she stayed for a few days … just to see how it goes …" Jackie began.

"I could always come up and collect her – both of you, if necessary – if there was any cause for worry," said Geoff. "How does that sound?"

"Okay by me," said Marnie.

"Is that agreed, then?" said Geoff.

"I think so," said Jackie hesitantly. "I don't think there's any risk, really. It'll be a nice surprise for her." Within moments Anne appeared, carrying the teapot and the milk jug. She put the teapot on the table, poured milk into her mother's cup and looked at their upturned faces.

"Shall I get my things out of the car and put them in the washing machine?" she said.

❦ ❦ ❦ ❦

It was quiet in Knightly St John that Saturday afternoon in high summer. Though many of the villagers had gone to the opening of the County Show, the pub had a steady flow of visitors, coming to stare secretly at the church that had featured all week in the media. With scarcely a breeze to ruffle the treetops, the cottage gardens and vegetable patches dozed in the warm sunshine, abandoned to the flitting of butterflies and the droning of bees.

Down at Glebe Farm could be heard the droning of the tumble-drier as Anne's clothes completed their restoration. Anne herself uncharacteristically dozed for two hours in a deck chair, while Marnie pottered about on *Sally Ann*, happy to have her friend back again. In the time while Anne was away, they had both come to see their friendship in a new light. Anne had first come to Glebe Farm as a schoolgirl needing experience of work, of life and of personal freedom. Now, she had returned as an indispensable member of the team, a close friend and confidant. At about seven o'clock, Anne stretched her arms to the sky and Marnie came to sit on the grass beside her.

"How are you feeling?"

"Better than I was."

"You've had a long day already. Do you feel like eating anything? Or an early night?"

"I feel quite rested, but I couldn't eat much, not after two pieces of your Dutch apple cake."

"Same here. Suppose I put together a tray of crudités? We could have something simple, perhaps a spritzer. We could go for a walk along the towpath. Not too far ... help you loosen up a bit. Have a restful day tomorrow. You'll be good as new after the weekend."

"Sounds great." Anne smiled with contentment. "Just what I need. I *am* sorry about the holiday, sorry for Mum and dad, but I'm glad to be back. I know that sounds horribly selfish, but I know they'll enjoy their trip on *Sally* and that makes me feel better. They'll really like that. It was so nice of you."

"I hope so. At least on board *Sally* they'll be in the best place if there's another flood."

"Marnie, over supper will you tell me what happened ... all of it? I want to hear it from you."

Marnie sighed. "That's what I was afraid of."

"You really can't talk about it?"

"Actually, of all people, you're probably the only one I *can* really talk to."

"And I'm the one you don't want to talk to about it, aren't I?"

The meal could not have been better chosen. Marnie had plundered *Sally Ann's* store cupboards and the table was laid with small dishes brimming with good things, olives stuffed with pimientos, anchovies and almonds, feta cheese, dates, houmous, radishes and beetroots, prawns and mayonnaise, pitta bread warmed in the oven. Anne had collected a bunch of marguerites, sweet peas and roses from the overgrown cottage gardens, and stood them in a small glass vase on the table. They sipped spritzers as they picked their way through the flavours, while Marnie related the events of the past week and Anne listened in silence.

"So you can see I made rather a mess of my contacts with the police. I got off to a bad start and went downhill after that."

"You were in a state of shock," said Anne. "I know just how you felt. When I saw the paper it was as if I'd fallen into a black hole. It was ages before I even realised I was crying."

"Well, Roger says I ought to make a full statement of everything I know, even if the police *do* think I'm crazy trying to find out who killed the vicar in the Civil War."

"What does Ralph think?"

"He's still in Seattle, but he's coming back early next week, if he can get a flight. He's worried about us being here with a murderer on the loose. Oh, sorry, I didn't mean to sound alarming."

"It's all right. I don't feel scared. What bothers me is the vandalism ... how it might be connected with everything. You'll have to show the police the smashed stones in the crypt. They're evidence."

"Yes, and we're the only ones who know about them."

"Apart from the vandal," said Anne.

Marnie frowned. "Quite. I wonder if he, assuming it *is* a he, knows what we did with the stones."

"Do you think he might try to take them away?" said Anne.

"They're evidence. If he knew where the grave was, perhaps he knows where we hid the pieces."

"He can hardly move them in broad daylight with the police swarming about," said Anne.

"But they aren't," said Marnie. "They're all in Buckingham at the show. Everybody knows that."

"Tomorrow they're using the church for services … Mrs Appleton told us."

"Right," said Marnie. "So that leaves only today when the place will be left empty. Presumably someone will have been in during the afternoon doing flower arrangements ready for tomorrow."

"That only leaves this evening," said Anne.

❦ ❦ ❦ ❦

It was nearly ten, as early as they dared, before they drove up the field track in the gathering dusk. Any earlier would add to the risk of being seen. Any later and the chance of meeting someone else with a similar intent would be increased. They were in jeans and dark sweaters, though Anne had suggested she should wear a balaclava helmet to conceal her pale blonde hair and thought Marnie could try a few twigs in her hair to complete the picture. Both knew the humour was forced but it kept up their spirits. They each carried a torch. Anne had stuffed hers into a small black shoulder bag.

"What do you need the bag for?" said Marnie.

"I've got the Polaroid. I thought I'd take some photos of the stones where they are in the crypt. I know it wouldn't be real evidence, but it would help back up your story."

"Good idea. And you're a witness, of course."

"Or accomplice," said Anne. "Depending on how you look at it."

"Bartlett treats everything I do with the utmost suspicion, but I don't see what he can make of this. All we're doing is preserving the evidence of the vandalism from interference."

"Are you *really* sure we shouldn't tell him about this and let the police handle it?"

"The police are all away tonight, and tomorrow could be too late. Anyway, I don't think the police would take me seriously. That's the trouble. And this is virtually all the evidence we have."

"I suppose so," said Anne.

Marnie squeezed Anne's arm reassuringly. "Okay, let's go."

They cruised slowly past the church. From the road they could see nothing but its outline in the darkness that was thickening by the minute. They drove on for half a mile and pulled up in the entrance to a field beyond the last cottages. Marnie switched off the engine and turned out the lights.

"Just as we thought," she said. "We'll be sheltered from view by the trees in the churchyard. If we approach from Martyrs Close, we can reverse up to the wall by the back gate. We ought to be out of sight there in amongst the bushes. Nobody's going to be around at this time of night."

"Marnie, what do we do if we meet the vandal? We haven't talked about that."

"I'm not sure. It depends on the circumstances. Run like hell, I suppose. I'm rather counting on the timing being on our side. If he *is* planning to do something, I think he'll wait till after the pub has closed and nobody will be about to see him. If it worries you, it's not too late to change our minds."

"Does it worry *you*, Marnie?"

"Of course."

"That's all right, then. I thought it was only me. By the way, I've got the mobile in the bag with the camera ... in case we need to call for help."

"Good," said Marnie. "You'd better make sure it's switched off until we want it. It'd be a pity if it rang just as we were holding our breath two feet away from the vandal. Mrs Jolly might just decide to find out how the apple cake turned out."

They headed back to the village, this time skirting the groups of cottages to arrive at the new executive houses in Martyrs Close. They turned quietly at the end of the cul-de-sac and reversed along the path, coming to a halt two metres from the gate in the churchyard wall among the brambles. There were lights visible in some of the houses, while others were showing a porch or hall light and one or two were in darkness. Marnie reached up and flicked a switch overhead.

"What's that?" said Anne.

"Interior lights, so they don't come on when we open the car doors. Got everything you need?"

"In the bag."

"Right," said Marnie, fingering the padlock key in her pocket. "Let's get going. Try not to slam the door." They eased themselves out and waited for a moment in silence before they turned to the gate. It opened easily with a faint grating of its hinges. They stepped inside the wall, pushed the gate shut and listened. The glow from the pub lights cast shadows of the yew trees across the churchyard. Marnie swallowed at the sight of the ancient gravestones, some of them tilting at strange angles, reminding her of graveyard scenes in old black-and-white films. All that was missing was the hooting of an owl and the mist rolling across the ground. She leaned over to Anne and squeezed her hand.

"Okay," she whispered. "This looks fine, well, sort of fine. Come on. Keep to the grass. Don't walk on the gravel." Crouching low, they made their way quickly and silently to the door of the crypt, hidden in deep shadow. Marnie groped for the padlock and inserted the key. In mid-turn she stopped.

Anne leaned forward to whisper in Marnie's ear. "What is it?"

"Torch." Anne pulled out the penlight, half shielding it with her hand. In the thin beam the padlock looked normal, but the wood had been splintered in a failed attempt. or perhaps an interrupted attempt, to prise it open. It was loose but the lock still held. "Put out the light. Do you want to go on?"

"We've got to, haven't we?" Anne whispered. "Now that we're here." Marnie turned the key and removed the padlock from its hasp, pushing its bulky shape into the pocket of her jeans. The door creaked loudly in the night air as she pushed it open. She shivered. They slipped inside, easing the door shut, inch by inch. The air was stuffy and cold.

"I'll go first," said Marnie. "Don't put on your torch until we're well clear of the door." She trod carefully, conscious of Anne's hand touching her shoulder, like gas-blinded soldiers walking in line in the First World War. After three steps she put on the torch and swept its beam across the floor. "They were over here," said Marnie. "Be careful where you tread. Yes, look: they're still here. That was the last one. Toni brought it here by herself." There was a moment of silence.

"I'll photograph them before we disturb them, shall I?" said Anne.

"Right." Marnie stood back lighting the stones with both torches.

"I'm not sure if this'll really work," said Anne, "but the flash ought to do the trick if I get close in." She took several exposures with the Polaroid, waiting for each one to develop itself and roll out of the machine. It was too dark to tell if they were successful. "The shadows are tricky, but they'll have to do."

"Can you get one or two of these tools?" Marnie showed her the hammers.

Anne took two more shots. "That's it. Anything else?"

"No. We can go now." Anne put the photos into her bag, slung the strap over her head and stooped to pick up the nearest stone. Breathing heavily from their exertion, it took them three trips to fetch all the pieces and load them into the boot, the last trip carrying the largest piece between them. By now more accustomed to the dark and the gravestones, Marnie went back alone to replace the lock, feeling like a Victorian grave-robber. Treading through the darkness, she kept to open ground, clear of trees or the larger tombs that might be places of ambush and held her torch in a firm grip. She closed the padlock and headed back towards the gate at an easy pace. Somewhere not far away a dog howled and the words from a book she had read at school and all but forgotten came into her mind: *The hounds of Hell are loosed this night ...* She could no longer recall the name of the book or the author, but she gave him the benefit of the doubt and quickened her pace to a steady jog.

"Did you find another stone?" said Anne, when Marnie was in the car beside her.

"No. Why?"

"You're breathing heavily."

"I think I'm too old for this kind of thing."

"Well, I'm definitely too young."

❦ ❦ ❦ ❦

Back at Glebe Farm they decided to leave the stones in the car until the next morning.

"Where do you want to sleep, Anne?"

"Anywhere will be an improvement on last night. I don't think I'll have any trouble dropping off."

"Let's check your room ... see if it's aired." They opened the office barn and Anne climbed the ladder to her loft. She called down to Marnie, waiting in the office.

"Seems okay. You've changed my sheets, Marnie." There was no reply. "Marnie?"

"Yes, when I knew you were coming back early." Anne poked her head through the trap at the top of the loft ladder and looked down.

"What are you doing?" Marnie was standing looking down at her desk, frowning.

"The answering machine says I've got a message, but whoever it is just hung up. I could tell there was somebody there. They just didn't speak." Anne scrambled down the ladder.

"Perhaps they knew you had a mobile and tried to ring you on that number. Could it be Ralph?"

Marnie shook her head. "He'd have left a word to say he'd tried to get through. Strange ... I wonder who it could be at this time on a Saturday evening."

"Try one-four-seven-one," said Anne. "That'll give you the number of the last caller." Marnie picked up the phone and pressed the four buttons.

"*You were called by ...*" She fumbled quickly for a pen and scribbled the number on the pad.

"Same STD code as here, somebody local." She put down the phone as Anne read the number.

"Do you recognise it, Marnie?"

"I'm not sure." She looked at her watch. "Nearly eleven. Probably too late to ring back now."

"Did the message say when the call was made?"

"Ten forty-two ... I suppose I could try." She dialled the number, leaving the handset on the machine so they could both listen. It rang three times before replying.

"*Hallo. This is Toni Petrie at the vicarage. Sorry to miss you, but please keep in touch by leaving a message after the tone. God bless.*"

Marnie pressed the button to end the call, staring at the telephone. Anne cleared her throat.

"Why don't you get your things and come and sleep on *Sally* tonight? The camp bed's not too bad, is it?" Anne climbed back into the loft in silence and returned moments later with a bundle under her arm. They locked up and walked through the spinney.

"It isn't a game, is it?" said Anne quietly.

"No." Marnie half regretted that she had allowed Anne to stay, but wondered now how she would cope without her. "No, it isn't. And it's not too late for me to take you home. What do you think?"

"We may as well sleep on it," said Anne. "I could do with a cup of tea."

"Good idea. I'll make mine a brandy."

On board, Anne sat in the saloon while the kettle boiled and Marnie lit the two oil lamps to save *Sally's* batteries. Dolly followed them in and curled up on one of the safari chairs. Anne fumbled in her shoulder bag and pulled out the photos.

"Well, at least they show the stones were there. You don't think the police will be angry because we've moved them, do you Marnie, accuse us of tampering with the evidence?"

"I thought of that," said Marnie. "No. I don't think that matters in this case. They'll find traces of stone by the grave outside the walls if they're interested. Are the photos clear enough?" Anne studied the photos more closely.

"There's not a lot of doubt what they are, but they could be anywhere, I suppose. The lighting was hopeless." She turned the photos to see them better in the glow of the lamps. "Actually, you can read the inscription – what's left of it – in this one. The flash must have caught it at just the right ..." Her voice petered out and Marnie glanced over her shoulder from the galley.

"What's the matter?"

"There's more writing on this one ... near the bottom."

Marnie stirred the pot and brought it to the table. "Can you make it out?"

"It's another name, I think ..." She slid the photo across the table to Marnie.

"John," said Marnie, squinting at the image. "It says John. That's odd ... and this looks like a number. *I know!* It's a Bible reference. St John's gospel. It's a quotation ..." Before she could finish, Anne raised a hand, turning her head towards the curtains.

"Listen! What's that?" They stood up, straining to hear. "Something wailing ..."

"It's the car alarm!" said Marnie. She thrust the photo at Anne and headed for the door, grabbing her torch from the worktop. Anne chased after her, seizing the meat tenderiser mallet from the galley. Marnie took a different route through the spinney from the usual path. They stooped low, moving as quickly and as silently as they could in the dense darkness, stopping beside the office barn. The car stood alone in the yard, lit up by the automatic security lighting, its hazard lights flashing, siren howling.

"What makes it do that?" Anne whispered. "Has someone tried to steal it?"

"Any movement can set it off. Wait there a moment." She advanced cautiously out of the shelter of the barn, looking in all directions, and stopped by the driver's door.

Anne followed her. "Is it all right?"

"Seems okay. She pressed her key to stop the alarm and made a quick tour of inspection while Anne kept watch. "Windows and doors all right ... tyres untouched ... wait a minute ..."

"Something wrong?" said Anne. Marnie was squatting, running her hand along the boot.

"Someone's been trying to break in here," said Marnie. "Look." Anne glanced down, not daring to take all her attention from the yard. Anne squatted beside her. The bodywork was buckled where an attempt had been made to lever it open. "I'd say this was caused by a sharp implement ..." As she spoke the light went out. Anne gasped. Marnie touched her arm and stood up. Immediately the light went on again. "Don't worry. It goes off after a while if there's no movement in its range."

"I nearly had heart failure!" Anne was breathless.

"I suspect our visitor was equally surprised by the lighting and the alarm. That's why he didn't manage to spring the boot open."

"But he could still be around," said Anne, her eyes wide open.

"I doubt it," said Marnie. "Too big a risk that we'd call the police at the first sound of trouble."

"Might not be a bad idea," said Anne.

"Let's get back to *Sally*." Marnie led her friend swiftly, giving her no time to be afraid, holding her by the arm until they reached the boat. In the glow from the cabin door, Marnie looked at Anne.

"What are you smiling at?" said Anne. Marnie pointed at the mallet.

"You look like Attila the Hun!" She turned the girl and guided her down the steps into the cabin, colliding with her back when Anne stopped suddenly without warning.

"Marnie ..." Anne's chair was lying on its side on the floor. On the table the cup had been knocked over, the tea spreading in a puddle like a pool of blood, dripping steadily onto the rug. Marnie bolted the double steel cabin doors behind them. She picked up the chair and Anne began mopping the tea with a dish cloth, wringing it out in the sink. Dolly emerged from under the bed and stretched.

"If only Dolly could talk," said Marnie and poured her some milk. She stood up with a sudden movement. "The photos ... they've gone ... *damn!* Oh well, at least we've still got the stone pieces."

Anne reached into the back pocket of her jeans. "And we've got this one," she said, "the one with the bible reference." Marnie took it from her and held it to the light. She pulled open the map drawer and found the magnifying glass, holding it over the photo.

"It looks like John 15: 23–25." Without a word Anne fetched the old paperback Bible that Toni had given her and searched through the New Testament.

"This is it. Shall I read it out?" Marnie nodded.

"He that hateth me hateth my Father also. If I had not done among them the works which none other man did, they had not had sin: but now have they both seen and hated both me and my Father. But this cometh to pass, that the word might be fulfilled that is written in their law, They hated me without a cause."

Part 26

Sunday 6 August

That night was a restless one for the crew of the narrow boat *Sally Ann*. Marnie lay in bed, weary but unable to close her eyes, the adrenaline of the evening's excitement and exertions still running, as she rehearsed again and again the visit to the crypt, the attempted break-in on the car and the mystery of the inscription on the headstone. She was convinced that whoever had splintered the door of the crypt had also tried to get the boot open. The two locks swirled together in her mind as one image, the sharp point pressing in to snap them open. Both times she had foiled the attempt. This presumably meant that both times she had come close to the vandal. Who else could it be? That person was out there somewhere, perhaps just outside. At first the idea did not worry her. It would take more than a tin-opener to break through *Sally Ann's* thick coat. But then Marnie realised that they did not need to break though the steelwork or the doors. It would be easy to smash one of *Sally's* big windows and throw in a petrol bomb. In seconds she and Anne would be roasted alive where they lay. Suddenly cold and sweating, Marnie resisted the temptation to sit up for fear of disturbing Anne.

On the camp-bed in the saloon, Anne could not switch off her brain. Over and over she repeated the text from the gospel to herself in the darkness, mouthing the words soundlessly, her lips moving like a monk at prayer. She had read it only a few times, but it had become indelible in her brain. She knew that she would be able to chant it like a mantra when she woke in the morning.

He that hateth me hateth my Father also. What did it mean? Why were Sarah Anne Day and her father hated?

If I had not done among them the works which none other man did, they had not had sin: but now have they both seen and hated both me and my Father. It seemed to be for something they had done. Well, obviously, she thought. Why else? People cannot hate you for what you think. Could they hate you for what you believe? Could that be different?

But this cometh to pass, that the word might be fulfilled that is written in their law. Something to do with the law ... what law had they broken? Was she taking this too literally?

They hated me without a cause. Worst of all, Sarah Anne believed herself to be innocent, hated for no reason. Yet she still committed suicide. Why do people commit suicide? They lose all hope. Shame? Despair? Guilt? But she did not think she was guilty of anything.

Her last vision, before exhaustion dragged her down, was of the stonemason's chisel chipping at the headstone, neatly writing the inscription all those hundreds of years ago. And then it began to swing through the air, changing into the sledgehammer that had been lying on the dusty floor of the crypt, flying through the air to smash the headstone to pieces. Anne was too exhausted to resist the blow and she fell down the deep dark stairs of the tower into a troubled and tormented sleep.

❦   ❦   ❦   ❦

Marnie sat up in bed and turned onto her side to look round the partition into the saloon. "What are you doing?"

"Reading the Bible," said Anne, sitting at the table, already dressed, her bed folded away.

"That's a fine and proper thing for a good girl to be doing on a Sunday morning. What time is it?"

"Eight o'clock. I've put the kettle on and the croissants are in the oven."

"That's fine and proper, too. Shall I fetch your shawl and bonnet?"

Anne gave her an old-fashioned look. "Do you hear that? The church bells have been ringing for the past ten minutes. I expect it's in memory of Toni."

"There'll be a morning service," said Marnie.

"Eight o'clock matins," said Anne. "I've been thinking about the inscription."

"So have I."

"Do you know what it means, Marnie? Is there something you haven't told me that might explain why they were hated, Sarah Anne and her father?"

"You know everything I know."

"And you don't know why she killed herself?"

"All I know is that she committed suicide. It was in her father's will. Ralph showed it to me."

"I wonder how she did it ..." Anne's face became sad and thoughtful.

Marnie sniffed. "I can smell the croissants. We don't want them to burn. Do you want to wash?"

"You go first. I'll have a shower after breakfast."

Marnie emerged five minutes later from the heads to find the table laid outside and Anne carrying the breakfast tray. It was a peaceful scene on a fine summer's morning, faint sunlight, shining water, birds singing, steam rising from the lip of the pot, the smell of coffee.

"I'm certainly ready for this," said Marnie. Anne poured coffee into *Sally's* best and only china.

"It would be an awful shame if anything spoilt all this, wouldn't it?" said Anne. She offered Marnie a croissant. There was a crock of fresh butter on the table and home-made strawberry jam.

"Nothing's going to spoil it," she said.

"But I think that's what you're worried about."

"Who said I was worried?"

"Well, I can't be the *only* one," said Anne. "It's understandable after what happened last night."

"You came back, so things can't be too desperate here. I think we should have some ground rules ... just a few sensible precautions. There's no point in doing anything silly."

"I'll make a list, shall I?" said Anne.

"Naturally. For example, we won't go through the spinney alone after dark. For the next few days, we'll both sleep on *Sally*. We'll keep her locked when we're not on board and we'll both carry a torch in the evenings. Oh, yes and definitely no weapons."

"*Weapons*? We haven't got any weapons."

"Meat tenderiser mallets count as weapons."

"Just a precaution," said Anne.

"Well, if there had been anyone there and they'd got hold of it ..."

"Before I have my shower ..." Anne began.

"You feel a list coming on?"

"No. Well, yes. But I was thinking ... we could move the stones from the boot of the car. Do you know where you want to put them?"

"I know the very place," said Marnie without hesitation.

❦   ❦   ❦   ❦

While Marnie and Anne shifted the pieces of gravestone, heads were bowed in the church as prayers were said for the soul of Toni Petrie. The congregation was full as the Reverend Jim Fowey, brought out of retirement as a caretaker minister, spoke the words from the Authorised Version.

There were many tears shed in church that morning, and many in the congregation who searched their consciences for feelings of guilt for the dreadful event that had shaken Knightly St John to its foundations. Everyone present took comfort in the familiar form of the service as they had known it for most of their lives. Confusion over motives and beliefs was rife and, while all felt regret, one in their midst was suffering a mortal anguish, an aching in the soul brought on by the knowledge of personal complicity in a most dreadful and shameful act.

The murderer of Toni Petrie was present in church that day.

❦ ❦ ❦ ❦

Monday 7 August

On Monday morning a grey mist hung in the air as if autumn had come early. It hovered over the surface of the canal and coated *Sally Ann* in condensation. Marnie and Anne walked briskly through the spinney enjoying the cool moist air, both of them wondering what they might find as they approached Glebe Farm. But all seemed normal. Marnie went to inspect the car while Anne opened up the office barn. It was seven-thirty, a new week and there was work to be done. Anne glanced at the answerphone as Marnie came through the door.

"That's strange. Look at this, Marnie. Did you know we had messages on the machine?" She pressed the playback button. The machine peeped. Silence. Only the sound of the tape running. "How odd."

"Perhaps someone mis-dialled," said Marnie. "It wouldn't be the first time." The machine peeped again.

"It's Ralph. I'm stuck in New York! You wouldn't believe the hassle. It looks as if I won't be back until early on Tuesday. As soon as I reach Heathrow I'll give you a ring. Hope you're OK. Bye!"

"He sounds a bit fraught," said Anne.

"Yes," Marnie sighed. "I hope he's not messing things up for himself with his American colleagues. He was supposed to be going on to Harvard. I think they want to offer him a chair."

"He must be very concerned about you," Anne said with a twinkle in her eye.

"No doubt, but I don't want him to damage his career because of it."

"He's too intelligent to do that," said Anne. She surveyed the office. Marnie felt proud of her efforts at keeping it tidy. "This place could do with straightening out," Anne continued, "but I think I'll do it at the end of the day. We've got plenty to get on with for the moment." Marnie sagged mentally.

It was just after nine, and Anne was boiling the kettle for the first coffee run to the builders, when she crossed to the door and announced the arrival of a car in the yard.

"What sort?" said Marnie from her desk.

"Cavalier like ours. Dark grey."

"How many people?"

"One. A man. Looks quite pleasant. Like a sort of uncle."

"That'll be Sergeant Marriner. He's not too bad, especially when he's alone."

"I'll get another cup out."

"Don't bother. They always refuse." Marnie rose as the detective came into the office. She was determined to give full, clear answers and hold nothing back.

"Good morning, sergeant. This is my colleague, Anne Price. I expect you'll want to talk to her."

"That's right, Mrs Walker, I will do, but not at the moment. I'll come back with a WPC, though I'm not sure when that will be." Anne felt as if she had arrived at the dentists to be told her treatment was being postponed. Marriner continued. "There's something I need to ask *you*, actually."

"Would you like a cup of coffee, sergeant?"

"No, thanks. I can't stay long. Have you seen the former vicar, Mr Hughes, recently?"

"Yes. He came here early last week. We chatted briefly. I haven't seen him since."

"Have you any idea of his whereabouts?"

Marnie reflected that only a policeman would ask a question in that way. She concentrated on the facts. "No, I haven't. I did try to ring him the other day, but he wasn't at home."

Marriner nodded, as if she had given the right answer. "Yes. We know about your call. Why did you ring him, Mrs Walker?"

"I was concerned about him. When he came to see me, he looked terrible. Blamed himself for what had happened. Said it was all his fault ..."

Marriner's eyes narrowed. "What did he say exactly?"

"Something like ... his fault because he'd urged Toni not to go to the police about the vandalism. He didn't want there to be a lot of trouble and hoped it might go away. That's why he blamed himself."

"He wanted to keep her quiet?"

"Only in the sense of avoiding a row so soon after he began his new post as Rural Dean."

"And you have absolutely no idea, no idea at all, where he might be at the moment?"

"I haven't seen him or spoken to him since that day. I'm sure he felt as shocked as anyone at what happened and felt guilty at his part in it. I feel the same way."

"Was he jealous of her success in taking his place, would you say?"

"*Jealous?* He'd just been promoted, sergeant. His new job was a step up the ladder."

"So he's an ambitious man, in your opinion?"

"I hardly know him. But it stands to reason he must have been glad to get on."

"And it would be a pity if he suffered a setback because things went wrong from the beginning."

"I really don't know him well enough to be able ..."

"Coming back to my question, Mrs Walker. You didn't give me a direct answer. Have you any idea at all where he might be at the present time?"

"Sergeant Marriner, I think you're getting the wrong end of ..."

"Mrs Walker. Will you please answer my question." The voice was quiet but the tone was firm. Marnie wondered if she had said too much already. Why did Marriner distort everything she said? Would it be better for the police to contact Randall for his own good? Would there be more trouble if they found out that she had been at the vicarage?

"The other day ..." Marnie began. "It was Saturday morning ... I went to the vicarage and happened to notice that there was a car in the garage. I don't think it was Toni's old Allegro. It was a different colour ... dark blue I think ... and a different make. It's just a thought ..."

"Do you know what car Mr Hughes has?" said Marriner. Marnie shook her head.

"A VW Beetle," said Anne quietly. "Dark blue. I don't know what the number is."

Marriner made a note on his pad. "Why did you go to the vicarage, Mrs Walker?"

"I've been getting strange phone calls. Nothing unpleasant, just silence. The other day I got one and afterwards I dialled one – four – seven – one. The call had been made from the vicarage."

"You're quite sure?"

"I got Toni's voice on the answerphone."

"And you went round there because you thought you might find what exactly?"

"I thought Randall might be there, in a disturbed state. I thought it might have been a cry for help. This time I didn't want to let someone down."

"Of course, you can't prove any of this," said Marriner.

"Oh come on!" said Marnie. "Look, I'm trying to help. Can't you just believe me?"

Marriner took in a deep breath. "Your track record for helping us isn't exactly brilliant," he began.

Suddenly Anne stood up. "I can give you evidence," she said and pressed the answerphone *Play* button. "Listen." The messages came on, the first of them a silence, then Ralph's message. "We found these when we arrived at half past seven this morning," said Anne.

"Were you with Mrs Walker when she went to the vicarage on Saturday morning, miss?"

"No. I was on my way back from Scotland with my parents. We got here in the afternoon."

"So no-one saw you at the vicarage?" he said to Marnie.

"Yes. George Stubbs saw me. We chatted for a minute or two about the upkeep of the garden."

Marriner took more notes. "Now we're getting somewhere. These are facts." He stood up. "Thanks for your help. We'll be in touch."

"Coffee?" said Anne. "If he's the pleasant one, I can't imagine what the other one's like."

"I thought you got on well with him," said Marnie.

"But he twisted everything you told him, as if you were making out a case against Mr Hughes."

"I expect that's just their way of probing."

"So that call wasn't someone wanting our fax machine," said Anne, unscrewing the coffee pot.

"No. Probably not."

"And you were trying to protect me from what's going on."

"It's a fair cop. I'll come clean, guv'nor," said Marnie. "The only thing is, I get the impression you're better at this than I am."

"Or maybe I just say what I know because I can't see the implications," said Anne. "I hope I haven't made it worse for Mr Hughes."

"I'm sure you haven't. Here, let me take the tray over to the site. I have to have a word with Bob."

❦ ❦ ❦ ❦

Marriner cupped his hands against the side window of the garage, discovered that it was empty and jumped back into the Cavalier. Within minutes, all units were instructed to keep a lookout for the dark blue Beetle and its driver, who was to be apprehended for questioning. Care should be taken when approaching him.

❦ ❦ ❦ ❦

Bob the foreman took the tray from Marnie. "Have you got a minute, me dook?" he said.

They walked through into the first cottage, stepping over stacks of sockets, switches and junction boxes. Bob led Marnie up a new staircase, as yet unprimed, and into a room where the old floorboards had been removed, revealing joists that had been cut in places to make gaps for water and heating pipes. The fresh copper of the pipework shone red as it snaked its way across what was to become the bathroom. Stud partitions were in place, almost covered with plasterboard, dividing off a corner of the room. Marnie looked around, poking her head through the open doorway, freshly fitted with architrave, taking in the layout of the rooms.

"It's coming on well," she said. "Are you pleased?"

Bob puckered his lips. "Yes and no, really. It all fits together okay. Compact but not poky. Don't get too close to that wall, me dook. You'll make your clothes dusty."

"But something's bothering you."

"Just some of the details," said Bob.

"Such as?" He guided her over to the corner of the bathroom.

"In here, like." He pointed at the wall, the original external wall of the old cottage.

Marnie raised a questioning eyebrow. "Go on."

"You said you wanted to keep the character of the place, didn't you?" Marnie agreed. "You said you didn't want us to put in lots of new plasterboard and make the existing walls all smooth and, er ..."

"Featureless," said Marnie.

"Right. But look at this part." He ran his hand over the wall. It was rough, the stonework covered with old lime plaster that was bubbling and cracked all over its bumpy surface.

Marnie peered in to see it from close up. "This is the airing cupboard, isn't it?"

"Yes. We're fitting it out with slatted shelves over the hot water tank. The thing is, me dook ... well, if it was me ..."

"Come on, Bob. I think I know what you're telling me, but I'd like to hear it all the same."

"Well, if it was me, I'd replaster in here to make a proper job of it, like. You know what I mean?"

"Yes. Will it actually be visible to anyone?"

"Well, only to whoever's putting things in or taking them out."

"You don't think it will usually be full of towels and sheets, so that the wall will be hidden?"

"I suppose so, really. But it won't be properly finished, will it? And it doesn't make any difference to the character, doesn't make it featureless ..."

"In a way," said Marnie, "one thing cancels out the other, but I take your point. Okay. Please go ahead and plaster it. It'll make a better job." Bob led the way downstairs.

"That really bothered you, didn't it," said Marnie, "even though no-one would ever see the place?"

"Maybe," said Bob. "But *I'd* know it had been left like that and so would *you*. I wouldn't want to think I hadn't done a proper job."

❦ ❦ ❦ ❦

Anne looked up from her desk as Marnie came back to the office. "Frank Day rang while you were on site." She liked using terms like *on site*. It made her feel professional. "He said not to disturb you, but could you ring him on his mobile when you had a moment."

"Right. Thanks." Marnie wondered whether that meant she should phone him when she was alone. She decided to make the call later in the day. For the rest of the morning they worked steadily, and it was nearly noon when Anne filled the kettle. She went out to fetch the tray from the builders.

"I'll make them their midday tea. They prefer tea with their sandwiches."

"It's dusty work," said Marnie absently, ticking off a list. "Tea's good if you're thirsty. When I was in number one this morning, I was amazed how much dust was in the air."

"You didn't say what Bob wanted to talk to you about," said Anne. Marnie explained about the plaster in the airing cupboard while Anne rinsed the mugs quickly with hot water as the tea brewed.

"They said I spoil them. They'll always want clean mugs from now on because of me."

"It's nice that you look after them so well," said Marnie. "I'm sure that's one of the reasons why Bob likes to do a good job for us."

"Well," said Anne, her voice booming deeply. "If it was me, me dook ..." They both laughed.

"Yes," said Marnie. "That's exactly what he said."

"That's what he always says," said Anne. She picked up the tray and headed for the door. "He really does care about his work, doesn't he?"

"Oh, yes," said Marnie. "He's a real craftsman."

❦   ❦   ❦   ❦

Anne volunteered to go back to *Sally Ann* and put together a sandwich lunch while Marnie continued with her designs. She reached for the phone half a minute after Anne had set off. The line was patchy but clear enough for Marnie to make out the strain in Frank's voice.

"I really do need to talk to you, Marnie."

"What's the problem? Are you able to talk about it now?"

"No, but it's about my family ... you know ..."

"Would you like to come over for a sandwich? We could talk in private on the boat, if you wanted."

"Thanks, but I'm on the road, following the van. We're just outside Leeds at the moment. I probably won't get back until early evening. We've got to collect some more stuff on the way down."

"Do you want to ring me when you know what time will suit you?"

"Yes, I will. I've got to talk to you ... got to talk to someone who understands."

"Is this about Toni or the other vicar, Frank?"

"Yes. I mean both, in a way. Marnie, I know what happened."

"Are you sure?" There was a silence and Marnie thought the connection was broken. "I can't hear you, Frank." She waited.

"I should've warned her. It's a pity about the gravestone. She shouldn't have interfered. She got in the way. I wanted to warn her, but then it was too late ..."

"Frank, what are you telling me?"

"You're the only one who can know what happened, Marnie. You must see that."

"I'm not sure I really ..."

"Look, I've got to go now. This is our turning."

"You'll ring me later?"

"Later. Yes." He was gone.

"*The only one,*" Marnie repeated to herself. "Again."

❦   ❦   ❦   ❦

On the drive to Brackley, Marriner spoke to Cathy Lamb on the radiophone. She said that Bartlett was in a meeting with Superintendent Bragg, Head of CID. It would be a difficult discussion. Bartlett was short on results, had no clear idea how the crime was committed, no murder weapon and no prime suspect, and at any moment the media could decide to make an issue of the case.

"Tell the CI that I'm going to Brackley to Randall Hughes's house. He may have been camping out in the vicarage at Knightly. Oh, and I'll need you to come with me to Glebe Farm later today. Mrs Walker's assistant has come back early from holiday. I'll want you there when I talk to her. She certainly seems more co-operative than her boss."

He found the house of the Rural Dean tucked into a quiet corner of the town, at the back of the church, approached by a cobbled footpath with iron railings. It was early Victorian with a paved forecourt and tubs of flowers. Mrs Partridge was waiting to let him in and kept up a steady nervous chatter as she showed Marriner from one room to another. He said little, concentrating on the house, looking for anything unusual. There was not even a newspaper lying around as evidence that someone actually lived there.

"Is it always like this? So tidy?"

"Oh yes. He's very fussy is Mr Hughes. Can't stand mess. Of course, his study isn't the same – lots of books and papers – but even there, he knows where everything is …"

"I'd like to see it," said Marriner. "I'll probably need to have a good look at it."

Mrs Partridge took him upstairs to a large room with a bay window looking out onto the garden and the rooftops of the houses beyond. The desk was covered with folders and books, leaving a space in the middle. Built-in bookcases lined two of the walls, all filled with books, and cardboard boxes as yet unpacked stood against a wall. At the second mention of the need to spend some time checking out the study, Mrs Partridge took the hint and offered to make him tea or coffee.

He had never seen such obscure book titles. There were commentaries on the Old and New Testaments, concordances, and learned works on subjects that to him were meaningless. To his left was a pile of folders and he pulled them towards him. They contained the draft of Randall's thesis, pages of long sentences in long paragraphs, interspersed with quotes, some of them in Latin or Greek or Hebrew. There were notes in the margin scrawled in tiny writing like a pattern round the borders.

The top folder was well worn in faded green, with an equally faded title in blue felt tip: Current Chapter. It contained about twenty pages of typing, plus a few sheets of notes in the now familiar minute handwriting. He flicked through the papers, determined not to miss anything that any reasonable Chief Constable could construe as evidence. Marriner reached the last page, convinced he was wasting his time. Here again was a decorated border that seemed to be composed of tiny flowers, but on closer examination it was made up of words joined together without spaces between them round the edge of the page like a maze or a crown of thorns. It seemed to be a single phrase repeated again and again. He put his eyes closer to the page and tried to make it out.

"Christ," he muttered. Mrs Partridge, who was at that moment coming into the room with a tray of coffee and biscuits, was shocked.

❦ ❦ ❦ ❦

"Hey, this is a real treat," said Marnie. "I didn't realise you were going to do something like this." She took a large bite out of the egg and bacon sandwich, craning her head forward over the plate. Beside her, Anne could not reply because her own mouth was full. They chewed on in silence and then reached for their glasses of cider at the same time.

"Dad made them on the last day of the holiday as a treat because the weather turned cool and cloudy," said Anne. "That's what gave me the idea. Of course, I just had egg in mine."

"This is *wonderful*," said Marnie.

"I'm glad you like it. I wondered whether you might find it a bit hearty for lunch." In mid bite Marnie made conciliatory noises and shook her head.

Suddenly, a strange sentence came to her. It made her shudder. *The prisoner in the condemned cell ate a hearty breakfast.*

❦ ❦ ❦ ❦

Marriner arrived back at HQ and went down the corridor leading to Bartlett's office as his boss was converging on it from the opposite direction. Bartlett rang through for sandwiches and coffee. "God almighty, I can do without that sort of grilling." He motioned Marriner to a chair. "So what's new? Cathy said you've seen the missing assistant. What's she like?"

"Just a kid," said Marriner. "I think she'll be more helpful than Marnie Walker, though. But look at this." He laid a sheet of paper on the desk in front of Bartlett, who screwed up his face, straining to read the tiny writing, his nose almost touching the page. "What's it say? Bloody funny writing. It's all joined together. What the hell is this, Ted?"

"Start in that corner and you'll see it better." Bartlett twisted his head to focus on the words.

"Oh, yes, I see. What does it say?" He began reading out loud, slowly and carefully like someone just learning to read. "*Vengeance – is – mine – I – will – repay.* Blimey." He looked up at Marriner. "I want every available unit. I want roadblocks, searches, press, radio, television."

"All in hand," said Marriner.

"Helicopter out?"

"Not yet."

"Do it. Now."

❦ ❦ ❦ ❦

Anne finished wrapping the parcel and looked up at the clock. It was nearly five. "Just in time to get the design into the post," she said. "Do you want anything special from the shop?"

Marnie looked up from her concentration. "Oh, I hadn't thought about that. Let me think. I know there are some things we need ..."

"Don't worry," said Anne. "I've already done a list. I just wondered if you wanted anything else."

Marnie smiled. "Where would we be without your lists?"

"I really don't know how you coped while I was away. Okay, I'd better be off then. See you!"

"Hang on a sec," said Marnie. "I've just thought. Can you get some nibbly things? Frank Day's coming round for a chat this evening. I'll need something to go with a glass of wine."

"I didn't know that," said Anne. "Right, I'll see what they have." She opened the door.

"Anne, I'd like you to be there as well. Sorry I forgot to mention it. I've had my head down today."

"You don't have to invite me."

"Of course. Please."

"Okay. Thanks." Anne turned to go and raised a hand to shield her eyes. She turned back to Marnie. "There's that helicopter again. It's been going backwards and forwards all afternoon. I wonder what it's doing." She strained to see it as it passed in the distance. "I think it's police."

"Can't be doing a traffic survey here," said Marnie. "I bet it's Bartlett keeping an eye on me."

"Isn't that what they call paranoia?" said Anne.

"Doesn't mean they're not out to get me," said Marnie. Anne stuck her tongue out and set off.

❦ ❦ ❦ ❦

Talk about headless chickens, thought Marriner, as he pulled into the police station car park. He had spent the entire afternoon driving round in the vain pursuit of Randall Hughes. As the day wore on, he became increasingly convinced that his suspect had probably gone off to visit relatives and forgotten to mention it to his cleaner. In the entrance to the station he ran into WDC Lamb.

"Hallo, sarge. No luck?"

Marriner shook his head. "I'd better go and tell Bartlett," he said. "He *will* be pleased."

"He's not in. There's a meeting in the Super's office. He said he won't be back till after six."

"Oh well, I suppose that gives the chopper a bit longer to come up with something."

"It doesn't, I'm afraid," she said. "The chopper's grounded. Low cloud developing."

"What a balls-up," he muttered and, grateful for small mercies, headed towards the canteen.

❦   ❦   ❦   ❦

"That was a nice supper," said Anne, clearing the table. "Coffee now, or when Frank Day arrives?"

"I think I'll have one now. Goodness knows what time he'll turn up. How about you?"

"Perhaps I'll go and do my tidying up and have something when he gets here." Cloud cover had brought a premature half-dusk as she hurried through the spinney.

Marnie meanwhile put on a tape, thinking about what Frank had said on the phone that lunch-time. Had he really said he knew what had happened? Restless and longing for a cigarette, she picked up the folder of papers that Ralph had given her.

It was a strange assortment: copies of deeds, bills for work carried out for the church and the lord of the manor. Most striking was the photocopy of a letter from the Northampton Grand Committee, informing the vicar of 1647 precisely what order of service was permitted. The letter looked so new that Marnie had first thought it was modern.

She began to set the papers in order: background, the Day family, church bills, other village matters, Fellheimer's commentary and finally, her own list of questions and notes. Among the bills the name Day regularly reappeared. Sarah Anne's father, Jonathan Day, was the village blacksmith, like his father and grandfather before him. He had been badly wounded at Huntingdon in 1644 and had not returned until after the death of the vicar. He could have played no part in the murder.

She searched back through the papers and found that his father, Joseph Day, had worked on the rebuilding of the church tower thirty years before. He had submitted bills for *sundry ironworks*. In the tower? What ironworks? thought Marnie. Perhaps in the belfry? All the papers were there, giving the names of stonemasons and apprentices. After each mason's name was the title *master mason*. Obviously a matter of pride. They were craftsmen. Now, centuries later, there were more craftsmen working in the village, taking similar pride in their work, even though the technology had changed. But why were the men who restored the tower content with the timber partition? Why did they not finish the tower properly in stone? Bob would never have tolerated that standard of work, so why did they?

Marnie turned up the oil lamps. She loved this time of the evening when the lamps lit up the cabin. It was magic. Every colour shone, the tongued and grooved boarding, the Liberty print curtains, the polished brass rods. A memory came into her head, of Peter the engineer at the boatyard in Oxford.

"You have to do your best all the time, even if no-one can see it. You know it's been done properly and that's what matters."

She read on through the documents. It was then that she noticed the faint scrawl after the signature on the will. At first she had taken it for the date, but realised it was a word, or a collection of letters. *PSlOB.* She fetched the magnifying glass from the map cupboard. It may have been *PsIO8 or even Ps10 8.* Anne's last remaining photograph from the crypt lay beside her on the table, with its reference to St John's gospel. Marnie fetched the old Bible. The only book that began with *P* was the Book of Psalms. *Ps.* She looked up Psalm 10 and stopped at verse 8. Her cheeks began to tingle.

Well, me dook, if it was me ...
They hated me without a cause ...
The murderer must have been in the tower ... it's the only logical possibility ...
Perhaps it was the same murderer both times ...

Marnie felt hot and dizzy. She put a hand to her head and tried to think clearly, breathing in deeply, suddenly seeing everything as it must have been. Her head spun. She reached into the cupboard for her torch, pressing the switch to check the batteries. She had to know, could not bear to wait another minute. And she had to go alone. There would be time to tell Anne later, once she had found out the truth for herself. At least now she knew what she was looking for. Nothing was going to deflect her this time. She picked up the church keys and, as an afterthought, the thick file of papers and made her way out quickly and quietly. She skirted round the back of the office barn.

❦   ❦   ❦   ❦

Anne could still hardly believe her good fortune. Surveying the office, she wanted to turn cartwheels of joy, though all she had done was a little filing, some dusting and general tidying up. The pleasure was disproportionate to the effort, but it was *her* office and *her* job and she did it for Marnie.

Next, she climbed the loft ladder with clean sheets over her shoulder. Before setting to work, she turned on her cassette player and loaded a Vivaldi tape borrowed from Marnie. She hummed the *Four Seasons* to herself as she put her room in order.

❦   ❦   ❦   ❦

Frank Day turned off the motorway after parting company with the van and headed towards the south of the county. He pressed the buttons for Marnie's number on his mobile. In the window flashed a message: BATTERY LOW. Damn! He thought about looking for a payphone, but realised that by the time he had found one, he would be almost on her doorstep. He decided to press on.

❦   ❦   ❦   ❦

Marnie approached the church from Martyrs Close, trying to look inconspicuous, walking unhurriedly with her file tucked under her arm. She slipped through the gate and walked round to unlock the main door, pulling it behind her, confident that she had not been seen. She walked straight towards the tower door and pushed it wide open, hesitating for a second. It was the first time she had been in the church since Toni's death.

Flicking on the torch, she hugged the file to her and made a determined effort not to stare down at the place where she knew Toni had been found. She climbed carefully up to the landing to look closely at the wooden partition. How she had not realised that this must have been the key to the whole mystery she could not imagine. Anne, with clear logic and straight thinking, had to be right, and this had to be the place. Systematically, Marnie ran the fingers of her free hand over every inch of the surface in the powerful beam of the torch. Minutes passed, but she followed the torchlight until she finally came to the bottom of the dark oak panel. Her search had revealed nothing and she turned her attention now to the surrounding stonework.

Again she ran her fingers down the rough surface, looking for any loose stone that might give access behind the panel. She cursed that she had not thought to bring a penknife, but suspected that it would not have been necessary. First one side and then the other. Nothing. All that remained was the lintel and the flagstones beneath her feet. She stepped backwards onto the nearest step and inspected the floor of the landing. Certainly, one of the stones wobbled, while the other was rigid. This must be significant, she thought, and pressed down carefully at each corner with her hand, watching the partition in the torchbeam for any movement. There was no reaction.

Despite the lack of success, Marnie's determination and certainty did not waver. She leaned back against the outer wall and considered her position, muttering that she would stay there all night if need be. It occurred to her that perhaps access could be gained from above or below the landing and she walked down to the bottom of the stairs to look at the plans in the file. They revealed nothing new and, to gain a clearer perspective, she decided to slip outside to look at the whole structure. She eased the door open and stepped out to survey the tower from the shelter of a yew tree.

Gradually a plan began to take shape in her mind. What if she took out the partition? It was only the size of a door. She could cut it out with an electric jigsaw. Why not? She could probably do it in the daytime and complete the work before anyone realised what was happening. Bob and his men could fill in the gap with matching stonework. The tower would finally be completed to a high standard after all these years. Or was it crazy? Technically of course she would be tampering with a listed building without permission, but was that important if it solved the mystery of two deaths?

Marnie peered round the yew tree and saw no-one. Quickly she jogged back to the main door. As she went in she heard a car go by. Reaching the landing again, she had one last look at the panel and made her decision to return the next day with the power tools and an extension cable. She would reveal nothing of this to Frank, but would listen to what he had to say with an open mind.

Outside in the street, while Marnie was thinking of her action plan, a car came to a halt a short way beyond the church. Frank Day wondered if his eyes had deceived him. Had he really seen someone going in through the church door? He reversed the car and pulled up at the lych gate.

❧ ❧ ❧ ❧

When Anne completed her work in the office barn, she decided to return to *Sally Ann*. The dull evening had become even gloomier since she had first left the boat and she was surprised not to see any lights burning on board as she approached through the spinney.

"Hallo! Marnie!" she called and stepped down into the cabin. Dolly was curled up on one of the chairs, but the boat was otherwise deserted. She walked through to the galley and picked up the mobile phone. No messages had been left. There were papers standing in piles on the saloon table beside a half empty cup of coffee. She turned on a cabin light and examined the documents. Where was Marnie? They could not have missed each other in the spinney. She would have heard the car if Marnie had driven off and would have heard Frank's car if he had arrived. Anne picked up the magnifying glass and twisted it in her fingers. She opened the map cupboard. The torch was missing. She checked the key hooks. The ornate church key had gone. She picked up the mobile again and checked the last call. It was a mobile number that she did not recognise. Frank Day?

Anne turned at once, stuffed the phone into her back pocket and left the boat. She jogged past the farm buildings and up the track, feeling in her hip pocket for the pen-light she always carried.

❦   ❦   ❦   ❦

Marnie found no other possible way into the hidden chamber from either above or below the landing. Her mind was now made up and she was determined to cut out the panel. From near the top of the stairs she began to make her way down, when she heard a sound from somewhere below. At first she wondered if the clock was about to chime. Perhaps a door shutting in the pub car park opposite? Instinct told her otherwise and she waited in the semi-darkness. The acoustics were deceptive. She resumed her descent, treading silently, memories of being trapped in the crypt uppermost in her mind. A feeling came over her that she was no longer alone in the building. Reaching the landing, she paused, steadying herself against the stonework, one hand gripping the torch, the other clutching the thick file of papers. There was a click somewhere nearby. Instinctively she retreated onto the dark landing. She tottered unsteadily on the uneven step, both hands full, and reached up to regain her balance, pressing the torch against the stone surface above her head.

It was at that moment that the killer struck, having waited patiently for so long in the darkness. It was a vicious blow, a murderous blow aimed straight at the heart and it could not miss.

❦   ❦   ❦   ❦

Anne had slowed with a stitch in her side at the top of the field track and was now walking as briskly as she could towards the church. Rounding the bend, she could see a car parked near the gate. It looked familiar. Frank must have asked Marnie to meet him here instead of on *Sally Ann*. Strange that Marnie didn't tell me, thought Anne. She was turning in through the lych-gate, when she saw a sudden movement in the doorway. Instinctively, she crouched down beside a tombstone. It was Frank Day running out of the church. In the dim light Anne saw clearly his face, aghast. He crashed through the gate, scattering gravel and leapt into his car. He pulled away, making a U-turn and driving at speed down the high street.

A wave of fear hit Anne and she swallowed hard, her heart pounding. She leapt to her feet and sprinted into the church, reaching for her pen-light. The tower door was open, and she leapt headlong up the stairs, coming to an abrupt halt round the first bend. There were papers everywhere like feathers after a pillow-fight. Suddenly she saw another shape, sprawled face down on the stone stairs. Anne knelt and cradled Marnie's head in her hands, afraid to move her. She pulled off her sweatshirt and rolled it into a pillow, gently sliding it into place. *Oh God, oh God, oh God …*

"Marnie!" she half whispered, half shouted. "Oh Marnie! Marnie!" she sobbed. Think girl, think. What do I do? Get a grip on yourself. Quickly! Fighting shock and horror, Anne pulled the mobile out of her pocket and pressed three nines. She made the call and slumped forward to put an arm round her friend who lay motionless on the hard stone. Anne put the phone down on the step and saw that her hand was covered in blood.

❦   ❦   ❦   ❦

Marriner risked a surreptitious glance at his watch when he thought Bartlett was not looking. That day he seemed to have been working for ever. Everyone in the briefing room at HQ was slumped in chairs round the room which had gradually filled with a fug of cigarette smoke. Bartlett droned on.

"Right. That just about summarises where we are at present and you know what your duties are for tomorrow and the next day. I want action, I want results. I shall personally go to Knightly to interview Marnie Walker and, er, Anne Price. Cathy, I'll want you in on that. Ted, you deal with tracking down Hughes. And have a word with the old farmer, Fletcher. Okay?" Marriner nodded.

"Will we be going to Knightly first thing, sir?" said Cathy Lamb.

"Meet me here at eight and we'll go in my car. Any other questions? Can you get that, Ted?" A phone was ringing and Marriner was already on his way to it as Bartlett was speaking.

"Marriner. What? Is she … Right." His reaction had drawn the attention of everyone in the room.

"What is it?" said Bartlett.

"The murderer has struck again in Knightly St John … in the church."

"Do we know who the victim is?"

"Oh yes, we know who it is," said Marriner. "Marnie Walker."

"*Christ almighty!*" said Bartlett.

Part 27

Monday 7 August
Beth and Paul sat at Marnie's bedside in the Intensive Therapy Unit. They seemed mesmerized by the panel of numbers and symbols, each row in a different colour, above the bed. Neither had spoken since the consultant had taken them into a small office an hour ago, when Marnie came up from the theatre, to give them an explanation of what was happening. When he told them to prepare themselves for the worst, Anne had fainted, falling from the chair so suddenly, without a sound, that no-one had been quick enough to stop her hitting the floor. Now she lay sedated in an adjacent guest room, while attempts were being made, so far without success, to contact her parents.

Quietly and calmly the nurses went about the business of constantly monitoring the equipment that was keeping Marnie alive. Beth watched them coming and going, conferring with each other in hushed voices, occasionally adjusting the dosage in a drip, recording changes on a chart and checking the numerous tubes. The police had spoken to the consultant after his interview with Beth and Paul, and a young WPC was now sitting some distance away, keeping watch. The numbers seemed to be changing without any constant pattern like an erratic machine running out of control.

Beth heard the nurses murmuring "... kidney function ... kickstart ... boost the adrenaline ..." One of them noticed her staring and smiled at her. It was a grim smile.

❦ ❦ ❦ ❦

Bartlett walked out of the church and climbed back into his car. He called the station on the radiophone. "Any news?"

"Still breathing, but that's about it, sir."

"What about the girl who went with her in the ambulance?"

"They're keeping her sedated. She knocked herself out, apparently. Fainted. They say we can't talk to her again until tomorrow morning."

"Bugger!" said Bartlett. "Can you get Ted Marriner to contact me."

"He's on his way back to Knightly, sir."

"Right. I want to know as soon as there's any development."

"Yes, sir."

We all know what that means, thought Bartlett. He was tired, frustrated and angry. If Marnie Walker had only told him everything she knew, they might not be in this position now. To make matters worse, he had been bawled out by the duty pathologist who had been summoned from a concert in Northampton, only to be told the corpse was still breathing and on her way to the General.

❦ ❦ ❦ ❦

Beth turned over in bed for the hundredth time and looked at the clock. She had dozed fitfully since they had been told by the consultant to get some rest at midnight. She could hear Paul breathing regularly in his sleep as she strained to read the time. Quarter to five. She slid out of bed, silently opening the door and walking back to the unit in her dressing gown. The double doors were locked and there was a keypad on the wall. Access could only be gained if you pressed the right code. Beside this was a push button and an intercom. Beth hesitated. Could she disturb the unit at this time? Through the glass panels of the door she could only see to the end of the empty corridor. The unit was round the corner to the left out of sight, where Marnie lay. Beth could not bear to wait, could not bear to prepare herself for the worst without seeing her sister. She pressed the button. She put her hands in her pockets and leaned against the wall, fingering her wallet of photographs.

The intercom hissed and Beth bent down to speak into the microphone. "It's Marnie's sister, Beth." There was a buzz and the door clicked. At the end of the corridor she was met by a nurse, and she dreaded hearing what she might say. The nurse was young, fresh, with auburn hair tied back in a pony tail and a hint of freckles. "I'm Marnie Walker's sister, Beth" she repeated.

The nurse gave the slightest of smiles. "Yes. You can come through." Her accent had a hint of Australian. They both spoke in hushed voices as they walked along.

"I wasn't sure if it would be allowed at this time of day. I couldn't sleep ..."

"There's no restriction. Any time, day or night, is permitted here. We usually only allow two or three. There's only one other visitor at the moment." Beth could see the curtains partly drawn round Marnie's bed, but could see no-one there. In the chair by the wall a policeman was seated.

"One other visitor?" she said in disbelief. "Visiting Marnie?"

"She's been here since four o'clock," said the nurse. They reached Marnie's bed and there, sitting close beside her, talking quietly in her ear, sat Anne. Marnie lay utterly still, her dark wavy hair pulled clear of the tubes, the skin stretched tight against her cheek bones. The girl did not notice them arrive. She was leaning forward, elbows resting on the edge of the mattress. Beth could just make out her voice. It was calm, almost businesslike.

"... and that leaves the other two, and the head office ... Now that's more complicated than the other schemes. I'll do you a special list for that one ..." Anne looked up at the panel. "All readings normal now for twenty minutes, but you've got to manage it yourself without the machines. Okay?"

Beth swallowed. She sat at the foot of the bed. Anne looked round, her face drawn and pale, her left cheek bruised and swollen from the fall. She smiled. "They told me she could probably hear me if I spoke to her and would understand what I said, even if she made no sign."

"Was that right, what you said about the readings being normal?"

"Yes. The nurses have been explaining to me what they've been doing and I've told Marnie. It's very complicated, but everything is controlled by the equipment at the moment."

"So Marnie's not actually better?" said Beth.

"Not yet. She has to be able to carry on without help from the machines and things." The nurse returned and checked the readings. Beth stood up and went round the bed to her. The nurse was entering figures on a list, adding a line to a graph. She looked at Beth.

"We've got her stabilized at the moment. That's a good sign."

"Does it mean she'll be all right?" said Beth.

The nurse paused. "It's a good sign," she said. "Still too early to tell, though."

"Is it all right for Anne to talk to her like that? It won't stop her resting?"

"It's fine." Beth went back to her seat. Anne was wearing a Carlsberg T-shirt to replace her own blood-soaked one. The girl looked like a waif, but she was part of Marnie's lifeline and Beth could not help but love her for it and admire her determination and presence of mind. Anne had placed her hand on Marnie's arm and was whispering encouragement to her. Another nurse came by, checking the graphs before passing on.

Anne turned to Beth. "It's like this the whole time," she said. "There's always someone around. No wonder they call it *intensive care.* Would you like to sit here?"

"No. It's okay," said Beth. "You carry on. I'm sure you're doing a lot of good."

"She knows you're here too," said Anne. "I told her." Beth felt a pricking behind her eyes. Anne continued. "I've told her that Ralph will be back today and I'll let him know where to come."

"He'll be jet-lagged," said Beth. She took out her wallet of photographs and glanced at them.

"He won't notice it," said Anne. "Nor will we until afterwards … until after we know she's better, I mean." Beth looked again at the coloured readings and at Marnie, white and still on her pillow.

❦ ❦ ❦ ❦

Far out above the Atlantic Ocean, Ralph closed his eyes in the dimly-lit cabin of the 747 but could not sleep. Twice he had almost pressed the service bell to ask for a brandy, but changed his mind. He needed to have a clear head when he arrived at Heathrow. The rest of his journey was already fully planned and he was determined to bring *Thyrsis* up to Knightly and remain there, moored beside *Sally Ann,* until the murderer had been caught. He could scarcely believe he had left Marnie and Anne to face the situation alone. Well, this time he was not going to abandon them. This time he would see it through, come what may.

❦ ❦ ❦ ❦

Tuesday 8 August

At six, the next shift of nurses came on duty. There was only one other patient in the unit, a young man injured in a motorcycle accident, and his parents were taking it in turns to sit with him. The nurses going off duty briefed their incoming colleagues in detail on both patients before they all began a thorough examination of them. Beth and Anne moved away and wandered down the corridor. Through the large windows they could see the sun already climbing. It would be another fine day.

"This would be a good time for me to go and dress properly," said Beth looking down at her bath robe. "Are you all right for clothes, Anne?"

"They lent me this." She pulled the T-shirt wide to show how large it was. She wore it like a dress.

"Okay. When I get back, perhaps we'll have some breakfast. You ought to eat to keep your strength up. Marnie's counting on you." She turned to go.

"Beth? Can I look at your photos?"

❦ ❦ ❦ ❦

Marriner could not believe how tired he was, as he pulled into the forecourt of the central police station at six-thirty and picked up Cathy Lamb. Bartlett was already on his way to the church and two other cars were out, one searching for Randall Hughes, the second going to Rooks Farm.

"We've got to speak to the girl," said Marriner. "She may have seen something."

"She won't be much good for a while if she's concussed," said Cathy.

"We'll have to see about that. Did you speak to the DCI before he left?"

"Oh yes. He's like a man possessed this morning. He says he's going to personally supervise the search of the grounds and not stop until the weapon's found."

"We'd better get all the facts we can about the knife wound, size of blade, depth of penetration …"

"You sound as if they've already got the autopsy booked," said Cathy.

"What? Oh, well, you know what I mean. Have you had any report from the hospital?"

"I checked just now. The consultant said she'd be lucky to last till morning."

"Then we'll soon find out," said Marriner.

❦ ❦ ❦ ❦

Anne sat on the broad window sill wondering when she would be able to go back and sit with Marnie. She looked down at the grey plastic wallet in her lap.

The first photo showed two little girls on bikes. The darker one was astride hers, both feet firmly on the ground, her hair in bunches, short shorts, long white socks, looking confidently straight at the camera. The other was sitting with one foot down, seeming less sure of herself, even though she was evidently the older. The next picture was a family group with ponies. This time the younger girl, probably about twelve, was smiling down from the saddle, while the older was leaning forward to pat her mount on the side of the neck.

Anne worked through the wallet and saw Marnie growing up. Here she was picking pears from a tree, legs dangling over a bough, Beth covering her head below. Here they were in a sailing dinghy, Marnie hanging out over the side and Beth clinging on beside her.

Towards the back of the collection they were older. Marnie sitting on the bonnet of a red Mini tearing her L-plates in half, Beth looking out from inside the car. There were other cars: a green and white Citroën 2CV, the two sisters standing up inside, their heads sticking out through the open roof; an elderly Triumph Spitfire with the hood down; a single-seater racing car in front of the pits at a circuit. The next batch showed Marnie with friends, obviously at college. Several of the shots featured a strikingly handsome young man and Anne guessed this was Simon. At the end, a group was sunbathing beside a dazzling blue sea, and the young women were sunbathing topless. Anne thought, "It's a good job Mr Stubbs can't see this. His eyes would come out on stalks." Her smile vanished at once as she recalled the image of how Marnie looked at that moment.

Just then the consultant came round the corner and walked towards Anne, his expression serious. Her stomach churned and she slipped down from the window sill, her mouth suddenly dry. Behind her, she heard a sound and looked round to see Beth tapping on the doors at the end of the corridor.

"Shall we go and let her in?" said the consultant. He put a hand on Anne's shoulder as they walked along together. "There's no news, I'm afraid. Nothing has changed."

Anne breathed in deeply. "It could be worse," she said.

"Yes. The battle isn't over by a long way."

"You mean she'll be all right?"

"It's not as easy as that. I'll tell you as soon as there's any development." He pulled open the door and confirmed the situation to Beth.

"I think I'd better get you some breakfast," she said to Anne.

"But I'm not hungry. I couldn't eat anything … really I couldn't."

"A little fruit juice," said the consultant. "You need fluids. You're not going to be able to help Marnie if you don't look after yourself. I could quite easily confine you to your room, you know. Technically, you're a patient here too." His voice was firm but kindly.

"I don't want to leave Marnie. Could I drink it up here?"

"Out here," he said. "Not in the unit. Anne, the police want to question you. They said it's very important. I've told them you're in no state to talk to them at present."

"I'll do anything I can to help," she said.

"I know, but you may not be as strong as you imagine." He turned to Beth. "What do you think?" Beth looked at Anne and saw a thin, pale girl of sixteen, with a bruised face and dark smudges under her eyes from lack of sleep, her skin unhealthily translucent and in the aftermath of shock.

"I think," said Beth, "that Anne is as solid as a rock."

The consultant considered this for some seconds before he spoke. "Two minutes, then."

❦ ❦ ❦ ❦

It was just after 08.00 when the Jumbo touched down at London Heathrow and rolled down the runway to its stand at Terminal Three. Twenty minutes later Ralph retrieved his luggage and went through customs. He stopped briefly in the arrivals hall to ring Marnie's number. The answerphone clicked on and he left a message that he was on his way. In five minutes he was boarding a cab.

"What's your price to take me to Northamptonshire?"

❦   ❦   ❦   ❦

"How are you feeling now?" They were sitting in the office in the Intensive Therapy Unit, Anne, Marriner and Cathy Lamb, under strict orders to be quick and not put Anne under any stress.

"All right," she said.

"We have to ask you some questions so that we can find out who did this," said Cathy. "Do you think you can help us?" Anne nodded.

"Did you see anyone at the church yesterday evening?" Anne was surprised how painful it was to think back. Her head began to throb, her breathing quickened and she began to ache all over. She became even paler. "Would you like some water?" said Cathy. Anne took the glass and held it without drinking. She tried to find the words, but felt she might pass out again and closed her eyes. Marriner leaned forward to speak, but Cathy put her hand on his sleeve and shook her head slightly.

"Take your time, Anne," she said softly. "No hurry. We can wait." Marriner sat back and restrained himself. Slowly Anne opened her eyes. In her mind she saw a face twisted with pain and fear. She took a sip from the glass. The water tasted like dust. Faintly, she muttered a single word.

"Frank?" said Marriner.

"Frank Day. He came out of the church ..."

"That was before you went in and found her?" said Cathy.

"He was scared ... ran out ..."

"Are you sure it was him? It was dusk. Did you see him close up?"

"He ran past me by the gate ... he was scared ..." Anne spoke quietly, staring ahead of her.

"Was he holding anything?" Anne tried to picture him, but it made her feel worse. She shuddered.

Marriner whispered in Cathy's ear. "We need to know if he was stained with blood." She had found it hard enough to ask Anne to think about the murder weapon. This was even worse.

"Was he holding anything?" she repeated gently.

"Don't think so. Don't remember." Anne could recall only the face, the staring eyes.

"Can you remember his clothes?" said Cathy. She was almost whispering now. "What was he wearing?" Anne struggled to remember. What did it matter? she wondered.

The door opened and the consultant came in. Immediately Anne's head snapped up. "Is Marnie all right?"

"Still the same." He turned to Marriner. "That's really all I can allow for the moment."

"I'll need to talk to you, sir," said Marriner, "but first I've got to follow up what we've been told."

"Of course. You know where to find me, sergeant."

❦   ❦   ❦   ❦

"Where exactly do you want, guv'nor? Northampton itself, is it?"

"It's a village in the south of the county. Knightly St John. It's on the canal near Stoke Bruerne."

"You might have to give me directions when we come off the M1. Do you know how to get there?"

"Yes, I'll tell you. Come off at the junction before the Northampton turn. I'll guide you from there."

"Righto."

♣ ♣ ♣ ♣

On the radiophone Marriner rang the station while Cathy drove. "Suspect is Frank Day. Lives at Priory House, village of Yore, near Towcester."

"We've got him, sergeant," was the reply.

"*Got him?*" said Marriner.

"He's at Towcester police station. DCI Bartlett is interviewing him now."

"How did that happen? We've only just found out he was involved."

"Turned himself in about an hour ago. The DCI says you're to join him at Towcester."

"We're on our way," said Marriner. Without waiting to be told, Cathy flicked the indicator, and swiftly crossed two lanes of traffic in the unmarked grey police car. She accelerated firmly away, heading south out of town, while other drivers, taken by surprise at the Cavalier's rapid change of direction, exchanged glances, shaking their heads in silent testimony to the vagaries of women drivers.

♣ ♣ ♣ ♣

The cab-driver reached behind him and slid the glass partition aside. "Funny that," he said over his shoulder. "Until this morning I'd never heard of that village, now they're talking about it on the radio. Always the way, innit?"

"The village?" said Ralph. "Knightly St John? What did they say?"

"Been a murder there. Some woman."

"It was the vicar," said Ralph. "A couple of weeks ago. Have they made an arrest?"

"No. This was just now. Last night, it said. Must be another one."

"Are you sure? What did they say *exactly*?"

"I didn't catch all of it. I heard the bloke say Knightly St John. I thought they said there'd been a murder in the church. Someone's helping the police with their inquiries. They always say that."

"Could you let me know if they mention it again?"

"Righto."

♣ ♣ ♣ ♣

Marriner and Lamb arrived at Towcester police station as Bartlett decided to take a break from interrogating Frank Day. The DCI met his colleagues and took them to the canteen.

Bartlett seemed even more exasperated than usual. "What's the situation with Marnie Walker?"

"No change," said Marriner. "Still alive, just, in intensive care."

"What are the odds?"

"Not good. The man in charge gives her an outside chance at best."

"So she could *survive*?" said Bartlett in surprise. "How many times was she stabbed?"

Marriner looked uncomfortable. "Chief, we came away as soon as we got the statement from the girl about Day. The consultant gave us two minutes. We got the name and contacted the station. They said to come here at once. We thought – I thought – that should be top priority."

"Okay. I'll want a full report on Walker after we've finished here. Did you see her?"

"What there was to see. She's covered in dressings and tubes. The machine's keeping her alive. What about Day?"

"You're not going to believe this. He says he found her and ran out to phone for an ambulance."

"That's rubbish," said Marriner. "The *girl* rang for help."

Bartlett shook his head. "Switchboard have confirmed. They logged two calls. The first was from the phone box in Knightly ... a man. It came in less than a minute ahead of the girl's."

"Then why didn't he go back afterwards?" said Marriner. "Guilt, most like."

"He said it brought it all back ... the other murder. He said he couldn't stand it."

"He's confessed to murdering the vicar?" said Marriner.

"Not quite."

"But he was involved?" said Cathy.

"Like I said," Bartlett continued. "You're not going to believe this ..."

❀   ❀   ❀   ❀

On the M1 there were roadworks between junctions 10 and 11, causing the traffic on both sides to queue for several miles. Ralph's cab was stationary when the next radio news bulletin was given.

"Can you hear this, guv'nor?" The driver slid the glass panel open for Ralph to listen.

"... *was taken to Northampton General Hospital, where she underwent emergency surgery during the early hours of this morning. The victim is believed to be a local businesswoman and close friend of the Reverend Toni Petrie, who was murdered in similar circumstances ten days ago. A man is helping the police with their inquiries. In the City, share prices have regained some of their earlier ...*"

"Did they give a name?" said Ralph.

"No. Just said it was a woman." The traffic began to creep forward. "Someone you know?"

Ralph was overwhelmed by fatigue and almost despair. *Close friend ...* Who else could it be? *Emergency surgery ... murdered in similar circumstances ...*

"Look, can you go on to Northampton, please? I don't know the town, but we can ask someone the best way to the General Hospital."

The driver could think of any number of humorous replies to that question, but, seeing the desolate expression of his fare and hearing the anxiety in his voice, he thought better of it.

❀   ❀   ❀   ❀

Time passed. As the morning dragged on, Anne sat close to Marnie's head, talking to her about work, telling her what was happening around them, looking up occasionally at the readings, wondering what would happen if the machine was switched off. A momentary panic gripped her as she wondered how long they would keep Marnie alive by technology. She had never seen anything like this before, except on television, where serious-faced doctors were usually wrestling with their consciences before telling tearful relatives that there was nothing more they could do. Here, there was only calm efficiency, nurses constantly monitoring and adjusting. Half an hour ago they had suddenly conferred with the consultant and taken the motorcyclist off to the theatre again.

Beth was sitting beside Anne, having sent Paul to the canteen to have some coffee, when Marriner and Cathy Lamb returned. The detectives were shown into the consultant's office.

"I'd like to ask you about Mrs Walker," Marriner began, "about her condition."

"She has serious multiple injuries and a considerable degree of trauma. She has lost a great deal of blood and part of the operation involved the treatment of haemorrhaging. X-rays suggested a punctured lung, but we found that this had not occurred. There are two broken ribs, a possible impact injury to the spine and a head injury that has certainly caused severe concussion but does not appear to have fractured the skull. The main concern derives from the possibility of internal bleeding, particularly in the brain, which could lead to sudden haematoma with disastrous results."

"How sudden would that be?" said Marriner.

"In layman's language, depending on the rate of haemorrhaging in the brain, Mrs Walker could die at any moment."

"Is it a good sign that she's in a stable condition?" said Cathy.

"Not necessarily." The consultant spoke in a quiet, even tone with no trace of emotion. "The stable condition, as you put it, is brought about by our equipment. Mrs Walker is heavily sedated and the machines are regulating her systems artificially."

"Doctor," Marriner began. "There's something I'm not clear about. You've described her injuries, but our understanding was that Mrs Walker had been stabbed, like Reverend Petrie."

"Mrs Walker has not been stabbed, sergeant. Or, if she *was*, something deflected the blade. Of course, it's true that she has sustained a chest injury. The two broken ribs are the fourth and fifth, located roughly over the heart." He put a hand on his own chest by way of illustration. "I cannot say how the injury was caused, but I can tell you it was a very severe blow and could easily have been fatal."

"No idea what could have caused it?" said Marriner.

"It would take a thorough examination of the area to arrive at an understanding of what precisely happened. Even then, it wouldn't necessarily explain what had caused the injury."

"Are you still of the same opinion about her chances that you explained earlier?"

"Yes. We have to monitor what's happening and take action, but it's still too early to tell what the outcome will be."

"Further surgery perhaps?" said Marriner.

The consultant stood up. "Sergeant, that would be speculation. We just don't know at the moment. In her present condition, even to move her could be dangerous."

❦ ❦ ❦ ❦

"I don't think we've got any case at all, sir," said Bartlett. He was ready to hold the phone away from his ear if the Assistant Chief Constable bawled him out.

"But what about the confession?"

"He said he felt guilty about not going back to the church after ringing emergency. He said – you're not going to believe this, sir – that his family were responsible for killing the vicar in the Civil War and he thought history was repeating itself ..."

"Is he a nutter or trying to pull the wool over our eyes?" said the ACC. "What evidence is there?"

"We've done a thorough search of his house. We've checked all his clothes. We've had him clinically examined from head to foot. He's clean. *Totally* clean."

"There must have been some blood on him, *surely?*"

"Not a drop, not a *speck*. He says he went straight for the phone as soon as he saw her."

"On his shoes?"

"Nothing. He didn't go near her."

"Bullshitting? Covering up?"

"I don't think so, sir," said Bartlett. "He's a complete bag of nerves, but I don't see how we can seriously regard him as a suspect. There's just nothing to go on."

There was a pause at the other end of the line. "What about Mrs Walker?"

"Ted Marriner's just rung. He's seen the doctor in charge of the ITU. She could go at any time."

"Not able to speak?" said the ACC.

"No chance, in a coma. Marriner's spoken to the girl again, just briefly, told her not to say a word to anyone. Morton's keeping an eye on her, won't let us question her again, says she's in shock."

"Any luck with the old farmer ... what's his name?"

"Fletcher. Yes. Dodds and Bathurst ran into him in the village, seemed normal enough, just goes on long walks, ... always has done. They asked him if any of his implements were missing. He said he thought everything was in its place but they were welcome to check. Waste of time there."

"Okay, but make sure they check him out," said the ACC. "What about the missing priest?"

"No sign yet," said Bartlett, "highly suspicious. Time we put out another call: press, TV, radio."

"Agreed. Go ahead. Keep me posted."

❦ ❦ ❦ ❦

Why did I do it? Why did I do this dreadful thing?

He had walked this land all his life and knew every path, every spinney, all the fields by their names. From where he sat, on a fallen tree-trunk, in the shade of a blackthorn, he could look out across the shallow valley and see the outline of the villages that had been his neighbours for over seven decades. The only movement now in his view was the slow progress of a narrowboat on the canal. There were no roads to be seen, no railway, only the reflection off the water in the distance. On the horizon he could make out the contours of his fields, once his grandfather's fields and now technically his son's. His eyesight was still good enough to detect the sheep grazing in Long Meadow.

More than anything, as time went by, he clung to what had gone before and saw it as the only lasting reality and value in life. Owning land and belonging to the land was the only thing that made sense to him. Anything that contributed to the stability around him and his family he held dear; anything that threatened this sense of order, he opposed. The modern world could go its own way, just so long as it left him in peace.

How could I have done such a thing? How could I have committed a mortal sin ... a mortal sin?

Soon after the outbreak of war, he had joined up on his eighteenth birthday. He had cycled into Towcester without waiting for his call-up papers and volunteered at the recruitment centre. In the days waiting to receive his orders, he had walked these paths and fields, wondering if it would be the last time he would see his home land, realising what mattered to him in life. He had fought to protect his country, his home and family. He was prepared for ever afterwards to fight to protect what was his.

❦ ❦ ❦ ❦

"Excuse me." The Australian nurse bent forward to speak to them quietly. "There's another visitor outside, says he's a friend of Marnie."

"That'll be Ralph," said Anne getting up from her chair.

"That's right," said the nurse. "The thing is, we don't normally allow more than three visitors unless the patient is ..."

"Feeling better," said Anne quickly. She turned to Beth and Paul. "Shall I go and have a quick word with him? He can have my place."

The nurse walked part of the way down the corridor with Anne. They could see Ralph standing outside the glazed door, looking grey and tired. Anne attempted a reassuring smile.

"I'm sorry about the rules," said the nurse. "This is someone special?"

"Very," said Anne. "I'll just talk to him for a moment ... let him know what to expect."

"Good idea. When you want to come back in, press 3-4-6-2 on the keypad to open the door."

Ralph listened carefully to Anne's description of Marnie and her outline of what the consultant had told them. When she reached the end of her narrative, he blinked a few times and took a deep breath.

"Let's go in," he said softly. "You lead the way." Anne pressed the buttons on the pad and pushed the door. They walked in silence up the corridor together, neither noticing the warm sunny day in the world outside. Telling Ralph the details of Marnie's condition had brought it all back to Anne and she felt the energy draining from her. Ralph's return gave them his extra support, but ultimately it did not change anything. Anne realised that Ralph must be feeling the same fears, the same desolation, and she reached across to take his hand. He squeezed gently. They walked together.

❦ ❦ ❦ ❦

Randall walked over the farm bridge from the towpath, crossing the Grand Union Canal and climbed down from the parapet into the field beside the water. He picked his way through the trees and undergrowth that lined the uneven edge of the waterway and squatted on a horizontal bough.

By the waters of Babylon we sat down and wept, yea we wept when we remembered Zion.

He understood the feeling, though he was too drained to be able to weep. And what good would it do now? It was far too late for anything other than guilt, shame and regret. He put his head in his hands, shifting to move the buckle of his trouser belt to prevent it digging into his stomach. Closing his eyes was a mistake. His mind filled with images of blood, images that had haunted his every attempt to find sleep in the past week. He saw the blood on the walls of the tower, felt the shock of the blade striking the victim, heard the stifled choking at the last intake of breath and the thud that followed the headlong pitch down the hard narrow steps, the crumpled body sprawling out, the arms spreading as if crucified. His soul howled like a dog in the wilderness. How would he ever atone?

❦ ❦ ❦ ❦

The police car cruised the main road, PCs Dodds and Bathurst becoming increasingly frustrated with every tour. This time they were heading for Yore and Great Hanford, under orders to check every pub car park, every side road and any place that could not be seen from the helicopter.

"We're on a hiding to nothing," said Dodds. "Find the bloody thing and all we'll get is *About time, too* ... don't find it and we're incompetent."

"Yeah," said Bathurst, "there are no Brownie points in this one, unless we find it straight away."

"Some hopes," said Dodds.

As they pulled off at the 'Village Only' sign into Great Hanford, they were unimpressed by the fourteenth century church with its early English stained glass windows. There was nowhere nearby that could conceal the dark blue VW. They pulled round to the King's Head and drew up in the empty car park. PC Derek Bathurst turned the car and set off through the village. He stopped at a field gate beside the canal. Across the field stood a lonely barn, its corrugated roof pitted with holes.

"Yore?"

"I suppose so," said Dodds. "This is a bloody waste of time. He's miles away by now."

"What about that barn?" said Bathurst.

"What about it? The gate hasn't been opened for ages. Look at that spider's web."

"Right." Bathurst turned the car and drove off.

❦ ❦ ❦ ❦

"Have you eaten today?" said Beth softly.

"What day *is* today?" said Ralph, not intending a joke.

"Exactly. I know how you feel, but you and Anne should both try and eat." She looked at Marnie, death-white face on the fresh white pillow. "They've got her stabilised for the moment. I'll come and fetch you if the doctor wants to talk to us." Ralph tried to remember food and drink, hunger and thirst. He glanced at Anne, her head resting on the side of the bed near Marnie's pillow, her lips moving.

"Where's your husband?" said Ralph.

"Paul's in the lobby."

"Okay. Thanks. I'll take Anne to get something, and I'll ask Paul to come through." He put his hand on Anne's shoulder. They went downstairs where Anne rang her parents. In the canteen they drank coffee, Anne holding her cup in both hands, elbows on the table, like an orphaned refugee. They each had a sandwich untouched on a paper plate.

"Do you feel able to tell me about things?" said Ralph. Anne's eyes seemed bigger in her thin face. In her mind she saw Marriner, his face close to hers. *You must not say a word to anyone about what you know ... do you understand? ... not a single word to anyone at all ... anyone at all ...*

"Yes of course. I'll tell you everything I know."

"Only if it causes you no pain." He touched her hand lightly. She took hold of his fingers.

"It will always cause me pain, Ralph ... whatever happens."

❦ ❦ ❦ ❦

"It's good of you to see me, Dr Morton." said Ralph. "My friends have told me the situation. Could you give me an idea of what's likely to happen in the near future?"

"The short answer is that I don't know exactly. Marnie is stable at present and we're monitoring progress. Unless there's a sudden deterioration, we can keep her like this for some time."

"At what point might she regain consciousness?" Morton had many years' experience of not raising hopes and not provoking despair where either was unnecessary. He had seen many patients die suddenly, but his watchfulness and thoroughness had undoubtedly saved the lives of patients who had only the faintest of chances.

"That will depend on a number of factors that are not yet clear. I know this isn't helping very much, but she has sustained severe injuries that not everyone would have survived. She's basically fit and strong and something helped diminish the impact of the blow ..."

281

"The papers," said a quiet voice beside the two men. They looked at Anne. "The file of papers about the church. They were all over the steps."

"Something certainly cushioned the blow," said Morton. "Without that ..." He spread his fingers and shook his head. "As it is, I think there is a *chance* that might be better than evens. It all depends on whether there's substantial haemorrhaging. If you need to make plans or arrangements, I suggest you do that today, this afternoon. After that, we shall see ..."

❦ ❦ ❦ ❦

The old man looked down at his hands. They were big with strong fingers, the skin hardened with years of physical labour.

How could I have done it? How could I have done what I did?

❦ ❦ ❦ ❦

Anne seemed to take note of her surroundings only as they were driving out of the hospital car park. Ralph had led her down to the entrance and installed her in the car, but in her thoughts she had remained upstairs in the ITU.

"Is this your car?" she said suddenly.

"No. I hired it while you were sitting with Marnie. We should be in Knightly by about five."

"I'll be glad to have a shower and change clothes," said Anne wearily. "I seem to have been wearing these for ever."

"Me too," said Ralph.

"Of course. You must be exhausted. I bet you didn't sleep on the plane."

"Or anywhere else," said Ralph. "By the way, have you got keys for Glebe Farm?"

"No. I'm sure I rushed out without them. We'll be able to get in, though. The boat'll be unlocked."

They found the doors to *Sally Ann* wide open and Dolly sitting on the hatch. Anne fed her, made Ralph a cup of coffee and checked everything on board. She decided to have a shower while Ralph inspected the buildings. The office barn was closed but not locked. He returned to the boat to find Anne standing on the aft deck in a white dressing gown, towelling her hair.

She smiled as he approached. "At least I feel more civilised after that."

"Good. Before I forget, we need the key to the barn to make it secure. Now, you've got to eat. I'll make something. No arguing."

She gave him a pale smile. "For both of us," she said. He made an omelette that he sprinkled with herbs from the tub on *Sally's* roof and they made the surprising discovery that they were hungry.

"What are your plans, Ralph?"

"Good question. My brain's rather befuddled at the moment. The main priority is to get back to the hospital. On the other hand, I've got no clean clothes with me. Perhaps I ought to fetch some things from Oxford. It's not very far, half an hour or so."

"I'd like to get back as soon as possible," said Anne, aware that Ralph was her only transport.

"Well, I could buy some clothes in Northampton. I wouldn't need much."

"And they have showers beside the guests' rooms in the ITU ..." said Anne.

"Okay. You finish drying your hair and I'll clear away." Anne went round to sit on the bed with the towel while Ralph washed up. "Anne, do you want to go back to the barn to get some clothes?" There was no reply. "Anne?" He looked round the partition. She was lying on her side, fast asleep. He removed the damp towel from beside her. Somehow the sight of Anne sleeping increased his sense of loneliness. He reached down to the hem of the dressing gown and covered her legs. She did not stir as he drew the duvet over the bed and gently wrapped her in it where she lay. After a few seconds of thought, he returned to the galley, scribbled a note that he left on the table and went out. He locked the doors and poked the key back into the cabin through the narrow gap at the top.

Stopping only to ring the hospital from the phone box in the high street, Ralph set off for Oxford while he still had the energy. It would simplify everything if he could sort matters out while Anne rested. No need to have to go traipsing round Northampton. He would be able to give Marnie his complete attention with nothing to distract him. With any luck, he would be back before Anne woke.

DCI Bartlett left the interview room and rang the County's Police HQ. He spoke to Superintendent Bragg, Head of CID. "Still the same story in every detail."

"What do you make of it?" said Bragg.

"At first I thought he was lying, but we've got no evidence to contradict him. The only other thing that I can see is … well, I think he fancies Marnie Walker …"

"Lovers' quarrel, you mean?"

"No. Not really. I don't think they're involved."

"Talking of which …" said Bragg.

"Still alive, sir. I've got a message from Marriner. He's been checking the hunt for Hughes and now he's back at the hospital."

"Drawn a blank there as well," said the Superintendent. "Not doing very well, are we?"

Bartlett got the message. "I think I'm going to have to release Frank Day, sir."

"Not yet. We can hold him a while longer. Keep him in overnight. It'll get the press off our backs for the time being. No statement, pursuing inquiries, usual line."

Randall had no idea how long he had sat in the shade by the water's edge. The sun was still bright but it was lower in the sky, moving towards evening. All day his head had been filled with visions of blood and broken limbs, Jesus on the cross, the smell of death. A waking nightmare. A spasm of pain pierced his skull and arrows of light flashed through his brain. There was a roaring in his ears and as he sat, feeling the rough, unaccustomed stubble rubbing against his palms, a message came to him, clear and unequivocal. A voice crying in the wilderness. There was a way and it demanded a sacrifice, another victim.

Quite suddenly, the pain had stopped. A calmness came over him, a feeling of acceptance and peace. There would be no more days and nights of torment. For the first time that day he found his hands were no longer shaking. His head was clear. It was all quite simple. He almost smiled to himself at the knowledge of what he had to do. With a firm step he crossed the bridge over the canal and turned to walk down the tow-path in the direction of Glebe Farm. There was no other way.

In the cabin, Anne slept a deep dreamless sleep. She lay motionless, breathing steadily. There were no ghosts now. She did not stir when Dolly jumped up onto the bed, turned twice, three times round and curled into a ball near her feet.

It had been all right until the new vicar had come. New ways, new services, new language … everything new. Change, change, change. Then it was the other one. A woman priest! It made no sense. It could not be right. It was like a heresy, or so he had thought. Was he right? Did any of it matter? Nothing could excuse what he had done. May she rest in peace. Yes.

He knew what he had to do. He stood up, stiff in his joints from sitting so long on the fallen tree-trunk. His guilt hung on his shoulders like a cloak, but he shrugged it off and began walking over the fields. He had to confess everything. He would tell the newcomer. There was no other way.

❦ ❦ ❦ ❦

Ralph left the car on double yellow lines outside the college entrance and dashed through to the inner quadrangle. The head porter in the lodge had never seen him move so fast. In fact, he had never seen anyone in college move so fast. Ralph ran through the cloister, up the corner staircase and left his door open as he dashed into the bedroom. He threw the clothes into his overnight bag and set off back to the entrance.

The head porter shook his head as Ralph flashed past the window and jumped back into the car. He had never known Dr Lombard forget his post.

❦ ❦ ❦ ❦

Beth and Paul had long since given up trying to make conversation at the bedside. Occasionally Beth would whisper something to Marnie, but it made her self-conscious and in any case she could not think of much to say. She wished Anne was there with her non-stop murmuring in Marnie's ear.

They had grown accustomed to the constant coming and going of the nurses. In the late afternoon the degree of activity increased as one nurse first took the readings, then summoned a colleague, and they were finally joined by the consultant. Beth felt her mouth go dry as she watched the three of them on the opposite side of the bed, talking in quiet voices. She sensed that something had happened and looked up at the readings glowing in different colours, the numbers flickering by the slightest of margins, no more than a decimal place of variation. The medics remained talking, heads close together, faces serious in concentration. One of the nurses walked away and returned in moments with a new plastic bag of fluid to replace one of the existing drips. She made notes on a chart and rejoined the discussion. Beth strained to hear what was being said and suddenly felt Paul's hand touch her own. If only they would talk to us, she thought, and held her husband's hand in a tight grip.

Dr Morton turned and looked in their direction. He spoke to the nurses again and walked round the bed. Beth wondered how often he managed to smile in his work. "We're going to reduce the level of sedation," he said. "Now that everything is stable for the moment, we're going to bring her back up to the surface."

"Is that a sign of progress?" said Beth feebly.

Morton gave the merest hint of a smile. "One step at a time," he said.

❦ ❦ ❦ ❦

Marriner and Lamb followed Dixon, the estate agent, from room to room in the vicarage. Already it was beginning to smell of neglect. It was cold with a threat of dampness.

"Hard to tell," said Marriner standing in the master bedroom. "What do you think, Cathy?"

"It's all neat and tidy, sarge." She went over to the window and looked down into the garden. "Same as outside. It's all being looked after."

"That's Mr Stubbs," said Dixon. "He's arranged to have the garden maintained."

Marriner stood by the bed. "It doesn't look as if anyone's sleeping here," he said.

"Is that what you think is happening?" said Dixon. "Someone living here?" There was no reply from Marriner or Lamb. "You can always tell when someone's got in. We see it all the time. There's usually a terrible mess. You wouldn't believe what goes on. I mean, some of the bathrooms ..."

"Yes, of course," said Dixon. "But there's no evidence of a break-in, is there? And the garage was locked. The house looks just as it was when I checked the services after the Reverend Petrie ..." His voice trailed away. Marriner looked grim. Another blank. Bartlett would go through the roof if they did not find something soon. Cathy lifted up the edge of the counterpane and looked under the bed.

"Thank you," said Marriner, turning to leave. "If anything comes to light, I'd be glad if you'd ..."

"Sarge?" Cathy was pulling something out. "Have a look at this. It seems to be ..."

"A sleeping bag," said Dixon. It was a good quality piece of equipment.

"Do you know if this was here when you came before?" said Marriner.

Dixon frowned and shook his head. "Sorry, can't help you there. I certainly didn't see it." Suddenly his expression lightened. "Just a minute." He opened his file and studied it closely. "There's no sleeping bag shown on the inventory. It *might* have been put there in the last week or so."

"Right," said Marriner. "Let's check the whole house again for any other signs, now that we know someone *has* been here."

"It could just have been overlooked, sergeant. How could anyone have broken in? There's usually a broken window or a lock forced. I know for a fact that everything was secure."

"Who might have a key to the property?" said Cathy.

"A key? The vicar, of course, but all her things are still being held at the police station. We keep one at the office. There may be a spare somewhere ..."

"Is that all?" said Marriner. "Anyone else?"

"No ... Oh, the previous vicar might still have one, I suppose ..."

❦   ❦   ❦   ❦

Ralph tried not to notice the tiredness as he turned the hired car out of Oxford towards the by-pass. He sustained himself by thinking of Marnie in hospital and the need to get back to Anne as quickly as he could. Somewhere on his list of priorities was a shower and a change of clothes. The first indication of a problem was the flashing of warning lights up ahead. There was a tailback on the approach to the A34 roundabout. The problem was that the roundabout was still a long way off. Everything was at a complete standstill.

❦   ❦   ❦   ❦

Anne stirred in her sleep and was instantly awake. She sat up, trying to remember why she was lying on the bed on *Sally Ann*. The sudden movement caused the cat to stretch and yawn.

"Hallo, Dolly," Anne said automatically. She looked at the sleeves of the unfamiliar white dressing gown and suddenly felt a weight in the pit of her stomach at the thought of Marnie. She stood up to check the time. How long had she been asleep? Where was Ralph? She must have stood too quickly, for she was momentarily dizzy and had to sit down in the saloon. Her eyes focused on Ralph's note. He had written the time of his departure. Just over an hour ago. With luck he should be back any time now. She rang the ITU. No change.

Her clean clothes were in the loft in the office barn and she belted the bath robe around her as she set off through the spinney. All was quiet in the early evening. Anne loved this place, despite all that had happened, and she wondered if Marnie would ever walk here again. She quickly put the thought out of her head. It was a kind of heresy, and that was a word she had learned to hate.

The first sign that all was not right was the door to the office barn. Anne could not believe that Ralph would leave it open. She stopped and looked carefully for any other abnormality. There was nothing for it but to go on, advancing from tree to tree to the edge of the spinney. It was then that she heard the sound. A chair scraped on the floor. Could it be Ralph? All her instincts told her that it was unwise to assume too much these days. She crept to the side of the barn and listened. A low murmur from inside. Anne took a silent breath and looked round the corner into the office. She gasped.

Two men were in the middle of the office, one kneeling, the other lying in front of him. Anne could not see who was on the floor, but at once recognised the back of Albert Fletcher. Her gasp caused him to turn and, as he saw her, his eyes grew wide. Anne could now see the man lying there. Randall Hughes, as pale and as still as death. On the ground lay a heavy pocket knife, its blade unfastened.

Later, looking back on that moment, Anne could not remember why she acted as she did. She had wanted to run away as fast as her legs would take her. But there was something pathetic about the scene, Albert Fletcher kneeling, staring at her, desolate. She rushed forward and knelt beside the old man, saw the dreadful bruising round Randall's neck and the remains of a belt in the farmer's hands. The end had been sliced through by a sharp blade. The other part dangled from the beam over their heads. Randall Hughes groaned, his eyes flickering.

"You're shaking, Mr Fletcher. Are you all right?" He stared at her, and she got up to fetch a glass of water. "Here. Try some of this." While he sipped, she grabbed the cardigan from the back of Marnie's chair, rolled it up and put it under Randall's head. She could think of nothing else to do.

"I thought you were ..." the old man began. He could not continue. Anne urged him to take another sip of water. Tears filled his eyes. "I have done a wicked thing ... I will never be forgiven ..."

"I think you've saved his life, Mr Fletcher." She looked up at the piece of leather belt hanging down. "I couldn't have done that. Your sharp knife saved him ... that and your strength."

"But I have done wicked things ..."

"No, no. That's not true. You've saved his life."

"I saw them – Marnie and the vicar – at the gravestone, when I was walking ... I saw what it was. I thought it was heresy ... I thought it was my *duty* to smash it ... Now it's come to this ..."

"He'll be all right," said Anne, desperate to know what to do. "Would you like some brandy? Marnie keeps some in the cupboard for emergencies." She fetched a cognac and raised the glass to his lips. He coughed.

Anne wondered whether to pour a few drops onto the lips of Randall Hughes who was now regaining consciousness, breathing raggedly. She jumped at the unexpected sound of the mobile ringing in the pocket of the dressing gown.

"Anne? It's Ralph. Look, I've been held up but I'm clear of Oxford now. I'm in Bicester. Should be with you soon. Are you okay?"

"Yes. Ralph, there's been an accident. I'm not sure what to do. Mr Hughes is injured ..."

"How?"

She lowered her voice. "I think he's tried to hang himself ..."

"*What?!*"

"Yes, in the office barn. I'm here now with Mr Fletcher. He cut him down and saved his life. What should I do? Must I get the police? I'm really out of my depth here."

"Oh, god," said Ralph. "Are you in danger?"

"No."

"What state is Mr Hughes in? Does he need emergency treatment?"

"He's coming round."

"And the old man?"

"I've given him some brandy, but he's very upset."

"Sounds like you're doing all the right things, Anne. Look, ring Mr Fletcher's family and get someone to pick him up. Ask for someone to stay with you and Mr Hughes till I get back. I'll be about twenty minutes." She rang off and did as Ralph had said. Randall Hughes was still not fully conscious and the marks on his neck were becoming increasingly dark and livid.

"I wanted to atone," said the old man, putting a hand on Anne's shoulder. He closed his eyes. "I could not believe what I did ... such a wicked thing ..."

"You don't have to tell me, Mr Fletcher. It's all right. Talk about it when you feel better."

"No, no. I want to tell you. I *have* to tell you. You're a good girl, Anne. When I saw you come in, I thought you were her ..." He raised his eyes towards the beam.

Anne wondered who he meant. "What you did was very good, Mr Fletcher."

The farmer shook his head. "No. I desecrated the gravestone ... smashed it to pieces ... a dreadful sin ... and I damaged the car ... took the photos from the boat..." He hung his head. "Her gravestone ... her who hanged herself." Anne stared up at the beam, at the hook that hung near her desk, where she worked every day, under the loft where she slept every night.

"Never mind," she said with difficulty. "No harm's been done and you've saved Mr Hughes. I think that pays it back, don't you?"

The old man looked intently at her face. "You don't know who killed the vicar, do you?"

"No," said Anne. "I've no idea. Do *you?*"

"No ... but I know it wasn't *him*." He looked down at Randall.

Anne was shocked that anyone could have suspected him. "Of *course* not," she said.

"He's not a bad man ... just wanted different things." The old farmer searched Anne's face with a desperate stare. "You can't go on hating for ever ... it's wrong ... evil."

"I know. You're right."

"God forgive us ... and God bless you, my dear child." Anne was relieved to hear the Land Rover pull into the yard. She helped the old man to his feet as Leonard Fletcher and Molly Appleton rushed into the barn.

"Thanks for phoning me. I picked Molly up on the way down. Maureen's busy with the kiddie."

Molly knelt beside Randall and loosened his collar. She dampened a tea towel at the sink and applied it to his forehead. He groaned. "Leonard, you take your dad off home. We'll be all right."

"What happened, exactly?" said Leonard. Anne pointed to the belt hanging from the beam.

"Your father cut him down." She picked up the knife, closed the blade and handed it to Leonard.

"Have you phoned the police?" he said.

"No. Only you. Ralph said just to phone you."

"It's just ... for everyone's sake ... it may be better not to ..."

"I know," said Anne. "Don't worry. Ralph will do what's right."

Randall began to come round after the two men had left. He grimaced and raised a hand to his neck, swallowing painfully. Molly put her hands on his shoulders.

"Just lie still for a bit, vicar," she said. "You've had a nasty shock." His eyes opened slowly, and focused on the belt hanging above him. Molly turned the damp cloth on his head. "Just take it gently."

"He's going to be okay, isn't he?" said Anne.

"He'll mend. We don't want any more unhappiness in this village. We've had our share."

"We don't need to tell anyone, do we?" said Anne.

"That may depend on what your friend says. But I think Leonard was right."

Minutes later Ralph arrived. Anne gave him an account of everything that had happened. Molly sat on the floor beside Randall, who was now awake.

Ralph took Anne to one side and spoke softly. "Anne, what do you know about Mr Hughes?"

"He's been in hiding."

"You mean from the police?"

"I suppose so ... from everyone."

"He's a suspect?"

I don't know. I do know Marnie's been very worried about him."

"Did she think he was dangerous?"

"Only to himself. He told Marnie it was all his fault ... that he let Toni down."

"And Marnie wasn't afraid of him? You're sure of that?"

"Absolutely. I think she was afraid he might do something like this. I'm sure she didn't blame him. Nor does Mr Fletcher." She looked at Randall, resting on one elbow, rubbing his neck. "Nor do I."

"I see." Ralph thought hard.

"If Marnie was here," said Anne, "I know she'd help him. She thinks he's suffered enough already."

Randall spoke softly, his voice unsteady. "Where is Marnie?"

Ralph knelt down beside him. He put his hand on Randall's shoulder. "Why did you do this?"

"God knows ... or perhaps he doesn't. I thought I could atone in some way for what I did. If I hadn't told Toni not to report the vandalism to the police, she'd be alive today."

"Do you know who killed her?"

"I truly have no idea."

Ralph looked at Randall intently for some seconds. "How do you feel?"

"Foolish is the short answer." His voice was hoarse.

"Are you in pain?"

"Discomfort."

"Do you know the police are searching for you?"

"Oh, God. I really couldn't face anybody."

"They know where you were ... or at least, they have a pretty good idea."

"Pity. I'd rather not ..." He swallowed. "I'd rather not be seen by them in my present state."

"No," said Ralph. "I understand. It's a pity you couldn't disappear temporarily."

"I couldn't agree more."

Ralph offered Randall the remains of the brandy and held the glass while he sipped. Randall coughed. Ralph said: "Do you know Murton?"

"Village outside Oxford?" said Randall.

"That's it. My cottage is there. It's quite secluded, all by itself down near the river. It's the sort of place I might offer to a friend while I was away, a friend who needed a break to think things over."

Randall considered the implications. "You're not going to call the police?"

"What for? It wouldn't help matters. Under stress this could happen to anyone."

"You have no idea," said Randall, "what a comfort it is to hear you say that."

"We'd better act quickly." Ralph outlined his plan. Randall's car was concealed in a barn not far away. He would stay at Molly's house until nightfall and she would drive him to the barn. Randall would go on minor roads to Ralph's cottage and make himself at home there.

"Act surprised if you get a sudden visit from the police," said Ralph.

Randall was incredulous. "How on earth would they know I'm there?"

"I shall tell them," said Ralph. "That's the whole idea."

"You'll tell them," Randall muttered vaguely. "I see ... yes, of course. Sorry. Brain's not working."

"What about food?" said Molly. "Why don't I put together some things for you?"

"That seems a good idea," said Ralph, taking the cottage key from his key-ring. "The important thing is to avoid main roads. You know the area. Tell me, are you fit to drive?"

"Oh yes," said Randall, smiling weakly. "I'm a new man."

"Good," said Ralph. "Now we really must get on our way. Ring me on Marnie's mobile if you need to. I'll have to remember to drop you casually into the conversation when the opportunity arises."

Anne quickly wrote the mobile number on a slip of paper and gave it to Randall. "I must get dressed," she said and made for the loft.

"My special thanks to you, Anne," said Randall. "I'm sorry you had to be involved in all this. By the way, where is Marnie? You didn't say."

"Molly will explain after we've gone. I won't be a minute, Ralph." Turning to climb the ladder, she hesitated and looked back at Randall. "You must make sure no-one sees those marks on your neck."

"Don't worry. A dog-collar can hide a multitude of sins."

❦   ❦   ❦   ❦

Beth came back to Marnie's bedside, tucking the used phonecard into her wallet. "I spoke to mum," she said quietly to Paul. "Apparently dad's in a terrible state. I didn't want to worry her, but I told her they'd better get here as soon as possible."

Neither she nor Paul noticed the nurse coming up until she was beside them. "Excuse me, can I ask if you'll be wanting to stay in the guest room again tonight?"

"If that's possible," said Beth.

"It's fine, only we've got someone coming in from out of town and the family will need a room. We only have three rooms and we're going to be full tonight, I'm afraid."

"I see," said Paul. "We'd better talk to Ralph."

"Is that Dr Lombard?" said the nurse.

"That's right."

"If you see him before I do, will you tell him the police want to talk to him? It's Sergeant Marriner."

"He wants to see Ralph this evening?"

"No. He's gone, but he said he'll be here tomorrow morning."

"Here he is now," said Paul. Ralph and Anne walked in, pale and tired.

The events at Glebe Farm had exhausted Anne, and Ralph was running on reserve. The nurse gave him the message while Anne kissed Marnie on a part of her face that was not covered with tubes and sat down beside her.

"That's good," said Ralph. "I didn't want to see them before tomorrow if possible."

"Of course. You must be exhausted." said Beth.

"That," said Ralph, "and other reasons I'll explain some time."

"Ralph, we have a problem – no, not with Marnie. There's only one guest room available tonight."

"We're going to be full, I'm afraid," said the nurse.

"Perhaps Paul and I can go to a B and B ..." Beth began.

Anne stood up. "It's okay. Unless you think we ought to stay, we can go back to Glebe Farm."

"Officially, I think we still regard *you* as a patient," said the nurse. "But I don't think anyone will object to you going home. We have a number and can reach you if we have to."

❦   ❦   ❦   ❦

Leonard Fletcher came into the kitchen where his wife was laying carefully folded sheets on one of the shiny lids of the Aga. The room smelled of warm, fresh cotton.

"How is he?" she said.

"Asleep. As soon as his head touched the pillow, I think. Out like a light."

"Do you think he's all right? When you brought him home, he looked shattered. And he's not been himself for a while."

"Oh yes, he's all right now. I haven't seen him so settled for a long time."

❦   ❦   ❦   ❦

The meeting room at the police station was stuffy and hot, the air stale and smoke-laden. DCI Bartlett seemed to have aged in the past week.

"Any questions?" he said to the group of officers sprawled around the room.

"If there's no evidence, sir, why are we holding Day?" It was a young DC on his first murder case.

"Good question. We're going over all the facts again ... probably release him in the morning. Anything else?" No-one spoke. Bartlett dismissed the team. Only Marriner remained in the room.

"Not a lot to show for our efforts, sir," he said. "Is that why we're keeping Day in?" Bartlett nodded. Cathy Lamb looked in.

"I've rung the hospital," she said. "No change. They won't say what her chances are. 'Ask us tomorrow' is the best I could get."

"Tomorrow ..." said Bartlett.

"We'll get over to the hospital," said Marriner, "have another talk with the girl and see Dr Lombard."

"I'll probably join you there," said Bartlett. "I've got a meeting with Bragg and the ACC first thing."

"Well, let's hope things start to go our way tomorrow," said Marriner.

"What the hell's become of Hughes?" said Bartlett. "He's disappeared into thin air. I'm sure he's the key to all this ..."

❦   ❦   ❦   ❦

Randall arrived at Murton around eleven o'clock after a zig-zag journey over unmarked roads. The cottage was old and beamy with chintz covers on the sofas and shelves of books everywhere. Surrounded by trees and a slightly over-run cottage garden, it was sheltered from view at the end of a narrow country road.

Randall had parked under a rose-covered carport and let himself in at the back door. Despite the warmth outside, the thick walls made the interior of the house chilly and Randall opened windows to let the building breathe.

Ten minutes after arriving, having switched on the immersion heater for a bath and put on the kettle, Randall sat on a sofa in front of the inglenook fireplace. This was what he needed more than anything, peace and solitude, space, time to think. The pain in his neck was unpleasant, the skin sore from the chafing of the belt against his throat and an ache at the top of his spine from the pressure of hanging. He closed his eyes at the thought of it. In the kitchen he could hear the kettle switch itself off. He opened his eyes and looked down at his hands. They were firm and still.

He put his palms together and slipped down from the sofa to kneel on the floor. In his prayers he remembered the people of Knightly St John down the centuries and asked for their souls to rest in peace. He prayed for Toni Petrie and asked for forgiveness for his part in her tragedy. He prayed for Albert and Molly, for Anne and Ralph, who had all helped him towards a new start. Kneeling there in the quiet cottage, he did not know that a word of prayer for Marnie would not have gone amiss. In their haste to be away, he had forgotten to ask Molly why Marnie had not been there that evening.

⚘   ⚘   ⚘   ⚘

By eleven o'clock that night, Ralph was feeling mesmerised from looking up at the instrument panel beside Marnie's bed. Anne had been in her usual position, resting her head near Marnie's, talking to her quietly, threatening her with even more lists when she was better. It was Beth who came up from a break in the canteen and told them it would soon be impossible for Ralph to drive, and Anne would fall asleep where she sat. They agreed to go back to Glebe Farm, while Beth promised to sit with Marnie till midnight and return again as early as she could in the morning.

"Will you be all right to drive?" said Anne as they got in the car.

"As long as you talk to me on the way and don't let me nod off."

"It's my best talent. Hadn't you noticed?"

"Actually," said Ralph, "since that shower and the change of clothes, I feel more human, but I'll certainly be glad to rest my limbs." They pulled out of the car park and turned south.

"You know," said Anne, "I can't help wondering what made Marnie go out by herself like that, without saying anything to me."

"You were in your room in the barn, weren't you? And you were waiting for Frank Day to turn up."

"Yes, but we were going to talk together. I just can't understand it. The whole point was to hear what he had to say. It doesn't make sense."

"You don't think he could've rung again and asked Marnie to meet him at the church?"

"Maybe ... only I don't think Marnie would've gone without saying anything. She was so careful about us not being alone after the business of the gravestone and the photos being stolen ..."

"Well, something made her leave in a hurry. Perhaps we'll never know what it was ..."

"Don't talk like that!" The sudden vehemence of Anne's cry made Ralph jump. The car swerved and he had to struggle to regain control. "Oh Ralph, sorry, sorry, I'm so sorry, I didn't mean ..."

"No, it's okay. I'm the one who should be sorry. I didn't mean it like that ... of course I didn't ..."

"I'm just *so* tired," said Anne. "My nerves are all on edge. So are yours, I know.

You must be absolutely shattered. I'm really, really sorry." She reached across and put her hand on his arm.

He placed a hand over hers. "I know. We're both sorry and we're both tired and we're both on the same side. I'll tell you something else. Marnie could never have a better friend than you."

"Or you, Ralph. She couldn't have a better ... well, you know ..."

"Yes, I know ... And we'll be able to think more clearly when we've had some sleep."

"I'll write a list of points tomorrow, shall I?"

"I rather thought you might. And the first one will be a question. What did Marnie find that made her go out by herself? When we get near an answer to that, we'll be starting to get on the right track."

As good as her word, Anne kept up the conversation all the way back to Knightly St John. She told him about the plans for Glebe Farm and her own ambitions to go to college and train as a designer. Ralph enjoyed listening to her. It brought him closer to Marnie and her life. He felt the comfort of a child hearing a favourite story. If only it could have a happy ending ...

When they pulled into the yard the security lights came on. Anne pulled the torch out of her bag. "Shall we check *Sally Ann*?" she said. "I expect Dolly will want feeding. I hope she doesn't feel neglected." True to form, Dolly came trotting along the roof of the boat, warbling a greeting laced with more than a hint that a night-cap saucer of milk would be acceptable. In the galley, Anne obliged and added some cat biscuits for good measure. Purring filled the cabin. "Marnie used to say ..." Anne corrected herself. "Marnie says that's her favourite sound. Would you like something, Ralph?" She put a finger on the top of the brandy bottle that was standing on the work-surface.

"For medicinal purposes, perhaps?" he said. Anne brought out a brandy goblet from the cupboard and poured a glass. She fetched herself a mineral water and they sat at the table.

"Plan for tomorrow?" said Anne.

"Back to the hospital first thing. Also, I want to talk to Frank Day at some point. Is there anything you have to see to here?"

"I'll need to talk to the bank about paying the builders. There's a payment due this week. Could you help me with that, Ralph? I think the bank manager will pay more attention to you."

"Of course."

They were both aware of their fatigue. Anne was propping up her chin. She yawned and blinked her eyes. "I'm not sure I want to go back to the barn tonight," she said.

"No," said Ralph. "Is it locked up?" Anne nodded. "Would you like first go in the bathroom?" She nodded again and stood up wearily. In minutes she emerged wearing the white bath robe.

"I'm not a very good hostess," she said drowsily. "I ought to be looking after you."

"Don't worry. You're doing well."

Anne sat on the bed and ran a brush over her short hair. Ralph got up and took the brush from her. He swung her feet up onto the duvet, pulling it over her as he had done before. He kissed her on the forehead. She smiled and was already asleep as he turned back to the saloon.

🌷 🌷 🌷 🌷

Wednesday 9 August

"Are you sure you've had enough sleep?" said Anne. Ralph was folding up the camp bed in the saloon. It was the most primitive device he had ever seen.

"This," he said, "is more luxurious than the Savoy, the Ritz and the Dorchester put together. I can't remember the last time I slept so well."

"Oh, good. I'll just ring the hospital and then I'll make breakfast." Ralph had a quick luke-warm-hot-cold shower. Anne set the table outside so that he had space to dress.

"Ralph!" she shouted from the aft deck. "She's awake! She's come round!" Ralph dashed out to find Anne perched on the stern rail, gasping for breath like a marathon runner, her cheeks flushed. Weakly she handed him the phone. Worried that she might faint, he put an arm around her.

"Hallo. This is Ralph Lombard. Is she all right?"

It was the Australian nurse. "On the mend, Dr Lombard. We reduced the sedation early this morning and she began to regain consciousness about two hours ago. We're going to do some more X-rays. I must stress, she's not out of danger yet, but things are looking better."

"Is she in pain?"

"I'm afraid she is at the moment, but we can keep that under control."

"Can we see her?"

"Of course, but not just yet. We've got a lot to do."

"And you don't want us in the way, of course. When would you suggest?"

"If you could leave it until about noon, that would help a lot."

Ralph thanked her and gave the news to Anne. "You've gone pink," he said.

"*You've* gone white." They stood and hugged each other.

Ralph had not taken his first sip of coffee before the list of the day was in progress. Between noting down the items, Anne bit her lip, smiled, sighed and shook her head. Her world was starting to come together again. After toast and coffee they set about their tasks. Anne prepared a letter on the word-processor explaining about Marnie to send to all their friends and colleagues. Ralph had just finished a call to his college when the phone rang in his hand.

"Who is this, please?" The voice was hesitant, subdued.

"Ralph Lombard. I'm a friend of Marnie. And you?"

"It's Frank Day. I wanted to ask Anne if there was any news about Marnie."

"She's getting better, Mr Day. She's conscious. We're hoping things will be all right."

There was a pause at the other end of the line. "Thank God ..."

"Are you okay?" said Ralph. "You sound fatigued. I was rather hoping to talk to you."

"I haven't slept." His voice was almost a whisper. "I've been worrying all night, in the police station. They've just let me go. I'm so relieved ..."

"We all are."

"I must tell you I had nothing to do with what happened to Marnie. You must believe that."

"You didn't see anyone there, anything suspicious?"

"I've told the police everything I know. I just ran out to phone for help. My mobile was dead, so I went to the call-box. When I got back there were people coming from the pub. I suppose I panicked."

"Perhaps we can talk when you're feeling better," said Ralph.

"Yes. I'll be in touch."

Anne was humming to herself as she printed the letters and licked the stamps for the envelopes. She made them into a neat pile and ticked that item on her list. "There's just the bank now," she said. "And I'll make coffee for the builders before we go." Ralph was glad to see Anne looking so happy, flitting about the office barn as if she had wings on her heels. For that moment he did not want to spoil Anne's elation, but they would have to stay vigilant. At the back of his mind a voice was telling him not to drop his guard. The problem had not gone away. This was only a temporary reprieve from the horror that had fallen on the village once again. The murderer was still at large.

❦   ❦   ❦   ❦

Marriner looked at his watch for the hundredth time. Ten past eleven. Everyone was determined to thwart their progress on this case. At the hospital no-one would even give him an idea of when he could speak to Marnie. The girl, who was supposed to be a patient, had been allowed to go home. The medics had told Ralph Lombard to stay away for the whole of the morning. It would be typical of this case if Bartlett rang him from the ACC's office and demanded an update on progress. He rang in and asked for any news on the search for Randall Hughes. Nothing. *Not a bloody thing.*

"How about coffee?" said Cathy Lamb. "I don't think there's anything useful we can do here." On the way to the lifts they met Anne and Ralph walking quickly towards them.

"Mr Lombard?" said Marriner. "I'd like a word with you, please. You got my message yesterday?"

"Yes, I did," said Ralph without stopping. "Excuse me. I'll be with you in a minute."

Marriner's jaw dropped. "I don't believe this," he muttered to Cathy. "Anyone'd think I was invisible." He hurried after them and almost caught up as they reached the doors to the ITU, confident that he had them cornered. "You won't be able to go in there. It's locked." Anne quickly pressed four buttons on the keypad and pushed the door wide enough for her and Ralph to slip through. Marriner was caught wrong-footed and, by the time he reached the door, it had locked itself again.

"*Jesus!*" he clenched his fists at his side. "Did you see what numbers she pressed?" Cathy shook her head. "*Bugger it!*" He pressed the bell. At the end of the corridor, Anne and Ralph turned the corner. "I could have him for obstructing our enquiries. *Bloody cheek,* walking past me like that!"

He was still muttering a minute later when Cathy pointed down the corridor. Ralph was returning. "Didn't you know I wanted to talk to you urgently?" Marriner began. Ralph raised a hand.

"Of course. I'll do all I can to assist you, but first things first. You are Sergeant Marriner, I take it?"

"Yes. And I want to talk to you and the girl. Now."

"Her name is Anne, Anne Price. She needs a moment or two with Marnie. Talk to me first."

"I *hope* I'll get some co-operation."

"Of course. I didn't mean to be rude, but we have a lot on our mind. I know you do, too. You look as if you could do with a cup of coffee, sergeant. Come on." For the second time that morning Marriner found himself chasing Ralph. At the lift, Ralph turned to Cathy and held out his hand. "Ralph Lombard. We haven't been introduced." He spoke as if they were attending a college dinner or an embassy reception. Cathy needed all her willpower not to laugh and did not dare look in the direction of her sergeant, who was struggling to regain his usual calm.

"Cathy Lamb. Detective constable." She smiled charmingly and shook his hand. Marriner rolled his eyes and took a deep breath.

In the canteen, Ralph bought them coffee and biscuits and chose a quiet table. Marriner's temper subsided and Ralph gave him his absolute attention. In response to Marriner's questions, he gave a succinct account of his movements since leaving Seattle, but omitted the incident involving Albert Fletcher and Randall Hughes. Cathy Lamb took detailed notes in shorthand.

"Thank you for that, sir," said Marriner. "You've been very helpful." Cathy closed the notebook.

"I haven't finished," said Ralph. Cathy flicked open the pad.

"You have something else to tell us, sir?" Marriner waited while Ralph composed his thoughts.

"You will find this strange, sergeant, but what I'm going to tell you seems to me to have a bearing on your enquiries. I must ask you to be patient while I explain." Ralph began to outline the events that had taken place in the Civil War. He told them about the unsolved murder, the will, Fellheimer's research notes, the suicide of Sarah Anne Day and the finding of her headstone. Cathy wrote quickly and carefully, occasionally hesitating over an unfamiliar word, once asking him to repeat the reference for the Bible quotation. At the end, Ralph folded his arms.

"That seems weird," said Marriner. "What could a murder committed all that time ago have to do with the murder last week?"

"That is precisely why Marnie did not want to talk about it. No-one wants to seem a fool, especially a young professional woman talking, if you don't mind me saying this, to a middle-aged man."

"They can't be connected," Marriner said quietly. "It's impossible."

"You thought the vandalism to the gravestone was connected," said Ralph. "Perhaps it was part of the same thing. Old animosities, bigotry, prejudice ..."

"Yes, but that was a recent crime. Mind you, we've found no trace of the headstone ..."

"It's hidden in the builder's rubble at Glebe Farm," said Ralph. "Marnie and Anne put it there. You'll find it at the back of the main farmhouse."

Marriner looked startled. "Why didn't she tell us any of this?"

"She was going to, but before she could do so, she was nearly murdered. Nearly but not quite, by the look of it this morning ... Tell me, sergeant, do you have a prime suspect?"

The sudden change of direction caught Marriner off guard and he struggled to find the right words. "That's really a matter ... not the sort of thing we can ... you understand, sir."

"So you don't have one," said Ralph. "I see. Anne suspected as much."

Marriner looked unsettled. "We're investigating a number of leads at the moment and we're still trying to contact Mr Hughes," said Marriner. "You've not mentioned him ..."

"Hughes?" said Ralph innocently. "Randall Hughes, the former vicar of Knightly?"

"Yes. Did you know him?"

"Of course. We met at a village event several weeks ago. We got on quite well."

"He's gone missing," said Marriner.

"No, he hasn't."

Marriner gave a start. "What do you mean? We've been searching everywhere for him. I expect you'll know where we can find him as well, sir?" There was an edge of irony in the tone.

"I can give you his precise address," said Ralph. He turned to Cathy. "Shall I spell it for you?"

※　※　※　※

Strangely, seeing Marnie half conscious was almost worse than when she was lying as still as a corpse on the white sheets. Ralph could sense her suffering now that they were letting her come round. Her serenity had gone, the statue stillness had been replaced by restless movements, her freedom limited by the tubes and dressings. Worst of all, she tried to smile when she saw him and for some seconds he could not find words to speak. He sat beside her and kissed her hand, too frightened to touch any other part for fear of breaking something. Anne was sitting as if in a trance.

"Marnie, oh Marnie." He held her hand as firmly as he dared. In the corner of his eye he saw the tracks of tears on Anne's face. He put his free hand on hers. "We will find who did this," he said.

"Yes, we will," said Anne falteringly. "I promise you, Marnie."

❦　❦　❦　❦

"I really don't think it's a good idea," said Dr Morton.

Marriner sighed loudly. "Doctor, we are trying to find who did this. We need a break and every minute could count. I wouldn't ask if it wasn't vital."

Morton sat thinking. "I doubt if she can help you at this stage. She's suffered severe concussion; she's lucky not to have broken her skull. Strictly speaking, she's not off the danger list yet."

"All the more reason for letting us see her," Marriner insisted. Morton frowned.

"I will have to be present," he said. "You'll leave the moment I tell you. Is that understood?" He led them into the unit and explained to Ralph and Anne, Beth and Paul what he had decided. The three adults moved away to give the police space by the bed. Only Anne remained where she was. Marriner cleared his throat by way of introduction. Anne raised a finger and leaned forward.

"Marnie," she said. "Marnie, are you awake?" There was a slight turn of the head towards her. The eyelids flickered. "Listen, it's the police, Sergeant Marriner. He wants to ask you something."

He kneeled down beside her. "Mrs Walker," he said softly. "Do you know who did this to you?" Marnie's eyelids flickered again and her breathing quickened, but she made no attempt to speak. Across the bed, Morton shook his head at Marriner.

"Ask me," Anne said. He whispered in her ear. She looked surprised. "Marnie, was it Frank Day? Did he do this?" The eyelids flickered again and this time Marnie's mouth started to move. She licked her lips and Anne moved in closer.

"What did she say?" said Marriner.

"She said 'there' … or it might have been 'not there'."

"Is that all? What does that mean?" said Marriner. "Ask her was it Randall Hughes."

Anne glared at Morton before relaying the question. "She said 'no'."

"Are you proposing to try the name of everyone in the village?" said Morton. Marriner ignored him.

"Ask her if she saw who did it." This time, Marnie began to whisper without Anne's intervention.

Anne turned to Marriner. "She said 'yes'!"

"Who was it?" said Marriner, straining forward.

Anne listened and turned back. "She said 'no'."

"No? But she just said …"

"I think it means she can't remember," said Anne.

"That's all you're going to get for now," said Morton. "She's too tired to be able to help you. That's what she means."

❦　❦　❦　❦

The two police cars pulled into the lane blocking it completely. Bartlett led the way to the front door, sending three constables round the back of the cottage, with a fourth standing beside him on the path. He knocked on the door. There was a sound of movement from inside and Bartlett braced himself. The door opened and Randall Hughes appeared. Wearing his long black cassock, complete with dog-collar, he looked surprised but otherwise at ease, holding a green plastic watering can.

"Good morning," he said affably. Bartlett eyed him warily and held up his warrant card.

"Detective Chief Inspector Bartlett, Northamptonshire CID."

"Randall Hughes. How do you do. This is unexpected. Won't you come in? I was just watering the plants in the conservatory. Would you like some tea?"

❦   ❦   ❦   ❦

Marnie spent much of that day undergoing further tests to determine the full extent of her injuries. She grew weary of being told how lucky she was, especially as every breath caused her pain.

Anne spent as much time as was allowed sitting beside her, no longer keeping up the constant words of encouragement, but simply being there. Each time Marnie woke, her first sight was Anne. Ralph phoned the bank, the builders, the brewery, suppliers, everything needed to keep Marnie's world moving. Anne had given him a list. Beth and Paul were on standby to fetch parents from the airport.

❦   ❦   ❦   ❦

Marriner and Lamb returned to the police station in Towcester for a meeting with Bartlett who had 'invited' Randall Hughes to come with him for a 'discussion'. Borrowing a friend's cottage for a few days and forgetting to leave a note for the cleaning lady was not yet an indictable offence, but Randall agreed to accompany the police in his own car. The fact that some of his property, namely a sleeping bag, had been found in the vicarage was one further regrettable example of his forgetfulness. The excellent condition of the plants at Ralph's cottage were a testimony to his caring nature.

"So you were in no way involved in the murder of Toni Petrie?" said Bartlett.

Randall's face clouded over. "I cannot, in all honesty, say that. I am partly to blame for her death."

Bartlett and Marriner exchanged glances. "Would you like to explain that statement, sir?" said Bartlett. Cathy Lamb waited, pencil poised over her notebook.

"It was on my advice that she said nothing to the police about the vandalism. If the two incidents are connected in any way, I bear part of the guilt. We neither of us wanted any scandal in our new jobs." He looked down at his lap. "I am ashamed of my behaviour. It was selfish and unforgivable."

"And that is why you wanted to go away for a few days," said Bartlett.

"Yes," said Randall truthfully. "I needed time to think and pray ... time to repent."

"And Dr Lombard allowed you to use his cottage to complete your repentance?"

"No. That's not strictly true," said Randall. "I shall never *complete* my repentance, as you put it. I shall go on repenting for the rest of my life."

❦   ❦   ❦   ❦

"What will you do now?" said Anne. Ralph steered out of the hospital car park and pointed his car in the direction of Knightly.

"That rather depends on you," he said. He looked at the dashboard clock. Two-forty-five.

"You must have important things to attend to, Ralph. I'll be all right at home if you have to get back to Oxford. We can meet later."

"Mid-evening?" said Ralph. "They said she'll probably sleep until eight or nine. Suppose I come back at about seven?"

"Fine. I'll be home in time to see the builders and make their tea. I've got plenty to do."

"You'll put the mobile on charge?" said Ralph.

"Yes, I won't forget. I'll be okay."

"Promise?"

"I promise, Ralph. Don't worry about me. I'll be perfectly all right."

Part 28

Wednesday 9 August

Anne was in her element. She set about giving the office barn a thorough sorting out. She told the builders briefly what had happened and assured them she would see to anything they needed, including all payments. They promised to press on as before. She rang her parents and suggested they wait until the weekend before coming up to visit Marnie in the General. Within an hour of arriving, the office looked as it had been when they first came to Glebe Farm, apart from a pile of papers that Anne had collected from in- and out-trays for attention. At five she collected the tray of mugs from outside and waved the builders on their way up the dusty track in their old Transit.

She bundled the papers into a spare folder and pocketed the mobile phone. Time to turn her attention to *Sally Ann*. It took half an hour to make the interior of the boat as orderly as the office barn and Anne made a cup of tea while Dolly ate her supper. Settling herself at the table, she began to sift through the papers in the folder, putting them in piles for filing and action.

In the middle of the bundle she came upon an A4 pad that she had not noticed before. The cover had some of Marnie's doodles. The first pages contained sketches of the church and the porch from different angles. The drawings were annotated, and some of the pages had notes in more than one handwriting. With a pang, she recognised the small neat characters of Toni Petrie in a list of dates along with the bold angular writing of Mike Thomas. Anne made a note on her own pad to speak to Mike about the porch job. On the next few pages Marnie had written notes of her meetings with Toni to tackle the renovation: timetable, budget, action and so on.

The last meeting was the week before Toni died and Anne turned the page expecting that she had reached the end of the notes, only to discover that the writing continued. At first, she could not make sense of what she saw. There were names she did not recognise, dates copied from the church history booklet, the names of vicars at the time of the Reformation, question marks beside the gaps in the list, places where battles had been fought in the Civil War. Anne read on and found yet more notes, lists, questions. Suddenly she felt weary at the thought of reading the whole story again and she closed the pad, dropping it onto one of the chairs. She returned to sorting the office papers.

Anne poured a second cup of tea, and Dolly sat washing herself on Marnie's notepad on the chair opposite. All that remained now was a few odds and ends from her shoulder bag that she spread out on the table: leaflets about hospital visiting times, plans of parking areas, a form for donations to an equipment appeal. In among the papers she came across Beth's photographs.

Marnie had been a pretty child from a comfortable background, her father successful in business, her mother an art teacher. A secure home and a settled, happy childhood. Both sisters had set out to make careers for themselves and had succeeded. Anne wanted nothing more than to do the same.

She followed Marnie's growing up, from bicycle to pony to sailing dinghy to cars. She wondered about the racing car photo. Marnie had never mentioned this as an interest. The photo showed Marnie in a dark tunic, perched on the front wheel of a single-seater, helmet in her lap. Behind her stood Beth, smiling. Anne found the answer on the reverse: Marnie's 21st – Brands Hatch Racing School, a birthday present from her sister. Anne looked at the confident, intelligent face and saw no vanity, but a willingness to accept a challenge. She remembered Marnie saying that she believed in the Royal Marines school of management ... *take the high ground.* It was said with humour, but Anne had learnt the importance of taking the initiative and seeing a job through to the end.

❦ ❦ ❦ ❦

"That wasn't too bad, was it?" The nurse rearranged Marnie's sheets after changing her dressings. It had been a tiring process with every movement causing a pain in some part of her anatomy. Marnie smiled weakly, too weary to speak, her head still throbbing and the feeling of nausea never far away. They had told her she would feel dizzy for some days after losing so much blood, but they would be able to keep the pain under control. The fact that every part of her seemed to ache constantly made her realise at least that her systems were in working order. Marnie could see a window at the end of the unit. It was a fine day. She had no idea of the time and wondered what was happening at Glebe Farm, content for now to let Anne and Ralph handle things. She began to drift into sleep again, just as another nurse came to check her readings, one of the almost constant visits.

The nurse looked down at her and smiled. Marnie smiled back and gave a slight cough. The pain began in her chest and travelled round the inside of her head, across her back, down her spine and came to a temporary halt around the knees. Marnie hoped there would be no repeat performance for a while. The nurse entered some details on a graph. When she had finished writing, the nurse turned and adjusted the needle connecting the back of Marnie's right hand to a drip. She leaned forward to speak softly. "You know, Marnie, you're a *very* lucky lady ..."

Marnie tried to shout 'hooray!', but the words would not come.

❦   ❦   ❦   ❦

Ralph had picked up a bundle of post at the porter's lodge and walked round to his rooms on the first floor at All Saints. After opening the windows, he sat at his desk and was sorting his letters when the phone rang.

"Ah, you're back."

"Hallo, Randall. How are things? Are you okay? I was going to ring you."

"Much better, thanks. Look, I really don't know how to ..."

"There's no need. Please. You don't have to. Have you been contacted?"

"They came round this afternoon. I've just got back. Ralph, they told me about Marnie ..."

"Yes, an awful business. Narrow escape. So how was it?"

"Not such an ordeal as I feared, really ... I managed to tell the truth most of the time and I don't think I actually lied, just side-stepped some of the questions. They were obviously pissed off with me for having disappeared like that, but that's hardly a crime, is it?"

"No, it's not. And you're feeling better? You certainly sound better."

"A new man. I can't tell you how grateful I am. I never thought I'd owe so much to Albert Fletcher. Look, I'm sure you must be wanting your cottage back ..."

"Do you want to stay on for a while? You're very welcome. I'll be back at the hospital this evening and then probably at Knightly. I'm keeping an eye on Anne until things are sorted out."

"Well, if it's no problem. A day or two more would be great. I'm getting myself back together."

"Good. Be my guest. If there's anything you need, just help yourself."

"Ralph, I wanted to tell you I really have no idea who was responsible for what happened to Toni or to Marnie. It's a complete mystery to me. That wasn't why I tried to ..."

"I didn't think it was. The trouble is, I don't have a clue either and I don't think anyone else has, including the police."

After they had hung up, Ralph turned to his pile of letters and opened the first. It looked like a routine matter from the Senate of the university. He read the first sentence and his eyes widened.

❦   ❦   ❦   ❦

Anne emptied the rubbish into a black plastic sack and dumped it on the aft deck of *Sally Ann* ready for the skip. She felt restless and perched on the stern rail, watching the water, looking at the trees and brambles lining the canal. Everything was still, everything except her mind.

She wandered down into the cabin and through to the galley, opening the photo album on the bench. Here was Marnie in action. There, in the hospital, was Marnie the casualty. One often led to the other, Anne thought. Warriors were wounded; drivers crashed; sailors were shipwrecked. The difference between them and ordinary mortals was that they took action, took the high ground. So why had Marnie gone off like that? The reason came to Anne in a calm, clear voice speaking in her head. *Marnie had found the answer.* She wanted to resolve matters without waiting for anyone else to help her, or face danger with her, perhaps. She had gone for the high ground and it had nearly killed her. But w*ho* had tried to kill her?

Anne sat down with Marnie's pad and the file of papers. She had read through all the notes and was just starting on those she had not studied before, when she heard footsteps. Too early for Ralph. She froze, eyeing the meat tenderiser mallet on the workbench. A shape passed the window. She heard a footfall on the deck and felt the boat move gently at her mooring. Anne stood up.

"Anyone on board?" A man's voice, raised, strained, familiar.

"In the cabin," Anne called out. "Who is it?" The man came down the steps into the cabin.

"It's only me Frank I said I'd come and talk to you and Ralph. Is he here?"

"No, not at the moment." She hoped the anxiety would not show in her voice.

"Will he be long?" Anne was not sure how to handle this. Either way could be the wrong answer.

"I'm not sure, really. Can I give him a message? Get him to call you, perhaps?"

Frank stood still. He looked dejected, as if he had made an effort to get there. "I should've phoned first. I thought he'd be here. Silly of me. I didn't mean to intrude."

"No. That's all right. Ralph said you'd be in touch. He wanted to speak to you."

"Do you think I should wait? Would that be okay? I'll come another time if you'd prefer ..."

"Er, no. It's just that I'm not sure how long he'll be ..." This is getting ridiculous, she thought. Either tell him to come back later or ask him to stay. One thing or the other. Stop dithering. Take the high ground! "Would you like to wait for a while? I'll put the kettle on." She walked confidently to the sink. I'm out of my depth again, she thought. What had Marnie said? *Not there* or *there*? Behind her Frank sat down.

"I've disturbed your work," he said, looking at the papers on the table. "Sorry about that."

"It'll keep," she said. "Don't worry."

"It's funny," he began. "I've got loads of notes just like this, all about this horrible business."

"I'll tidy them away in a minute," said Anne fiddling with a match at the cooker.

"This is very thorough," said Frank turning some of the papers round to read them. "I didn't realise anyone could find the will and all these other things. How did Marnie do that?"

"She didn't. It was Dr Fellheimer at Oxford, at the university. He showed it to Ralph."

"There are loads of things I'd not seen before. All this Civil War stuff ..."

"Yes. I don't think I'd be very good at that kind of research." Anne brought the tea-pot to the table. "It's all very complicated." She reached into the cupboard and produced cups and saucers.

"I don't know," said Frank. "You're very organised. You could probably work it all out for yourself, Anne, if you had the time." There was something odd in his tone.

"Have *you* worked it all out?" Anne wished she had not spoken, as soon as she opened her mouth. She also wished Ralph would come back earlier than planned. She rummaged in the cupboard for the sugar bowl.

"Only so far," he said. "I know the name of the person who did it ... It was Day, of course."

Anne jumped and dropped the sugar bowl, spilling white granules all over the floor. "Sorry, Frank. That was clumsy of me. I haven't had enough sleep, I expect." She pulled out the dustpan and brush.

"I don't take sugar, actually," said Frank. "Are you sure you're okay? Oh look, you must have bumped into the table. There's tea on some of the papers." He took the tea towel from the front of the cooker and began mopping up. They finished and sat down, Anne wondering if her dizziness was caused by standing up too quickly. "I think we could both use some of that tea," said Frank. Anne poured two cups while he continued looking at Marnie's papers. "Are these your notes?"

"No. They're Marnie's."

"And these are her questions ... Let's see if we can answer them, shall we?"

"I'm not sure I'm up to it at the moment," said Anne.

Frank read the list in silence, as if he had not heard her. "This is good. Marnie's covered everything. You see, the logical person to have done it was Jonathan Day, Sarah Anne's father. The trouble with *that* theory is that he was miles away in Huntingdon, badly wounded. It's in his papers. He didn't leave much in his will because he was so badly injured, he could no longer work at his craft."

"Was he a stone mason?" Anne was taking interest despite herself.

"No. He was a blacksmith. The Days were the village blacksmiths for generations."

"*Blacksmiths?*" said Anne. "I don't understand ... why was he working on the tower?"

"What do you mean?"

"Well, we don't have anyone like that working on our building. That explains the bill from Jonathan Day ... *sundry ironwork* ... and the notes about his father working in the tower years before."

"Where did you get that from?"

"It's in Dr Fellheimer's papers. I've just read it." She shuffled through the documents and pushed one across the table. "There it is, you see. Marnie's put a question mark next to it. I couldn't understand about ironwork in the tower."

Frank studied the paper with intense concentration. "Why do you think it's odd?" he said.

"Well, what was there for a blacksmith to do? I can't make out why a blacksmith should be working in the tower at all."

"Because they were doing something to the clock mechanism, presumably."

"No," said Anne, "surely that was Sarah Anne's *grandfather,* about a hundred years before. What was her *father* doing in the tower? That's what I don't get."

"Yes," Frank muttered. "I see what you mean." He pulled the other papers towards him. "What does this mean, this here?" He pointed to a note in Marnie's handwriting: *Bob – pride in work, esp. for the Church.* And what about this: *wooden partition – why not done properly?* Who's Bob?"

"He's our foreman."

"So is this about your building work, then?"

"I don't think so," said Anne. "I hadn't seen that before. Or any of these notes."

"She's put a circle round it. She must have been thinking about it. And this *sundry ironwork* ... Marnie was asking herself the same question as you."

"Did Marnie know he was a blacksmith?" said Anne.

"I think I mentioned it to her at some point, yes." Frank was leafing through the papers and stopped at the will. "She's made a note here as well ... she's circled something after the signature ... It's very faint. I can't make it out. Your eyes are probably better than mine. Can you read it?"

Anne screwed up her eyes. "Try this," she said, reaching round for the magnifying glass.

Frank took it and held it over the document. "Ps 10.8. Can't be the date ..."

"Another Bible quotation?" said Anne.

"Of course!" said Frank. "Psalm ten, verse eight. It *must* be. We need a Bible." Anne reached over to the bookcase and produced the old paperback. Frank took it quickly from her hand.

"Have you got it?" said Anne.

Frank looked astonished. He sat there with his mouth open, his eyes working from side to side. He began breathing faster. "Yes, oh *yes*." His voice sounded strange, almost manic.

"What is it?" said Anne, with another quick glance towards the meat tenderiser mallet. Frank lurched to his feet, dropping the Bible under the table. *"Oh God! I see it ... I've got to stop him!"* He pushed the chair aside and rushed to the doors.

Anne called after him. "Who? *Frank! Who* have you got to stop?" He crashed up the steps. From the window she saw him running through the spinney. She saw again in her mind the terrified face at the church, the night Marnie was attacked. *What do I do? What do I do?* She reached down for the Bible, searched for the Psalms and thumbed her way through the thick book to Psalm ten, running her finger down to verse eight. How strange ...

8. He sitteth in the lurking places of the villages: in the secret places doth he murder the innocent.

She read no further. A cold hand seemed to have gripped her throat and her cheeks tingled. All her thoughts jumbled together, screaming at her to understand. The Bible text seemed to fly off the page into her face ... *the lurking places ... the secret places ...* the shoddy partition ... Bob not happy with substandard work ... especially for the church ... *sundry ironwork ...* a blacksmith in the tower ... *hateth my father also ...* who hated her father? ... why? ... was it guilt at something he'd done? ... *They hated me without a cause ... why? ...* Of course ... because it was *my father* who had done it ... *he* was the murderer! But *how* did he do it? Anne steadied herself at the table. Marnie must have worked it out. She went to the church, to find the secret place. Then who hid there had tried to kill *her*? ... Yes ... Yes ... The truth became clear. It was obvious.

"I was right all along," she whispered. But if the murderer could attack Marnie, he could kill Frank as well. Anne raced out and sprinted through the spinney, all thoughts of her own safety left behind in the dust from her heels. She came to a halt, gasping, at the top of the field track and willed herself to press on. She ran as fast as she could, ignoring her fatigue. Up ahead she could see Frank's car parked by the church gate, one door wide open, an indicator light still flashing. Wishing someone would come into the deserted street to help her, wishing she had a weapon, something solid to hold, she felt the mobile phone bumping in her pocket and realized that she was racing unprotected into a situation that had killed two people, nearly three.

She skidded round the gate, sliding on the gravel path, showering the grass with stones as she pitched forward. The church door was ajar and she hesitated a moment on the threshold, wondering if she should phone for the police, but by the time anyone arrived, it would be too late. It was probably too late already. Anne slipped into the building and raced towards the tower. As she approached, she could hear banging from high up. She took a deep breath and climbed the worn stone steps as quickly as she could. The noise of the banging grew louder, the mad, desperate hammering of a fist on wood. Frank seemed to be trying to smash the partition to pieces, but it was solid oak, hardened for four centuries ... *He sitteth in the lurking places of the villages: in the secret places doth he murder the innocent* ... Anne willed herself up the steps to the final bend. In this frame of mind he would take no notice of her! And he would be killed!

"Frank! Frank!" she screamed as loud as she could in the semi-darkness. Startled, Frank half turned, his arm still raised. The movement unbalanced him and he tottered on the loose step, grabbing at the air to save himself from falling, his hand seizing the stonework above his head. He did not see the partition swing open behind him, but Anne saw it and launched herself forward, grabbing him at the waist in a clumsy rugby tackle, pulling him on top of her, aware of a rushing sound above them as they crashed down onto the landing. The impact of the fall winded Anne and she struggled to free herself. Frank cried out in agony.

❦   ❦   ❦   ❦

Sergeant Marriner was getting ready to leave the station on his way to the hospital. In all his years of investigating crimes he had never reached a point where every line of enquiry had come to nothing. No murder weapon, no firm evidence, no prime suspect. Cathy Lamb knocked on the door and they walked down the corridor together. They scarcely spoke, both of them deflated, aware that Marnie's evidence was likely to be unreliable. Severe concussion rarely produced good witnesses.

"Do we know if she's actually awake, Cathy?"

"I rang ten minutes ago and she was sleeping. The nurse said she'd probably wake up this evening, but she couldn't say when."

"Another wild goose chase," Marriner muttered, "Still, we've got nothing else to go on."

"But if she saw who attacked her ..."

"*If* she did," said Marriner. "And *if* she can remember ... The way things are going on this case, I wouldn't be too optimistic ..."

"Sergeant Marriner!" An officer in shirt sleeves called from the door. He held up his hand to his ear, thumb and finger splayed, imitating a telephone. "Call for you, sarge. She says it's urgent."

"Who is it?" He wondered if this would be bad news from the hospital, after all.

"A girl. Anne Price. Very agitated."

Marriner feared the worst and hurried along the corridor. He picked up the phone. "Marriner." Cathy Lamb had followed him back and saw him frowning as he listened.

"Are you in danger? ... Right, we're on our way ... with you in ten minutes." He put the receiver down and barked orders at the duty officer. "Ambulance and paramedics – Knightly St John – the church – get Dodds and Bathurst to meet me there immediately – tell Bartlett. Got that?" He raced to the car park, Cathy doing her best to keep up, both of them relieved at last to have some action.

"What is it, sarge?" said Cathy breathlessly as they clambered into the car. "He's bloody struck again!"

❦   ❦   ❦   ❦

The ACC lit another cigarette. He had been going to give up for the umpteenth time before this case had come along. He offered the packet to Bragg who refused and Bartlett who accepted.

"You reckon he was hiding out at the vicarage all along, but now he has this alibi ... this convenient stay at Lombard's cottage ... but you don't believe it."

"No way," said Bartlett. "It must have been Hughes. It was his sleeping bag under the bed, his car in the garage. Not a word to his cleaner or the church authorities. People don't just vanish like that, unless they've got a particular reason."

"He said he had," said Bragg.

"Wanted time to pray. He lives next door to a bloody church! He could've prayed in there any time he wanted!"

"But there's no firm proof, is there?" said the ACC. "He could've left the sleeping bag at the vicarage. No-one can swear it *wasn't* there. Marnie Walker couldn't be certain it was his car in the garage. What about the neighbours at the cottage?"

Bartlett shook his head. "It's tucked away. No-one could be sure if he was there, or if it was him or Lombard. The place isn't overlooked."

"Well," said the ACC, "if he sticks to his story, true or not, Lombard's given him an alibi. And there's not much we can do about it." The phone rang. "Hallo? ... Yes, he's with me now ... go on ... *Christ!* ... I'll tell him." He put the phone down. "You'd better get over to Knightly straight away."

Bartlett stood up. "What's happened, sir?"

"Your murderer's been flushed out of the woodwork ..."

❦   ❦   ❦   ❦

Ralph had thought about ringing Anne before setting off from Oxford, but decided against it. Better to get on the road. He made good time and was ten minutes early as he drove down the high street and past the church. A few people were standing outside the pub talking, and he noticed a parked car and someone walking on the church path, otherwise all was quiet. Ralph was glad the village had at least the appearance of returning to normal.

A moment's apprehension came over him as he swung the car through the field gate. He had felt uneasy at leaving Anne and now wished he had phoned to see if all was well. He put the thought aside and was reassured at the sight of the rooftops and chimneys of Glebe Farm, against their backdrop of trees, homely and secure. It was a good place to come home to.

Ralph became aware that all was not as he expected when he caught a glimpse of a car boot protruding from behind the barns. It looked familiar and he tried to place it. Molly Appleton was standing in the yard. There was something odd about her, not fear or distress, but perhaps an unease. Ralph pulled up and got out quickly.

"Hallo, Mrs Appleton. I wasn't expecting to see you this evening."

❦   ❦   ❦   ❦

"You're getting to know the routine, I believe," said the nurse with a smile. Anne nodded wanly. The nurse continued. "Doctor will be here in a minute. We just want to check you over, see you're okay. Can you take off your top clothes in the cubicle and put on the gown."

Anne stood up and pulled off her T-shirt, dropping it on the back of her chair.

"Where's Frank?" She slipped out of her jeans, draped them over the chair and pulled on the gown.

"He's in radiology at the moment. We have to X-ray his leg."

"Is his ankle broken?" said Anne.

"Probably."

"He was in a lot of pain."

"We can control that, don't worry." There was a tap on the door and the doctor came in. He was a young man, Indian, wearing a turban, with a stethoscope slung over his shoulder.

"Anne Price, yes?" He spoke with a gentle voice.

"Yes."

"I'm Doctor Singh. I've come to see if you need treatment." He squatted on a chair opposite Anne and looked intently into her face. "What happened to you?"

"Frank fell on top of me on some stone steps."

"That's Mr Day?"

"Yes. He's being X-rayed. Do you know if he's all right?"

"He's fine. Don't worry about him. Let's concentrate on you."

"I'm okay."

"Where did he land on you? Can you show me." Anne pointed to her ribs.

"Let's have a look at you. Would you remove the robe and lie on the couch, please."

❦ ❦ ❦ ❦

When Ralph touched her hand, Marnie's eyes opened slowly and a smile spread across her face. He heard her breathing, saw her moisten her lips.

"Hallo," she whispered. Her voice was husky.

"Hallo, Marnie. Don't talk. Save your energy."

"What energy?" The smile returned. Ralph leaned forward and kissed her. She tasted of chemicals. A nurse came up silently and checked the readings, making the usual notes.

"How are you feeling, Marnie?" she said.

"Wonderful." This time it was a croak. Marnie cleared her throat and coughed.

"That's the anaesthetic," said the nurse. "We can get rid of the coughing, but it takes a while."

"I was expecting to find Anne here," said Ralph. Marnie looked surprised.

"She's downstairs," said the nurse. "She sent a message to say she'll be up in a minute or two." Marnie closed her eyes and the nurse made a signal to Ralph as she moved away. Ralph gave Marnie's hand a gentle squeeze and got up, following the nurse to the next cubicle.

She turned to him and spoke quietly. "Anne is in A and E, in casualty. As far as we know she has no injuries, but we always carry out a thorough examination in circumstances like this."

"Like what?" said Ralph. "I was just told she'd accompanied Frank Day in the ambulance."

"I really don't know more than that," said the nurse. "I was asked to pass on the message."

"Of course. Thanks. I'll find out from Anne. As long as she's all right ..."

"You'll have to get in the queue," said the nurse. "The police are waiting to question her as soon as she comes out of A and E."

❦ ❦ ❦ ❦

Dr Morton sat in silence for several seconds. Beth and Paul were by now accustomed to his manner and did not find the reaction to their question disconcerting. Morton drew breath audibly. "I would like to keep her here for two or three more days," he said with his usual deliberation.

"But you aren't worried about her?" said Beth.

"Not in the way you mean. On the other hand, a patient with such serious injuries always requires a great deal of care and I like to take no chances."

"Will she make a complete recovery?"

"As far as I can tell, she should return to full health. It may take time and she may have some discomfort for a while, the odd ache here and there. But once the ribs heal and the headaches subside, she ought to be as good as before ... and she *is* in good shape."

🌡   🌡   🌡   🌡

It was ten-thirty when Anne slumped into Ralph's car with a sigh. "It's been quite an evening for you," he said. "Let's take you home." The Volvo was old, but started at the first turn of the ignition.

"Just like *Sally Ann*," said Anne. "She always starts first time." They made their way out into the streets of Northampton and Ralph pointed the long bonnet towards the south.

"If it's all right with you, Anne, I'd like to stay at Glebe Farm tonight. I can go in the barn or stay on *Sally*, which ever you'd prefer. It's nice to think there's no danger any more."

"It's such a relief," said Anne. "To think that all that time, the murderer was there ... waiting ..."

"No wonder Bartlett and Marriner couldn't believe it," said Ralph. "It's the first time they've ever had the same murderer commit two crimes separated by three hundred and fifty years."

"Ralph ... do you think that's an end to it now? I mean ... all the hatred ..."

"Yes, I do."

"But what about Ireland?" she said. "You know Marnie often talks about the trouble there. It really upsets her. She says people shouldn't have to live in all that distrust and violence. I couldn't bear it. Perhaps it's the same in Knightly. Perhaps it never goes away."

"I think it's different here. Ireland is much more complicated, a bigger problem."

"But it's still people," said Anne.

"Yes. And the problem has persisted for generations. I'm sure one day things will change and everyone will want peace and be willing to work for it together."

"I hope you're right," she said.

So do I, thought Ralph. "Anne, things have changed in Knightly since Toni died. I think the village has suffered a severe shock to its system and things *will* be different from now on."

"Yes," said Anne. "I think Mr Fletcher has changed. Perhaps things will be better."

"That's my guess," said Ralph.

"You haven't asked me any questions about what happened," said Anne.

"You've been questioned enough for one day. You can tell me all about it when you're ready."

🌡   🌡   🌡   🌡

Thursday 10 August

It was a damp morning, one of those days in a long summer that warns of autumn coming. Moisture clung to every surface, dripping softly from the branches of trees in the spinney, outlining the webs of spiders, making the steelwork of *Sally Ann* glisten. It hung in a low faint mist over the surface of the canal and the air smelled of leaf mould and the good earth.

Dolly had not stayed in for the night, preferring to roam outside. With the sun rising through the trees, she stood at the doors of the aft deck and meowed. It was a long persistent call and was heard by both the occupants of the boat. Anne heard it first and woke quickly. She glanced in the direction of Ralph who was on the camp bed in the saloon and saw that he had not moved. At once she leapt out of bed, anxious not to disturb him. She moved quickly because in the night she had slipped out of her dressing gown under the warm duvet. She felt the cool damp air on her pale body as she pulled open the bolts and let Dolly into the cabin. Pausing only long enough to take in the scene around them, she pulled the doors together and sprang back onto the bed. She saw that Ralph had still not moved and pulled the covers over her, enjoying the warmth of her cocoon. The world felt a different place now that the long nightmare had ended. Anne smiled to herself under the duvet and began putting on the white cotton robe, ready to get up and start a new day.

In the saloon, Ralph lay on the rickety camp-bed, wondering if it would collapse if he turned too suddenly. It seemed less luxurious than it had on his first night. He had heard Dolly's cry to be let in and had woken fractionally after Anne, only propping himself up on his elbow as she was reaching for the bolts to the stern doors. He had seen her pale, thin form, remarking how childlike she looked, and he had felt a great fondness for her, for this waif, this slip of a girl who had shown such courage and who had ultimately led everyone to the solution of a mystery that had been unsolved for centuries. He lowered himself quickly and quietly onto the pillow and pretended to be sleeping. He heard Anne stand up from the bed and step into her trainers. She went up the steps and out onto the deck, wrapping the robe around her against the faint chill in the air. It was a few minutes before she returned, and as she stepped down into the cabin she called out in a singsong voice:

"It's gone seven, Ralph! The morning's half over!" She walked through to the galley as Ralph stirred. "That's what Mum always says, anyway ..."

"Very wise woman, your mum. Good morning, Anne." Ralph found himself face to face with Dolly, purring loudly, asking for breakfast.

For Anne, the magic of the place had returned and even the most ordinary of tasks, mopping the deck and setting the breakfast table, was pure pleasure. Anne's gaiety was infectious and Ralph drew strength and optimism from her happiness. Over breakfast she narrated the events of the previous evening while Ralph listened in silence.

"So that was it, really ..." said Anne. "It was Marnie's notes that made me, made *us* – Frank and me – understand what had happened. Bob had made her realise that no craftsman would have left a wooden screen in the church. They would only have done their best work and that meant stone, a proper wall like the rest. And that bill for *sundry ironwork* was another thing. Only stonemasons were working there. One thing I don't understand is why he should've put in a bill anyway."

"Perhaps it was to explain why he was there at all," Ralph suggested. "No-one was likely to query it. He was just another tradesman. If he hadn't put in a bill, it might have looked suspicious."

"Yes, I suppose so. But the really creepy thing was that quote from the Bible, the psalm. *He sitteth in the lurking places of the villages: in the secret places doth he murder the innocent.* It made me tingle all over. When I saw that, I realised that I'd been right all along. The murderer *was* hiding in the tower on the night the first vicar was killed and was there all the time, like a boobytrap waiting to go off. It was the blacksmith's ironwork. I wonder why they never removed the killing machine."

"Probably never had the chance," said Ralph. "Jonathan Day was too badly injured to be able to do it and he couldn't have involved anyone else. They'd have shared his guilt and his sin."

"But Sarah Anne found out," said Anne.

"Yes, probably while she was caring for her father when he came back from the war. It would've been an intolerable burden to know that her own father had committed the murder of a priest."

"So that's why she killed herself."

"Yes. Also Marnie had an idea that Sarah Anne might have had a special feeling for the vicar. That would have made matters even worse, quite unbearable."

"Yes, I can see that," said Anne. "But they were *all* in it, the whole village ..."

"I can't imagine they'd all agree with killing the vicar," said Ralph, "apart from a few extremists, perhaps." They sat drinking coffee, watching the sun rise, dispersing the mist and warming the air.

"I understand about the boobytrap," said Anne, "but I'm not sure about why it was there and why they thought the vicar would go there anyway. How did the blacksmith know it would work?"

"Do you know what a priest's hole is, Anne?"

"A hiding place ... Was it for catholic priests when they were being persecuted? We did a history project about Tudors and Stuarts at school. But that was a lot earlier ... Henry the Eighth's time ..."

"That's right. It must have been a priest's hole, originally."

"But then the vicar would know about it," said Anne.

"Which is why it was so dangerous. I believe the hiding place was created when the new clock was installed in the mid-fifteen hundreds. That was the same time that priests were in danger if they refused to accept the new order of the Church of England. The blacksmith at the time, one of the Day family, would have been involved in fitting the clock mechanism into the tower. They would have needed metal frameworks and so on. They must have built the priest's hole when they did that work."

"So that's all it was originally," said Anne. "Just a hiding place."

"Yes. And the church would have accepted a simple wooden partition as the door and no-one would see it from outside. It was a clever plan."

"So that meant only the church and the blacksmiths would know about it," said Anne. "So did the blacksmiths change sides?"

"Good question. You have to remember that many people were attracted to the new ways and many could not tolerate what King Charles was doing. In a civil war people decide where they stand according to their own beliefs, not according to where they live."

"I know what you mean. In the church leaflet it said that most of the village wanted the Roundheads to win, but the vicar and some of the others supported the Cavaliers."

"That's the point," said Ralph. "The last thing the village wanted was a traitor in their midst, someone who'd be able to get up to a high place and give signals to Royalist soldiers in the area."

"The top of the church tower!" said Anne.

"The only tall building, with a built-in hiding place that the vicar thought only he knew about."

"So the blacksmith turned it into a trap to murder him. That's really gruesome."

"Well, I suppose there was a kind of harsh justice about it. The vicar was only in danger if he betrayed the villagers. If he signalled the enemy and then tried to hide, he'd put *his* life at risk, just as he'd put the community in danger by helping the King's men."

"And that was how it happened."

"Yes. The vicar must've been seen signalling from the tower. He saw their torches and went to hide. The trap was sprung and he was killed, leaving no evidence of a murderer."

"Do you think the villagers only pretended they couldn't find anyone, or did they know all along?"

"Impossible to tell. I expect most of them had no idea how it had happened, and if anyone did, they were hardly going to admit it, in case they were accused of complicity and sent to the gallows."

"Jonathan Day knew, but he was wounded in Huntingdon," said Anne.

"A perfect alibi ... as long as no-one knew he had built the trap."

"So poor Sarah Anne killed herself out of shame ... Why did her father put that quote from the psalms after his signature?"

"Hard to say. It may have been his private atonement. There was no priest at the time who could hear his confession. The murder must have weighed heavily on his conscience."

"Now he has two murders to bear ... and it could've been three or four," said Anne sombrely. "I wonder how the machine worked. It must have been very clever to be working after all this time."

"That I don't know," said Ralph. "But I'm sure we'll find out soon enough."

❦ ❦ ❦ ❦

The talk in the village shop was of nothing but the events surrounding the discovery of the infernal machine. The murder of Toni Petrie had filled the village with a sense of horror that ancient hatred should have come back from beyond the graves of generations to infect their lives all these years later. Pauline Fairbrother called in after being turned away from the church by the young constable guarding the entrance.

"He told me I couldn't go in with the church flowers," she said, incredulous. "As if I was going to disturb anything. But he said no-one was allowed in until the place was declared safe. I've left the flowers in the porch for the time being."

"They have to go through the proper form," said George Stubbs, who had come in for his regular order of cigars. "Talking of flowers, can you order me some from Interflora, Molly? I want to send a bunch to Marnie Walker in hospital."

"You're the third this morning," said Molly.

"Can you make sure I don't send the same as the others then? Poor girl will be bored stiff if she just gets pink carnations all the time!" Molly pulled the catalogue from under the counter.

"You can choose whatever you want, Mr Stubbs, and I'll tell you if you clash with anyone else." She turned the catalogue round towards him.

"I saw Anne being driven back last night by that friend of Marnie's," said Mrs Fairbrother. "Is he staying down there?" There was an edge of disapproval in her tone.

George Stubbs looked up from the catalogue. "I hope so, Pauline" he said firmly. "I'm quite sure her parents would prefer her to be looked after by someone like that, what I would call a gentleman, rather than have her left on her own after all that's happened to her."

"Oh yes," said Mrs Fairbrother. "I'm sure you're right, George. Molly, have you got a suitable get-well card?"

❦ ❦ ❦ ❦

The police car cruised past the shop as they were talking and came to a halt by the church gate. Bartlett and Marriner got out and walked up the path. The air in the church was cool, and Marriner led the way up the steps of the tower. When they reached the wooden partition, they switched on the temporary light that had been set up and examined the hiding place. The partition had been jammed open with a block of wood, creating a gap large enough to allow inspection of the interior.

"I'm not going to get my bloody head chopped off if I stick it through here, am I?" said Bartlett.

"Probably not, sir," said Marriner cheerfully. Bartlett knelt down and peered in. "At least," Marriner went on, "if you do, it can only happen once ..." He could not quite make out the exact wording of Bartlett's growled reply, but he got the gist of it.

"*Christ almighty!*" Bartlett exclaimed. "Oh, bugger, I shouldn't say that here, should I? Have you had a look at this, Ted?"

"Just a quick dekko last night, sir, before the light was put in. I had a torch."

"Have a look now," said Bartlett, crawling out backwards with extreme care. "Mind you don't touch anything. It's *amazing* ... the *size* of it ... and to think it's been hidden away all this time."

Marriner looked in. "No wonder Frank Day got his ankle broken," he said. "He was damn' lucky the thing didn't get him."

"It would have if that girl hadn't been there," said Bartlett. "How did he come to get his ankle stuck in the door, anyway?"

"It seems she grabbed him as the thing sprang open and they fell in a heap. The blade missed him by a whisker, but when he fell, his leg flew up and the door slammed shut on it. That's how we were able to see in. The paramedics forced the panel open to get him free and kept it wedged with kneeling pads from the church. I've asked one of the builders from Glebe Farm to prize it open so we can see what needs to be done."

"When's he coming?"

"Any time now," said Marriner, looking at his watch.

❦ ❦ ❦ ❦

Bob the foreman saw Anne and Ralph coming through the spinney and went down from the first floor of cottage number one to meet them. "Are you all right, me dook?" he said to Anne. "We were worried when we heard what had happened."

"Worried there'd be no-one to make your tea?" said Anne with a smile.

"Something like that. The police were here first thing. They want me to have a look in the tower and see what's what. He said to tell you that only I was to come, nobody else. Strict orders."

"We're coming with you," said Anne, looking up at Ralph.

"That's what he said you'd say," said Bob.

❦ ❦ ❦ ❦

The further Bob crawled forward to see round the wooden panel, the further his trousers slipped down at the back. Anne had heard of the term 'builder's cleavage' and now, despite the initial nervousness she had felt at returning to the tower, it was all she could do not to laugh out loud.

Ralph noticed her expression. "Things are looking up," he whispered. Anne spluttered and began coughing to camouflage it.

Bob's voice boomed from beyond the panel. "*Bloody 'ell!* Oh, pardon my French! You should see this bug ... er, this thing ..."

"Can you see how it works?" Bartlett called out to Bob's behind.

"Hang on a minute. What's this here? Oh, yes, I see." There was a series of mutterings and Bob inched backwards out of the gap. Everyone present on the crowded landing watched his every move for any sign that the machine might swing into action.

"May I take a look?" said Ralph. Before Bartlett could stop him, he knelt and looked in, studying the mechanism in silence for some seconds. "It seems to be a system of weights and pulleys."

"That's right, me dook," said Bob. "If you wobble the top step and then pull that stone up there over your head, it moves back just a fraction. Can you see?"

"Yes," said Ralph. "It moves a lever out of its slot …"

"That's it," said Bob. "And then that big stone in the leather sling drops down and makes the door swing open while the scythe blade flies out."

"It swings like a pendulum," said Ralph. "It must go at a tremendous speed." He looked up at the blade above him and realised that the rusty stains on it included the blood of Toni Petrie. He shivered. "What makes it close again?"

"That's the clever part," said Bob. "There's another stone in another sling and it acts as a balance. When the blade swings back, the lever catches in the slot and shuts the door fast. You'd never know it had been opened."

"And before the blade system was put in, moving the stone would just be a simple way of opening the door," said Marriner.

Bartlett shook his head. "It's a miracle that no-one else has been killed by it over the years."

"Do you think so?" said Ralph. "After all, it was designed to be hidden, and very cleverly designed at that. We couldn't spring it despite all our deliberate attempts. The first vicar knew how to open the priest's hole. As for Toni …"

"Cruel luck," said Bob.

Bartlett nodded. "It's certainly a miracle that Mrs Walker survived."

The group stood in silence, contemplating the awful ingenuity and the horror that it had caused across the ages. Suddenly, Ralph became aware that Anne was no longer with them. She had slipped away without a sound.

"Excuse me." He set off down the steps.

Part 29

A week later Anne made her way up to the ward where Marnie was continuing to make a good recovery. Her parents had finally arrived from Spain and had stayed in a hotel to enable them to make frequent visits. Now, they had gone to spend a few days with Beth and Paul in London. Ralph had gone back to Oxford for two days to sort out his affairs, but rang frequently for progress reports and would be returning at the weekend.

Marnie had had a succession of visitors, all of them timetabled by Anne, who organised a daily appointments list. George Stubbs had brought a Range Rover load up from the village and Anne's parents had come bearing home-made biscuits. Another time there had been Marnie's former colleagues from the office in London. On one day a deputation arrived from Little Venice, driven up by Roger Broadbent. Gary and Mrs Jolly were the first to walk in.

"Cor blimey, Marnie," said Gary. "You look like death warmed up." Mrs Jolly rolled her eyes to the ceiling, but Marnie gave her best smile.

"Oh good," she said. "I'm glad there are signs of improvement."

"*Improvement?*" said Mrs Jolly.

"Yes," said Marnie. "I was admitted as a murder *victim*, after all."

"Well, fair enough," said Gary. "In that case you're doing all right."

Cards wishing Marnie well had arrived in great numbers, including many from people who did not know her personally, but knew of her through her donation of the drawings for the gallery at the National Canal Museum. This connection had led to media coverage of the attempted murder by the person dubbed 'the invisible man' in the popular press. The case had seized the public imagination with all its bizarre elements: the Civil War mystery, the murder of two vicars, the involvement of a woman vicar for the first time in a major news story. The miraculous survival of Marnie and, of course, the solving of the mystery by Anne, were the news editor's dream human angle. Ralph suggested that Anne should give one interview to a group of journalists and then keep out of the public eye. She had needed no persuading.

Anne turned into Marnie's ward and she was stopped in her tracks. The ward contained only four beds and Marnie was in the far corner. Today, it was barely visible behind a bank of flowers that cut her off from the rest of the world. A nurse bustled in with an armful of vases.

"Is anybody in there?" said Anne.

"Hack your way in," came a remote voice. "Try not to trip over the gorillas. I think I'll be the hospital's first case of terminal hay-fever." Marnie pulled herself up to sit straight but sudden sharp pains in her chest and back made her wince. The colour drained from her face.

Anne put a hand on Marnie's arm. "Are you all right?" she whispered.

Marnie opened her eyes, gave a weak smile and breathed in deeply but gently. "Fine," she said quietly. "I'll tell you something ... being murdered is no joke ... don't make a habit of it ..."

"I'll bear that in mind," said Anne, pulling up a chair. She waited patiently in silence.

"Getting there," Marnie said softly. "Tell me about Glebe Farm."

"Everything's under control." Anne produced a list from her bag. "The bank has paid the builders. Mike Thomas is coming up on Tuesday to see about tenders for the porch. Philip says Willards have approved the costings for *The Irish Navigator*, and work will start in three weeks."

"That's a relief," said Marnie. "You've done wonders. Are you getting enough to eat?"

"No probs. Molly Appleton has given me enough to feed an army. She's also given me tins of catfood for Dolly, who's become a serial mouser ... oh, sorry, I didn't mean that ..."

"Don't worry. What's she up to?"

"I think she means well ..."

"But?"

"It's just that she keeps bringing these mice on board, *live* mice. Probably thinks I need company while you're away. They run all over the place, but the exercise is doing me good."

Marnie smiled. "Anne? Have you got something to tell me?"

"What makes you think that?"

"Instinct. My antennae are twitching ... along with everything else just now."

"Well, I had a letter this morning ..."

"An offer to sell your story to *The Sun?*"

"My GCSE results ..."

"And?"

"I got an 'A' for Art, an 'A' for ..."

"So it's Anne with an 'A'!"

"Anne with five 'A's, in fact ... and three 'B's ..."

"Consider yourself well and truly hugged! Come here!" Anne moved closer and let Marnie kiss her on the cheek. "That's on account ... I'll dance a jig a bit later on. Hey, that's marvellous! We'll have to make sure we apply in good time for you to go to college after your year working with me."

"Brilliant," said Anne. "I've got some more news, actually. I hope I've done the right thing."

"I'm sure you have, but you can tell me all the same."

"You know Mrs Fairbrother, opposite the vicarage? Well, she came down with her daughter Jill last night. Jill's getting married and wanted to know if the cottages would be ready soon and if they were for sale. I said the first one would be ready late September, but they were to rent."

"That's right," said Marnie. "Although I'd thought we'd move into the first one before the weather changed in the autumn. When's the wedding?"

"Fifteenth of September."

"Honeymoon?"

"Two weeks ... Algarve."

"What did she think about renting?"

"Fine. They might have to move to Scotland in two or three years with her fiancé's job."

"Would she like to come in and have a chat about it?"

"I've booked her for fifteen minutes at the start of visiting tomorrow evening."

"Silly of me to ask, really ..."

"Oh, and can you give Ralph a ring." She pulled the mobile out of her bag.

"Now?" said Marnie.

"Now." Anne began pressing the buttons on the phone.

"Has this got anything to do with Ralph's sudden return to Oxford?"

"Possibly." Anne remained inscrutable. She handed the mobile to Marnie.

"Hi! It's me. Anne said you wanted me to ring ... You've been offered a job." Anne saw Marnie's expression become more serious "Does that mean ... and you've accepted it? ... so you won't be going to ...?" A smile spread across her face. "Congratulations! I'm delighted for you ... Yes, all right ... We'll talk about it at the weekend ... Well done, Ralph." She returned the phone to Anne. "Guess what? He's been offered a chair at the university, a professorship ... You knew all along!"

"That's one way to put some colour in your cheeks, Marnie. You're blushing."

"Nonsense, it's always warm in hospitals. Everyone knows that." Marnie wriggled gently to make herself more comfortable. "Anne, changing the subject, if this Jill Fairbrother is going to move in to number one, I'll need somewhere to live. It's all right for you; you've got your barn, if you're still happy to live in it after ..."

"I'm very happy, Marnie. I don't believe in ghosts. Anyway, Sarah Anne Day must know I'm a friend. Surely you can stay on *Sally Ann?*"

"There's absolutely no guarantee. After all, she is still Beth's boat. She could ask for *Sally* back and she's already made one attempt to sell her." Marnie leaned back, lost in thought.

Anne helped herself to some grapes "These are really good. I prefer the ones without seeds."

"I'm so glad. Anne, do you have strong views on moral blackmail?"

"Not so's you'd notice. I've never thought about it, really."

"It's highly reprehensible and should be deplored," said Marnie. She was looking better already. "Give me the phone, please." She pressed some familiar buttons and spoke into the receiver.

"You've done *what?*" said Beth.

"Bought a boat."

"Are you *serious?*"

"Yes. It's a really nice boat, too. Just what I need."

"But I thought you liked *Sally Ann*." Beth sounded bewildered, confused, even a little hurt.

"I do, but you want to sell her to Paul's colleague, remember?"

"He never mentioned her again. In fact, we've hardly exchanged two words since the day we talked about her." An old suspicion surfaced briefly in Beth's mind, but was as quickly rejected.

"Anyway, I've decided to buy this boat and my decision is final. I'm not going to let you mess me around any more."

"But after all the hard work you put into *Sally Ann* ..."

"You don't have to tell me."

"This is really sad. Only last night Paul and I were telling Mum and Dad about you and *Sally*, and all you've been through together. Are you saying you've really made up your mind?"

"Absolutely. There's no going back."

"Oh, well. That's it I suppose." Beth sighed. "So, where is this boat?"

"Little Venice. Towpath side, mooring number one." There was a pause. Marnie could almost hear Beth thinking.

"But ... that's where we keep *Sally*. That's *our* mooring."

"Not any more."

"What do you mean? There's no way we can give up that mooring as long as we have *Sally* ..."

"Good. That's agreed, then."

There was another pause. It took some seconds for Beth to understand. "You mean ... the boat you're intending to buy is *Sally Ann?*"

"Absolutely. And I'll tell you something else." Marnie paused a moment to get her breath. The conversation was beginning to tire her. "I'm getting her for a really good price. A bargain, in fact ... when I can afford to pay it." She lay back against the pillow and handed the phone to Anne, who pressed the stop button.

Postscript

After some weeks of lying outside the church in the warm weather, the flowers left in memory of Toni Petrie had withered, adding their own note of despair and decay. No-one knew what to do with them, though everyone wanted to be rid of this further sad reminder of mortality, and the whole village was relieved when Pauline Fairbrother walked quietly up to the gate one morning, knelt down and removed them to the sanctity of her compost heap.

♣   ♣   ♣   ♣